VANISHED

A GUARDIAN STORY

MORGAN VELA

CONTENTS

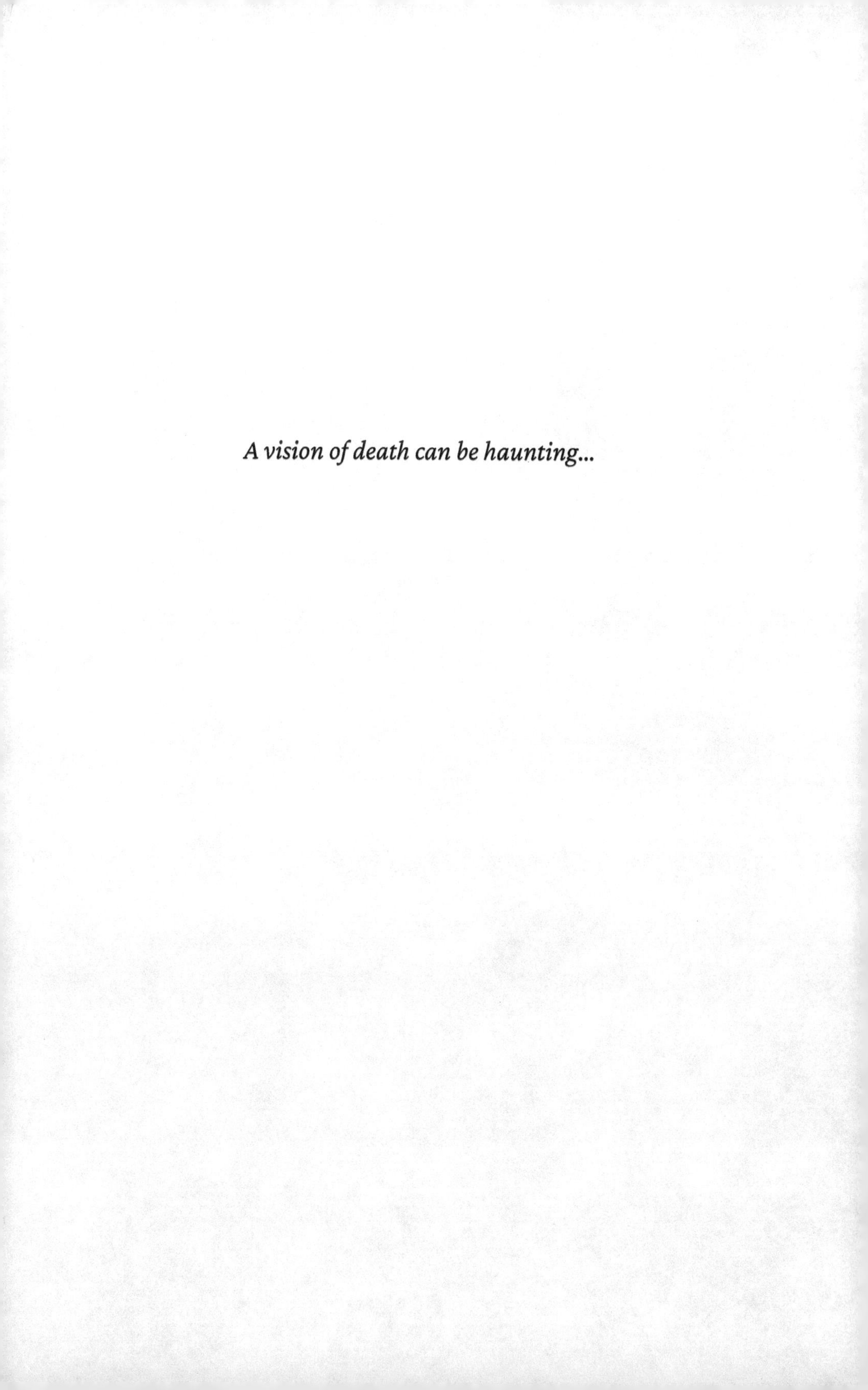

A vision of death can be haunting...

Yet, I see only hope in this revelation.

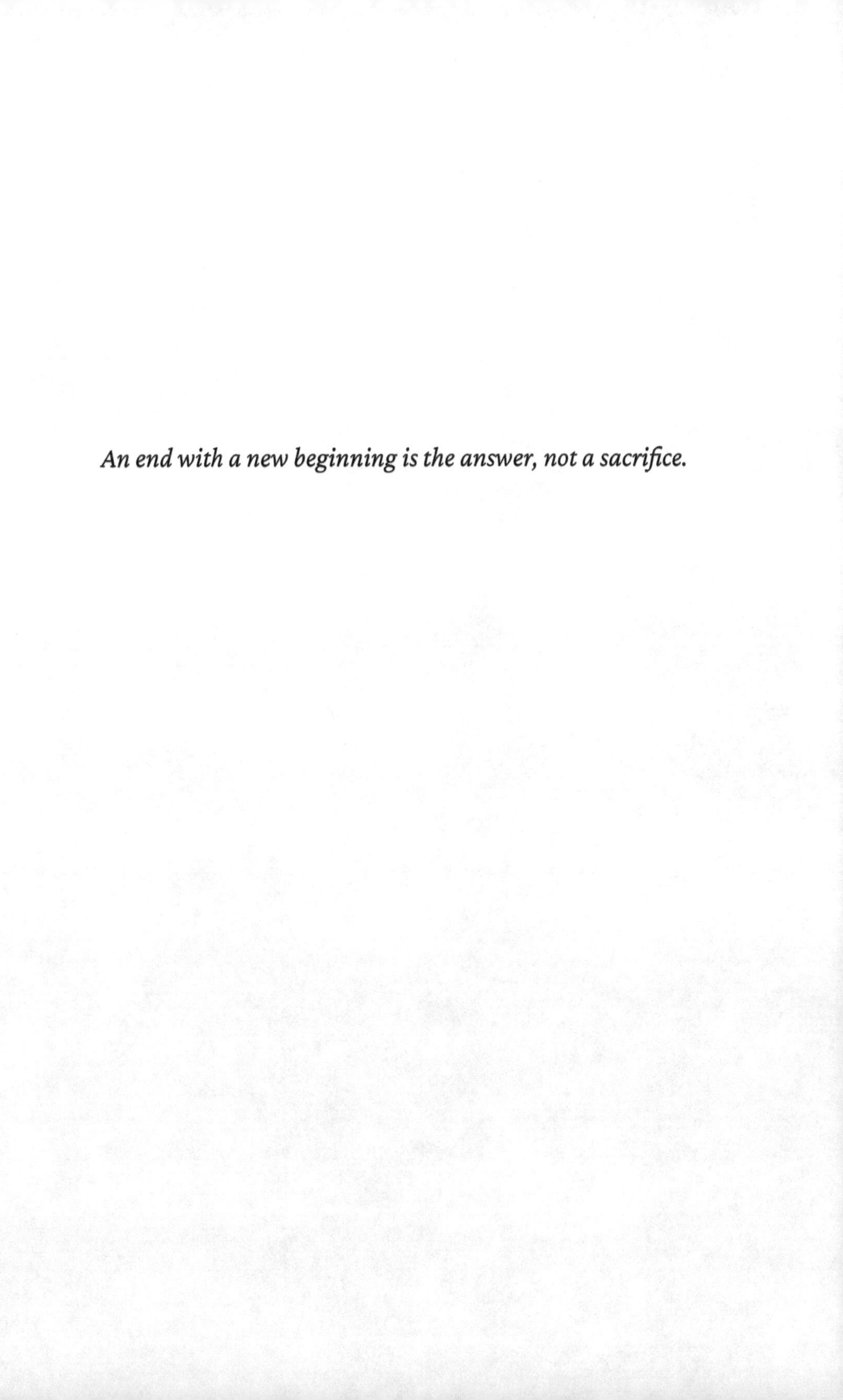

An end with a new beginning is the answer, not a sacrifice.

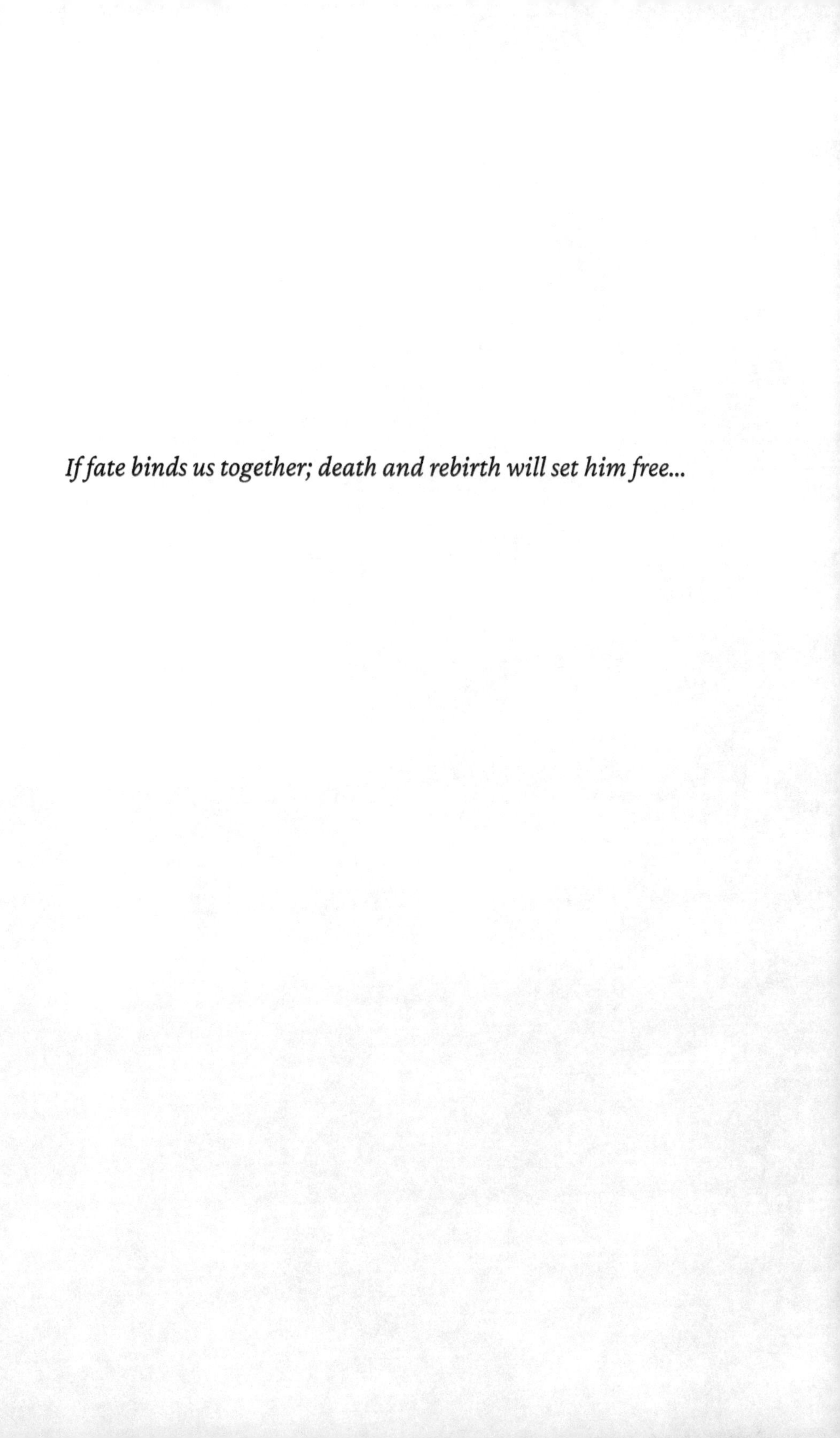

If fate binds us together; death and rebirth will set him free...

PROLOGUE

IN **THE MIDST OF THE STORM**, with the sword firmly grasped in both hands, I lifted it high towards the thundering skies and repeated the long-lost words: words that held the power to change my destiny.

"I conjure thee, Dragon!" My voice resounded into the night.

"Guardians of the shadow realm, I command you to release Xelraa. Unveil the portal of the dark shrine. Fire, release the forgotten gates. Bend thy will and grant Drake's passage, I command thee."

"Cum Saxum Saxorum, In Duersum Montum. Oparum Da. In Aetibulum. In Quinatum. Draconis, Draconis, Draconis."

As the last word escaped my lips, the sword's tip met with the silvery arc of a lightning bolt. In one fluid motion, I plunged the blade deep into the earth, precisely where the quartz lay buried.

Retreating to a safe distance, the crackling electricity tingled beneath my fingertips, a rippling effect of the power coursing through the ground. I watched in awe as the sword became aglow with a fiery red hue.

Beneath the surface, tendrils of electric energy unfurled from the sword's buried edge, slowly illuminating the etched pentagram.

The next bolt of lightning that struck the sword made me jump. I stifled a scream. My eyes fixed on the glowing sphere of light hovering above the blade.

As the brilliant orb dimmed, a sense of anticipation and dread filled my heart. Before me lay Drake, his form unmoving. A marble statue arched on the ground.

My knees buckled beneath me, and I collapsed to the ground, breathless and trembling as I grasped the severity of what I had done. Torn between fear and disbelief, I clutched the sacred book to my chest.

He was *real...*

My body shook—my mind became chaotic, and I suddenly found it difficult to breathe. I was terrified, my knees frozen to the ground.

Amidst the erratic thoughts, one particular fear took root. What was I going to do now? What was I going to do with him?

Slowly, his head stirred, his movements labored as though wracked with pain. He blinked, and my heart sped up; watching his eyes adjust to his surrounding, until eventually, they found me.

"Isabel..." His whispered plea barely reached my ears before he slumped, unconscious once more.

Fear had never felt more tangible in my entire life as it did at this precise moment. As I watched this man, this creature, before me, I fought the inexplicable surge—the need to go to him. Wondering if he was *hurt.*

I placed the book on the floor and pushed myself to my feet. Hesitantly, I took a few steps closer, sinking to my knees before him. Dry mud coated his body, and my fingers instinctively reached for his dark, matted hair.

A bolt of lightning tore through the sky, illuminating his grey eyes. The Dragon prince's eyes were startling. A hypnotizing grey-silver hue that seemed to glow in the evening shadows, drawing me in. He was dangerous, he was lethal— he was immortal. My hand stilled in mid-air, his expression daunting.

"Who are you?" His voice was stronger this time but tinged with anger. Drake scared me, and any coherent thought I could muster abandoned me.

"I will not ask again. Who are you?" He demanded, and the roar on his voice made me draw back.

He opened and closed his hand, assessing his movements, every muscle in his arm coiling, and yet despite the visible effort, evident by the hardening set of his jaw, he still managed to pull himself up to a seated position. His silvery eyes returning to me, filled with a thousand unspoken questions.

"I'm the one who freed you," I finally whispered, my voice trembling with false bravery or perhaps stupidity.

His expression transformed as he closed his eyes, angling his face toward the night sky. Inhaling deeply, his nostrils flared, and when he looked at me again, his eyes were no longer silver or grey—they were deep pools of onyx black.

"I can sense them," he growled, his fists clenching on the ground. "I can smell her," he added, his expression twisted in pain. "Lie to me again, mortal," he threatened, and a primal instinct to protect myself surged inside me for the first time.

Adrenaline poured through my limbs, propelling me. Without a second thought, I bolted. Sprinting blindly through the darkness, I brushed past trees and stumbled over rocks, the rain soaking my hair and clothes, but I never paused or looked back.

Fear of succumbing to the cold or exhaustion, as I fought to find my way back gripped me. When I finally emerged from the forest into the open field, the sight of the house in the distance flooded me with relief. Though my legs threatened to give out, I summoned every ounce of strength to push myself up from the muddy ground and press on.

As I drew nearer to the house, a wave of warm tears streamed down my cheeks. I was a coward, consumed by shame and guilt. Drake was alone in the woods, and it was my fault.

Never before, had I stopped to consider my actions and what the fruition of my plans would mean. What was I going to do with Drake? How could I justify his presence? How could I ever face him again?

The Drake I released, was a stark departure from the man who haunted my dreams and visions—the one who professed love to Isabel. This version of him frightened me, yet I found myself inexplicably drawn to his darkness.

Back within the safety of my home, I found myself yearning for the dawn to break. With every passing second,

Drake's presence became more of a tangible reality, one that I knew wouldn't vanish with the morning light as my dreams often did. I knew I had to confront him again, but not tonight. Tonight, I needed the solace of my thoughts to gather my courage and devise a plan.

I

REVELATIONS

BELYNDA

CUMMINGTON MASSACHUSETTS—The little bell at the library door tinkled in greeting, announcing my arrival. The red brick walls were real. Even the mountain of books waiting to be returned to their original resting place were tangible. It was my daily routine that grounded me; waking up to my normal mundane life was the only anchor to my sanity. It was proof that whatever my dreams were—they were far from being true.

Take a deep breath and return to the present moment. Mindfulness and focus are the keys. Frustrated, I paused the recording and removed my earphones. Sure, meditation was an effective therapy for most, but not for me. After years, I had come to accept that no amount of treatment could make sense of my life or put logic to my bizarre nightmares.

Celest, the library owner, sat like a statue behind the

checkout counter, completely lost in her latest research. Her posture as solid as her passion for books. Anyone who knew her could attest that she breathed and lived only for this forsaken place, which was more than could be said for her role as my legal guardian.

I'd often wondered if my life would have been easier had Celest chosen to believe in me. Instead, she co-signed my weekly therapy visits—years of therapy which had rendered me with a list of medications I refused to take, and a rather hefty bill for her to pay, which I often wondered how she could afford on a librarian's salary.

After my mother's death, Celest was left with the burden of my care. But, as I understood, that was by choice, not obligation. I often tried to comprehend her reserved and detached attitude, yet she remained an enigma. At times I felt I could trust her, and that she truly cared for me. But often, she chose to close herself off. The vague memories of Celest and my mother were hazy, but they had shared a genuine friendship. There was almost a sisterhood bond between them, and it was those memories which made me believe that a part of her cared.

Pushing the cart of old and dusty books, the screeching of the cartwheels against the worn wooden floor echoed along the silent corridor. Visitors glanced up in clear annoyance yet after offering an apologetic smile, they quickly returned to their reading.

As I reached the last section of the library, the pungent smell of polished wood, carpet, and dust carried me away from my troubling thoughts. It was the one thing I loved about this place, I found the peculiar fusion of scents reminded me of my mother.

Closing my eyes, I could visualize her, smiling as she brushed aside my hair and told me tales about dragons and ancient magic. My mother was beautiful, and she, too, had a passion for old books. We used to lay on these exact carpets as she read for hours, until my eyes could no longer stay open.

While I didn't think of her as often, being here always seemed to trigger those memories. It helped me to imagine her, watching over me in silent assurance that everything would be ok.

Mindlessly, I arranged the books in the cart before placing them back on the shelves.

"Belynda..." I jolted at the echo of Celest's voice, followed by the loud thud as the book I held landed against the floor.

"I'm in the back." The muffled sound of my reply echoed off the walls of books surrounding me. Celest appeared in the corridor just as I stepped off the ladder.

"You were so quiet; I didn't hear you come in."

"You were wrapped up in your reading. I didn't want to bother you." Really, she was just in her own world, but I reserved my opinion and instead reached for the book on the floor.

"How did your session go yesterday—any progress?" Rarely did Celest ask about therapy. But whenever she did, it typically triggered a familiar mix of apprehension and doubt about her true intentions.

"There's not a lot to say. I've been stuck in the same recurring dream I've had for years. But lately, it feels like there's been some sort of progression, like I'm witnessing the next chapter of a story unfold." Her expression shifted fleetingly, but I caught a glimpse of what seemed like fear or maybe concern, but she quickly regained her composure, masking it behind her stoic facade.

"I understand," she said softly, reaching out to lift my chin with gentle fingers. "Just know, I'm here for you," she added, her smile hesitant.

A part of me had ceased to hope that her interest in my dreams meant she was finally ready to believe me. I had longed for her acceptance, for her to acknowledge that my dreams were far from ordinary. I wanted her to recognize that therapy could only do so much for me.

She watched me for a moment, her gaze probing, as if silently trying to figure me out. "Thank you for helping with the books," she finally said.

"I don't mind," I replied, not looking up from the shelf I was organizing. "It keeps me busy."

That much was true.

Celest shot me a concerned look—an expression I had come to recognize all too well lately. "Belynda, you need to make some friends. You're almost an adult. It's a nice Sunday afternoon and it would help if you were out with others of your age, not cooped up in this dusty place helping me. I feel as if I'm to blame for this life of solitude you've found comfort in."

Perhaps she was onto something. I was becoming more like her each day: permanently closed off to the world.

"It's not your fault. I've told you before; I'm happy just the way I am, and I have friends at school." *Ok, that was partially a lie*—I had *ONE* friend. Apart from Lily, though that was likely because her mother was my therapist, and she had grown accustomed to seeing me over the years. "And before you say anything else, no, I don't need a boyfriend. My life is fine how it is."

"As long as you're happy and safe," Celest responded.

Did she really want me to be happy? I knew she didn't believe a single word I had just said, but she would act like she did. That was the mechanism of our relationship. She just let me be. Celest moved on quickly, and so did I. With a gradual smile, she walked away, leaving me alone with only the books and my thoughts for company.

Even though my relationship with her was unusual, to say the least, I was still grateful. I was sure my life would be much worse without her.

MINDLESSLY, I flipped through the old and heavy volume I had retrieved from the floor, scrutinizing the pages for any signs of damage. The book was ancient, obvious by its delicate texture as I traced my fingertips over the sheets. Turning the pages, I paused at one illustration. The image covered an entire page, and I was immediately captivated.

"The Dragon Kingdom and Guardians of the Realms," I murmured, my eyes fixated on the intricate details of the drawing.

The small text underneath the picture sent a chill through me.

The encryption tugged at a distant memory—something almost lost, yet not quite. *Yes, that's where I recognized it.* It was from one of the stories my mother used to read to me as a child.

My memory didn't fail me, and the subtle sense of Deja Vu was my confirmation. Celest and my mother always shared the same interests; knowing Celest's taste for the unusual and eclectic literature, it didn't surprise me that this was her reading choice. What I did find odd, however, was the other books discarded in the return cart like *"The Dragon Era" and "The Guardianship Legacy"*, all seemed related.

I dismissed the thought, neatly placing the remaining books back on their shelves before making my way to the front of the library.

Celest sat motionless at the front desk, her glasses perched halfway down her nose as she immersed herself in a book. Again, she didn't seem to notice me until I cleared my throat.

"Do you mind if I finish the rest tomorrow?" I asked, breaking her focus. "I still have some laundry to fold from, and I'm a little tired."

She looked up, momentarily startled, before nodding. "Sure, sure. Go ahead," she said, waving me off as she returned to her reading.

Stepping out into the cold air, I welcomed it, my lungs were grateful for the opportunity to take in fresh air once more.

As I walked along the sidewalk, I couldn't help but notice two unfamiliar faces. Visitors, I assumed — a rarity in a small town like Cummington, known more for its history and architecture than its tourist appeal.

Turning up the volume on my headphones, I tuned out the world around me, leaving the town center behind as I headed down a quieter street.

.   .   .

THE ROAD ahead disappeared over a small hill, with the Manor, my home, sitting silently at its peak. Passed down through generations, it was now my only inheritance, its history and charm a constant reminder of my childhood.

Lost in thought, I barely noticed the meditation music playing in my ears, the soothing sounds of nature and flutes blending together as I reached the porch.

I fumbled for the spare key hidden under the entrance mat, a small smile tugging at my lips as I stepped inside.

Celest was always insistent that I needed to make friends, but her taste in décor certainly didn't help. The gargoyle-like statues, angel figurines, and eccentric paintings scattered throughout the house were more likely to scare off potential guests than welcome them.

And then there were the books—endless piles of them, constantly making their way from the library to our home. Thankfully, Celest rarely ventured to the second floor, giving me some semblance of privacy within her organized chaos.

Glancing at the laundry basket sitting on my bed, I resigned myself to the task, knowing the clothes wouldn't fold themselves.

Soft rays from the afternoon sun still filtered through the windows as I folded the last piece of clothing away, the warmth of the fading daylight lingering in the room. With a sigh, I sank onto the bed, the exhaustion of the sleepless nights finally catching up to me.

The room bathed in a cozy glow that eased my tired eyes. I gazed up at the white tulle fabric cascading from the bed's frame, its delicate folds creating a canopy above me. I snuggled deeper under the duvet and glanced at the alarm clock on the night table. Celest wouldn't be home for at least a couple more hours. I closed my eyes and allowed myself to indulge for a moment.

I AWOKE *from the sudden heat — a heat that crawled from the soles of my feet and through my body like an electric current. My hands grasped aimlessly at the dark soil beneath me as I stared at the vast land ahead. The sun was fading, leaving behind dark orange and yellow tones.*

The foreign yet familiar surroundings had long ceased to unravel; this place and time had become my reality through these dreams—dreams which kept me in a strange state of awareness, where my consciousness was trapped between this nightmare and my reality.

I stared down at my body, dressed in the same gray tunic, allowing my feet to guide me down the path. A path I had followed countless times before, but only in this dream.

A cacophony of voices guided me toward the large rocks, were I always remained hidden. Giant boulders surrounded the cloaked figures, conveniently secluding their gathering.

They stood side by side, forming a perfect circle. Their voices flowed—almost like some poems do—creating an eerie symphony that echoed in the air. An unsettling hum filled the space, accompa-

nied by a chant in a language I couldn't understand. It grew louder, intensifying to a crescendo that sent shivers down my spine.

Frozen to the ground, I watched through the partition of the rocks. The filtering rays of the sun contrasted against their dark and long cloaks; the dim light casting shadows that masked their faces.

A figure broke from the assembly, stepping into the circle's center with both hands raised towards the skies. A hand disappeared beneath the cloak, retrieving a gleaming.

"As above, as below." Bellowed a man's deep and commanding voice, his words echoing above the stones, the sword raised to the skies.

In one rapid movement, he drove the sword into the ground by his feet. My hands became clammy, and my pulse spiked like it had the last time. I watched as the rest of the cloaked figures raised their hands to the skies in veneration.

"We release the gates of the worlds." The man in the center invoked.

"Cum Portal est Opaca, Unum..."

"Cum Portal est Opaca, Unum..."

"Cum Portal est Opaca, Unum..." echoed the circle in unison, their voices blending into a haunting chant that filled the air.

THE ATMOSPHERE SHIFTED, growing wickedly eerie as the howling wind whipped up spirals of dirt around me. I squeezed my eyes shut, trying to shield them from the stinging dust, and covered my ears to block out the piercing sound.

Forcing myself to my knees, I huddled against the onslaught of the angry elements, and the sense of impending danger creeping *over me. I couldn't explain the strange pull in the pit of my stomach, as if something bad was about to happen.*

I held my breath, bracing for the familiar sensation that always pulled me back to consciousness, but it didn't come this time. Instead, my heart fluttered with anticipation, waiting to discover what new revelations awaited me. Whatever lay ahead was uncharted territory—a new chapter unfolding in the ever-mysterious labyrinth of my dreams.

Lightning tore through the sky, illuminating the darkness with a blinding flash, and the rumble of thunder jolted me with pure fright. The bolt struck at the center of the circle, connecting with the sword buried in the earth.

A strangled cry broke from my lips as another bolt of light crashed down, this time causing an explosion of light at the circle's core. I stood frozen, caught between the realms of dream and reality, torn between fascination and terror. Despite the chaos unfolding before my eyes, the hooded figures remained motionless, stoic, a surreal sight.

The howling wind subsided, but the chanting was persistent, a haunting echo, refusing to be silenced.

The ground beneath me trembled, and the darkness began to retreat, replaced by a steady pulse of light emanating from where the lightning had struck. Slowly, the pulsating glow fused into a ball of fluorescent energy, or perhaps fire—it was difficult to tell, yet mesmerizing.

Another cloaked figure stepped towards the center of the circle, and slowly, the spectacle surrounding the buried sword began to dissipate. As the light faded, a palpable silence settled in the air. A Strangeness, that pulled at a familiar feeling buried deep in the pit of my soul.

I saw him then. Beyond the fading light—where the light engulfed the earth, a man was kneeling.

It wasn't possible. It defied all logic—how could someone materialize out of thin air? Yet, despite the impossibility, a strange sense of acceptance washed over me. A part of me recognized that I was dreaming, but another part felt an inexplicable familiarity with this surreal scene, drawn to the madness and the man in the shadows.

THE ANXIOUS FEELING refused to leave my body, unable to resist, I drew closer. My view was obstructed, but the overwhelming feeling of recognition was unshakable. The fluttering in my chest took flight as the kneeling person rose to their feet.

The man's sinewy muscles and broad shoulders betrayed his youth. But it was his face that struck me—a face that seemed familiar, though I couldn't place how or why. Some part of me—the one that seemed to belong in this place and time, recognized him.

An ear-piercing scream tore through my lips, as colossal wings unfurled from the man's body. For a moment, they framed his towering height, before dissolving into a black mist, that moved around him, like shadows.

My legs refused my command to run: a reminder that I had no control over these dreams. Instead, I shifted closer, drawn to him.

"Wake up, Belynda. Wake up." I willed the conscious part of myself to break free from the dream's grip, but it was no use. My feet moved against my will, carrying me towards him and as I emerged from behind the rocks, I was exposed.

Two of the cloaked figures broke from the circle, advancing towards me.

"Please, let him go. I just want to see him," I pleaded, my voice

sounding foreign and distant, as if it belonged to someone else. Everything felt wrong. Had I lost myself in this world of unconsciousness? Was I possessed by some unseen force?

The figures stood before me in silence, their faces concealed beneath the shadow of their cloaks. Slowly, they pulled back their hoods, revealing a set of familiar faces. I froze, disbelieve washing over me as I stared into Celest and my mother's eyes.

SWEAT TRICKLED down the back of my neck as I flung the blanket aside, gasping for air. Collapsing to my knees on the wooden floor beside my bed, I emptied the contents of my lunch in a violent heave. With uneven breaths, I waited for the queasy sensation to subside, pulling my knees close to my chest and resting my head against the edge of the bed.

A sense of helplessness washed over me. The dreams only seemed to be getting worse.

As my breathing settled, I summoned enough strength and clarity to rise and clean up the mess. With darkness already settling over the world outside, I knew Celest would return home any minute.

Pacing back and forth in the entrance hall, I wrestled with the idea of confiding in her about the latest development in my dream.

It had been a harsh blow for a nine-year-old to cope with the loss of a mother, and that dreadful time coincided with the beginning of these nightmares. Celest comforted me then, assuring me it was just a bad dream. Back then, it had been easy to believe her words, but the years passed and the nightmare continued, haunting me often.

At twelve, when I was old enough to research and reason, I realized it wasn't normal to have the same dream. Scared, I confided in Celest again.

Naturally, she was concerned, though in the end, she dismissed it once more: *"You'll be alright, Belynda. It's just a dream, nothing more," she reassured me.*

After that night, I stopped speaking about the dreams. Firstly, because at times, I questioned my own sanity. Secondly, there lingered the possibility that she was right, and it truly was just a dream. Lastly, that incident marked the onset of my mandatory therapy sessions.

Things had changed since then. For many years, until recently, the dream had remained the same: a repetitive scene playing out like a broken record. However, the recent revelations only served to torment me further. They were another chapter added to an already empty story—a narrative that didn't align with my reality, or anything of this humanly mundane world.

I HAD no illusions that confiding in Celest would offer any solution, but the uncanny resemblance between those women and both her and my mother compelled me to speak up. Perhaps it meant something, or perhaps admitting to witnessing a man with wings summoned from thin air by witches and their casting rites would convince her I'd completely lost my mind.

Lost in my thoughts, I set the dinner table, unaware of the front door opening.

"Guess what I got?" Celest chirped, waving a bag of Chinese takeout.

Knowing it was my favorite, I forced a smile. Silently, I watched as she placed the containers on the table.

"Here, I got you some noodles," she said, nudging a container my way, oblivious to the battle raging in my head.

"Thanks. Iced tea?" I swiftly changed the subject, hoping to mask my anxiety. Celest was usually perceptive, but she seemed preoccupied this evening.

"Yes, please. I'm famished. That's what happens when I skip lunch and attempt to survive on coffee," she joked, her humor only adding to my nerves.

The silence wasn't uncomfortable. We were both used to it by now. As I anticipated the dreaded conversation, a knot formed in my throat, making it impossible to swallow another bite.

"Aren't you going to finish the noodles?" Celest asked, breaking the silence.

"I'm not that hungry anymore. I'll eat the rest tomorrow," I replied, sensing her surprise turn to suspicion. I couldn't dismiss her observation so easily.

"Is everything alright? You don't lose your appetite often, and I know this is your favorite," she probed gently.

Numbly, I stared at my plate, the words tumbling out before I could stop them.

"Why do I have these dreams, Celest?"

I knew neither of us had an answer, but it was my way of

breaking the ice. Celest took a sip from her cup without meeting my eyes.

"I wish I could make them go away, but I think the therapy has done wonders for you. You should continue to focus on that," she finally offered. However, her encouraging smile didn't quite reach her eyes.

Rising from the table, she collected our plates and disappeared into the kitchen without another word.

I could see it was no different than any of the other times I had attempted to confide in her about my dreams. But this time I was afraid, and she was the only one I could count on. With resolve, I followed her into the kitchen.

"This morning at the library, you asked me about my progress, about the dreams," I began, and she shifted her attention to me.

"I'm listening," she spoke, her voice gentle.

"The dream came again this afternoon. They're happening more often now," I confessed. This dream was strange, different, and I swear that you and my mother were there," I explained, feeling a knot of anxiety tightening in my chest.

At my admission, her eyes widened with worry. "What do you mean?"

"The memory is a little hazy, and while I know it wasn't you or her, the resemblance was remarkable," I replied, my voice trembling slightly.

"Belynda, it's normal to dream about those in your life and even those who have left us. Seeing your mother or me is nothing to be disturbed about. Is it?" She didn't understand. Her words did little to alleviate my unease.

"It wasn't just their resemblance to you and mom. Everything else about this dream was odd." I hesitated unsure if to say more, but her eyes were encouraging. "I saw a man summoned out of thin air by a cult of witches, but I'm not even sure he was human. But more unsettling was that when I spoke, it wasn't my voice, I was someone else," I admitted, the memory of that strange sensation clear on my mind.

A tense silence filled the kitchen, broken only by the sound of running water. "The dreams haven't just changed, Celest, they frighten me. It's becoming harder to separate reality from illusion. I feel as if I'm living someone else's life," I confessed, my heart pounding in my chest.

The plate slipped from her hands and clashed in the sink, the noise echoing in the quiet kitchen. Her eyes reached mine. Her expression filled with worry.

"Belynda, have you spoken to the therapist about this? Told her how you feel?" Celest's voice was low.

"Not about this dream... it's only just happened, but they're happening often, and I don't know what's triggering them. Celest, I know you think therapy is the answer to my problems, but I'm not sure anyone can help me," I admitted, my voice tinged with desperation.

"Why didn't you say something sooner?" Celest's expression shifted to one of disbelief, and I took a deep breath to contain my bitterness.

"Because, you chose to believe it was all in my head and offered therapy as the eminent solution. You're ready to run away and have me committed even now. I can see it." I confessed, and it felt good to get the weight off my chest.

"Belynda, you don't know what you're saying. I only care that you are safe and happy. You don't understand what it's like."

"What is it like? I would if you would tell me. I have tried to understand you for years, but it's getting harder to do this when I feel that I'm all alone," I retorted, my voice trembling with frustration.

Celest couldn't meet my eyes as she spoke, her words tinged with sorrow. "You will never be alone, child; you're just growing so fast." Her thoughts seemed distant; lost in an abyss I wished I could reach. I was almost certain the glassiness in her eyes were contained tears.

"Do you trust me?" her question caught me off guard.

She pinched the bridge of her nose—a sign of worry. "I want to. I do," I admitted, despite my previous reservations to confide in her, she was all I had.

"Then believe me when I tell you that everything will be okay," she urged, finally meeting my gaze.

My hysterical laugh morphed into a broken sob, which I stifled with my finger over my mouth. "You don't know how much I want to believe that. But how can you be sure? Is there something you haven't told me? A magical potion that can solve my madness?"

The thought of her hiding something poisoned my mind, and I took an unconscious step back. Though I thought I glimpsed pain in her eyes, I wasn't sure of anything anymore.

"Belynda, if I had an answer or a way to stop the dreams, I would tell you. Believe me. All I want is for them to go away so you can be normal and happy," Celest pleaded, her voice filled with anguish.

"I don't think I will ever be normal," I choked out, fighting the tears. Celest reached hesitantly rushing her fingers along my cheek.

"It's okay to cry. Everything will be alright. Believe me, this will pass. Just forget this crusade of figuring out why and how, just concentrate on your life in the meantime. Stop chasing after the ghosts of your dreams, please. I will have a word with the therapist tomorrow. Perhaps you should take a break from that too. It might help to clear your head. Would you like that?" Celest's asked with unusual gentleness and understanding.

"Yeah, I guess," I mumbled, wiping away a tear that escaped the corner of my eye.

"We will figure it out. I promise." She kissed the top of my head and pulled away with a soft smile, before retreating down the corridor and into her office.

As I watched her disappear, a sense of relief washed over me. At least this time, she hadn't made me feel crazy or dismissed my nightmares. Though, in essence, what she was proposing was not much different.

I couldn't silence my thoughts any more than I could stop the dreams from happening. Celest had asked for the impossible. Yes, I would continue to live my life, yet nothing would change. While a part of me wanted to believe her, when she said that everything would be alright— I knew that promise was beyond her reach.

CELEST

In the office, my trembling hands reached for the phone, dialing the only person I trusted at that moment. It must have been just after two in the morning in Rome, but he would understand. *Come on, Seymor, pick up!*

"Ciao. Celest?"

"Yes, it's me. Mi dispiace per l'ora tarda. But it's important."

"Of course. Is everything alright?"

"It's Belynda. It appears that what we thought was dormant has awoken. Seymor, I don't think we can avoid it any longer. I fear her mother was too hopeful to shield her from this."

"I thought the binding had worked and her visions were under control?"

"As did I, but something is changing, they're progressing. She has seen visions of the covenant...and the fire bound."

"Celest, I am sympathetic with the cause, but you know my position and my opinion on all of this. You and her mother have tried to go against fate from the beginning, and while I understand your reasons, they are not enough to stand against what should be. What will be..." I knew he would say that, but at this point, he was the only one I could turn to.

"Has she been in contact?" He was silent for a moment, and I knew I shouldn't have asked.

"I'm afraid not. But if things are changing, she must know. She has the gift."

"What do I do then? Sit and wait?"

"There is nothing we can do to change what is to come. But it's time she knows the truth. A good start would be to retrieve the prophecy's manuscript from the reliquary."

"That will raise suspicions," I hesitated, but Seymor was right.

"We've always known there was a possibility this time would come, and I'm aware retrieving it doesn't come without risks for you and the girl, but she will need it soon if things are as you say. It's her legacy, and it will bring some clarity for her when the time comes."

"I know. I'm trying my best, I just don't know if it's enough anymore," Seymor was silent at the other end of the line. We both knew everything was about to change.

"Just be careful," I stared at the portraits hanging in my office with a heaviness in my chest. My brother was right. I had to retrieve the manuscript, it was the only way to move forward.

"I know it's late, I won't keep you any longer. I'll be in touch soon."

"Be careful," Seymor repeated.

"I will. I promise." I hung up the line, feeling the weight of the world on my shoulders. Seymor was right, we were fools to think it was possible to keep her destiny from finding her.

BELYNDA

"What is wrong with you?"

I examined my reflection in the bathroom mirror. The more I tried to make sense of it all, the harder it became. Celest had a point. I had to let it go and stop fixating. It was exhausting—physically mentally, and emotionally.

My body sloped against the wall and the cold tiles of the bathroom floor welcomed me. My eyes fell heavy. *Don't fall asleep...fight it,* my mind repeated. The tightening in my chest deepened dreading the idea of returning to that feeling of helplessness and despair that I experienced in the last dream.

The warm water from the tub spilled over as I stepped in. My body sank willingly into the inviting warmth and the muscles on my neck and shoulders relaxed instantly.

Eventually, the aroma from the lavender oil and restless nights caught up to me, yet I feared what I would face if I dreamed again. Though it proved inevitable, and I despite fighting it, I eventually succumbed to the darkness.

The heat stirred me awake, again, I followed the voices to the circle where they chanted as one. The wind came, shadowed by lightning and the winged man that rose from the light. I recognized myself within the dream, yet felt detached as if observing in slow motion, only this time I took in every detail I had missed the last time like the wings which were striking. Dragon-like.

"Please, let him go. I just want to see him," It was eerie, hearing myself speak yet not recognizing my own voice. It felt alien, not my own.

The women who looked like Celest and my mother stared at me. The resemblance was remarkable yet there were differences; they were not my mother or Celest. The lady with my mother's likeness stepped closer, her expression stern.

"You shouldn't be here, Isabel. You know the rules; you're not allowed," she hissed, her anger palpable. Confusion clouded my mind. Who was Isabel?

She was wrong. I wanted protest, to say that my name was Belynda, but my mouth and thoughts betrayed me. Once again, I was a mere puppet in this nightmare.

"Please let me go, mother. I love him. Do something. I beg you," I pleaded, but a hand stifled my pleads.

"Don't you dare say another word. He doesn't belong with you. The covenant forbids it." Her poisonous voice rang with authority and finality.

"Then I don't belong here either. Punish me, not him." I pleaded, tears streaming down my cheeks and I was no longer sure if they were my own, or Isabel's.

"You know I won't allow that. The council has decided. I can only protect you, but you will never see him again, is that understood?" she declared, her tone firm. The finality of her words swallowed me.

"How could you do this? He would give up his immortality to stay with me, they have the power to change him. You know that! They can change this stupid rules. Please do something. You can stop this." I cried out, desperation in my voice.

"Isabel, you know that's impossible. You are my daughter. I don't like to see you hurting but I can't turn against the guardianship, you foolish girl. You don't understand the position you have put me in and yet you ask me to break everything I stand for? I am trusted to protect the balance between the realms, not break it." Turning to the other woman, she handed her a book that was hidden within her tunic.

"Esther, take this. Return to the circle; they won't be able to hold the portal open much longer without us," she commanded and the woman obeyed, spinning around to join the others.

Facing me, she stared into my eyes and tenderly cupped my face in her hands, as if that would help me accept her actions.

"Isabel. He will spend the rest of his days in Xelraa—let him go," she urged softly.

Pain clawed at my chest, unbearable—it threatened to choke me.

"Nooo, mother, I beg you. Please. It was us—both of us. Send me to Xelraa too!" I held her robe and fell onto my knees, pleading desperately. "He doesn't deserve that. He won't survive the shadows. Please don't do this!"

Grabbing my wrists, she forced me to my feet.

"He is not human. He will adapt," she insisted, disgust flickering across her face. How could she think him, or his kind were any less worthy than us? Only a monster would condemn an innocent whose only crime was to love.

"Why are you so blind? Why can't you see that there is more humanity in him than in your coven of monsters?"

"Keep your voice down!"

"You'll never silence me. I will never rise to my seat. That's my promise," I vowed, catching a fleeting glimpse of guilt before her mask of composure returned.

"If you persist, you will pay the consequences, too. You must understand, his noble blood does not excuse his actions. The rules are there for a reason. The consequences of your decisions are bigger than you both. He has accepted responsibility and agreed to the council's terms. He has made his peace and chosen to live with the consequences, and you should, too."

"It's wrong. You will all burn for this," I screamed, hatred simmering in my blood.

"That's enough. Leave now. That is an order," she commanded,

pulling the cloak over her head, before retreating to the circle. I felt the energy pulsating from within its boundary, in sync with my beating heart.

I FOUGHT to catch my breath, inside the grip of the now freezing water, but this time, I could not bring myself to cry. Emptiness coursed inside of me, the feeling threatening to extinguish me forever.

The images replayed in my head. It was becoming clear that these dreams were not my own—no, they had to be the memories. Someone else's life. No dream could be that vivid or visceral and I knew the difference between a dream and a nightmare. This was neither.

The only rational explanation was that these memories belonged to another soul, intertwined with mine in some unfathomable way. No therapist could help me—perhaps I was possessed but not by the ghost of an earthly entity. *No.* It was too fictitious for rational human understanding. Even I recognized the humor behind the idea of being possessed; yet it was either that or accepting instead that I was descending into madness.

It was cold in the bedroom, but I didn't realize how much until I was finally under the warmth of the covers. The clock on the table marked ten past midnight, but I couldn't sleep. Instead, I took the journal and pen from the drawer and captured the details of the dreams while they were still vivid in my mind.

THE JARRING NOISE jolted me awake, the sound intensifying like a relentless drilling in my head. With a groan, I dragged myself upright and silenced the torture device. Blinking away sleep, I noticed the faint light slipping through the edges of the curtains.

I shivered as my feet hit the cold wooden floors. With less than five hours of sleep, I could almost predict how my day would play out.

Grimacing at the tangled mess atop my head, I quickly smoothed it down before applying a touch of pink lip gloss and mascara to counter my pale complexion. Despite my efforts, the puffiness of my eyes and the blotchiness of my nose remained visible though I doubted anyone would care, or notice.

"Shoot. I Can't miss the bus," I muttered to myself, quickly slipping on the jeans and cream sweater. With my book bag slung over one shoulder, I dashed downstairs, wrestling my boots onto my feet as I went.

The ground floor was silent and deserted as I reached for my coat, but I noticed Celest's car still parked outside. I debated sharing the details of the dream with her, but she had asked me to stop chasing after them. Perhaps it was best to keep this to myself for now. After all, what could she do to help? Unless... I was seriously considering possession. I shuddered at the thought, pushing it aside. Best not to entertain such desperate possibilities—at least, not yet.

An engine rumbled in the distance, and my stomach lurched as the bus appeared on the hill. An empty stomach, a sleepless night, and a Monday morning—a *recipe for a long and painful day.*

The driver's impatient honking echoed through the quiet morning, despite spotting me by the roadside. With a roll of my eyes, I climbed aboard and settled into a seat at the back.

The ride to school was quiet, with most students now opting for cars due to the pressure of popularity. Even Lily, had succumbed to the craze.

The first person I saw as I stepped off the bus was her. Waving at me frantically. As usual, I ignored her and headed the opposite way. I had no idea why she wasted her time inviting me to the table with that group of idiots. Whatever benefit Lily saw by hanging out with them was beyond me. She wasn't pretentious or arrogant like them, yet her role in the cheer team somehow made her part of that circus. That was one thing where Lily and I would never see eye to eye. I preferred my privacy and solitude.

Taking refuge under the shade of a cypress tree, I opened my copy of Pride and Prejudice, flipping through dog-eared pages until I found my place.

Glancing up from the book, I spotted her crossing the field with a look of sheer determination, forcing me to acknowledge her presence, so I waved.

Lily stood before me, her expression a mix of annoyance and mischief, her hands firmly planted on her hips, her perfectly styled hair framing her pixie-like features. I admired her morning energy, wondering how anyone could be so lively at this hour.

"Ouch, what's that for?" I protested, nursing the spot on my arm where she had just delivered a karate chop.

"That's for ignoring me," she snapped, a smirk replacing her earlier irritation.

"Do they realize how weird you are?" I teased, aiming to rile her up for my arm's sake.

"Says you," she retorted, flopping down next to me against the tree trunk.

"Can we move past this and talk about the party? I know you're dying to tell me all about it," I urged, noting the excitement dancing across her face.

"You won't believe it. Ben asked me out!" she squealed; her happiness contagious. Ben, though popular, had always been different, just like Lily. I was pleased he'd finally mustered the courage to make a move.

"Does that mean you're officially an item now?"

"Baby steps. First comes the date, then the dating," she explained, blushing at the prospect.

I nodded knowingly. Ben's shy nature meant their journey to official coupledom would likely be a slow one. Lily beamed, clearly excited at the prospect.

"But you haven't heard the best part," she continued, but my gut stirred with unease at her excitement.

"Let me guess, someone got embarrassingly drunk?" I ventured.

"No, even better," Lily chortled. "Oliver confessed he likes you."

I sputtered. "You're joking. Is this payback for missing your party?"

"I wish it were. He's been asking questions about you. At

first, I found it odd, but when he blurted out your name when asked about his crush, I knew it was real. He's been fixated on you ever since. And he wasn't even drunk when he spilled the beans," she mumbled on, making absolutely no sense.

"I think I'm going to be sick," I muttered, rising to my feet, Lily following suit.

"Come on, it's kind of sweet that he likes you. And let's be real, half the girls at school would kill to be in your shoes," she reasoned and I didn't even know why she was still talking about this.

"If they want my shoes, they can have them," I quipped, feeling a mixture of disbelief and dread settle in the pit of my stomach.

The bell rang, just in time. Lily veered toward her class as I made my way to English. As the warning bell chimed, I slid into my seat.

OLIVER

My father's words reverberated off the stone walls, rattling me to my core.

"You obey without question. Understand?" he ordered.

"Yes, father. But why her? Why now?" I countered.

"How do you expect to inherit my seat if you can't follow orders without questions? Befriend that girl, by any means necessary. I need access to that house, to her aunt. Am I clear?"

"Yes, Sir."

. . .

As the bell rang, I pushed aside the thoughts of my father's demands and entered class deliberately late. Standing out was second nature to me—being the best, the one everyone revered—except in my father's eyes. No matter my efforts, I could never meet his expectations.

"Apologies for being late, Mrs. Gill," I said, interrupting her attendance call.

She didn't bother lifting her gaze from the sheet. My habitual lateness went unnoticed, a privilege perhaps attributed to my charm and looks, though in reality, it was my father's generous contributions to the school that shielded me from the consequences.

My thoughts, drifted back to the night of the party.

"Sorry, what was the question?" I asked, trying to regain my focus.

"Come on, Oliver, spill it. Tell us who your crush is. Is it Bonny?" one of the girls whose name I could not recall, asked.

Truth or dare. The alcohol blurred my senses, but truth came easy. I had no crush. I could have any girl. The only problem was the lie I had to tell to pave my way into Belynda's world. If they bought it, she would too. It was either that or face my father—an unacceptable option.

Glancing around, I spotted her, seated alone at the back, just as I had anticipated.

BELYNDA

Though I wasn't a fan of Oliver, or his friends, I couldn't deny his appeal to most girls. He had the looks, and the charm, not to mention he was tall and his ranks in the football team ensured he stayed fit. However, he was undeniably a jerk. Ignoring his grand entrance, I pulled out my literature book and journal.

The class had settled when the chair next to me screeched against the floor. I jerked in response and glanced up in a panic, staring into the eyes of the devil himself.

"Do you mind if I sit here?" Oliver's green eyes gave me chills. I had never seen them this close, but they were a jade green that looked almost sinister in a strange likeness to mine. I broke eye contact, immediately returning to writing the notes on the board.

I didn't care if he was being polite. Hopefully if I ignored him long enough, he would get the hint and find a seat else-where. However, I wasn't that lucky. Oliver settled beside me with a thud, disrupting my peace.

I wouldn't let him get to me. I moved my book to the side of the table, trying to build an invisible barrier between us.

Everyone's eyes fell on us, and I could see that this new attention from Oliver was going to be an issue.

"This is boring," He muttered. "Can I borrow your notes from last class?"

I didn't look away from my book. *Oliver's attempt at small talk only fueled my suspicions.*

"Ok. Listen here, Oliver. To be clear, I'm not interested. I don't want you to sit next to me. In fact, I'll rather not have anything to do with you." His face hardened, but his resolve to annoy me was greater than the embarrassment of rejection. Collecting himself, he let out a forced laugh.

"You're very defensive, aren't you? I didn't know you had such personality, or I would have spoken to you sooner." He added, smiling like the confident fool he was.

"Oliver, is there something you want to share with the class?" The teacher asked.

Everyone turned to stare at us.

"No, Mrs. Gill. It was Belynda... she was being funny, that's all," he replied smoothly, earning a warning glance from our teacher.

I was going to kill him.

There were so many things I wanted to say to him, but instead I bit my tongue. The wise choice was not to encourage him any further. Oliver didn't try to speak again during class; I figured it was due to the vibe I was sure he could sense radiating from me.

As the bell sounded, I hurriedly gathered my things, ready to make my exit. But before I could flee, my book bag straps were yanked, forcing me to face the devil himself. My expression must have been murderous as Oliver took a step back.

"Okay... okay, I'm sorry. Just give me a sec, okay?" he pleaded, hands raised in surrender. "Look, I know I'm a jerk. I just can't help it, sorry."

Well, at least he was self-aware, I thought, suppressing a sigh. Being an idiot seemed to come naturally to him, but perhaps there was more to Oliver than met the eye. I searched his face for any clue about his intentions, but he remained unreadable.

"This should be interesting," I said, humoring him. He smiled awkwardly, seeming out of his element for once.

"I only wanted to ask you out for coffee, or maybe I can give you a ride home after school sometime," he offered tentatively.

I couldn't help but feel a pang of embarrassment for him. Whatever his game was, he seemed uncomfortable. But what if it wasn't a game? What if, beneath his hard-to-get exterior, he genuinely liked me? The thought softened my hostility towards him slightly, but I remained cautious.

"I'm sorry, but I can't," I declined politely, turning to leave.

"Wait, you don't mean that. What about this weekend?" he persisted.

"It's not going to happen, I'm sorry," I repeated a bit harsher this time, hoping he'd understand.

"Oh, come on. You can pick the time and place," he pressed on, his tenacity irking me.

I sighed inwardly, realizing he wasn't taking no for an answer. I needed to be direct, to spare him further embarrassment.

"Oliver, I'm not interested. It won't happen, today, tomorrow or ever," I stated firmly, cutting off any further debate. His surprised expression told me he rarely received such candor.

"I'm sorry. I have to go. I'm going to be late for class," I added, turning to leave.

"You should know I don't give up easily," he called after me as I exited the classroom. There had to be a way to make him leave me alone, to rid myself of this unwanted attention once and for all.

By LUNCHTIME, my mood had improved. I sat alone, lost in music, trying to escape my thoughts. The day passed quickly after that, thankfully. Lily didn't bring up Oliver when she stopped by my locker, and I didn't either. With Lily, less was best, especially since I had enough complications to deal with —like unraveling the mystery of Isabel and why she haunted my dreams.

2
FINDINGS

CELEST WASN'T HOME—her car wasn't in the driveway, which was odd, considering she usually closed the library early on Mondays. After hanging my coat, I discovered a note and two twenty-dollar bills on the kitchen counter.

Belynda, help yourself to the leftovers from last night. I should have mentioned something sooner, but I didn't get a chance yesterday. I'm heading out of town for the day to a librarian conference.

I'm hoping to be back by tomorrow. Please open the library tomorrow after school if you do not hear from me by then. Be careful and call me if you *need me. I have left you some money in case of an emergency.*

Stay safe, Celest...

A LIBRARIAN CONFERENCE? It seemed odd, but I wasn't complaining. With the house to myself, I crumpled the note and tossed it aside. Enjoying the temporary freedom, I emptied my book bag onto the counter and tackled my English and math homework, though I abandoned the last few equations. Numbers weren't my strong suit. After packing everything away, I found myself gazing up at the ceiling.

Every young adult's dream was to stay home alone, yet I found myself with nothing exciting to do. The recent development with Oliver made me hesitate to call Lily. Instead, I retrieved the nail polish box from the bathroom and returned to my room. As rain began to fall outside, I settled onto the cushioned bench by the window and painted my nails, the gray sky mirroring my mood.

Lost in daydreams, I gazed out at nothing in particular while the polish dried, finding peace in the empty road and the sway of the grass in the wind. My stomach protested, snapping me out of my reverie. As I stood, my foot cramped, causing the unscrewed polish bottle to topple over, spilling thick burgundy gloss onto the bench and wall.

"Crap. Crap. Crap. Great. Just great!" I cursed, horrified as the burgundy seeped into the rug.

Raiding the kitchen cabinets for cleaning supplies, my stomach grumbled again. I devoured the leftover noodles in a few bites, hastily grabbing a bottle of water, some napkins, and a spray can from the cleaning supply room.

Relief washed over me as the stains began to fade. Considering my recent bad luck, I deserved a break. Only a stubborn speck of paint remained in a small fissure where the wall met the bench. Grabbing some scissors, I attempted to dislodge it, but there was a loud crack, followed by an explosion puff of dust.

I jumped back. "Damn it!" I cursed again, as I stared at the top of the bench now separated from the wall.

Moving closer to inspect the damage, I prodded the wooden bench and to my horror it opened wider like the top of a chest. Sitting up on my knees, I peeked inside the opening—a dark and dusty space, long buried and forgotten. I couldn't see a thing, so I pushed harder on the top until it finally gave.

Hesitantly, I moved my hands about the space, removing the spider webs that cloaked the opening. A few objects rested at the bottom, blanketed in a thick layer of dust. My heart fluttered and my mind raced with a million questions. Was it my mother's? Perhaps a secret or hidden treasure of hers? Whatever lay within my reach sure hadn't been disturbed in a long time. This old and forgotten space smelled of decay and the faint stench of humidity, reminiscent of the old section at the library.

With the light from my cell phone, I illuminated the darkened crevice and reached inside with apprehension, taking hold of the first item my hand touched. It was cold and heavy, undoubtedly ancient—a chalice. The timeworn brass metal was dented, resembling artifacts found in museums or shrines. Inspecting the heavy metal in my hand, I couldn't help but wonder whose cup this had been—my mother's or one of my ancestors, without a doubt. But why was it hidden? Perhaps it was a prized family heirloom.

Using my sleeve, I wiped away some of the dust and noticed a symbol scored into one of the sides of the cup. The mark looked like three eyes, all interlaced at one end.

Goosebumps prickled my skin, and a surge of electricity shot down my spine—an unusual reaction. The cup held secrets my ancestors had guarded, but why remained a mystery like everything else in my life it seemed. It made me think about my dreams, prompting a chilling notion: perhaps madness ran in the family.

A sudden wave of heat, dizziness, and numbness overwhelmed me, as I cleaned the cup's base. Inscribed across the bottom was a name—Isabel. *Was I dreaming?* The possibility seemed plausible, yet as I brushed my fingers over the name, the strange sensation I usually felt while dreaming was not present this time.

In a panic, I hurled the cup back into its hiding spot and slammed the top shut.

The more I tried, the less I managed to grasp a logical explanation. Was I losing my mind, or was I truly being haunted by Isabel's ghost? *No, it had to be a dream—although the most vivid I'd had.*

Reaching for my dream journal, I searched for my last entry...

Isabel's name was in almost every line, scrawled in my handwriting. I reached for my cell phone and checked the time and date, desperate to convince every logical part of myself that I wasn't dreaming. Still, the truth was that any other alternative was just as scary — if not worse to consider.

I went downstairs to clear my head. Everything was just as I had left it. Returning to the couch, I skimmed through the channels aimlessly, before shutting the TV off. Glancing at Celest's note, discarded in the trash, the inevitable question stared back at me: if I wasn't dreaming, was I losing my mind? Or was it possible that somehow, there were supernatural ways that could connect something so old—and likely dead—to this world? Some unexplainable method that no rational human mind could understand.

HEART POUNDING, I rushed upstairs with determination. Ignoring the facts wouldn't solve anything. For years, I'd wished for answers to stop the dreams. If this was a divine sign, I had to take it. With resolve, I shut the door, entered the dim room, and flicked on the bedside lamps. Sitting on the floor, I steeled myself before the bench once more. Though part of me hoped it was all in my imagination, I knew I had to face it head-on, however scary it seemed.

Taking a deep breath, I pushed up the top of the bench, my heart racing as it creaked open. Unsure what terrified me more —losing my mind or confronting the truth. I reached inside and recoiled at the touch of cold metal. It was real. Trembling, I retrieved the chalice, its weight heavy in my hands, the name "*Isabel*" carved upon it.

Isabel. Isabel. Isabel. The name stared back at me as if daring me to deny its existence.

I wanted to believe there was a reasonable explanation;

but my whole being told me otherwise. I tried to deny it, but the electrifying connection as I held the chalice in my hand was unexplainable—as unexplainable as my firm belief that this Isabel and the one from my dreams were the same. If she was one of my ancestors, it could explain why her belongings were hidden here.

I tried to reason with the warring in my head, but there was nothing normal about having dreams that defied logic: like magic rituals and winged men. This cup wasn't justification enough to believe in something so unimaginable. No, I needed more proof.

With a sigh, I set the cup down and reached into the opening once more. My fingers touched the edges of a box-shaped object, heavy enough to require both hands to retrieve it.

Carefully, I placed the box beside the chalice on the carpet and unwrapped it from its dusty cloth covering. Contrary to my initial assumption, it was not a box, but a large and ancient book. Running my hands over its weathered cover, I felt a sense of awe. Despite my experience with old books from working at the library, none had ever compared to this one.

The first page displayed an inscription in an unfamiliar language, its delicate paper threatening to crumble under my touch. But as I turned the page cautiously, I found myself able to decipher some of the faded text: *"Manifest (IV) The Sacred Knowledge."*

Though much of the text remained legible, its meaning was lost on me. The first pages delved into the uses of herbs, oils, and stones, many entirely foreign to me. Beyond the introduction, intricate symbols adorned the pages, one of which matched the mark on the cup. I leaned in with curiosity and read about the *Three Quetrus*—a symbol representing the realms of sky, sea, and land, as well as the mind, body, and soul connection. It also made mentions of its uses as a protective talisman.

Feeling overwhelmed, I couldn't deny the possibility of magic anymore. If this were true, then the unrealistic elements of my dreams might hold some truth too: the ritual, the thunder, and the mysterious winged man that haunted my thoughts. It meant accepting that my world was a façade, to a bigger reality, one my mother and ancestors appeared to have been aware of.

But beyond the unsettling truths lay Celest. Perhaps she knew more than she let on. As I wrestled with these revelations, I realized it would take time and more evidence to fully grasp this new reality. For years, I'd yearned for answers to my dreams, hoping for a simple solution. Now, I was faced with supernatural possibilities, which promised the answers I sought, however accept them, seemed too great a risk— possibly inviting more trouble than relief.

Turning the pages further, I discovered detailed instructions for sacred rituals, outlining tools, ingredients, and favorable timings. The complexity of the spells filled me with fear, the idea of beings vanishing or portals opening seeming too farfetched to be true.

When I reached the section on casting circles, I snapped the book shut and set it down beside the cup, my mind reeling with the weight of all this new knowledge.

• • •

ONCE MORE, I reached into the compartment, using my phone's light to illuminate the space. A piece of cloth caught my attention, and as I pulled, one of the floorboards came loose, revealing the final hidden item. With trembling hands, I retrieved the heavy piece, hesitation warring with curiosity.

My heart raced as I removed the cloth. Everything slowed. The metallic crash of metal echoed through the room.

Frozen, I stared at the sword on the floor. Encrusted stones adorned the hilt, while ancient symbols graced the blade.

I reached for it, my hands pricking as they felt its weight.

Gripping it by the hilt, I raised the sharp blade, mesmerized by the intricate details. Its craftsmanship was flawless, holding a sword, aroused a sense of power I'd never experienced before.

Amidst the fascination, a slew of new thoughts and questions swam in my head, all without rational explanations. I stared at the items before me, hoping for some semblance of normalcy to return.

In a desperate attempt to shake off the surreal feeling, I pinched myself and took a cold shower. Yet, upon returning to my room, the objects remained there, their presence undeniable. They seemed to challenge me, like Isabel's name on the cup, daring me to deny their existence.

I wasn't sure how long I stared at the cup, book, and sword, but eventually, I returned them to their dusty hiding place. With them out of sight, I felt a wave of relief wash over me. I could convince myself they were just figments of my imagination, products of my overactive mind.

Yet, despite my attempts at denial, I couldn't shake the unsettling thoughts that plagued me. After reading the contents of that book, I could picture Isabel as some sort of witch or malevolent fairy tale creature, sent to torment me. What would come next? Vampires, werewolves, dragons, fairies, and ghosts? Overwhelmed by fear and confusion, I ran to the bathroom, retching in horror until there was nothing left inside me.

HOURS PASSED, and I slowly regained some semblance of calm. Eventually, I mustered the strength to get up and brush my teeth. As I splashed water on my face, I stared at my pale reflection in the mirror and for a moment, I felt a prickling sensation, almost as if I were being watched. I dismissed the thought, knowing I was only susceptible by my recent findings.

Glancing at the clock on my nightstand, I realized Celest wouldn't be returning tonight and for the first time, I was scared.

I climbed into bed, but sleep remained elusive as a million thoughts thundered through my mind. *What are you, Isabel? And what do you want from me?* Unable to shake the unsettling feelings, I glanced at the bench beneath the window. The cup, the book, and the sword seemed to pulse within their dark and hidden space, taunting me.

WHEN THE FIRST light of morning filtered through the windows, I was already dressed and seated at the breakfast counter. The whirlwind of thoughts in my head showed no signs of slowing, even after a few sleepless nights. And to add to my discomfort, the cursed items remained as real as ever this morning. A fact, I had confirmed as soon as I opened my eyes.

As I stepped off the bus at school, I silently prayed for a day without Oliver. Mentally, I couldn't handle dealing with him today, or any other day for that matter.

"What happened to you? You look like hell!" Lily's voice broke through my internal shatter, mirroring my earlier thoughts when I caught my reflection on the bathroom mirror.

"Just tired, that's all. No worries, though. You're bubbly enough for the both of us," I replied, attempting to divert her attention away from me. As we approached the building, the bell rang.

"Oh, by the way. Could I ask you for a small favor?" I began, hoping she would say yes.

Lily smirked in response. "What is it? You never ask me for anything, so whatever it is must be good."

"Well, I hate to disappoint you, but I only need a ride. I need to go to the library right after school."

"Boring..."

"I'm not sure what you expected."

"I don't know. Maybe you wanted me to send a message to a certain person," she teased, wiggling her eyebrows suggestively.

"Hell would have to freeze over," I deadpanned, knowing exactly who she meant.

"I guess you're right. Why I expected more, I have no idea. Anyways, I got to run."

"Wait, is that a yes?" I called after her.

"Of course. See you later."

• • •

I WAS RELIEVED to find Oliver absent from class; my only struggle was battling sleepiness. By the time school ended, I felt like a walking zombie.

The temperature had noticeably dropped. "Oh god, it's freezing," I shivered as I hopped into Lily's warm car and was greeted by a look of concern. "Belynda. Are you sure you're alright?"

"I told you I'm fine. Just haven't been sleeping well," I assured her.

"Then you should be resting. Just know I'm here for you, anytime," she offered, her voice soft with genuine worry.

"I know. Thanks," I replied, grounded by her kindness, and decided to try to be a better friend. "Why are you going to the library anyway?" she asked, after a brief pause.

"It's a favor for Celest. She's out of town and asked me to open the library this afternoon."

"You're home alone! I envy you."

"Trust me, it's not as exciting as it appears," I replied, recalling yesterday's events.

"You say that because you don't know how to have fun," Lily teased.

"You're probably right. But seriously, who in their right mind thinks about going for ice cream in this weather?"

"Honestly, I don't care about the ice cream. I'm only going because it's supposed to be Ben's shift."

"I'm happy for you. Maybe we can all hang out together sometime?" I suggested, hoping for a distraction from my own thoughts. I figured it was a normal gesture of friendship.

"Are you serious? Oh, this is epic. EPIC," she beamed, her excitement making me laugh.

"By the way, I meant to ask you. Did anything happen between Oliver and you at school yesterday?" I hesitated, considering whether to tell her what had happened, but I couldn't bring myself to lie.

"He asked me out, but I said no," I confessed, feeling a pinch of irritation at the memory.

"Why didn't you tell me?"

"You know me. I don't share much, and I didn't want you to get any ideas about Oliver and me," I explained.

"Well, you must not have been clear enough, because he's under the impression that you and him are an item," Lily blurted. I stared at her in shock.

Forget about being sleepy and tired, I was ready to murder Oliver.

"You have no idea how furious I am right now. You do know he's lying, right? He needs to back off and stop spreading rumors," I fumed, my frustration bubbling.

"Ignore him. He'll get over it soon enough," Lily said, trying to make me feel better.

"I hope you're right. There is too much going on in my life without adding an Oliver-sized headache to the mix," I sighed, feeling the weight of my troubles closing in.

"Is everything ok? I know you don't like to talk about your life much, but you know you can trust me," Lily reminded me again, with visible concern.

"I know I'm not the best of friends and I'm sorry for being so closed off. It's just that my life is a little complicated. I don't tell you my problems, not because I don't trust you, but because I can't even make sense of them myself," I confessed with a smirk.

"Yes. Mom mentioned last night that your aunt canceled your sessions." I nodded, realizing Celest had made good on her promise. "Look, it's ok if you don't want to tell me every-thing. I understand. I only want to know that you're alright, that's all," she assured, her voice gentle and understanding.

"Honestly, although things have been a little crazy, I'm starting to find some clarity. I guess what I'm trying to say is that I'm alright. You don't have to worry. I mean it, I'm good," I reassured her, feeling a sense of relief at being able to share some of my burden with her.

"Ok, then. So, your birthday...what are we going to do?" Lily changed the subject, attempting to lighten the mood.

"Nothing. That's not until next week and seriously, you know I don't make a big deal of it," I replied, surprised that she always managed to remember. She rolled her eyes, a clear indi-cation she wasn't heeding my words.

"Thank you for the ride," I said as we reached the bend outside the library.

"Anytime. Text me when you've finished, and I'll pick you up. Unless you prefer to sleep up there in the book dungeons," Lily laughed, the sound, bringing a smile to my face.

"I'd rather not," I smiled. "Oh, and Lily? Please try to discourage Oliver's notion of me," I added before getting out of the car, my frustration still lingering.

"I'll see what I can do. But I can't promise anything."

"Thank you. Be safe," I said before hurrying into the library, feeling the chill in the air and my worries settling back over me.

. . .

I FLIPPED the library sign to open and switched the lights on, illuminating the room. Throwing my book bag on the couch, I glanced at the overflowing return cart. *Unbelievable.* With a heavy sigh, I contended with the idea of having to re-shelve the books again. Reluctantly, I pushed the cart, appreciating the echo of my footsteps as I moved through the silent library. Savoring the peace.

Returning the books to their individual places, I made my way toward the back shelves. As I reached for one of the last books, a strong sense of déjà vu washed over me. I turned the book over, recognizing it immediately as the one I had shelved Sunday afternoon, the one that had fallen to the floor.

With piqued curiosity, I flipped through the pages until I landed on a familiar picture: *"The Dragon Kingdom and Guardians of the Realms."* Celest's stubborn interest in this book made my skin prickle. The words on the page resonating, with my recent dreams.

"The Guardian of Realms and Dragons..." I murmured to myself; the words echoed those from my dream journal. A shiver ran down my spine. It was as if the universe was orchestrating events to drive me to madness.

Stepping down from the ladder, I carried the book back to the front of the library, my mind buzzing with fear and uncertainty.

I IMMERSED myself in the text on the right page, instantly drawn into the hypnotizing tale. It unveiled the origins of the first guardians, twelve children chosen by the Goddesses of destiny. These children, born with unique gifts, were raised, and educated in the craft of magic with the purpose of protecting the secrets of the elemental realms from the human world, and guarding the portals between the worlds. The passing down of their knowledge and responsibilities became a sacred tradition, where only the firstborn inherited their parent's gift.

The legend recounted the birth of the first pureblood, a girl born from two guardians under the Cromwell legacy. She was said to possess extraordinary power and the gift of sight. Raised amidst the creatures of the realms, she grew into a formidable young woman. The dragons, rulers of the fire realm and closest allies to the guardians, were depicted: as immortal beings with control over fire with the ability to shape-shift.

The tale took a romantic turn when the pureblood fell in love with the prince of the fire realm—a Dragon, defying the most sacred rule. The council's discovery led to the severance of her lineage's rights, causing division among the guardians. Some were believed to oppose the ascension of the pure blood's lineage out of fear of her powers.

This division marked the separation between the Guardians and the magical realms. The pureblood, resolved to remain with the prince, attempted a forbidden spell to grant him a mortal life beside her. However, her defiance resulted in the guardianship condemning the Dragon prince to the shadows of the dark realm—a placed described ed as a prison for immortals. Despite this, the dragon accepted his fate, opting to endure the sentence to uphold peace among the realms, understanding that no suffering could compare to losing her.

• • •

I HELD the book in my hands, its weight a tangible reminder that it wasn't a mere figment of my imagination. Terror crept over me, wondering how many before me had seen it as nothing more than a beautiful tale of myth. Little did they know, it was a nightmare brought to life, haunting my dreams with tragic outcomes that somehow intertwined with my own existence.

As I sat on the couch, re-reading the story, I couldn't deny the truth vibrating in my bones. Isabel, the protagonist, was undeniably real, and her love for the immortal Dragon mirrored the connection I felt with the winged man in my dreams. Another important piece of information I'd learn, was that the stolen book, *"The (IV) Manifest,"* triggered the legacy's downfall, marking the loss of sacred knowledge and the guardianship's access to all realms.

Closing the book, I took a deep breath. For the first time, I prayed for the dreams to come, eager to discover Isabel's fate and my purpose in this nightmarish tale. Accepting this newfound reality was frightening, especially considering the supernatural world it unveiled. Yet, despite the confusion, I saw some clarity, shedding light on Celest's fascination with these books and my family's secrets.

Moving forward, I had to tread carefully around Celest, I couldn't shake the betrayal of being kept in the dark for so long, suffering without explanation. The realization was sobering. I was alone—the one person I thought to count on, I couldn't trust.

. . .

RETURNING the book to its place on the shelf, I typed out a quick message to Lily. The afternoon had been slow, with only a couple of girls from school visiting.

As the front door swung open, Celest entered, struggling under a pile of books. "Hey," I greeted in surprise.

"Do you mind giving me a hand?" she asked, setting the books down on the counter.

"Sure," I replied in an awkward attempt to put aside my mistrust. I helped her with the books, suppressing the urge to voice the questions in my head. For now, I had to keep up appearances, hide my suspicions until I knew what her true role was in this story.

"How was your trip?" I asked as we worked to unload the rest of the books.

"It went well. I got some new material for the library," she replied. "But I miss my bed. I hate sleeping in hotels."

"I'm glad it worked out," I offered, stepping back to grab my bag.

"Where are you going? We can leave together. I'm just about done," she said, and I froze.

"Actually, I made plans with Lily. She's picking me up, if that's okay," I explained, grateful for the excuse Lily unknowingly had provided.

"Of course. I'm happy that you're spending time with your friends," Celest said with a genuine smile, momentarily catching me off guard. I reminded myself of her manipulative nature, steeling my resolve.

"Yeah, Lily's great. I'll ask her to come over one of these days," I replied, my tone more forced than I intended.

"You can bring her anytime you want. I would love to see her," Celest added before my phone buzzed, with Lily's reply.

"Speaking of the devil. I have to go," I said hastily, grabbing my bag.

"Just don't be home late. It's getting dark out and it's a school night," Celest called after me as I hurried out to of the library.

THE SKY WAS a mixture of black and gray, and the cold had not diminished. A particular smell lingered in the air, the same smell that often came before it rained.

Lily sighed. "You probably had more fun in the book dungeons, than me."

"Did you get to see Ben?" I asked, her face fell.

"He didn't show up," she replied, thoughtful for a moment. "Neither did Oliver, actually. I wonder what kept them. They didn't answer their phones either, which is odd."

"Maybe his phone died," I suggested, "I'm sure he has a good explanation," she grimaced, so perhaps I wasn't helping.

We had barely made it to the front of the house before the first drops of rain hit the windshield. Lily still looked sad.

"Thank you for the ride. Please text me when you get home."

She nodded as I shut the door.

BOUNDING UP THE PORCH STEPS, I shielded myself from the rain with my book bag. The house, usually welcoming, now seemed eerie in the darkness. Despite turning on the lights, I couldn't shake off the unsettling feeling lingering from my recent discoveries.

After a quick shower, I slipped into my comfortable pajamas, seeking solace by the window. The rain pounded against the glass, its relentless rhythm mirroring my restless thoughts.

As Celest's car pulled into the driveway, the storm outside intensified, shrouding the sky in darkness and thunder. Though I wanted to avoid her, I knew I couldn't hide in my room forever. I hurried downstairs to grab a snack, intending to bid her good night and excuse myself quickly.

I had barely finished my juice when Celest entered, soaked from the rain. "It's crazy outside," she shivered, hanging up her coat.

"Yeah. You should change quickly," I advised, eyeing the water pooling around her.

"I know. I'm ready for a warm bath. I'm going to bed early; it's been a long day," she said wearily, and I could see the exhaustion in her eyes. I imagined, keeping up such deceit could be tiering. I *almost* felt sorry for her. *Almost.*

"Do you want me to fix you something to eat?" she offered, interrupting my thoughts.

"No, that's okay. I just had some juice," I declined, watching her move about the kitchen.

"Okay. I'll take some tea with me to bed. You should rest; you look tired too," she suggested and the kindness in her voice felt so sincere—I didn't know what to make of it.

"I will. Goodnight," I replied, turning for the stairs.

"Goodnight," Celest said, hesitating before adding, "Um, Belynda. I know I might not say it often, but you know I love you, right? No matter what?" Emotion welled up inside me, choking me. I wanted to believe her, so I nodded and forced a smile before fleeing to my room, tears spilling as I closed the door behind me.

Settling by the window once more, I wrestled with conflicting emotions. Celest's words were like a knife, stirring up doubts. If she cared, then why lie? She had to know about the magical things hidden in our home, concealed beneath the chest by the window. Her interests in the books at the library were confirmation that she knew something. Whatever her motives, I decided to keep my guard up until I found out all the facts.

Thunder rumbled, and lightning pierced like lashing tentacles through the darkness. Thoughts of Isabel swirled in my head, each possibility on our connection, more bewildering than the last. Despite the fear and uncertainty, eventually, exhaustion pulled me in and this time, I welcomed whatever dreams or nightmares it brought.

THE SKIES WERE ALMOST DARK. *Down on my knees, the only thing I could focus on through the angry tears was my mother's retreating figure as she returned to the circle.*

"I hate you!" I shouted, overcome with rage., but she wasn't moved.

How could they? They knew nothing of his essence, his humanity. They considered themselves almighty, yet they were monsters—

compared to him. Without him, I was lost. Curse my pureblood, curse the fates, curse the rules that condemned us.

Driven by a frenzy of anger and pain, I rose to my feet and sprinted towards the glowing circle. I cared not for their rules; I needed to see him one last time. He had to know I would fight for him until my dying breath.

Drawn by his presence, I stumbled towards him, unable to tear my gaze away. By the fates, I loved him. Standing tall and defiant, armed with strength and dignity in the face of injustice—as though nothing could touch him. The royal blood that flowed through his veins, was evident in every line of his regal form. I knew his pride forbade him from bowing to anyone, even in the face of his imminent fate.

His fists were clenched tightly by his sides, his anger barely contained. His jaw and shoulders tensed, he was fighting to contain his fire.

"I will not lie to save myself. If her and I are a mistake, you can sentence me now as I am guilty," he declared, his once-soothing voice now dripping with fury. Pain gripped me, tearing me from the inside.

Though his grey eyes avoided mine, he was very aware of my presence. However, his control was already hanging by a thread, if he looked at me, broken it would end him. He was a warrior; he would fight his element as long as possible to retain his human form. He didn't want to be judged as a monster; losing control was out of the question.

In this surreal moment, reality blurred with the dreamlike state. Boundaries between Isabel and me dissolved, her pain became my own. I yearned to reach out to him, to feel the safety of his arms around me.

. . .

As the elder pronounced his sentence, time slowed to a crawl. With every syllable, the weight of impending doom pressed down on me. When he uttered the final word, 'Xelraa', I acted on instinct, hurling myself through the circle, past the startled guardians, and into Drake's arms.

It took him only a moment to realize what I had done but, as he felt my arms wrap around his torso, he responded, bringing me closer. His warmth chased away my fears, and for that second in time, I was unafraid. In his arms, I felt whole.

We had always shared this connection—an attraction too powerful to fight. It felt like destiny, even if others couldn't see it.

As he gently kissed the top of my head, I focused on his lips. His touch was gentle as he cupped my face, his nose tracing along my cheek barely grazing my skin until finding the hollow beneath my ear. Warm currents pulsed through my body as his lips met mine.

"It will be ok, Isabel. I promise," he whispered, trying to reassure me. "Don't worry about me."

His eyes pleaded with mine, willing me to believe, but I knew better. There was nothing he could do, except fight them all, and he wouldn't do that. He wasn't the monster they thought.

My heart broke all over again as I brought my hand to his face, memorizing every detail. He leaned into it. His silvery eyes almost glowed as my fingers traced over the dip of his lips, his warm breath sending currents of heat searing down my spine. Bringing one hand to my lower back, he kept my face in place and slowly leaned forward and claimed my lips for a kiss—a kiss that had the bitter taste of finality. I gripped his shoulders refusing to accept his fate.

"That's enough, Isabel. You too, Drake," my mother called, interrupting the last moment I had left to claim.

"No, you can't!" I clung to him, unwilling to move.

"Isabel. Look at me, please." Drake implored, wiping away my tears. "You need to be strong now for the both of us. I cannot leave in peace knowing you cannot deal with this choice—this life," the calmness in his voice, infusing me with resolve.

His eyes shone, and so many emotions burned within them. He was right. We couldn't let this be the end.

"I promise you, this is not goodbye," my tears flowed as I spoke. "We will find a way back to each other. I don't know how or when, but I will not rest until that day comes."

"Just promise me that you will be safe. For me. Promise," he pleaded, desperately searching my eyes for confirmation.

I bowed, unable to say the words as he pulled me into his arms.

"I will set you free. I will make this right, I promise. I don't care how many lifetimes it takes. I will find a way," I whispered, my cheek cradled against his chest.

"I'm yours," he whispered, leaning his forehead against mine. "Forever."

Before I could speak, I was torn away from him by two of the council guards.

"Let her go!" Drake commanded; and yet they hesitated. "I said. Let her go!" He took one step toward us, his voice no longer calmed.

I struggled against their hold, and this time, they released me, and Drake turned away from me, staring at my mother.

"Just get this over with," he growled.

"Are you certain you're ready to proceed without your parent's

presence to offer their goodbyes?" My mother questioned, with hesitation and I knew she only did it for the queen's sake.

"I have made my peace. They know I have made my decision. Cast your sentence," Drake thundered.

Mother bowed her head in agreement and glanced at me before speaking the words that would condemn him to the shadows.

Their chanting took flight and as the wind picked up, I fought to keep my eyes open. It wasn't long until a deafening silence surrounded me, and as I opened my eyes all that was left were ripples of dirt, trails of light, shadows, and the memory of him.

THE CRUSHING lack of oxygen jolted me awake, my chest tight with a suffocating pressure that left me gasping and heaving for air. Tears streamed down my face as I realized I was back in my room, trapped in a nightmare from which I couldn't escape. How could Isabel's memories evoke such intense emotions within me? It was irrational, yet I felt the weight of her love for him pressing down on me—*Drake*. I trembled as his name echoed deep inside my mind.

Wrapped with anguish, I watched the dawn break through my window. When I finally summoned the strength to rise, dizziness overwhelmed me, sending me sprinting to the bathroom.

Collapsed on the cold tiled floor, I struggled to control the spinning sensation. Celest's gentle knock at the door pierced through my haze. *Please not now.* The bathroom walls danced around me in circles every time I tried to open my eyes.

"BELYNDA, you're going to be late for school," she nocked again. "Belynda...are you alright?" I cringed, surprised when I felt Celest's hand on my forehead.

"I think it's just my stomach." I mumbled, attempting to downplay my misery.

"What happened?" Celest pressed with concern.

"I don't know. I just got nauseous."

"Have you been crying?" Her direct question caught me off guard.

"No," I lied; bracing myself for further interrogation, but it never came. Silence hung between us, broken only by Celest's sigh. Slowly, I was able to open my eyes and shift my head to meet her gaze. Her brow furrowed. She was worried.

"You should have had some dinner last night. Juice is not a meal, you know!" Celest chided gently.

I was relieved she didn't push the issue further.

"You don't have a fever, so that's good," she added, placing her hand against my forehead again. "Can you stand?"

I nodded and grabbed onto Celest, who supported most of my weight. This time, the walls didn't spin.

"Ok, back to bed. You can't possibly go to school like this. You can barely stand on your own!"

I wasn't going to argue—not about that or anything. I couldn't even think about her betrayal; all I could do was push my anger aside and be grateful as she helped me back to bed.

"Just rest for a while. I'm going to make you some broth for later. I'm sure you'll feel better after you have some." She tucked me in, the weight of the covers comforting, before leaving the room.

The anguish rooted in my heart matched the weakness in my body. As I lay there with my eyes closed, the sickening feeling began to settle. Eventually, exhaustion overtook me, and I fell asleep.

WHEN I WOKE, it was past noon, but the spinning and nausea had subsided, leaving only a lingering weakness. I felt suddenly famished as I descended the stairs and found Celest in the kitchen.

"You're up," she said, surprised. "I was on my way to check on you. Are you feeling better? Hungry?" She smiled, making her way towards the stove.

"Better. Smells good."

She watched me silently, and I knew the wheels in her mind were turning. Likely wondering why I had been so upset, though I knew she wouldn't ask.

She served some soup and handed me a spoon, urging me to eat. "You'll feel better."

"Thank you," I said, digging in. It was the first decent meal I'd had since yesterday's lunch.

"Are you feeling well enough to stay by yourself for a while? I was hoping to get some things ready at the library for the book fair on Saturday, but I can stay if you need me to."

"No, go ahead. I'm feeling much better. I completely forgot the fair was starting this Saturday. I'm sure you have a lot of catching up to do."

She smiled and I returned it, choosing to set aside our differences for the time being.

Walking to the entrance hall, she grabbed her keys and coat. "Just call me if you need anything, alright?"

"I will, don't worry." I heard the door close behind her, followed by the rumble of the car engine as it left the driveway.

CELEST'S TIES to my mother and the family remained a mystery. She was hiding things—I didn't doubt that now, but I had no proof. However, her concern for me today, her nurturing, brought things into perspective. She couldn't be so heartless; she must have reasons for lying to me. Until I figured out what those were, I was forced to keep my recent findings to myself. My main concern now was Isabel. These dreams or memories were clear indicators that she wasn't at rest. She needed something, and I had to figure out what. Helping Isabel and deciphering the messages of the dreams—that was my priority.

After rinsing my dish, I sprawled across the couch. For the first time, I glanced at the gargoyle-like statues with different eyes. They no longer represented something impossible or dark. They reminded me of Drake, and for some reason, I felt a sense of belonging. Even the strange décor in the halls pulsed with meaning. I was living in a world where magic was no longer fiction. It was a revelation, and I wondered how I hadn't noticed it before. Then again, it wasn't every day that one woke up and discovered that the world as we knew it was a lie.

As I stared at the ceiling, the crisp images from my dream resurfaced. Although physically I felt better, the hollow sensation inside of me remained. The unexplained sadness lingered. Closing my eyes, I almost felt Drake's touch and the warmth of his arms around me. Unconsciously, I touched my lips, recalling how he had felt. *The memory of his eyes...*I couldn't grasp the strange emotions now evolving and threatening to drown me. First, Isabel, and now Drake too. Slowly, these dreams sucked me into an abyss.

I tried to piece together recent events, but there were too many unanswered questions. Isabel was not a figment of my imagination; that was clear. Experiencing her pain and sorrow, especially after learning her story from the library book, gave her existence new meaning. The connection we shared, despite the gap in time and space, was proof of something beyond the ordinary. Whatever supernatural force was responsible for it, there had to be a reason for it.

HEADING BACK TO MY ROOM, I noticed Celest's office door slightly ajar, odd, since she usually kept it locked. Curiosity lured me in. Before I knew it, I was closing the door behind me.

The room lay in shadows cast by the desk lamps, giving it a gloomy feel. I wasn't sure whether it was the brown carpet or the aged mahogany desk, but something seemed to drain the life from the space. Despite being my mother's office once, I couldn't recall visiting it often. As a child, it remained off-limits, a fact I never questioned, though now I wondered if there was more to it, something they sought to hide.

The facts compelled me to believe that our lives were intertwined with the supernatural, so I could sympathize with their need for secrecy. *But why the conspiracy to keep me in the dark? Were they afraid I wouldn't believe them or understand?* It wasn't fair to blame my mother for my struggles; after all, it wasn't until after her death, that my dreams begun. But I wondered, if perhaps had I known then, what I knew now, if accepting the fairytale, the bizarre would have been easier than contending with the idea that I was losing my mind.

Pushing aside the unsettling thoughts, I opened the first drawer to find only office supplies. The second held old newspapers, which proved more disappointing. The third, however, was locked, a peculiar choice for an office that remained closed-off. Despite searching the desk, I found no key. As my gaze fell on the caller ID, one entry caught my attention—a Sunday evening call to an international number. Celest had never mentioned contacts abroad. Scribbling the number on a post-it note, I tucked it into my pocket.

Glancing at the certificates adorning the wall, my mother's name caught my eye. Knowing that Celest still maintained my mother's presence alive, somehow reinforced my inclination to give her the benefit of the doubt.

I couldn't tear my gaze from the imposing portrait dominating the left wall of the office. As my fingers brushed the coarse canvas, I felt the weight of history beneath them.

Thousands of names and dates were meticulously etched, into the surface, but one name stood out: *Sir Lucas W. Hershton (1745-1795)*. Hershton, my surname, inherited from my mother due to the lack of a paternal figure. Strangely, after his name, the entries ceased. Some names were accompanied by intricate miniature family crests, while others stood alone.

Tracing my fingers over the names, made me wonder about

the lives and legacies recorded here. My heart skipped when I ran over a familiar name: *Cromwell*. The entry from the library book echoed in my mind: *"born under the Cromwell legacy"*. *Isabel...*

Her name wasn't hard to find. It stood alone, devoid of descendants, more tangible now than ever: *Isabel Adams Cromwell (998 - 1024)*. The dates beneath her name brought on a quiet sadness. No matter how many times I counted, I couldn't bring myself to accept the truth. *Twenty-six.* Too young to die.

In my dreams, I was a vessel, experiencing Isabel's world through her eyes. Her age had remained a mystery until now. The notion of her premature death and the possibility of the guardians' involvement left me frozen, stunned by the implications for both her and me.

Leaving the office, I closed the door behind me, feeling a sense of determination settle inside me. Now more than ever, I needed answers, for Isabel's sake. My instinct told me the dreams were her way of seeking for help, but I wasn't sure of my path. I needed more answers.

The startling ring of the doorbell snapped me from my thoughts, and peering out the window, recognition twisted into suspicion. Why was he here, at my doorstep? My confusion morphed into irritation as I descended the stairs.

With a swift pull, I swung the door open. "What are you doing here?"

"Hello to you, too..." His tone dripped with sarcasm.

I resisted the urge to snap back, rubbing my forehead as a

headache began to bloom. "Oliver, this isn't a good time. Just tell me what you want."

"Can I come in?" *No absolutely not, I wanted to say,*

Please?" he added, and while I knew I might regret it later, his politeness softened my reluctance. After all, he was harmless. Just an idiot.

"Sure, whatever." I conceded reluctantly.

Inside, he commented on the eccentric décor. "It's kind of scary in here. I like it."

I rolled my eyes, shutting the door behind him. "Don't touch that," I warned as he reached for one of Celest's statues.

He shrugged, producing a couple of folded papers from his pocket. "That's the homework," he said, handing them to me.

"You could have just given that to me outside, you know..."

"Jeez. Thank you. That's all you had to say," he retorted, crossing his arms. B*e polite, be polite. He brought your homework,* I reminded myself.

"Thanks. You really shouldn't have bothered."

"I know, but it's worth two grades, so I figured it was important." I glanced down at the sheets of paper in my hands; his justification softening my tone.

"Thanks. Would you like something to drink?" I headed to the fridge.

"What do you have?" He asked, trailing behind me.

"I have soda, tea, water, and—milk," I replied, scanning the shelves.

"I'll take the soda." He settled on a stool in the kitchen without invitation, but I held my tongue, attempting civility.

Handing him the soda, I noticed his gaze, uncomfortable and irritating. "Stop that," I snapped.

He seemed confused. "You're staring at me—it's weird."

"Has anyone ever told you how stubborn you are?" he deflected.

"Look, I don't mean to be rude, but I have a headache; maybe you should leave."

"Why are you being difficult? Just go out with me once. Please. I promise I'll leave you alone after."

"I don't understand why you're so invested in me if you're willing to settle for one date. It's clearly not that important to you, which makes me wonder about the real reason you're so interested in going out suddenly?"

He hesitated, taken aback by the question, fueling my suspicion of his motives.

OLIVER

I knew that convincing Belynda to agree to this date would require extreme measures. The type of girl I was used to dating would not question my motives for liking them—hell, they would jump at the change, no questions asked. I never expected this to be a refreshing challenge. While part of me pursued her to please my father and keep watch over her and her aunt—I found her attitude and rejection equally refreshing, and strangely I became intrigued by the girl's life. I never shied away from a challenge, and this was no exception. Besides, defying my father's orders wasn't an option; I had to play along, even if it meant humbling myself and pretending to have feelings for her.

"Ok, I'll admit I already told everyone at school that I was taking you out and I'm sorry. I just didn't think you'd say no to me," I confessed, hoping for some mercy.

That's as much truth as I could offer but, from the look on her face, it wasn't helping my case.

"That's what you get for being so presumptuous," she shot back.

"I deserve that," I conceded.

"Look, I'm grateful that you brought me the schoolwork, but do you not think your behavior is strange?" she questioned, gesturing between us.

"It's not strange to me. I would like to get to know you. I see nothing wrong with that," I replied, though her skepticism was clear. I knew I'd have to beg.

"Not strange? We have never spoken more than two words to each other, and yet suddenly you're interested in hanging out. I'm not like you, Oliver. You and I are worlds—no *universes* apart. We couldn't be more different."

She was right, but I needed her to like me, or at least take pity on me. "Please, Belynda. Just one date, only to salvage my name in school," I pleaded, knowing it wasn't enough but hoping it would open the door to her closed circle. "That's all I'm asking."

BELYNDA

I realized he wouldn't give up, not with his reputation on the line. His determination might cause even more harm in the end. Yet, there was a surprising honesty in his motives, and for a fleeting moment, I found myself reluctantly considering his request.

ailment was: Oliver. Now that I was away from his schemes, I felt perfectly fine. Though I couldn't avoid him forever, I would take any reprieve the universe was willing to offer.

Wandering through the deserted hallways towards the library, I slipped past the librarian unnoticed and settled at a secluded table at the back. I pulled out the old book from my bag, uncertain of where to begin. The task of granting someone a soul or making them human was foreign territory for me; my knowledge was reduced to the realms of fantasy movies and TV series. Yet, if such things were possible, they likely involved a ritual or spell. Whether I believed it possible or not, it was a starting point. Something inside told me that these items were connected for a reason and that I was chosen to uncover their mystery, to understand Isabel's story, and help her. It felt like fate was finally aligning in my favor.

Flipping page by page, I searched the text for any word that might offer a clue, hoping for insight into souls' mortality or rebirth. The realm of magic was unfamiliar and unnerving, but despite my fear, excitement and curiosity outweighed the unease.

As hours passed, anxiety began to settle over me like a blanket. I had poured over the book for almost three hours without finding anything relevant, or a single clue. Glancing at my phone, I realized I was about to skip my third class, but at that moment, I didn't care.

Taking a bite of my packed sandwich, I flipped the page once more, and the word 'vanished' caught my eye. Though the entry wasn't quite what I was looking for, the familiarity of the word echoed in my mind, sending a jolt through me. The uneasy ache in my stomach returned, mirroring the fear and loss I had experienced upon waking the previous day—the same sense of defeat and helplessness Isabel felt as she watched the Guardians vanish Drake.

As I scanned the page, my unease grew with each word, particularly as it described the opening of a portal to the Dark Realm, also referred to as the Shadow World. Swallowing hard, I pushed down the lump forming in my throat. I was certain that the Dark Realm was where Drake had been sent.

As I carefully contemplated my options, fear crept in with each breath. Who was I kidding? This was all too overwhelming. I had the dreams, a cup, a sword, and this book, but I was no witch or Guardian. What use did I have for this spell? This wasn't a fantasy; it was real, and meddling with forces beyond my understanding terrified me. I was utterly alone, and if things went awry, I'd have no one to turn to.

I was clueless about Isabel and Drake's fate beyond what I had seen on my last dream. He could be dead or alive, trapped in the Dark Realm, or back in his world. Or perhaps I had lost my mind entirely for even entertaining such possibilities.

The thought crippled me with anxiety. It seemed like madness, yet the idea of opening that portal and bringing Drake back was both terrifying and tempting.

One thing I knew for certain: if I succeeded in this ritual and brought Drake back, he might provide answers, maybe even silence my dreams forever. Failure would mean closure, accepting my fate along with the dreams. I had nothing to lose, except perhaps my sanity, which, given the circumstances, was already in question.

As I read over the details of the ritual, a sense of déjà vu swept over me, as if these words had crossed my lips in another life, though I knew they hadn't. Despite the slim chances of success, I entertained the bizarre idea, trusting my ability to follow directions. I was already invested, committing to it, would not worsen the outcome. My life could not possibly get any worse.

It was decided. I would proceed with the instructions outlined in the book, praying I wouldn't embarrass myself or face a worse fate. After meticulously writing down the necessary ingredients and tools, I stowed the book away just as the bell for fourth period rang.

THE EXCITEMENT of the tasks ahead made the rest of the day go by in a blur. The halls were almost empty. Closing my locker, I almost jumped out of my skin when Lily appeared out of nowhere.

"Jesus, you scared me half to death!" I clutched my racing heart.

"Oh, please. I've been standing here for five minutes, but your mind is elsewhere."

"Sorry, I've been a bit distracted."

"I noticed. Everything okay? I didn't see you this morning or at lunch, and you weren't here yesterday. I called, but no answer."

No, things weren't okay. I wanted to tell her, but I couldn't drag her into my chaos. Besides, would she even believe any of it?

"Yeah, everything's fine. Had a stomach bug yesterday, couldn't sleep last night. And Oliver's been pestering me." I scoffed, falling into step beside her.

"That he has. Everyone thinks you're secretly dating."

I stopped outside of school, tugging Lily to a halt.

"Lily, I *seriously* don't like him. There is nothing between us, you know that right?"

She snorted. "You think I don't know you and him? He's lying. And he's not your type; I see you go for the tall, dark, and mysterious."

Her words conjured up images of Drake, but I pushed them away.

"I don't know what to do. He came to my house, brought my homework as an excuse for a date. I said no, twice! I'm desperate."

Lily stared at me, taking it all in. "Oliver doesn't take no for an answer." *Tell me about it...*

"Yeah, I get it. Maybe if I play along, he'll back off."

"He wants what he can't have. Maybe if you give in, he will back off."

She had a point. Maybe playing along was the only way out.

"I'm not thrilled, but I'll consider it. Looks like I'm running out of options."

"Who knows, maybe you'll like him once you get to know him," Lily teased, and I punched her arm.

"That's what you get for being a smartass. What about you and Ben? Everything sorted out?"

"Yeah, it was nothing. They had to stay late for football practice. Miscommunication. We're good." She brushed it off.

"You two are great together."

"Thanks," she beamed.

"I've got to catch my bus," I said, nodding towards the approaching bus.

"I could give you a ride," she offered, but I declined. Asking for favors still made me uncomfortable.

"No, it's fine. See you tomorrow!"

I waved as I boarded the bus.

3
LETTING GO

IN MY ROOM, I RETURNED THE BOOK** to its safe place and pulled the list of items from my back pocket. Glancing at the list of things needed for the ritual for perhaps the tenth time now, I realized I had no idea what half of these things were, let alone where I could find them.

Black Sand

Cinnamon

Acacia Root

Dandelion

Dragons Blood Resin

Jezebel

Myrrh

Agrimony

Blood Root

Ashwagandha Root
2 Black, 2 Red Candles
White Quartz Stone

The candles and cinnamon were easy to find, but the other items would be a problem. With no local stores specializing in the occult or metaphysics, I turned to the boundless realm of the internet for assistance. After a quick search, I found two metaphysical supply stores nearby—one in Northampton and another in Amherst. However, getting to either would be a problem; it would take anywhere between thirty minutes to an hour. Asking Lily for a ride was an option, yet explaining the purpose of the adventure would be tricky. Alternatively, there was a bus route, but it would take even longer. Which meant I would possibly have to miss school, or venture alone on the weekend, and slipping away without Celest's suspicion was unlikely.

I dialed the number to the Northampton store, and a soft-spoken lady answered.

"Selene Mystical Realm, how can I enchant you today?"

"Um, hi. I'm interested in purchasing a few items and was wondering if you have them in stock before I make the trip?"

"Of course. What exactly are you looking for?"

I went over the list, "I'm not entirely sure if I'm pronouncing them correctly. I'm not familiar with these names." I admitted.

She was silent for a moment, either confused or writing the items down. "Hmm, I believe we have everything. Could you repeat the list?"

After repeating the list, I waited patiently in line as she checked the inventory.

"Hello, are you still there?"

"Yes, I'm here."

"Good. It seems we have everything you need except the Dragon's Blood Resin. It's not a commonly requested item, mainly used for more intricate spells. Is it for you?"

Caught off guard, I stumbled over my words, "Oh, uh, not for me."

I wasn't sure why I felt so nervous. Surely, someone dealing in such trades had to delve in the supernatural believes. I laughed silently at myself, feeling like a character from a fantasy novel.

"Well, whoever's using it should know what they're doing. The elements aren't to be trifled with."

"Yes, it's not for me," I repeated, feeling rather foolish now. Despite my obvious discomfort, the woman remained friendly.

"In that case, I might be able to source the Dragon's Blood from a friend, but it won't be until tomorrow."

"That would be excellent. I can—or rather, the person needing it can—wait. No rush. What's your name again?"

"It's Selene."

"Thank you for your help, Selene. Should I check back with you tomorrow?"

"I'm confident I'll have it for you. When were you planning to visit?"

I hesitated, not having thought out my plan yet. The fair started on Saturday and getting away from helping Celest would be impossible. My only option was Lily.

"I was thinking of possibly heading over tomorrow afternoon."

"Sure, that should give me plenty time. Your items will be packed and ready." *Perfect.* The less time I spent there, the less I had to explain to Lily.

"That would be great. Thanks again for your help. See you tomorrow."

"My pleasure, sweetheart. Have a good afternoon."

I was oddly surprised by how smoothly the conversation had gone. Now, I needed to craft a reasonable excuse to ask Lily for the ride. She picked up on the third ring.

"Hey, B. Twice in one week? You're setting new records here."

"Oh, stop it. Are you complaining?"

"No, not complaining, just pointing out the obvious."

"You're right. I'm a terrible friend, but I need another favor and I have no one else to ask."

"Will you stop that? I already told you I'm here for you. Asking for help is not a crime."

"Thank you. I know I don't say it often, but you are a good friend."

"Don't get all sappy on me now. Tell me, what am I good for?"

"I need a ride tomorrow to Northampton."

"Northampton... sure. What's going on?"

I felt the weight of my lies, but I had no other choice. "Celest is swamped with prep for the book fair and asked me to pick up a package for her. She offered her car, but you and I both know how that's a recipe for disaster."

Lily chuckled. "Yes, god forbid you take the wheel. Though you know you will only get better with practice, right?"

"I know. It's not that. It's just... how my mother died."

"I'm sorry. I know you don't talk about what happened, but I didn't know. I didn't mean to upset you."

"It's okay. It was a long time ago, and you didn't know."

"Now I understand why you're so against driving. I'm glad you told me."

"I don't think about it, really, but your mom says the fear is subconscious, so I guess I can't help it." I didn't feel bad confessing this to Lily, because it was what little truth I could offer of my life.

"I would probably feel the same way. Don't worry about it. I'll take you tomorrow after school."

"Thank you. I'm sure Celest thanks you too, but I thank you more for all of those poor innocent lives we are saving," I joked, trying to lighten the heaviness of the conversation.

"See you tomorrow then?" Lily asked hesitantly, perhaps feeling guilty for hanging up after discussing my mother. But I was okay.

"Yeah. Good night and thank you again."

"Please don't mention it. Night."

Never had been so committed in my decisions. Having a purpose and a plan made me feel driven, more in control of my life than ever before. Although everything I was doing was the opposite of normal, I felt as if there could finally be a way to rid myself of these dreams for good.

By the time Celest arrived, I was rinsing off my dinner

plate. She hung her coat by the entrance hall and came into the kitchen.

"It's freezing outside and I'm starving."

"I heated up your frozen lasagna. It's still warm."

"That sounds like heaven right now. I've been surviving on coffee all day."

"Still organizing for the fair?" I asked while she served herself, before perching on the counter.

"Yes. The trip this week set me back a bit but I still have tomorrow." She replied between bites.

I felt proud of myself for not allowing our differences, or her lies, to prevail over civility. I owed Celest; although I didn't know her reasons for lying to me, the time would come when she would have to answer for them.

"If you're not too busy tomorrow after school, I could use your help." Celest asked, and I stilled for a moment.

"I can't. I agreed to go out of town with Lily after school. Maybe after, if we don't come back too late?" She glanced up from her plate with disbelief.

"I'll have to admit that I'm surprised but, in the same sense, pleased." If she only knew what we were really doing, she wouldn't be so pleased. "I'd hate to jinx it, but it looks like maybe stopping the therapy was a good decision after all."

"I guess. Maybe I don't feel as pressured. Lily is friendly too, so I don't mind her."

"Well, whatever the reason, I'm glad. You should bring her for dinner sometime. Maybe having someone normal around will help..." She trailed off, realizing where her conversation was headed. She didn't have to finish; I knew what she wanted to say.

"Yeah." I conceded, breaking the awkwardness.

"You go and enjoy yourself. We can get an early start on Saturday."

"Sounds like a plan."

"Thank you for all of your help. You know I really couldn't do it without you."

"I don't mind. I know it's important." She took another bite of her pasta, and I saw my opportunity to get away.

"I'm heading up. Have a good night."

"Mm hmm. Goodnight."

As I reached the stairs, I glanced at her closed office door. "Oh. You forgot to lock your office yesterday," I mentioned casually, observing her reaction. "I noticed the plaques on the wall from Mother and I got curious. I hope you don't mind," I added, noticing her growing discomfort.

"No...not at all." *Liar*, I smiled.

"Thanks. Goodnight."

"Yes...goodnight."

PULLING the hood tighter to my face, I stepped onto the school bus. Despite the biting cold, the sun shone and I was happy. It was Friday and I couldn't wait for the magic supplies to start preparing for the ritual. I had not had any dreams since Wednesday, and I felt rested.

Though to my utmost horror, Oliver was waiting as soon as I reached the school. I kept walking, refusing to sour my good mood this early in the day.

"Belynda, wait up." When I didn't stop, he grabbed my arm.

"Oliver, not now. Please," I pleaded, wiggling my arm free from his hold.

"You promised. You said you'd think about it. Please."

I took a deep breath to clear my head.

"Oliver." I looked up at him, lips pursed. "Be honest with your friends. Or, I don't know, tell them that you changed your mind about me. Give them any reason you want."

Surely, he could do that without ruining his reputation.

"I can't. Why are you being so difficult? Just once and I'll leave you alone. That was the deal."

"What deal? I didn't agree to anything."

"No, but you said you would think about it. You implied that you would help me." I stopped, releasing a sigh of frustration while he smirked, enjoying the predicament. "You know I won't give up, don't you?"

Yes, I did. I knew that very well!

"Why can't you just leave me in peace?" I snapped. Perhaps there was no other way to get rid of him.

"There is only one way I'll do that, and you already know my condition."

Unbelievable. I was being blackmailed for a stupid date. *One date!*

"A date, Oliver. The only one you'll get. After that, if you don't leave me alone, I will find a way to hurt your precious reputation. I swear."

"In that case, how does next week sound?" I wanted to argue, but as I watched Lily across the schoolyard, an idea popped into my head.

"That's fine. As a matter of fact, we can go with Lily and Ben," I smiled. "Double date." He didn't seem happy.

"That's not really what I had in mind," Oliver argued. His phone buzzed, and his face transformed as he read the message. "Uhhh, for fuck's sake," he mumbled before turning to me once again. "Next week then." Without another word, he walked away. I wasn't sure if it was irritation or concern written across his face, but it was good to know that at least someone was able to get under his skin. I called it karma.

OLIVER APPEARED to be in a lousy mood and failed to show up for first period. For that small reprieve, I was happy.

I tried to concentrate on the board, attempting to drown out the background chatter, though it was difficult when I was the topic. Agreeing to the date with Oliver no longer seemed like a good idea. Maybe it would have been less irritating to have Oliver annoy me than to be the talk of the school. Yet I had made my bed, and now I had to lie in it.

I was ready to run and hide by the time school finished. People walked up to me in the hallways, congratulating me as if my non-existent relationship with Oliver was something to celebrate. The perils of high school gossip. Lily was already by my locker and refrained from making any funny comments. It must have been the look on my face.

"Are you ok?" she asked with genuine concern.

"Yeah," I said, releasing a heavy sigh. "I'll be ok. I just have to ignore them. I'm sure it will die down in a few days."

"See, that's the spirit. Ready to go?"

"I've never been more ready to leave." I slammed the locker door and followed her to the car.

• • •

I usually avoided spending time with Lily outside of school. She wasn't privy to the chaos of my life, so it felt nice to enjoy some normalcy with someone close to my age. What I appreciated even more was her ability to recognize the topics I preferred not to discuss and how she respected my boundaries without judgment. When I mentioned the idea of a double date with her and Ben, she was ecstatic.

As Lily sped past the outskirts of town, I watched the scenery blur by while she cranked up the volume on the radio. Her laughter filled the car as she rolled down the windows and sang out the lyrics.

"Don't be shy. I know you know this song," she said, and I joined her in between fits of laughter as we shouted the chorus.

"I haven't laughed this hard in a long time. Thank you. I needed this," I admitted.

"That's because you're a hermit who never wants to do anything fun," she teased, hitting a bit too close to home.

"You mean parties, drinking, and dealing with the obstinate lot that you hang out with?" I retorted, and she couldn't argue with that. Oliver unequivocally fell into the obstinate category.

"Parties can be fun, you know," she insisted, but I knew it wasn't for me.

"With the right kind of people, maybe. Sometimes I wonder how you manage to be friends with them. Honestly, you're nothing like them," I said, genuinely curious.

She laughed and shook her head. "You're being biased because you detest socializing. I don't personally like everyone, but it doesn't mean I can't be civil. I don't particularly appreciate how they behave sometimes. Besides, you know me. I'm easygoing."

"You're right," I admitted.

"About what part exactly?" she asked.

"That I detest socializing," I replied with a small smile.

Lily laughed and changed the station. "Well, you're not getting away from our double date next week, that's for sure!"

I cringed inwardly at the reminder. "Please don't remind me. At least you and Ben are coming along."

"That was a great idea. I wish I could have been there to see his face," she said, and I smiled, recalling Oliver's annoyed expression when I invited them along.

LILY ATTEMPTED to parallel park outside the shop, and I seized the opportunity to escape.

"You don't have to get out. I'll be back before you've parked," I said, opening the car door and stepping out before she could argue.

Bells chimed as I entered the shop, greeted by the pungent scent of incense saturating the space. The lady behind the counter wore a pleasant expression, quite different from what I expected. She appeared to be in her mid-late forties, just like Celest.

"Welcome. How may I help you this evening?" she greeted me warmly.

"Hi. I'm Belynda. We spoke on the phone yesterday," I replied, smiling back at her.

"Oh yes, of course. I'm Selene," she said, extending her hand, which I shook briefly.

"Thank you for helping me."

"Well, that's what I'm here for. Give me a minute," she said, disappearing behind curtains at the back of the shop, painted with a golden sun and silver moon.

As I waited, I glanced around at the vast collection of crystals, incense, stones, candles, books, and strange-looking tools. It was truly fascinating. I picked up a deck of tarot cards and examined it closely.

"You're a reader?" Selene's sudden question startled me, and I quickly returned the deck.

"Oh no. Not me. I don't," I replied, feeling a bit flustered under her gaze. She averted her eyes noticing my discomfort, almost as a silent apology for the intrusion.

"It will be forty-five dollars even," she said, placing the small box on the counter and smiling.

I handed her a fifty-dollar bill from my monthly allowance and told her to keep the change.

"Thank you," she said as I took the box, but I felt her gaze linger on me as I walked away. Before I reached the door, her words chilled me to the core.

"I didn't mean to unsettle you. There just seems to be something special about you. The light in your aura is bright and powerful: a light I've only felt in old souls," she said.

I turned to her with picked interest. "I...I'm sorry. What does that mean?"

"Perhaps a past life. You know, reincarnations. That sort of thing," she explained.

Her words struck a chord within me. Could this be my connection with Isabel? Selene's theory only solidified my own suspicions, making the possibility of magic alongside other things I never knew possible more tangible.

"Be careful. Magic is not a game. Some things just can't be undone," Selene warned, glancing at the box in my hands, her eyes softening. She was special herself and wise, so I dropped the pretense that the items were not for me.

"Thank you again, Selene," I said gratefully as I left the shop, almost crashing into Lily, who was coming to find me.

"I was starting to worry a witch might have turned you into a rat in there," Lily joked.

I laughed nervously. "Only you could have such an active imagination."

"What did your aunt want from a place like that anyway?" she asked curiously.

"Books. For the fair. Just books," I replied, trying to brush off her curiosity.

It was almost dusk when Lily drove past the town center. I was relieved Celest hadn't taken me up on my offer to help once I returned. I was exhausted. It had been difficult to smile and maintain a happy face on the drive back. Selene's words circled my mind like a vinyl on repeat. I did not doubt her abilities, even though they surpassed logic. A few weeks ago, I would have laughed at her, but things had changed. I had begun to abandon the beliefs that tethered most people to what was expected and believable, embracing the notion that this world was far from ordinary and mundanely dull. Yet, one fear remained: the indecision of what I had to do and what the consequences could mean.

"Some things just can't be undone..." Selene's words resonated, urging me to tread lightly with my exploration of magic.

"Belynda!" Lily's shout jolted me from my thoughts.

"I'm sorry. What?" I asked, shaken.

"You know, sometimes I truly wonder what goes on inside that head of yours. It's like you're on another planet," Lily wasn't laughing this time, concern was written on her face.

"I'm sorry. It's a bad habit. I tend to shut myself off a lot, but I'm ok. I promise. You know me better than anyone else if it's any consolation. It takes me a while to open up but you're on the right track," I reassured her.

"I don't know about that...but I guess it's a start," Lily conceded.

"It is a start," I agreed.

"So, your birthday next week..."

"No. Forget it. I'm not letting you ruin my weekend talking about my birthday. I told you I don't like celebrating it."

"Fine. Whatever. We'll talk about it next week. Because you're not getting off that easy."

I rolled my eyes and stepped out into the cold evening.

"Thank you again for the ride. I had fun."

Lily smiled, pleased by my admission. "No problem. I'm always down for road trips or hanging out."

Her phone rang, and she glanced at the screen. "It's Ben."

"Take it. It's freezing out here anyway."

"Ok, see you next week then."

"Good night," I called and waved as she drove away.

Back in my room, I thought about starting my notes and research for the ritual, but I was exhausted. The thought of helping Celest with the book fair this weekend was an inconvenience. It meant sacrificing precious time, but I had no choice.

I was already tucked into bed when Celest's car pulled up.

THE DAY WAS BEAUTIFUL, with scattered clouds and a soft breeze visible through the bedroom window. Watching the grass sway across the road was soothing, tempting me to stay cocooned in my cozy room, however, duty called.

Working at the library today was unavoidable. The book fair was a significant event for Celest, as it typically accounted for a substantial portion of her annual book sales. She was already sipping her coffee by the time I made it downstairs.

"Good morning," I greeted, pouring myself a cup. "Ready for your date with books?"

"As ready as I'll ever be." She looked tired. The strain of the late nights evident. *Or maybe it was all the lies and conspiring.* Pushing aside the negative thoughts, I decided not to start the day on a sour note, considering I was to spend the day with her.

"I can't wait for it to be done and over," I admitted, taking a seat at the counter. Celest placed a muffin in front of me.

"Thanks. You look exhausted."

"Yeah, another late night. But the worst is over. You know how neurotic I get about everything being perfect for opening day. Once it's past, I can relax a bit."

I nodded, aware of Celest's perfectionism when it came to her books.

As we drove into town, men worked on setting up rides

and confection stands. Soon, our town center would be transformed into a freak show. It wouldn't be ready until next Friday, but the sight reminded me of my date with Oliver—something I wasn't looking forward to.

Tents rose along the town center's sidewalk as small businesses prepared for the market fair. It was a tradition preceding the carnival's opening, that provided locals with a chance to boost their profits.

THROUGHOUT THE DAY, I assisted Celest in setting up her tent and organizing tables outside the library while she sorted the books into categories. She seemed to think I was her good luck charm, assigning me the task of pricing and collecting money. I had a different theory, though. If I were to guess, it wasn't so much luck but rather my charming face that attracted customers. I chuckled at the realization, especially after the fourth male customer—none of whom struck me as readers of romantic fiction. The male species was simply beyond comprehension.

To pass the time, I picked up one of the many romance novels on display. Despite frequently reading about love and passion, I had yet to experience those emotions myself, even in my teenage years. Watching a couple stroll by, thoughts of Isabel and Drake stirred something inside me. Would I ever find someone I felt that strongly about? For the first time, I found myself contemplating the future, wondering about the possibility of leaving my dreams behind and finding peace in an ordinary life, meeting someone special along the way. However, it didn't seem like my life was headed in that direction—on the contrary. The more I delved into the mysteries of the magical world, the further that wish seemed.

Pushing aside the thoughts, I set down the novel to assist a lady who looked like a potential buyer.

By six, Celest and I had stowed away all the books inside their protective plastic boxes. I waited in the car while she returned the cash box to the library and closed up. Eager to begin working on the ritual, I tried to compartmentalize my feelings toward Celest as I watched her from afar. It was evident she was hiding things from me, though her motives remained unclear. While I knew she cared for me and vice versa, I couldn't bring myself to trust her—not enough to reveal what I knew or my plans.

"I'm glad that's over," Celest remarked as she got in the car. "Do you want anything to eat?" she asked, adjusting the heat.

"I'm good. I'm still full from the sandwich and pastries," I replied.

"Yeah, me too."

After a few minutes, Celest pulled into the driveway, and I followed her inside.

"I have some papers to go over. Do you want some tea?" she offered.

"No, thank you. I'm tired; I'm going to take a quick shower and head to bed. We have another early morning tomorrow too," I declined.

"Ok, get some rest."

"Good night," I called back as I dragged myself upstairs.

. . .

AFTER A REFRESHING SHOWER, I felt rejuvenated. Locking my bedroom door, I retrieved the book from the secret compartment beneath the windowsill.

I found the page containing details of the ritual and read the instructions on what to do with the ingredients. Most needed to be ground together until it formed a paste-like consistency. We had a mortar and pestle in the kitchen, and I was certain I could find matches to light the candles as well. The problem was all the different steps which had to be done before the ritual took place: ground cleansing, circle casting, element calling...I had no idea what any of it meant or how to do it.

Turning to my laptop, I ran a search on ground cleansing for rituals. The results were extensive but not as straightforward as I'd hoped: cleansing for home energy, spiritual cleansing, cleansing for the new year, cleansing crystals. After sifting through several websites, I noticed a common theme among most cleansing rituals: the use of smoke and water. Burning sage leaves was the most popular option, although some people preferred other herbs like lavender, cloves, basil, or pinecones. Most smoke cleansing instructions were simple: start in one area and move clockwise, circling back to the starting point.

Some websites also mentioned using all four elements symbolically for cleansing, with salt and water representing earth and water, and fire and smoke representing air and fire.

Grabbing my notepad, I began writing down notes:

Ground cleansing: candle, salt, water, sage, or lavender.

Light Candle and the Sage or Lavender. Ask the elements of Fire and Air to cleanse the space for the ritual. (Walk around the area clockwise, spreading the smoke for cleansing.)

Mix the salt and water, then ask the elements of Earth and Water to cleanse the space for the ritual. (Walk around the area clockwise, sprinkling the saltwater for water cleansing.)

I wasn't sure if this was what the book referred to as ground cleansing, but it was the best I could find for now. I'd have to make do with the resources I had from the internet. Finding an extra candle around the house would be simple, but sage might be a problem. Lavender, however, was always a possible option.

My entire body ached as I stood. I placed everything back into the secret compartment before climbing into bed. Too tired to think about the ritual, I closed my eyes and drifted into sleep.

"Please don't go. I need you."
"I'm right here. Look at me."

THE INTENSITY of those grey eyes jolted me awake, and I threw the blankets aside, running my hands over my face. Those grey eyes burned into my mind, and I knew just who they belonged to—*Drake.* Taking a sip of water, I tried to shake off the strange sadness that lingered. Although it wasn't my usual dream, it still left me feeling unsettled. Empty. Perhaps all those thoughts about finding someone special had seeped into my subconscious. I made a mental note to stop reading romance novels.

To my horror, Sunday turned out to be much like Saturday. I helped Celest at the book market; despite my earlier apprehension about the effects of reading the romance novel, I finished it during slower times.

By the time we got home, I was exhausted and tempted to postpone working on the ritual until the following day, but the memory of a pair of haunting grey eyes, compelled me to do what I had set out to do. As I sifted through the pages in search of the ritual, I stumbled upon a section titled *"The Sacred Circle."*

The process of casting a circle for a ritual turned out to be far more complex and time-consuming than I had anticipated. Yet, having a structured guide was better than blindly guessing the steps. Reading over the information about the sacred circle, I felt a pang of regret for the hours wasted scouring the internet. Discarding the previous night's notes, I folded the page and tucked it into the book beside the instructions as a makeshift bookmark. I folded another sheet of paper, and placed it next to the steps for opening the portal to the Dark Realm.

The more I read through the process and familiarized myself with it, the more my anxiety grew. It was like reading fiction. Despite my growing acceptance of the supernatural, I couldn't help but laugh at the absurdity of it all. I fought between what I imagined could be possible and what I had known to be real my entire life. I questioned my ability to open any portal and, even more so the ability to bring another creature into this world. Truthfully, part of me still wondered if Drake and Isabel had been real or if I was just delusional. Yet, another part wanted to believe—the part that knew my dreams were beyond ordinary. That part clung to the facts: the book, the sword, and Isabel's cup. If didn't hang on tight to those beliefs, as irrational as they were, I would be lost, and I was determined to give a chance to the impossible.

My bones ached from the cold as I waited for the bell to ring. I hadn't seen Lily this morning meaning she was either late or not coming, which wasn't good for me because I had planned to ask her for a ride back to the library after school. I couldn't wait for the book fair to be over, yet rushing this week meant bringing forward the weekend and the date with Oliver—something I was not looking forward to. I made my way to class with a few seconds to spare; I could no longer stand the cold.

As usual, Oliver waltzed into class after the teacher called attendance.

"Good morning Mrs. Gill," he greeted, before strolling over and taking the chair beside me.

"Good morning," he smiled, nudging me with his shoulder. I pulled away and looked at him like he had gone mad.

"Seriously? We're not friends, and we're definitely not pretending to be boyfriend and girlfriend. I agreed to one date, and we both know it's only because you practically black-mailed me into it. So, I'd appreciate it if you didn't sit next to me at all."

"Is that all?" he replied, his tone filled with sarcasm and a smirk. *Yeah. He had no plans to move.*

"Look, we do have a deal. But the whole point of the date is to salvage my reputation. I shouldn't have lied and I'm sorry, but I can't just pretend I don't know you. People won't believe we're seeing each other if we don't spend any time together. So please, just for this week, bear with me. After our date on Saturday, you can dump me, okay?"

I stared back at him, wondering why I had allowed myself to get caught up in this mess.

"Remind me again what I actually gain from doing this? I could just walk away and be done with you now."

"You could," he admitted, his tone surprisingly sincere. "But you won't, because you're not the type to ruin someone's reputation like that. Besides, if you did, I'd be obligated to annoy you every day for the rest of your life."

"You find that amusing, don't you? I'm basically being blackmailed into saving your lying behind."

Oliver let out a laugh, drawing the attention of the entire class.

"Now, Mr. Radcliff, if you insist on being late, at least have the decency to pay attention," Mrs. Gill called him out, her tone firm.

"Apologies, Mrs. Gill," he replied with the least bit of regret.

I lowered my head and covered my mouth, trying to stifle a laugh. He deserved that. Facing me again, he smiled, not caring one bit that he was humiliated in front of the entire class. Instead, he pulled his chair so close to mine that our elbows touched.

Just a few more days, just a few more days. I reminded myself.

The bell rang, but Oliver took his time gathering his things.

"Shall we? I'll escort you to your next class."

"No way!" I laughed but this time without humor. *He was out of his mind.*

"People need to believe we're a real couple. Either I walk you to class or we engage in some PDA. Take your pick."

"Try anything funny and you're dead. Do you hear me?"

If anyone had told me last week that I would have Oliver Radcliff walking me to class, I would have called them a liar. But life had a funny way of taking you places you never expected.

The walk from English to History was the most awkward thing I had ever experienced. Oliver acting like my personal bodyguard, hovering close to my side while I tried to hurry and keep the distance between us. I cringed every time I caught someone staring at us, while Oliver seemed to revel in the attention, greeting his friends with high-fives along the way.

He pulled from my book bag, and I halted right outside of class, turning defensively.

"You touch me, and you're a dead man Radcliff," I warned.

At my comment, he laughed without restrain. "Can I at least give you a kiss on the cheek?"

"What part of *touch me and you're a dead man,* do you not understand?"

"Relax. Christ. It was just a joke. Would it be such a terrible thing if you liked me even just a little?" His tone was odd, almost vulnerable and for a moment, I wondered if he was starved for genuine affection.

Don't even think about it, Belynda. Do not go there. Whatever his issues are, they're not yours.

"I'm just going to ignore that question since we both know the answer."

"Yeah. we do. See you at the end of class."

Without another word, Oliver turned and walked away, leaving me to wonder, what was his deal? One minute he was smirking and the next, he sulked in unspoken misery.

WHEN THE CLASS FINISHED, just as he had promised, he was leaning against the wall of the hallway. He seemed more himself, but I sensed some sadness that hadn't been there this morning. I tried to remind myself that I didn't care.

"Shall we?" He pushed off the wall, taking the bulky history project board from my hands without a word.

"I might as well contribute," he remarked, and I didn't protest. He had a point.

We walked in silence into the cafeteria, feeling the stares and hearing the whispers from anyone who happened to catch a glimpse of us. I wondered what they thought when they saw us together—*the strange and quiet Belynda with Oliver.*

"I take it this deal includes sitting with me for lunch as well?"

He nodded, and while I wanted to kill him, I felt kind of sorry for him and curious to know what his deal was. So, I took it as my opportunity to pry into the devil's mind.

"What are you having?" He asked.

"Pizza for me, thanks. Oh, and a salad, chips, a coke, and an apple."

He rolled his eyes, knowing I was taking advantage of him as payback.

"Sure, babes. Anything else?"

I pretended to think while he waited, as the line filled up behind us.

"Maybe some ice cream as well, sugar plum."

His eyes narrowed. "Are you seriously planning to eat all of that?"

I mockingly gasped, covering my mouth. "Are you implying I'm overweight?" A few students walking by overheard and caught Oliver's eye. He plastered a smile on his face, and strode off to get our food.

When he returned with two overfilled trays, and the most irritated face I had seen yet, I laughed.

"What? Is this relationship not turning into everything you hoped it would be?" I smiled, but he just glared back.

"I have to say it's different, but I enjoy a good challenge," he smirked and I knew he was trying to turn the game around.

He dug into his burger while I took a few bites of my pizza in silence, competing in a glaring contest.

"I want to see you eat all of that."

Oh, he wasn't the only one who loved a challenge, but I wasn't aiming to please him. I was desperate to annoy him so, instead, I ate two bites of the salad, one bite of the apple, a few bites of pizza, maybe two chips from the bag, and most of the ice cream.

When I said I was finished, he glared at me like I expected;

however, he surprised me when he picked up the pizza and finished it, then the salad, the apple, and the chips—on top of the burger he had just eaten.

"Seriously. Where do you put all that food?"

"I just hate throwing away food like that. There are too many starving people in the world. Besides, I'll burn it all off in football practice."

I stared at him, confused. Was this the same Oliver I knew? Since when did the football jock care about wasting resources or worry about anyone else but himself? I found myself at a loss. The Oliver I knew didn't fit with this person here with me now: a person with a conscience.

"Are you alright?"

"You know, I thought I had you figured out but then you say something like that, which makes me think there might actually be some humanity in you. I don't know; it's just strange, that's all. I never pegged you for someone with a conscience," I said.

He seemed surprised by my observation. "One thing I've learned is that there is always more to a person than meets the eye," he replied, cryptically, leaving me to wonder how much of that was true.

"Perhaps you're right about that." After all, there was much more about me than what others perceived. Maybe there was much more to him too. "So, can I ask you a question?" I asked, sipping my coke.

"We're technically dating, so ask away," he smiled. I rolled my eyes, but his comment didn't deter me from satisfying my curiosity.

"Why me? You could have picked any girl you wanted from school to annoy. So, why me?"

He became lost in thought for a moment, making me question if he had an ulterior motive for this tireless pursuit. The longer the silence, the more convinced I became that he had no valid reason for picking me at all.

"Why not you?" *Was he serious?*

"You can't answer a question with a question. Unless you have some dreadful evil plan, you're trying to cover up?"

"No. That's not it. It was just a drunken truth or dare game that got out of hand. They wanted to know if there was someone I liked and, for some reason, I said your name. After that, I couldn't take it back. The lie grew and I had no choice but to approach you."

I knew there was some truth to this story because Lily had told me about the game, as well as his drunken state. I guess subconsciously, a part of me felt terrible; still, it wasn't like I had any feelings for Oliver.

"Fair enough," I said, dropping the matter.

"You sound relieved?" he seemed puzzled by my reaction.

"Well, for one, it's easier knowing you don't have genuine feelings for me, it will make the end of this painless for both parties," I smiled, trying to lighten up his suddenly sour mood.

"I never said I didn't care about you. But I guess I deserve your indifference. After all, this is only a temporary arrangement," he crushed the empty can in his hand, and diverted his eyes. There it was again—that look of sadness.

"Why do you do that?" I questioned.

"I'm not doing anything!" his eyes returned to me, defensive.

"You do. You get serious and detached; you did the same earlier when you asked if it would be so horrible for me to like you, even a little, and you did it again now."

He stayed silent, staring at me as if seeing me for the first time and, at that moment, I knew that Oliver was nothing but a lost and misunderstood little boy. He hid behind his egotistical and narcissistic ways to cover up the pain behind his loneliness. I had gone through enough therapy sessions to recognize this mechanism. He put up a clown mask, so people never discovered that underneath all of that crude exterior, he felt undeserving of love—holy *crap.*

"I see you, Oliver Radcliff. You can't fool me. We both know that you're nothing but a scared little boy underneath that cool and collected face you project. You're scared to show your true feelings and, even worse, you're scared that others don't love you enough."

"Are you crazy? Keep your voice down with all that nonsense. You don't know a thing about me!"

"That's too bad. For a minute, I thought I might have been mistaken in my previous assumption of you. I even thought that perhaps we could find common ground and be friends." It was a feeble attempt to coerce him into admitting there was more to him, yet I realized it was true as I said it. I could be friends with him, if only he would be himself and stop pretending to be who others expected him to be. But I knew that was not possible. Not from the fuming look now on his face.

"I'm starting to think this lunch thing was not such a good idea after all."

"Well, I'm all for canceling this charade right now." Heck, I didn't know getting deep with Oliver would be my ticket to freedom; otherwise, I would have done it much sooner.

"Don't get too excited now. I just think lunch is a bit much. Perhaps we can narrow it down to twice this week. I'll find a way to make myself busy with practice or something, but I'll see you on Friday for your birthday." He smirked and his mask was back on.

I was not getting through to him. After all, what did I expect to accomplish in one lunch after a lifelong practice of hiding?

"Whatever. See you then."

"I have to go the opposite way to the gym, so I can't walk you to class. I'll see you tomorrow?"

"Does it look like I'm bothered one bit? Need I remind you I was forced into this extended arrangement just this morning?" I took a jab at his feelings, and sure enough, he took the bait.

His eyes darkened, and the silence spoke volumes. It bothered him beyond words not to be liked, not to be accepted. His reputation was so important to him that he would go to great lengths to squash even the smallest of doubts from those around him. Poor Oliver, it was an exhausting way to live—living to please others.

"Sure. See you tomorrow, babes."

"Bye, sugar plum," I called after him. A few students nearby stared.

I no longer cared what they thought. Perhaps I wasn't so much in Oliver's clutches as he was in mine. I knew how to get to him, and I would enjoy torturing him even if the more sensible side to me knew it was wrong and feared he might not entirely deserve it.

With Oliver distracting me, I had forgotten entirely about Lily. I tried her cellphone, and she didn't answer, so I sent her a quick text.

-Hey. Are you ok?

Her response came a minute later.

- Had the migraine from hell, and I started my cycle. My Mom will write me a note. But I'm better now.

-Well, I'm glad you're better. I'll see you tomorrow.

-Thanks, see you :)

THE REST of the afternoon went by in a blur. I found myself caught in between thoughts of the ritual and, to my horror, stupid Oliver. I felt no romantic interest in him, it was a nagging sense of guilt that plagued me. He didn't deserve my pity, but I couldn't help it. What he needed in his life were people that genuinely cared for him—perhaps I could care for him as a friend. I could give him that chance as long as he understood the boundaries.

When the school bell rang, I took the bus straight home, bypassing the front door to drop off my history project board on the porch before retrieving my bike from the side shed. The library was my next stop.

"Hey. How was school?" Celest smiled, as I arrived.

"Ok. Same as always, I guess?" I offered, settling down to do my homework.

I finished my Science and Math assignments and passed the rest of the time helping a few customers. As the sun began to set, I was eager to head home.

"Could you take the cash box to my office while I put the books away?" Celest asked.

I didn't hesitate. Grabbing the cash box, I made my way back into the library. It was shrouded in darkness, with only the front desk illuminated in the absence of customers.

I retrieved the key to Celest's office from under the empty register and flicked on the light switches, as I walked down the corridor.

My first thought as I entered her office was that nothing had changed since my last visit. Books were scattered across her desk, and the looming old Armoire stood against the wall eerily. I always thought of it as a prehistoric wooden monster but, for the first time, curiosity drew me in.

I placed the cash box on her desk and approached the Armoire. The wooden doors were intricately carved with animals, trees, and faces. Something I had never noticed. I hesitated as I pulled on the doors, surprised to find them unlocked. The contents blew my mind. "Wow...Celest. You are full of surprises, aren't you?" I whispered.

Inside the wooden monster, I discovered an extensive collection of small bottles with labels dotting the shelves: herbs, oils, incense, candles, and stones, among other items I did not recognize. Clearly, Celest was not indifferent to supernatural beliefs. *But why keep it a secret?*

As I scanned the shelves, I spotted a bottle labeled 'Dragon's Blood Resin,' the one ingredient, Selene had to find. I grabbed a small white candle from a box she had, knowing she would not miss one. Then, read through the labels and, found the bottle containing sage leaves, taking a few.

Closing the cabinet, I rushed out of her office, feeling a rush of adrenaline. Technically, I was stealing, but given Celest's deception, I figured it was a fair trade. I stashed the candle and sage in my book bag which laid the couch before leaving the library.

"You can leave your bike inside. We'll take the car. Maybe you can get a ride tomorrow," Celest suggested.

"Ok." I brought the bicycle inside, and Celest locked the door. Clutching my bag for dear life, I couldn't shake the thought that she would somehow know, but deep down, I knew I was being paranoid.

Exhausted from the long day, I showered and climbed into bed, making sure to stow away the candle and sage leaves with the rest of the supplies in the hidden partition.

As I lay there, I found myself scrolling through moon calendars online. According to the book, the circle to open a portal had to be drawn on the dark moon. Various lunar calendars confirmed that this Thursday would be the next dark moon, leaving me with only a twenty-four-hour window to cast the circle for the ritual. The tight timeline made me anxious; it was barely any time to assemble everything. However, if I didn't proceed with the ritual this week, I would have to wait another month. Perhaps delaying it was the wiser choice. After all, I felt more frightened than excited at the prospect of opening a portal and summoning an immortal being. The weight of the consequences made me question if I was truly ready to gamble with my life.

I woke up feeling refreshed, grateful that the haunting dreams hadn't returned for the past couple of nights. It was a relief, but I couldn't shake the feeling that there was still much I didn't know. Perhaps Isabel could sense that I was trying to help and had stopped invading my dreams, at least for the time being.

As I got to school and stepped off the bus, I was met by Oliver.

"Good morning."

"Morning," I grumbled.

"I take it you're not a morning person," he teased following me towards my class.

"Are we starting with this again? Isn't it a bit early? Why don't you spend time with your friends? I don't want them to think I'm monopolizing you," I said, glancing at the rest of his group, Lily included, who sat with Ben, and waved at me.

"Don't worry. I know my priorities."

"Sure you do," I muttered under my breath. He didn't know the meaning of priorities even if they smacked him in the face.

"Just sit down. You're making me nervous just hovering," he took his seat next to me in class, as his phone buzzed. I watched as he texted back with a frown.

"Will you come?" Oliver asked, taking me by surprise.

"Where?"

"To the game," he said, as if his question had been obvious enough.

"You already know the answer to that, besides, I don' like football. I don't get what all the fuss is about. It's just a bunch of guys throwing a ball or running behind it." Oliver stared open-mouthed, watching as if I were insane.

"You are the only person I've met who doesn't like football," he laughed. I glared at him.

"Well, maybe you just don't know many people."

Thankfully, we had an essay to work on, so he didn't have much time to annoy me. Though as I headed to history class, he hovered next to me, just like the day before.

"Do we honestly have to do this every day?"

"Are we discussing this again?"

"I just don't see the point. Yesterday it was interesting news and today nobody cares, so what's the point?"

"We just started dating."

"In your dreams," I corrected, and I watched as he bit back his anger.

"You know what I meant. People will question, if we don't spend time together."

"Whatever, so I guess I won't be seeing you for lunch then?"

"No, I think I drew the line after you attempted to dissect me yesterday."

"Cry baby," I teased him, then walked into class.

. . .

When the final bell rang, I met Lily in the parking lot as planned, grateful that she had agreed to drop me off at the library. We jumped as tires screeched right in front of us.

"Are you out of your mind?" I yelled as the devil rolled down his window. Lily laughed; she was enjoying this way too much.

"I'm taking Belynda to the Library. She's helping her aunt with the book fair."

"I can give you a lift if you want. I'm heading that way anyway."

"When hell freezes over."

"Are you going to make Lily go in the opposite direction just because you're stubborn and don't want to get in my car?"

"I don't mind," Lily added, but I couldn't help the guilt.

He was right; but damn, I really didn't want to go with him, and I certainly didn't want to explain his presence to Celest.

"You know what, it's ok. I'll let Oliver take me. You're seeing Ben after anyway, so it's not fair for me to make you go to town for no reason."

"Are you sure? I don't mind."

"Yeah. I'll see you tomorrow."

I jumped in the passenger seat next to Oliver and clicked on my seat belt.

"See you tomorrow," Lily called after us. I waved as Oliver drove out of the parking lot.

"I guess hell must be freezing over right about now."

I rolled my eyes, knowing he wouldn't miss the chance to throw that in my face.

"You know I don't mind walking, right?"

"Would it kill you to be nice?"

"Would it kill you not to be such an ass?" I rebuked. He stared at me for a moment, then turned back to the wheel.

"Sorry for being an ass," he said with genuine sincerity.

"Thank you for the ride," I added.

"You see. That wasn't so bad, was it?"

I ignored him and looked out the window, breathing in the smell of his car: leather and pine. It was nice.

"I like your car."

"Thanks, I guess." He looked at me and frowned.

"That was me being nice, in case you were wondering," he laughed out-loud, and I smiled.

"I can see that. It's just hard to believe, that's all."

"Well, don't get used to it."

"Trust me. I know better."

The ride was short, but it wasn't painful or awkward like I had expected. We actually managed to get along when we weren't bickering over inconsequential things.

As we entered the town circle, I asked him to drop me off a few stores down.

"Just leave me here," I insisted.

"I thought you said you were going to the library. That's still a block away."

"I know where the library is. I can walk from here. Thanks."

He grinned like an idiot; he wasn't going to stop.

"No. I think I'll take you all the way."

I removed my seatbelt, squirming in my seat and hoping to fly out of the car without Celest catching sight of me.

"That's your aunt right? He asked as he approached the sidewalk where the tent was set up.

"Yes. Bye, I'll see you tomorrow." I got out of the car in a flash and shut the door, but I could still hear his laughter from the sidewalk.

Walking under the tent, I felt Celest's curious eyes on me.

I prayed that the earth would open and swallow me alive.

"That wasn't Lily. Was that a boy from school?"

"Yeah. It's just Oliver. Don't worry about him."

"What do you mean? A boy is important. Are you dating?"

This was quickly becoming the most embarrassing conversation we had—ever had.

"NO. Nothing like that. We're just friends. I would tell you if it wasn't."

I could feel her eyes on me as she tried to decide if I was telling the truth or not.

But she didn't push it, and I was glad.

4

BLOOD BOUND

THE AFTERNOON FLEW BEFORE MY EYES.** Dinner was almost ready, and I made myself busy setting up the table.

"Smells good," Celest praised, entering the kitchen while still toweling her hair.

"Help yourself," I replied, placing two plates on the table before taking a bite of my pizza.

"I'm starving. Haven't eaten since breakfast this morning," Celest said as she sat down, and we settled into a comfortable silence as we ate.

For some reason, Celest's attempt to talk about Oliver earlier made me think of my mother. I wondered what she would have said instead if she had been there.

"Do you ever think of my mother?" I asked, surprising even myself. Celest looked at me with concern.

"Of course, I do. Not a day goes by that I don't remember

her, and you remind me of her so much," Celest replied sincerely.

"We grew up together and always considered each other family. Not having her around...was hard for me to accept too."

"You know, you never really told me the details of her accident. I realize I was too young then and as I got older; I was too afraid to ask. But I've been wondering about what happened."

"There isn't much more to tell. Your mother went on a trip and a week later, someone found her car at the bottom of a cliff on the coast," Celest explained, her voice softening.

"Yes, I know, but I mean...wasn't there an investigation into how it happened?"

"There was, but they determined it was an accident. She lost control, they said," Celest whispered, and I could tell she missed her.

"Thank you for everything. For what you've done for her and me."

"There's no need to thank me. I love you like a daughter Belynda, I truly do. Even if sometimes you struggle to believe that," Celest reassured me.

"Is there a reason you're thinking about this now?" Celest hesitated. "Does it have anything to do with your dreams?" she finished in a low voice.

I never expected her to be so blunt about the subject of my dreams. She had made it seem so taboo, only last week urging me to forget.

"No, it doesn't. But I'm glad you're mentioning them. You know I'm not irrational, right? These dreams are very real," I said bravely, meeting Celest's gaze.

Different emotions resided there including anger, yet also

fear. Her shoulders sagged as if carrying the heaviest burden; she was tired of fighting. Sensing her walls were ready to collapse, I didn't push her—out of fear that she would fortify them. Instead, I gave her time to say what she wanted to say.

"Belynda, I can only pray to the gods that you stay away from whatever has been haunting you. Sometimes it is better not to rise. Sometimes it is best not to become what we're destined to be. I don't want to see you walk down her path."

"Whose path, Celest? My mother's?" I asked, concerned by her reaction.

Celest looked frozen, as if her mind was traveling back through time, reliving memories until she found her voice again.

"There are things about your mother's past that not even I know about," Celest finally said, her voice distant, adopting a wise edge.

I couldn't make sense of anything she said and if there was someone out there who knew my mother best, it was undoubtedly Celest. Why would she say such a thing? Her chair scraped against the wooden floor, bringing me out of my haze. I heard her steps as she left the room, leaving me alone with the weight of her words—utterly lost once more.

I washed the plates and cleaned the stove, repeating the conversation with Celest over and over in my mind. The more I thought about it, the more troubled I became.

Why couldn't things be simple? Was that too much to ask? I was only seventeen. I should be living a carefree and happy life, overwhelmed with thoughts of boys and parties and friends. Instead, I was preoccupied with deciding whether I should listen to my dreams and help Isabel or take Celest's advice and protect myself from my demons, or at least that's what I understood from her cryptic words.

There was so much to consider. Mainly the uncertainty of not knowing if I was making the right choice. I wasn't sure which path Celest wanted me to avoid, but if it was my mother's—could death be the paying price for such a mistake?

I pictured my mother acting for the evil side, but I couldn't. Absolutely not. She had been good; she would have died fighting for what was right. That's what she taught me; I had to follow my instincts: my only guidance.

I needed to concentrate on the ritual and focus on the plan. There was a reason why I had found the sacred book, the sword, and the cup, and I wasn't about to give up.

IT WAS one of those starless nights where I could see the stillness of the surroundings through my window. There were no clouds; it was simply a quiet evening, a faceless canvas, but I could smell rain in the soft breeze. I closed the curtains and went to bed, hoping the morning would come soon. Somehow, all my fears seemed less frightening in the light of day.

THE COARSE SHEETS clung to my legs as I stirred in bed. My muscles felt like they had slept for days and the temperature in the room had risen above sixty degrees overnight. I opened my eyes a fraction,

searching for the time on my alarm clock, but it wasn't there. Nothing was.

Disoriented, I jumped to my feet, overwhelmed by the strange surroundings. I fought the haze in my mind, trying to understand where I was and how I had gotten here. It wasn't until my heart rate returned to normal and my eyes adjusted that I realized I was in my strange dream state—except there was nothing usual about this dream.

The chamber wasn't big; it was like a small log cabin. The floor was solid dirt and the only visible furniture was a simple wooden table, a chair, and the small bed where I had been just a moment ago. I walked around the bed, taking in every detail of the room.

There was a small fireplace, and above the stone mantle lay a few scattered books. The place was disorganized, but only because books lay everywhere. It almost reminded me of Celest. Glancing at the ones opened on top of the table, I realized they contained rituals and spells.

Every single item in this room was ancient. There was also an unmistakable smell of burnt candle wax, mixed with a dusty and humid stench which made my stomach turn.

I pushed open a door and walked into what seemed to be a chamber pot. A small wooden table, about waist height, rested against a wall, and a large metal bowl filled with water sat on top. On the wall above, there was an unfinished opaque piece of glass that provided a somewhat distorted reflection of oneself.

The only light filtering into the small space was through the narrow separation between the wooden logs. It certainly didn't seem like the place where I would find a light switch, which I confirmed when I noticed the half-burnt candle behind the metal bowl.

A sudden noise in the main room startled me and I turned

abruptly. Unfortunately, I wasn't quick enough as the person crashed into me or—more precisely—went right through me.

It felt strange, like a rush of icy winter air hitting my chest and making me shiver. She had gone right through me like I was a ghost. Shocked, I turned around and realized that it wasn't a figment of my imagination: there she was. I had never before seen her face, but I could feel it in my bones. Standing in front of me was Isabel.

This was unlike any other dream. I went from being the lead to the spectator, studying her every move. I found myself staring, completely baffled that I could see her rather than witnessing everything through her eyes.

I wondered if she could hear me.

"Hello?" I called, but she didn't move. Lowering her face close to the metal bowl, she splashed some water onto her cheeks. Completely unaware of my presence, she reached for a piece of cloth, folded neatly on the wooden table, and padded her face dry. It was the first time I had seen her face and I was surprised at how different we were.

Isabel had black hair whereas mine was honey gold. She was exhausted by the dark circles beneath her eyes, accompanied by a gloomy expression that showed a lack of care. Her brown eyes were void of emotion: lifeless, without light, and without hope. Staring back at her distorted reflection on the glass, she was silent as if expecting something.

The need to comfort her was overwhelming; she needed help or someone to reassure and be there for her. I could do nothing. I raised a hand towards her, somehow fearful of what would happen if I touched her.

"I'm not doing well on my promise, Drake."

My hand froze.

"I hope one day you can understand why I have to do this. Please, forgive me. I've tried, but there is no other way to free you. I'm so sorry for leaving you, Drake, but tonight we part." Her voice strained as she held back tears.

Running her hands over her face and through her hair, loss and hopelessness consumed her. Slowly, I withdrew my hand. I couldn't risk breaking the connection and waking from this dream; there was still so much more I needed to know.

She looked even more tired and broken now, as if her own words had stripped her soul. But I didn't understand, was she giving up on him, leaving him to his fate?

I felt conflicted. While I pitied Isabel, I couldn't believe she would break her promise to him. I thought her love for the dragon was eternal. It seemed like she would have given up anything to bring him back, but I must have been wrong.

Isabel whirled around quickly, and I barely managed to step aside to avoid the chilling sensation her body sent through mine. Keeping my distance, I followed her back into the main room, where she retrieved a small black book from the mantle. I stood a few paces away, still too far to read what she wrote so carefully. Even though she wrote with urgency, it wasn't her handwriting that worried me. Between her expression and the energy, she projected, she seemed on the verge of breaking down.

Her fingers moved swiftly over the pages, and my curiosity spiked. Slowly, I closed the distance between us, leaning over her shoulder to catch a glimpse of her writing. But I was too late. I only recognized a few words before she ripped the page from its binding and folded it neatly; my curiosity burned. Leaving the book behind, she grabbed the nearest candle and created a seal by pouring the *hot wax over the fold of the letter and pressing a metal stub over the top.*

Just watching her was incredible. She walked impatiently from one side of the cottage to the other; I could almost feel her anxiety vibrating. It was possible that whatever existed beyond these walls could sense her energy. I wasn't sure how long she paced like a caged animal within these four walls, but it had been a long while since the remains of daylight slipped through the small window. The only light was from the candles, which Isabel had lit as it grew darker.

"It is time," her quiet words broke the silence, taking me by surprise. What did she mean?

She opened a door where a few garments hung inside. On her knees, she pushed away some of the dirt with her hands and expose a wooden panel hidden beneath. Withdrawing one of the panels, a hollow space was revealed within. Expectantly I watched as she reached inside the partition and removed a sword. It was beautiful and magnificent, and I would have recognized it anywhere as it was the same sword now in my possession. She brought out her cup, followed by a few small leather pouches, a clay bottle, and something wrapped in cloth. Seeing her now with the cup and sword erased any doubt I might have had about their ownership. The one thing I had yet to see was the book.

Placing everything on the bed, she reached underneath to retrieve a box filled with candles. She grabbed a handful, then took the black book from the wooden table and threw it on the bed too. It was such an extraordinary and magical feeling to know that her things had survived through time, finding their way to me.

Her hands shook as she undid the buttons on the front of her dark purple dress, which fell to the floor around her feet and left her body bare. From the closet, she withdrew a simple white tunic and skillfully pulled it over her head, tying the ribbon around her back.

By tying the four ends of her bedsheet, she created a sack. Filled with the items she gathered, she swung it over her shoulder and placed the sealed letter on the wooden table. Her actions were clear. She wanted the letter found, but I wasn't sure who it was intended for. Perhaps her mother...

Grasping one of the lit candles, she stood by the door's threshold and stared back into the cottage with sadness. It was then that I realized what her words and actions meant. She was running away.

She took a deep breath and left the cottage, not bothering to close the door behind her. I followed Isabel quietly into the night, trying to stay close. As I walked, I realized how courageous she was to face this haunted maze of a forest alone. The night was dark and the soft light from the candle Isabel held swayed with the gentle breeze.

I wasn't sure how long we walked but it felt like a good mile. My nerves were on edge, and the constant fear kept my muscles alert. I heard the wicked rustling of leaves along the ground, twirling and dancing to the wind's symphony. The continuous singing from night critters that remained hidden from sight didn't help either.

I had to keep reminding myself that it was just a dream—I needed to stay calm. Isabel, on the other hand, never broke her stride. She was determined to reach her destination at all costs.

Abruptly, she stopped, and I walked right through her. It was such an intense feeling, and I didn't understand how it was possible. It was like I was transparent, without physical matter. Isabel resumed her stride, utterly unaware of my presence as I allowed some space to stretch between us, not wanting to collide with her again.

I sat by a tree as she placed the blanket on the ground. She grabbed a branch that had a few dry leaves from nearby and swept the earth around her. Her mouth moved in low whispers and after catching a few words, I realized she was cleansing the circle. I had read the same words when preparing the ritual.

I assumed she had meant to run away but instead, here she was, preparing for a ritual.

She swept a perfect circle around herself and left the space free of any debris, placing four lit candles evenly opposite each other around the circle. For the first time, I wondered if this was her way of guiding, showing me what I had to do in the ritual, so I made sure to pay extra attention to each move. Somehow, I felt drawn to the magic; it was scary being out here alone in the dark, but it was fascinating to watch her.

She removed the cork from the clay bottle and walked around the circle clockwise, pouring the bottle's contents onto the ground. Next, she picked up her sword and held it with both hands pointing away from her. This time, she walked across the purified earth with the sword's blade extended outwards, as if drawing an invisible line and closing herself within the invisible boundaries. Once she reached her starting point, she paced back to the middle of the circle and gracefully laid the sword on the floor.

Once more, she rose to her feet and took a few steps—stopping closely in front of one of the lighted candles. I caught the reflection of something in her hand, but it wasn't until her hand shot up above her head that I realized she held a small silver dagger. Then it came —her pulsating voice called out into the night like a torrent.

"Ego te Pegasi, a turre custodum usque ad aquilonem genius. Ecce testem invoco te, hanc circulus custodibus. Videte, meo. Salve et grata."

I was speechless. Every hair on my skin was on alert; her words, whatever they meant, emanated power. There were no visible entities, yet I felt their energies rushing from the soles of my feet. She walked to the next candle and raised her dagger once more.

"Ego te Aldebaran genius turre custodum usque ad orientalem. Ecce testem invoco te, hanc circulus custodibus. Videte, meo. Salve et grata."

She walked to the next candle and repeated the ritual several times..

"Et te defendat Regulus a turre custodum custos spiritus austri. Ecce testem invoco te, hanc circulus custodibus. Videte, meo. Salve et grata."

Then, the last.

"Ego te Antares a turre custodum usque ad occasum genius. Ecce testem invoco te, hanc circulus custodibus. Videte, meo. Salve et grata."

I watched in awe as her final words were swallowed by darkness. Returning to the blanket, she sat down with the black book opened in front of her.

I knew then it would be impossible to recall or describe the perfection of this moment. Though I didn't understand Isabel's words, I knew what the invocation meant. Her words called on the guardians of each element and from the electrifying energy that flowed, I knew they had indeed descended with her invocation. Everything outside the circle came together in unison. The wind howled and pushed at the dry leaves as giant spirals formed, stopping at the edge of some invisible wall that surrounded her circle.

The wild trees danced as if wanting to break free, and then came the rain. It was a perfect masterpiece as all elements came together. The last of them marked its presence as thunder erupted over the dark skies. There was no denying it. The guardians of the watchtowers were present in the form of their elements. The wind came for the air, the trees for the earth, the rain for water, and the thunder represented fire.

All the energies surrounded and protected the circle; everything was perfectly calm within its boundaries: no rain, no wind, just a perfect balance of flowing energy.

Isabel raised her hands and called out loudly into the night.

"All hail and thank thee for your presence. I, Isabel Adams Cromwell, bind these elements to carry and execute my will. I, Isabel Cromwell, bind the fate of the pure-blood to mine. I, Isabel Cromwell, pass on the burden of undoing the wrong that was done. Pure-blood, I bind thee. May your mind be free from the earthly rules of the guardians. I, Isabel Cromwell, bind my will and soul to thee pure-blood: born bound, raised bound, born chosen to break the balance and unleash the beast." Her words sent currents of electricity rushing through me.

"Hear me now, guardians of the watchtowers, gods, and guardians of the realms. Let my body be the instrument of passage. I offer thee. May the spirit of water help carry my soul and find its path to the chosen bounding. Hear my will and do my will. I bind these words with the powers that be. My will is done and cannot be undone."

Speechless and petrified, I sat. Each word spoken by Isabel vibrated in my mind, my soul. The authority in her words was powerful, and her tone demanding. There was no doubt in my mind that her wishes would be carried on; she was unequivocally the strongest person I had ever known.

Her powerful words caused a slight twist in the pit of my stomach; I hated to think about what her words meant. It wasn't a coin-

cidence that I witnessed this rite or had such a connection to her past. Her obscure words were difficult to decipher, but her wish was to bind her soul to a pure-blood, but she was a pure-blood herself. There was only one thought that made my stomach turn: the possibility that I could be a pure-blood, too. I hadn't known my father, so perhaps there was a slight chance. However, I wasn't bound from birth. It wasn't until after my mother passed away that the dreams began. I knew it was a foolish idea—but lately irrational explanations seemed to be all that surrounded me.

My thoughts were interrupted when Isabel spoke again. With the sword clasped firmly in her hands, she walked counter-clockwise, the sword's blade pointing outwards. I recognized her movements. She was opening the circle.

"Thank you for your presence. You may depart in peace."

I had goosebumps, for as soon as those words left her mouth, the branches of the trees stilled, and the rain subsided. Everything returned to normal in a mere second right before my eyes.

I drew my attention back to Isabel as she gathered everything on her blanket once more. She threw it over her shoulder, taking one of the candles to illuminate her way and disappearing into the trees. I got up from my spot and ran after her. Following closely, I noticed the bottom of her white dress was covered in mud as it brushed against the wet ground.

As I walked, I prayed to remain in this ghost-form, to live in the dream until I had more answers. The words from Isabel's ritual replayed in my mind but everything she had shown me was more puzzle pieces, not yet adding to a complete picture.

We hit a clearing and the most beautiful lake protected by a tall wall of trees stretched ahead of us. I could picture how breathtaking this place would be beneath a full moon.

Isabel lit up the rest of the candles and scattered them around. Sitting on the ground, she stared at the lake and I did the same— only sideways to watch her face. Tears streamed down her cheeks every time the dancing light from the candles illuminated the shadows under her eyes.

She brought her knees up to her chest and rested her chin on them, her broken sobs disturbing the quiet night. I wasn't sure how long she sat like that, drowning in her sorrow; the candles were half-burned, when she rose to her feet. Quietly, she walked to the lake's edge. The edge of the water touching her bare feet and the bottom of her dress.

"You promised. Don't fail me now," she whispered, bending down to graze her fingertips over the water.

Taking a few more steps, Isabel allowed the water to rise to her waist.

I decided not to follow her in; she needed space, even if she didn't know I was there. By the time the water covered her shoulders, I could barely make out her silhouette in the lake. I stood up, walking to the water's edge in time to see her head submerge. I waited for her to rise but I grew more impatient as the seconds ticked by.

Fear crept up inside me and I began to panic. "Isabel!" I screamed. "Isabel, please!" I called to her again overcome with panic.

I ran into the water, screaming her name frantically until I reached the spot where she had gone under.

"God, no. Isabel..." Through the hysterics, my brain replayed her earlier words and suddenly, it all made sense.

"May the spirit of water help carry my soul and find its path to the chosen bounding."

"No, no, no," I searched, trying to stir the dark waters, but they wouldn't move, reminding me I was only a ghost in this dream. I couldn't see her or touch her, yet I felt the tears running down my face. It was then that her lifeless body resurfaced. Her pale face, a haunting sight that seared into my mind.

EAR PIERCING SCREAMS tore from my lips as I lurched up out of bed. Tears flowed freely down my face. A strange sensation lodged in the back of my throat as if my lungs were burning.

It was hard to hang onto any semblance of reality after witnessing her lifeless face. Isabel had been real—she wasn't just a dream, and now I knew her fate. *Why had she submitted to such a horrible death?*

The truth about Isabel's fate hit me hard, I knew she had died at a young age, but that fact didn't prepare me for the crudeness of that vision. My mind couldn't process her loss, her choices.

After my screams, I braced myself, expecting Celest to come barging into the room. But she never did. Quietly, I walked to the bathroom and splashed water on my face, trying to shake off the unsettling feeling. But even as I returned to my room and opened the windows to let in the cold air, I couldn't shake off the numbness inside.

Outside, a storm brewed, mirroring the chaos in my mind. Drizzle fell, mingling with the cold wind that pushed tiny water drops through the window onto the bench where I sat, lost in my thoughts. I couldn't stop thinking about Isabel, her sacrifice, and its implications. Was I somehow linked to the future she had sealed her soul to?

Despite my doubts and fears, the sense of obligation didn't abandon me. I had to honor her sacrifice by attempting the ritual, even if I felt unprepared. I couldn't delay it any longer.

As I closed the window, my body stiff from the cold, I knew there was no going back. I had made my decision. But the night brought no relief, and I struggled to find any sleep before my alarm went off the next morning.

When I reached the bottom of the stairs, I was surprised; Celest was in her office, door slightly open while she sipped her coffee. I tried to pass by unnoticed but failed miserably.

"Belynda," she called and I had no choice but to turn.

She sat behind her desk, calmer than she had looked after our conversation the previous night.

"How was your night?" she asked, removing her glasses.

"It was disturbing," I responded. There was no use in pretending and I was tired of the façade. It looked like she had reached a turning point herself.

"I know you're suffering and I'm sorry. I am." Once again, she sounded genuinely concerned, but I didn't fully trust her motives.

I nodded and turned to leave, but she spoke again. "Just be careful, ok? You and I both know that there are things we don't have control over but just promise me that you'll be careful."

There were so many normal reasons why she would ask me to be careful, but I knew that she referred to none of them.

She was talking of darker reasons: the one I feared the most, the one linked to my mother's past and my dreams.

"Ok." My voice was raw with emotion as I fought back the tears. My vision blurred, and I had to make my escape.

I turned and left her office without another word. By the time I reached the edge of the road to wait for the bus, a few traitor tears had slipped down my cheeks.

OLIVER

I tried to avoid him just like the night before, but as the doors to his study swung open wide, I knew evading him was futile.

"Your inefficiency is beginning to test my patience, Oliver," his voice resonated, like the echo of my steps outside the hall. I took a pause, before advancing towards his door.

"Father... I don't believe she's involved with her aunt," I spoke, stepping to the threshold of his study.

"You are not here to think. Your task is to ingratiate yourself with the girl and be my eyes and ears in that house," he retorted sharply.

"It's that simple. She doesn't trust me. I need more time," I tried to reason with him.

"We don't have time!" His fist crashed against the mahogany desk, and I involuntarily froze. "She took those letters from the sanctum, and I need to know why. I have a feeling it's linked to the Sacred Book whereabouts, and she's hiding things from the covenant. If so, I must convene the council at once, but I can't do so without concrete evidence. Time is of the essence."

Whenever he got in this mood, it terrified me. "I understand, Father. I apologize," I managed to say.

"Apologies won't suffice. You're nothing but a disappointment," he seethed.

I took a step back, suppressing my anger for the way he treated me—for the way he made me feel.

"Tomorrow, Tyrus and you will thoroughly search every corner of the house," he ordered. I stilled at his request, internally questioning if the old man had finally lost his mind. Breaking an entry was pushing it but one did not argue with Stephen Radcliff.

"I'll do as you say, Father."

"I expect nothing less," he murmured, sinking back into his chair. "Close the door behind you."

With a nod, I shut the double doors and rushed away, eager to escape the hell that was my home.

BELYNDA

As usual, Oliver strolled into class after the bell, but he wasn't his usual arrogant self. He took the seat next to me without a word. Something was wrong. I tried to convince myself that his issues were none of my concern, but a small part of me cared, against my better judgment.

"Are you alright?" I ventured to ask, doubting he would share the truth.

"Do you even care?" he shot back; his gaze fixed on the board.

I wanted to lash out, but beneath the façade, I sensed he was already in pain.

"Maybe I do. Maybe I don't," I conceded.

A faint smile tugged at the corner of his mouth, but it seemed forced. "I'm okay," he stated, his tone more to convince himself rather than me. Though I felt a twinge of concern, I had my own demons to face.

When the bell rang at the end of class, he fell into step beside me, a ritual we'd unconsciously established over the past few days. As he exchanged pleasantries with his friends, I couldn't help but wonder if they noticed what I did. *Did they see the effort behind his smiles?* I wanted to shake him and yell at him to snap out of it, to stop pretending that he was alright—but who was I to judge?

"I'll see you tomorrow," he said with a forced smile, and I couldn't hold back any longer.

"Oliver, enough smiling. You're NOT ok. Stop acting," I admonished with frustration and the smile vanished from his face, replaced by a frown.

"What would you prefer? Should I wallow in self-pity? That's not who I am."

"I'm not asking you to mope around. Just stop pretending with me. You don't have to be okay all the time," I urged, my voice softening.

He leaned back, his expression shifting as my words sank in. "I'm sorry. Stop trying to figure me out," he muttered before walking away.

I listened to the teacher and pushed aside any thoughts of Oliver; I didn't wish him any ill—perhaps I might have cursed him a few days ago, but I knew him better now to know he didn't deserve it.

For the rest of the day, I succumbed deeper to the feelings

of loss that had plagued me since my latest dream. I didn't understand why Isabel would choose that fate for herself; she must have been confident that her binding spell would work to have given everything up just like that. Yet, I couldn't come to terms with her choices; I didn't know how.

The day dragged on much like the previous ones at the book fair, filled with the same monotony. Celest attempted to ask questions about Oliver, a conversation I swiftly brushed aside. Finally, I found a moment of relief as I pedaled my bicycle home from the library, just before the sun dipped below the horizon.

After a nice shower and a change into my cozy pajamas, I ate the remaining half of the sandwich Celest had picked up from the bakery, along with a cup of milk. Returning to my room, I sought refuge in the quiet evening.

Kneeling by the window, I lifted the lid of the bench, revealing the book nestled within. The shiny metal of the sword caught my eye, its craftsmanship far more impressive in person than in my dream. As I held it, a chill ran through me, remembering Isabel's hands gripping the hilt and the terrible end to her story. Shaking off the dark thoughts, I carefully returned the sword to its place.

Once again, I studied the instructions for casting the circle and reviewed the steps of the ritual. The thought of venturing alone into the woods at night gave me pause—I wasn't Isabel. I didn't have magic powers. But fear alone wasn't enough to deter me from what I had to do. I owed it to her to try. Yet, I couldn't shake the question of why Isabel hadn't succeeded when she evidently had power. What did I, or any other pure-blood, possess that she didn't?

My gaze fell on the answer—or at least, a possible one. Perhaps Isabel never had access to the book containing the spell to open the portal to the Dark Realm. Then there was the mystery of how her belongings and the book came into my possession—an enigma that suggested a connection within my family. Secrets that Celest, would eventually have to answer for. It wasn't a lack of courage that kept me from confronting her, but a lack of proof and trust. The timing wasn't right. I couldn't risk interference from her—or anyone.

As Celest's car pulled into the driveway, I replaced the book in its hiding spot and switched off the night lamp, lying on my bed and staring at the canopy above. My eighteenth birthday was just two days away, yet my life remained a tangled mess.

In a brief moment of empathy, I considered Oliver and whether I had been too harsh on him. Keeping people at arm's length was easier, something I had done most of my life. I had no right to judge him; if anything, I was more troubled than he was. I made a mental note to apologize.

EMERGING FROM A RESTLESS NIGHT, the ghostly remnants of a nightmare clung to my thoughts. Images of Isabel morphing into my own reflection haunted me, adding to the unease settling in my gut. Whether it was the nightmare or the looming ritual that stirred my discomfort remained unclear.

To my surprise, Celest had left for the book fair before me, leaving the driveway empty. School dragged on in a fog of worries and thoughts of the ritual, Oliver's absence barely registering amidst my haze of exhaustion. Lunchtime brought the impulse to tell Celest I'd be staying at Lily's tonight, but the fear of stirring suspicion held me back. Involving Lily in my lies wasn't wise, so I resigned myself to take my chances in the stealth of the night.

Alone in the school library during study hall, I carefully rehearsed the ritual steps in my head.

"I would give you a ride if it wasn't for the game tonight, but we need to stay for practice," Lily said, as we walked through the parking lot.

"I know. Don't worry about it. Have fun at the game," I smiled, through the headache I felt coming.

"See you tomorrow," she called, as I got on the bus.

The throbbing in my head escalated into a full-blown migraine, making me ache for my bed. As I stepped off the bus, my senses prickled and a sense of dread mounted over me, amplified by the sight of the wide-open front door and the absence of Celest's car.

Remembering Celest's earlier warning to be cautious, I hesitated at the threshold, yet a surge of adrenaline propelled me forward, crossing the door's threshold.

A chilling jab struck me as I watched the chaos laid before me. Everything was in disorder: cushions were slashed and thrown around, broken paintings and shards of glass were scattered everywhere. The intruder's intention clear, they weren't after valuables.

As the thought crossed my mind, I raced upstairs, flung open the door to my room, my heart hammering in my chest at the sight of the frenzied mess.

Running to the window, I pulled open the top of the bench that concealed the secret compartment. A tingling sensation rushed to my feet, and I breathed a sigh of relief to find everything untouched. Now more than ever, I needed to complete the ritual. If I ever had any doubt that this was the right time, this incident served to solidify my instincts—I couldn't afford to lose more time.

Catching my breath, I dialed Celest's number, my fingers trembling with urgency. She picked up on the third ring.

"Celest, you need to come home right away. Someone broke into the house; everything is a mess. I don't know if they took something. Just come over, please," I pleaded, panic thick in my voice.

"Belynda, slow down and take a breath," Celest urged, her voice tight with alarm. She never hung up; I could hear the shuffle of movement in the background as she got into her car. I disconnected the call the moment I spotted her car pulling into the driveway. She dashed across the entrance, pulling me into a hug.

"Are you alright?" The fear in her voice palpable.

"I'm ok. Just a little shaken," I admitted.

I followed closely behind Celest as she took in the chaos, her horrified expression mirroring my own.

"I don't think they intended to harm us," she mused, as she moved through the gallery of paintings.

"Me neither. It looks like they were looking for something," I noted. "The house is a mess, yet they didn't bother taking anything valuable," I pointed out, my brows furrowed.

"Oh, for the love of the Gods, what have they done?" Celest cried in disappointment, attempting to piece together her favorite statue.

"We'll have everything back the way it was in no time," I

said, attempting to cheer her up. She gave me a weak smile and nodded in agreement.

"I'll call the sheriff's office." I offered.

"No," Celest's responded too quickly. "I don't think it's necessary. I doubt the sheriff will do anything to catch someone for vandalism. I promise I will call them if I notice anything missing."

"But how do we know they won't come back?" I pressed, unsettled by her lack of concern.

Her refusal to involve the authorities only deepened my suspicions. What was she hiding? Who was she protecting?

"I'll call the locksmith tomorrow and have the locks changed," Celest declared, her tone final.

OLIVER

I followed Tyrus into the chamber, in an attempt to avoid my father's gaze, though I knew it was inevitable. As the council members departed, my father's agitation filled the room, evident in his brisk steps which echoed against the stone floors.

"Sir, I'm afraid we didn't find anything in the house," Tyrus reported, his voice tense.

My father's robes swirled around him as he paced, his frustration obvious. "Then we have to search the library."

"Father, it's a library. We'll be searching for a needle in a haystack," I cut in, trying to reason with him.

"I don't care if you have to burn the damn place down!" His voice cut through the chamber like a knife, leaving no room for argument.

Tyrus glanced at me, then back at my father with discomfort. "Sir, if I may be honest, the library might be a bit more complicated to access unnoticed."

Father's steely gaze fixed on Tyrus, silently demanding a solution. "But we will figure something out," Tyrus quickly added, attempting to appease my father's irrational demands.

"Exactly. In the meantime, I want someone to keep watch on that house. Keep me informed of any movement," my father commanded.

"Yes, sir," Tyrus replied, before exiting the chamber. I remained behind, studying the hard lines etched on my father's face.

"Is there something else you need from me?" I asked, but he never bordered to look up from his writing.

"Just get out," he dismissed me curtly.

I clenched my jaw, and left the chamber, suppressing the urge to speak my mind. Belynda's words echoing, reminding me to stay true to myself. Yet, I knew facing my father's authority, standing up to him was impossible.

BELYNDA

It took the rest of the afternoon and most of the evening to have everything restored to order, except for the few shattered items which remained beyond repair.

Throughout the cleaning, Celest remained unusually quiet, lost in her thoughts. She excused herself to bed early, claiming that she was tired, but her furrowed brow only confirmed my earlier fears. She was worried and hiding something.

My appetite had vanished in the wake of today's events

and the looming anxiety about the ritual. I managed to consume only half of my sandwich before abandoning the meal entirely. The break-in, stuck in my mind. It was a scary feeling to have a stranger invade our space in such a violent manner—not to mention that it had happened today of all days: the day I was set to venture out in the cover of darkness. Alone.

A hot bath offered temporary relief, yet the fear persisted. There was little I could do except wait until Celest fell asleep. Then, I would slip away unnoticed under the cover of night.

The part of me that had succumbed to terror saw today's events as a warning sign not to proceed. Yet, the rational side reminded me of how close I had come to losing everything, grounding my fears to the stark reality.

I couldn't afford to hesitate. I would attempt to bring Drake back, and even if I failed, I would find comfort in knowing I had given it my all.

5

CONJURE THE DRAGON

I **LAID IN BED, STARING AT NOTHING IN PARTICULAR.** I had memorized every denture on the ceiling boards in an attempt to distract myself and keep my tired eyes from closing. The clock on the nightstand mocked me with each passing minute, stretching the night into an eternity. Finally, with a glance at the clock—quarter to midnight—my heart sped up, and I knew the time had come to do my part.

Turning off my iPod, I slid out of bed, careful to keep the room encased in darkness. Black tights and a turtleneck sweater were my chosen attire, best suited for blending into the shadows of the night. I emptied my school bag, carefully packing the sacred book, the cup, and the ingredients. The sharp sword required special treatment, so I wrapped in one of my pillow shams for protection.

Despite my resolve to go through with the ritual, doubts still lingered. What would happen if the spell *did* work, and I managed to bring Drake back? I repelled the idea, refusing to think on it further, at this point in time, every negative thought was an excuse coursed from fear.

A change of clothing seemed appropriate, so I packed an oversized pair of sweatpants with a t-shirt that was always a size too big for me. I grabbed my running shoes from the closet before tucking the cell phone inside the bag.

As I came quietly down the stairs, I cringed at every creak of the steps. In the kitchen, I grabbed a juice bottle and the last box of matches before silently slipping out the front door, relief flooding over me once I was outside.

Sitting on the porch, I laced up my shoes, scanning the deserted road with apprehension. Today's break-in only heightened my paranoia. With a deep breath, I clutched the sword to my chest and dashed down the side of the house, adrenaline coursing through me as I cleared the open field.

Glancing back over my shoulder, I made sure there was a reasonable distance between the house and I before I slowed my pace.

The wild grass was about waist-high and though it was a moonless night, I could still make out the silhouette of the forest's border in the distance.

Clinging to the heavy sword, I ran the short distance until I was safely under the shadows from the first line of trees.

The dense foliage above covered the sky. Retrieving my phone, I used its light to guide me deeper into the woods.

The biting cold of the night air seeped through my thin sweater, sending a shiver through me. I cursed my lack of foresight and took a deep breath to steady myself.

Every rustle and whisper in the forest set my nerves on

edge. I worried about finding a clearing large enough to set up the ritual circle, urgency settling through my veins with every step.

A movement in the corner of my eye sent my heart racing, and I instinctively pressed against the nearest tree for cover. With trembling hands, I illuminated the area, only to be met by the gleaming eyes of a raccoon. Relief flooded through me as the creature darted away into the darkness. My bark of laughter broke the still silence of the night, and the sound served to ground my nerves.

Shaking my head, I pressed on, the chill of the night air, growing the deeper into the woods I went. Small clouds of breath escaped my lips, mingling with the frigid air. Despite the discomfort, I didn't turn around.

With numb fingers and stiffened muscles, I moved through the dense foliage, fighting a sense of unease that began to settle. Doubts crept into my mind, urging me to turn back. But then, almost as if by divine intervention, through the trees ahead, I caught sight of a large clearing, a beacon of hope in the darkness.

The clearing was the perfect spot. I arranged my belongings against the nearest tree and set about preparing for the ritual.

The lifeless branch I found to sweep the circle was no broom, but it would serve its purpose. With deliberate motions, I swept outwards in a circular pattern, reciting the chant I had committed to memory.

"Besom, Besom, magic Besom. Rising like the Sun, waning like the Moon. Sweep out darkness, cast out doom. Rid this circle's hallowed ground of negative energies all around.

Sweep this circle, sweep it deosil. Sweep out evil, make the round of the ground pure, where I do my will and so it shall be."

It was odd, hearing the words flow from my lips as if they belonged to someone else. Isabel's voice had been commanding and confident, unlike mine, shaded by insecurity and doubt. Yet, I pressed on.

Sweeping the dirt in a circular motion, I concentrated all my willpower into the branch, envisioning the negative energies dissipating from the sacred circle. Following the instructions from the ancient book, I repeated the sweeping three times until the space felt purified.

Discarding the branch, I collected my belongings, and moved them to the center of the circle, where I placed them carefully. Unwrapping the sword, I laid it on a makeshift mat fashioned from the pillow sham. Alongside it, I arranged the cup, the ingredients, and the book, its pages open to reveal the ritual.

The next step called for four candles to be illuminated. I placed them evenly across from each other along the circle's edge, interchanging a black and red candle. The flames provided a steady glow.

Absorbed in the ritual, I no longer felt the chill of the night air. Taking the crystal bottle I had prepared, containing only water and sea salt, I circled the perimeter once more, sprinkling its contents to symbolize the cleansing power of water and earth.

After setting the bottle aside, I lit the candle taken from Celest and burned sage leaves, filling the air with their smoky scent. According to the book, the smoke represented the element of air, while the candle's flame embodied fire.

With the cleansing complete, I grasped the sword to finalize the circle's closure. Drawing upon my brief research and the book's guidance, I understood the importance of this step in safeguarding the circle's boundaries against unwanted energies.

As the candlelight glimmered on the sword's handle, its precious gems came alive, emitting an almost magical glow. Extending my arm holding the sword, I walked around the circle, visualizing a radiant ring of light forming along its edge, sealing, and protecting its boundaries from external energies.

"In and around. Throughout and about. All good rest inside. All evil stay out."

It was a peculiar sensation, feeling safe within the circle's confines. Though I understood that was its intended purpose, I hadn't anticipated feeling its effect.

With sweaty palms, I finally felt prepared to summon the guardian spirits and protectors of the elements. Cradling the sacred book in my hands, I descended, pausing before the red candle which represented the north. I drew an imaginary star —what the book called an invoking pentagram—in the air with my hand. The symbol was necessary before reading the words that would summon and bring forth the elements.

"I call thee Fomalhaut; guardian, protector, and spirit of the watchtowers of the north," I bellowed into the stillness of the night. "I hereby call thee forth to witness, guard and protect this rite. Mark my will. All hail and welcome."

A surge of power rippled through the woods, heightening my senses. The energy, once dormant in the trees, now flowed with an intensity that was almost palpable. As I invoked the energies, each word surged, saturating me with a sense of power and conviction.

When I summoned the guardian of the last element, I was no longer afraid and insecure. Instead, I focused on the heavy raindrops pelting the earth outside the protective circle. The trees danced in harmony with the compass of the fleeing wind. Then, a streak of lightning erupted over the clearing, followed by a deafening clap of thunder that startled me into laughter, fueled by exhilaration.

Placing the book back on the ground, I seated myself and felt the earth beneath my fingertips, heightening my connection with the elements. Despite all my previous doubts, I couldn't help but marvel at the magic unfolding before me, a gift.

There was no logical explanation, at least not scientifically. Yet, as the elements materialized at my command, I embraced the realization that there was much more beyond our understanding. I knew with certainty, that nothing would ever be the same. Whatever doubts I had earlier about the spell working vanished; with every ticking second, I felt more confident in the believe that anything was possible.

My dreams with Isabel did not compare; this magic was my reality, my accomplishment.

Seated safely, within the protected circle, I watched the elements battle each other outside of the casted boundaries. A storm raged, rain poured from the darkened skies, as the wind whipped through the trees, invoking everything in its path. Thunder reverberated overhead, lashing at the skies without remorse. An echo of nature's raw power.

After the mesmerizing display of magic, I focused on completing the final steps to open the portal. I gathered the ingredients: cinnamon, acacia root, dandelion, dragon's blood resin, jezebel, myrrh, agrimony, a piece of bloodroot, and ashwagandha root, into the mortar. Slowly, grounding them into a red paste, following the instructions in the book.

Dipping my fingers into the paste, I drew an invoking pentagram on the ground, about five feet in diameter, as directed. Once the star symbol was visible, I carefully dug a small hole in its center and placed the white quartz inside, covering it with black sand.

Fear and uncertainty overcame me as I grasped the sword. This was the final moment, the proof I needed to confront Celest and provide closure for Isabel's sacrifice. But thoughts of the aftermath flooded my mind—what would I do with this newfound knowledge, and what about Drake?

Despite the rising anxiety, I knew there was no turning back. Taking a deep breath, I steadied my trembling hands and cleared my mind, ready to defy reason.

IN THE MIDST of the storm, with the sword firmly grasped in both hands, I lifted it high towards the thundering skies and repeated the long-lost words: words that held the power to change my destiny.

"I conjure thee, Dragon!" My voice resounded into the night.

"Guardians of the shadow realm, I command you to release Xelraa. Unveil the portal of the dark shrine. Fire, release the forgotten gates. Bend thy will and grant Drake's passage, I command thee."

"Cum Saxum Saxorum, In Duersum Montum. Oparum Da. In Aetibulum. In Quinatum. Draconis, Draconis, Draconis."

As the last word escaped my lips, the sword's tip met with the silvery arc of a lightning bolt. In one fluid motion, I plunged the blade deep into the earth, precisely where the quartz lay buried.

Retreating to a safe distance, the crackling electricity tingled beneath my fingertips, a rippling effect of the power coursing through the ground. I watched in awe as the sword became aglow with a fiery red hue.

Beneath the surface, tendrils of electric energy unfurled from the sword's buried edge, slowly illuminating the etched pentagram.

The next bolt of lightning that struck the sword made me jump. I stifled a scream. My eyes fixed on the glowing sphere of light hovering above the blade.

As the brilliant orb dimmed, a sense of anticipation and dread filled my heart. Before me lay Drake, his form unmoving. A marble statue arched on the ground.

My knees buckled beneath me, and I collapsed to the ground, breathless and trembling as I grasped the severity of what I had done. Torn between fear and disbelief, I clutched the sacred book to my chest.

He was *real...*

My body shook—my mind became chaotic, and I suddenly found it difficult to breathe. I was terrified, my knees frozen to the ground.

Amidst the erratic thoughts, one particular fear took root.

What was I going to do now? What was I going to do with him?

Slowly, his head stirred, his movements labored as though wracked with pain. He blinked, and my heart sped up; watching his eyes adjust to his surrounding, until eventually, they found me.

"Isabel…" His whispered plea barely reached my ears before he slumped, unconscious once more.

Fear had never felt more tangible in my entire life as it did at this precise moment. As I watched this man, this creature, before me, I fought the inexplicable urge—the need to go to him. Wondering if he was *hurt*.

I placed the book on the floor and pushed myself to my feet. Hesitantly, I took a few steps closer, sinking to my knees before him. Dry mud coated his body, and my fingers instinctively reached for his dark, matted hair.

A bolt of lightning tore through the sky, illuminating his grey eyes. The Dragon prince's eyes were startling. A hypnotizing grey-silver hue that seemed to glow in the evening shadows, drawing me in. He was dangerous, he was lethal—he was immortal. My hand stilled in mid-air, his expression daunting.

"Who are you?" His voice was stronger this time but tinged with anger. Drake—scared me, and any coherent thought I could muster abandoned me.

"I will not ask again. Who are you?" He demanded, and the roar on his voice made me draw back.

He opened and closed his hand, assessing his movements, every muscle in his arm coiling, and yet despite the visible effort, evident by the hardening set of his jaw, he still managed to pull himself up to a seated position. His silvery eyes returning to me, filled with a thousand unspoken questions.

"I'm the one who freed you," I finally whispered, my voice trembling with false bravery or perhaps stupidity.

His expression transformed as he closed his eyes, angling his face toward the night sky. Inhaling deeply, his nostrils flared, and when he looked at me again, his eyes were no longer silver or grey—they were deep pools of onyx black.

"I can sense them," he growled, his fists clenching on the ground. "I can smell her," he added, his expression twisted in pain. "Lie to me again, mortal," he threatened, and a primal instinct to protect myself surged inside me for the first time.

Adrenaline poured through my limbs, propelling me. Without a second thought, I bolted. Sprinting blindly through the darkness, I brushed past trees and stumbled over rocks, the rain soaking my hair and clothes, but I never paused or looked back.

Fear of succumbing to the cold or exhaustion, as I fought to find my way back gripped me. When I finally emerged from the forest into the open field, the sight of the house in the distance flooded me with relief. Though my legs threatened to give out, I summoned every ounce of strength to push myself up from the muddy ground and press on.

As I drew nearer to the house, a wave of warm tears streamed down my cheeks. I was a coward, consumed by shame and guilt. Drake was alone in the woods, and it was my fault.

Never before, had I stopped to consider my actions and what the fruition of my plans would mean. What was I going to do with Drake? How could I justify his presence? How could I ever face him again?

The Drake I released, was a stark departure from the man who haunted my dreams and visions—the one who professed love to Isabel. This version of him frightened me, yet I found myself inexplicably drawn to his darkness.

Back within the safety of my home, I found myself yearning for the dawn to break. With every passing second, Drake's presence became more of a tangible reality, one that I knew wouldn't vanish with the morning light as my dreams often did. I knew I had to confront him again, but not tonight. Tonight, I needed the solace of my thoughts to gather my courage and devise a plan. A plan that undoubtedly involved telling Celest.

6

A DATE WITH DESTINY

WAKING UP WAS RATHER PAINFUL. Every muscle in my body throbbed, and my half-asleep mind still hadn't fully processed the events from the night before. As I sat up on the bed, I still wore the same muddy clothes from last night.

I got up and every step was simply unbearable; every muscle ached, and my vision was fuzzy, but the realization of what I had gone through last night came back full force.

I glanced at my reflection in the bathroom mirror and gasped. My face was covered in patches of dried mud, while I had unknowingly decorated my hair with remains of dried grass. A few tiny cuts dotted my hands, but nothing that would spike curiosity.

The water from the shower ran while I freed myself of the dirty clothes. I washed my hair thoroughly, diligently scrubbing every inch of my body. The smell of the lavender soap invaded my senses, yet I still couldn't relax. An inescapable image remained stuck in my mind —the same vision I had endured all night before tiredness consumed me.

Drake. Even as I readied myself for school, all my thoughts returned to him and the haunted look in his eyes.

As the time drew closer to leave for school, I looked around my bedroom only to remember that I had no school bag and no cell phone. I covered my face with both hands and threw myself on the bed, allowing the mattress to muffle my cries of frustration.

How could I have been so stupid?

Celest was bound to notice the bag and missing cell phone, but they were the least of my worries. What I could never replace were the sacred book, the sword, and the cup.

A soft knock on my door stole me from my thoughts.

"Belynda, can I come in for a minute?" Celest said from the opposite side of the door.

I bolted upright with suspicion. She rarely came up here. *She must know something.* I began to panic.

I checked my surroundings to ensure there was nothing suspicious lying around. When I pulled open the door, Celest was smiling.

"Is everything ok?"

"Yeah. I was just getting ready for school."

"I know it's early, but I wanted to catch you before you left. Can I come in?"

Not good. Not good at all.

"Sure."

Celest stepped inside and I turned behind her, leaving the door wide open as if that would make her presence in my room any less awkward.

"Is everything ok?" I asked, dread evident in my voice.

"Everything is fine," she answered with a smile. "It's just that today is a special day for you. I have something that I have been saving just for the occasion."

My thoughts changed from panic to confusion. It took me a moment to catch up.

"Here you go, sweetheart. Happy Birthday," Celest's said, and I stared at the box in her hands, filled with surprise, wondering how I could have forgotten.

She lifted the top to the burgundy velvet box, revealing a beautiful, delicate silver necklace. Hanging from it was a beautiful diamond cut emerald.

"I hope you like it. It was your mother's," I glanced up at her admission. Sadness tinging her voice.

"My mother's?" I questioned, in awe. Returning my gaze to the stone.

Celest placed the box in my hands. "It a family heirloom. I'm sure your mother intended for you to have it one day." A knot formed on my throat.

"I love it," I cried, wiping the tears away with an attempt at a smile. "I'm sorry—I don't know what to say. This is more than I could have asked for."

"Here, let me help you with it." She took the necklace from the box, and I turned around, staring at my reflection on the mirror.

She undid the clasp and placed the necklace carefully around my neck.

"There," she smiled. "It looks beautiful on you, don't you think?"

It was quite beautiful. The green emerald accentuated my

hazel eyes and as I traced my fingers across the stone, I noticed a small symbol carved within it; it looked like a heraldic crest though not just any crest. I had seen it before in Celest's office —on *the family tree*. I gasped.

"You said it was a family heirloom? Is this our family crest?" I asked, staring at the symbol with curiosity.

"Yes, it has been in your family for generations," she said, and for the first time I knew she was speaking the truth.

"It's beautiful. Thank you. It means a lot to me." I turned to her, the knot on my throat tightening.

I wasn't sure if it was the necklace, the emotions bottled up from the past few days, or perhaps her kind gesture, but I surprised us both when I pulled her into an embrace. The need for comfort was overwhelming. "Thank you," I whispered, feeling a rare sense of happiness despite everything.

I waved goodbye at Celest from the porch. As she backed away from the driveway, the school bus pulled up the road. Pushing open the umbrella for shelter from the downpour, I ran the short distance to the bus while avoiding the large puddles that had formed overnight. Oddly, the weather hadn't improved since I called on the elements for the ritual. I hadn't thought of that before this moment, but perhaps the unfinished ritual was the cause. It would certainly be a problem if I didn't close the circle and released the elements properly.

The roar of thunder came, followed by the blinding light that illuminated the skies. Not much was visible through the foggy windows or the constant curtain of rain.

As the bus moved slowly up the hill, my heart leaped. I

wasn't sure if it was my imagination, but I thought I saw a man's figure by the side of the road. Although I couldn't be sure under the pelting rain.

Drake... No. I shook my head to dispel the thoughts of him. It was not the moment. But I would need to find him. Tonight. I had to. It was the least I could do—if he didn't find me first. I frowned at the thought.

SEYMOR

Sitting in the study of my London home, I listened to the murmurs buzzing throughout the chamber and those through the intercom come to a complete halt as High Council Stephen Radcliff called the assembly to order.

"This assembly is now open as we bring the guardianship to a full circle for the sacred duty bestowed upon us to serve and protect this realm and all others. Welcome, brothers and sisters," he declared, and the bustling voices rose once again.

"Silence. You know why we are here. Many of you sensed the high magic last night, yet we don't know how it was done, or who is responsible for it."

"Does this mean the Sacred Book has finally been located?" Sylvie from Denmark, a close ally, voiced over the intercom.

"I suspect it has," Stephen speculated, and I knew his intentions without hearing him voice them. "That is another reason why I have summoned this meeting. I have reason to believe that Celest has taken manuscripts from the reliquary. Information that has led her to the book, and yet she is keeping it from us."

"As a council member, I would like to speak for my sister, if

I may," I said through the intercom, aware that speaking out for her would put me on the line, but I had to cast doubt to buy her more time.

"Seymor, I urge you to keep an open perspective about this matter. She might be your sister but remember that the guardianship comes first. If she has kept the book from us, she will have to answer for it."

"Everyone present knows Celest. You know that she would never betray the service to the brotherhood," I said. Although in truth, only a handful of the members truly knew my sister. "Oh, and Stephen—I know the rules. I have always served this council and will continue to do so. Perhaps you are the one who should be reminded that you need proof before briefing an accusation, before summoning us to the chamber on official business." I pointed out, knowing deep down it wouldn't be long before he found what he needed to demand an in-person summon. "I suggest you keep your suspicions to yourself. Unless you have factual proof that my sister had anything to do with the stolen manuscript, the presumed location of the book, or the source of the high magic."

I didn't have to be in the same room as the man to know he would be furious, but I knew what cards to play and when. The few guardians I could call friends voiced their agreement that there should be no official accusation unless proof was delivered, forcing Stephen to back down. He was the head of the Council, but with a divided assembly, he had no power. He required three-thirds of our votes to make any move on Celest. I was counting on the few friends we had to make sure that didn't happen, even if he found enough proof to summon us all back to the chamber.

"Our focus should be directed to figuring out what was responsible for the high magic. We all know it would take the power of this entire council—and more, to do so. I cannot be the only one present who thinks this should be our priority," Benjamin, who was present in the chamber, added. The buzzing voices rose once again.

"We should also consider the prophecy of the pureblood," Ren's voice through the intercom brought the room to silence. Ren was an extremist when it came to lost causes; his fanatics for the prophecy made him a great ally.

"Let's not get carried away by old tales. A pureblood has to be sired by two guardians. So, unless you have a son or daughter with one of your fellow members that I don't know about, do not waste my time." Stephen dismissed the notion of the prophecy, and I was thankful for his ignorance. That meant less attention to Celest, fewer complications for the girl. She would be powerful—I had no doubts, what I never expected was for her gifts to spring this early. I had to speak with my sister.

"As agreed, this meeting is now dismissed until further notice. You will receive an official summons to the chamber once we have investigated further and found the facts."

Stephen would kill me now if he could. I was glad I was thousands of miles away in the comfort of my home, but I knew it wouldn't be long before those summonses came, and I had to be ready. I had to find Felsia and speak with Celest. We couldn't pretend anymore. The girl had to know what she was up against.

TYRUS

I stood post outside the chamber door, listening as the meeting came to an end. The departure of the members previously present was followed by loud, violent crashes inside. He was in a mood.

"Tyrus, come inside," his voice thundered through the doors.

I entered, bracing myself. "Yes, Sir."

"I need you to hire a man. Someone who can be discreet," he ordered.

I frowned at his request. "Sir, I can be discreet, as can any of my men," I replied confidently.

He shook his head. "No. I don't want this person traced back to us in any way."

"I understand, Sir. And the task?" I asked, dreading to find out in what new way I would have to compromise my ethics.

"Oliver is bringing Celest's girl to the fair tomorrow. I want to find out what she knows. By whatever means necessary," he said, staring at me with a chilling coolness. He didn't need to explain further; I knew how ruthless he could be.

"Sir, shouldn't we let Oliver know so that he is prepared?"

"Not a word to him or anyone. This stays between us. Do I make myself clear?"

"Absolutely, Sir."

"You are dismissed then."

I pivoted out of the room, questioning if I was doing the right thing. Wondering at what point I had lost my morals.

BELYNDA

As I dashed into the building, seeking refuge from the rain, a collection of floating colorful balloons greeted me, confirming my suspicions. Lily stood nearby, a wide grin on her face as she shouted, "Surprise!" loud enough for the entire hall to hear, as if the balloons weren't sufficient advertisement.

"I'm going to kill you," I teased.

"Come on, you only turn eighteen once. Suck it up. Here," she said, enveloping me in a bear hug while thrusting a card and a box of chocolates into my hands.

"I'll be nice, but only because these are my favorite," I smiled, not wanting to seem ungrateful. Plus, they truly were my favorite.

"Now, what exactly am I supposed to do with all of these balloons?" I laughed.

"You'll figure it out. See you at lunch?"

"I doubt you'll miss me in the cafeteria. I'll be the only one with the flock of balloons," her laughter traveled down the hallway.

I WAS SURPRISED to see Oliver sitting at our desk before anyone else. He smiled as I approached, the balloons trailing behind me.

"This is a first," I commented.

"Happy Birthday," he said, extending a card toward me. "I'm sorry I didn't get you any balloons," he smirked.

"I doubt you would have found any," I laughed. "How the hell am I supposed to function with them?"

Oliver glanced at my flock of balloons, then without warning, he stabbed one with his pen. Instantly, the balloon deflated and dropped to the ground. I smiled mischievously and took the pen from Oliver's hand.

I popped five more balloons but stopped when a group of students entered the class, followed by Mrs. Gill. I tied the last three survivors to the back of the chair and sat down beside a smirking Oliver.

"Remind me never to piss you off again," he added, and I was glad to see him finally showing some sensibility.

As everyone filed in, I opened his card and was surprised to find a one-hundred-dollar iTunes gift card.

"I can't take this," I protested, pushing the card back to him.

"Nonsense," he insisted, pushing it back toward me. "Besides, what would people think?" he smiled, and I had a feeling his gesture wasn't solely for his reputation's sake. Reluctantly, I accepted the gift with gratitude.

"You didn't have to get me anything, you know," I said.

"I know," he said sincerely, a departure from his usual demeanor.

"Thank you. I'm definitely going to use it."

"Ms. Hershton. Happy Birthday," Mrs. Gill called out, and felicitations rained from around the room, causing my face to flush with embarrassment.

"This is why I don't advertise my birthday. I hate the attention," I muttered.

"It's your birthday, enjoy it. The day will be over before you know it."

When the bell rang, Oliver walked me to my next class.

"What happened to you yesterday?" I asked, sensing our relationship had reached a point where such questions were acceptable.

"I had personal things to take care of," he answered curtly, and though I waited for elaboration, I knew the conversation had ended when he didn't offer any.

As he paused in front of me, his gaze fell upon my necklace.

"That's new," he observed.

"Yes. A birthday gift. It was my mother's," I said, but when he reached out to examine the crest, I slapped his hand away.

"I told you, no touching, remember?"

"Sorry," he said, moving away uncomfortably as the bell rang.

"I'll see you at lunch," I called after him.

The cafeteria buzzed with noise, but Lily's voice rang above all.

"No, you did not kill the balloons."

Damn, she was pissed.

"Sorry. That was my fault. I couldn't see the board with all of those damn balloons in my face," Oliver said, with an unapologetic smile."You are such an idiot," Lily scolded, but I was grateful that Oliver bore the brunt of her wrath.

Ben joined us too, but his presence was welcome. He was polite and sweet, simply wishing me a happy birthday without making a fuss like Lily did.

"I can't wait for tomorrow. We are going to have so much fun," Lily beamed, but I didn't share her enthusiasm. Even though Oliver and I were on better terms, I had more important matters to attend to, like finding the immortal Dragon prince I had selfishly abandoned.

By the time school ended, I was ready to murder Lily. Somehow, she had invited herself over to my house for some girl bonding time in the evening. How had she managed it? I had no clue.

Arriving home, I was plagued by a terrible migraine, just like the day before, and I was in a foul mood. The rain hadn't stopped, and it was beginning to worry me, that I could be to blame for it.

As I reached the front porch, fear replaced my worries. My school bag lay discarded on the floor, my cell phone inside. Anxiety washed over me; while the town was small, it wasn't small enough for Drake to locate me so quickly. Then again, he was a supernatural being, and I couldn't begin to understand his capabilities. Glancing around uneasily, I saw nothing but a curtain of rain.

Mindlessly flipping through TV channels, I found myself—for the first time since that morning—able to relax. Knowing Drake was alive eased my conscience. The mere thought of harm befalling him turned my stomach. How could I justify leaving him stranded and confused last night? I needed to face him, but I had no idea how. Tonight, would have been my chance, but the weather wasn't cooperating, and to make matters worse, I was committed to spending the evening with Lily.

I wondered if he was upset with me. It would explain why he left the bag without a word. I pushed the thought aside, fearing he might have left for good. If he had, I couldn't blame him. He didn't know me. Finding himself free after all these years was reason enough to not want to stick around. However, if he was gone, I'd be left with nothing: no sacred book, no answers. Strangely, the thought of never seeing him again bothered me more than anything else.

OLIVER

Practice was brutal. The coach had us running laps until our legs gave out.

"Ben, wait up."

"You're running soft, Radcliff?" he teased as we entered the locker rooms. Ben was like a brother to me, but sometimes his jokes felt like a reminder of the crap I had to deal with from my father.

"I think you've been hanging around my father too much lately."

His expression hardened momentarily.

"Sorry, bro. You know I didn't mean anything by it. Have you spoken to him lately?"

"Last night. He was in one of his moods."

"Yeah? I heard he called an emergency meeting this morning. My father had to go in early."

"Are you sure? I didn't know."

"You would've known if you showed more interest in the council," he quipped, sounding like my father once again.

"You know I try; I do. It's just that nothing I do is ever good enough for him. Honestly, I think when the time comes for him to pass up his seat in the council, he'll never give it to me."

"Well, from what you've told me, it's not like you're in a rush to inherit it anyway."

"Oh, I'm not. He can keep it. Forever. I was just stating the obvious. He doesn't think I'm worthy."

"You and your crazy ideas. Did you find anything else on Celest and Belynda?"

"Nothing. That's why he was fuming."

"Cut him some slack, Rod. You know he has all the responsibility of the guardianship. It's not easy constantly having to watch your back."

That was another thing I'd never agree with. Ben saw my father as someone to look up to, but he didn't know what that monster was capable of. My father only loved himself, and his people followed him out of fear, not loyalty or respect.

"By the way, did you notice Belynda's necklace?"

"I did. Why?"

"Well, you said you didn't find anything on the girl or the aunt, but I'm almost certain that the crest inside her necklace is one I've seen in the legacy chamber."

"Are you sure about that?"

He seemed as certain as I was, but if I could divert Ben's interest from Belynda's necklace, maybe I wouldn't have to mention it to my father.

"I'm almost certain, but I wasn't as close to her as you were. I don't know. I could be wrong."

"Don't worry. I'll confirm next time I see it. Besides, wasn't her adoptive mother part of the council?"

"Regardless, I'm sure that's something that would interest your dad."

Oh, I'm sure it would. I just wasn't sure if I was ready to tell him.

"Don't mention it. I'll deal with it."

Ben said nothing else on the matter, but I wasn't so sure I could trust him to keep his mouth shut.

BELYNDA

The sound of the front door lock clicking open had my heart racing. I wasn't sure who—or what I expected it to be, but relief washed over me when I realized it was just Celest. I guess a part of me was still jumpy from the break-in.

"Hey, how did it go today?" I asked, trying to quiet my racing heart.

"With this weather, I think it was a bad day for everyone. That's why I picked up early." She hung her coat and removed her boots by the entrance hall. "It's getting worse. I wonder when it's going to ease up."

I cringed at her comment with the sinking suspicion that my unfinished ritual might be to blame for the rage of the elements. I would have to find a way to fix it.

"Oh, I almost forgot. Lily said she might come over in a little while. I hope that's ok with you."

"Yes, of course. That's nice of her. How was school?"

"It was fine. Got some balloons, chocolate, and an iTunes gift card."

"I take it you weren't happy with all the attention," I smiled, realizing perhaps Celest knew me better than I thought.

"It wasn't so bad," I admitted.

"I'm glad. You are young; birthdays are meant to be celebrated! It means you are alive."

"You know why I've never liked making a big deal of it."

"I do. But I also know that your mother would have wanted you to enjoy it, so I'm glad you're coming around." Celest smiled and I did too. Today was a new day. I was turning eighteen and though my life was a mess, I chose not to feel guilty or sad—just for tonight.

The bell rang and Celest quickly answered it.

"Hi. How are you. Is Belynda home?"

"Yes, come in, please. Here, let me help you with that." Celest took the box Lily was carrying so she could take off her raincoat. Spotting me standing in the corridor, she grinned.

"I got you a cake."

"Of course you did. Thank you," I smiled.

"Lillian, how is Leonor?"

"Oh, my mom is good. Just overprotective as usual. She didn't want me out in this weather, but she eased up a bit when I told her I was coming over here. I can't be out too late, though."

"Well, I don't blame her. It's so stormy outside but I'm glad you were able to come."

At first, I feared it would be strange having Lily over, but it was nice to see her carrying on a normal conversation with Celest. She was the most social person I had ever met—technically, I hadn't met many people, but Lily was the definition of 'social'. She could talk up a storm, so I knew she and Celest could keep each other occupied, while I excused myself to take a quick shower.

When I entered my room, I found Lily sprawled on the bed, rifling through the music selection on my iPod.

"Hey." She responded, seeming quite comfortable on my bed.

"Do you even know the concept of privacy or manners?" I teased, as I stepped into my closet.

"No, never heard of it," she smirked.

"I can see that."

"Your aunt told me to make myself at home, so I did."

"You do know that she's not my aunt, right?" I was unsure if Lily, like most, also believed Celest was a blood relative.

Her silence told me that she had no idea.

"She's not?" Sitting up on the bed, Lily looked confused. I sat down beside her and took the iPod from her hands.

"Celest was my mother's best friend, but they were more like sisters. She was the one who raised me after my mother passed away."

"That was very nice of her. She must truly care for you to have done that."

Did Celest love me? I was sure she did—but having someone from the outside perceive the same felt reassuring.

I smiled, attempting to lighten the mood. "Is this what you call girl bonding time?" I asked, trying to divert the topic to something less serious. "I thought you were here to show me how to loosen up and have fun."

Her mischievous smile took over and without warning, she swung one of the pillows and hit me square in the face.

"You are in so much trouble," I grinned, taking the other pillow, and swinging it in her direction.

Lily fell onto the bed and I on the floor. My chest rose and fell in heaved breaths, and my throat felt dry. I hadn't laughed as much in a long time, and it felt nice to escape the negative aspects that made up my daily life.

Lily insisted on doing my nails, and I was unable to

convince her otherwise.

Before leaving, she and Celest sang happy birthday and cut the cake. My birthday wish was for Drake to be safe. The level of anxiety I was developing heightened every minute that passed, without knowing where he was.

When I said goodnight to Lily, she was still upset that I had refused to indulge in boy talk, when she had attempted to probe, under the bizarre notion that I was developing feelings for Oliver. The reality was that there was no boy to speak of. There was *Drake*... but he wasn't a boy, he was a *man*—an immortal man, and I knew better than to entertain such notions.

Celest and I stood in the doorway to see Lily off.

"She's a very nice girl. I'm glad you have her as a friend," Celest remarked, locking the door behind us.

"Lily's very determined," I added, smiling.

"I'm just happy you enjoyed your birthday. Goodnight, get some rest," Celest said. "I'm glad it's the last day of the book fair, but it's going to be a long day. I only pray that we have better weather."

"I hope so too," I replied with a frown. "Goodnight."

Once I retreated to the safety of my room, worry clawed its way back into my mind. I paced aimlessly, obsessed by the need to find Drake, to ensure he was safe. I imagined him out there, alone, as rain pounded against the window, a constant reminder of the unfinished ritual.

With resolve, I flung open the window and called out into the night, "Drake, where are you?" My words were swallowed by the wind and rain, met only by silence.

"This is nonsense," I muttered, unsure of what I had

expected. Extending my arms to touch the rain, I recited the few passages I remembered, unable to recall the exact words from the sacred book. "Guardian spirits of the elements, I release you. Thank you for your power, presence, and guidance. You may now go in peace. The circle is now open."

As I withdrew my hands, the torrent of rain persisted, and frustration crept in. But then, a tingling sensation danced up my arms, and I watched as the wind died down and the rain slowed to a drizzle.

The night became eerie and still; the soft, cold breeze caressed my face, and I marbled at the electrifying and thrilling sensation that coursed through me. My newly discovered abilities were nothing short of magical and they had transformed my reality. My life no longer felt ordinary and the dreams that once felt like a curse now seemed like a blessing.

Yet, beneath the thrill, there was still uncertainty and fear. I had no idea what the consequences of what I had done would mean. Like Selene had said, Magic wasn't a game. I leaned back against the window frame anticipating the severity of the consequences of everything I had done. Yet, despite the fear, I felt no regret for for releasing Drake. I found myself transfixed by the haunting memory of piercing grey eyes. The prospect of facing him again filled me with both dread and anticipation.

As MORNING LIGHT filtered into the room, I noticed the necklace still draped around my neck, a reminder of the events of the previous night. Unease crept over me as I realized I had no memory of returning to bed or closing the window. *Had I sleep-*

walked? The thought unsettled me, but I dispelled the idea, attributing it to exhaustion.

With a sigh, I resigned myself to the day ahead. The book fair awaited, the final day and the dreaded date looming ahead.

THE MORNING PASSED IN A HAZE, the sun rarely peeking through the heavy clouds. By late afternoon, my usually pale skin was flushed, whether from the high temperature, humidity, or the nerves about my impending date with Oliver, I couldn't tell.

Celest appeared to be in a good mood, likely due to the high sales or the fact the day was almost over. Whatever the reason, I took it as my opportunity to tell her about the date. It would be weird if Oliver just showed up at the house and I sprung the news on her without any warning. After helping her bring down the tent and put away the tables, I made my move.

"Celest, do you mind if I leave you to close up?"

"Do you feel unwell? You look a little flushed," she noted.

"I'm fine. I promise. Just planning to go to the fair with Lily and some friends," Celest, eyed me with suspicion.

"Will a certain someone be joining you?" she prodded, a knowing smile playing on her lips.

"It's more of a group outing, but yes, Oliver will pick me up," I admitted, aware that the less she knew, the better. After all, this was a one-time deal, and I didn't want her getting her hopes up.

She smiled pleased. "Mm-hmm. Is he important?"

"We're just friends, honestly," I assured her, though her

skeptical look suggested she wasn't fully convinced. Thankfully, she didn't push the matter further.

THE WALK home proved to be an unnerving journey. Leaving the town center behind and venturing into the deserted road, a sense of paranoia struck me. Despite the absence of any real threat, I couldn't shake the feeling of being followed, constantly glancing over my shoulder, and finding only the empty road stretching behind me.

By the time I reached the Manor, my nerves were tightly wound. My lack of experience in the dating scene added to my unease as I spent nearly an hour deliberating over what to wear. While my aim wasn't to impress Oliver, I wanted to feel comfortable in my own skin. I settled on faded blue skinny jeans paired with knee-high black boots, an aqua blue tank top, and a cream-colored jacket. A stark change from my usual dark choices, but somehow, this change represented a new vision of me of my newly discovered life and gifts.

As I reached the living room, Celest walked through the door.

"Did you manage ok without me?" I asked.

"Barely," she replied with a smile. "It's starting to look like a freak show out there."

I laughed at her remark, "Well, I guess I can add myself to the list of freaks then."

Celest grinned. "No, I think there's still hope for you."

Though I appreciated her good mood, I couldn't help but wonder if her happiness stemmed from an imagined relationship between Oliver and me.

The bell rang and Celest almost hurried to answer it. I followed closely behind, hoping to avoid any excuse to invite him in.

"Oliver, right?" Celest greeted politely as she opened the door.

"Yeah...Hi. I'm here to pick up Belynda," Oliver replied, surprise in his voice at seeing Celest.

"Oliver," I interrupted. "Ready to go?"

"Yeah," he said, with relief and eyed me with a smile.

I gave him a pointed look at the same time that Celest cleared her throat.

"Oliver, this is Celest. Celest–Oliver," I said, expediting the introductions.

"It's a pleasure to meet you, Oliver," Celest offered, extending her hand to him.

Oliver took her hand. "Thank you. The pleasure is mine," he responded politely.

"Do I know your parents?" Celest asked and I began to grow impatient.

"I don't know. My mother is Samantha, and my father is Stephen Radcliff." The way she stared at him was odd and her initial excitement transformed to a visible furrow on her brow.

"I'm sorry. Yes. I believe I've heard of your father, but I won't keep you waiting. Go on, you two."

"Let's go," I stepped past Celest, eager to end the awkward exchange, but Celest's firm grip on my arm halted me from following Oliver.

"Belynda. Please be careful." She begged; with real worry as she glanced at Oliver's retreating figure.

I nodded in understanding, promising to return early,

though I couldn't fathom why she was worried about Oliver. He may have been a jerk, but he posed no real threat. Oliver remained silent as he pulled the car in reverse.

"I take it your aunt doesn't like me much?" he remarked with a brooding expression.

"Does it matter? We're not planning to repeat this, so don't worry about it," I replied, hoping not to sound mean.

"Yeah, I guess you're right," he conceded, though his demeanor changed, and I remembered the one trivial thing I had learned about Oliver Radcliff: he didn't know how to deal with not being liked or accepted.

"If it's any consolation, this is the first time I've gone out. I'm sure she's just having a hard time letting go; it's nothing personal," I added as a feeble to ease his wounded pride.

"Sure." He didn't seem to buy my excuse but smiled, nonetheless. "You look good, by the way."

I rolled my eyes but thanked him.

"I'm not going to tell you that you look good too, your ego is big enough already. I don't want it getting to your head."

His bark of laughter filled the car.

"Well, it's the thought that counts, so thanks I guess."

The ride to the fair wasn't uncomfortable. Contrary to my initial beliefs, being friends with Oliver wasn't actually as unpleasant. There was no hint of romantic tension between us, which was unexpected but relieving.

THE FAIR WAS OVERWHELMING, and Celest's description of it looking like a freak show was an understatement. I hadn't visited the carnival since was a child and being surrounded by so many people made me uneasy.

When I spotted Lily, I was instantly relieved.

"You look stunning," she smiled, giving me a quick hug. I blushed self-consciously.

"Thanks. You look great too," I offered.

It was nice to see Lily so happy, especially with Ben by her side. They made a cute couple.

Oliver and Ben played a few games, trying to win prizes for Lily and me. It was a testosterone-induced battle that I didn't like much.

Secretly, I hoped Oliver would lose every game so I could witness his frustration. To my surprise, he did, although I couldn't tell if it was due to my silent wishes or if Ben was simply a much skilled opponent.

REFUSING to take Oliver's hand, we weaved through the crowds, following Lily towards another ride. A sharp bump against my shoulder diverted my attention, and scanning the crowd, I found myself transfixed on a familiar pair of grey eyes. Eyes that vanished as quickly as they appeared.

On instinct, I ran after them. Losing myself in the throng, I attempted to backtrack in search of those haunting eyes. Yet, the swarm of people made it impossible. I searched for him, left and right, but it was no use.

When I reached the more secluded part of the fairgrounds, lined with worker tents and trailers, I hesitated, deciding it was time to turn around. I knew what I had seen—*Drake*. He wasn't a figment of my imagination.

Just as I turned back to find Lily and Oliver, a hand clamped over my mouth, stifling out my cry. Another arm ensnared my waist, and I resisted, but wasn't strong enough to free myself from the man's grasp. Through my terror, only one thought was on repeat: *not you, Drake. It can't be you.*

Panic blurred my senses, as I found myself dragged behind a tent, not a soul in sight. I wrestled against the man's hold, and attempted to scream, but his hands only clamped that much harder.

My entire body trembled with fear as I felt his tainted breath against my neck.

"Stay still, little princess. I've got some questions for you," he commanded, and I obeyed, a mix of fear and relief flooding through me as I realized it wasn't Drake's voice.

"I need you to tell me the truth. Understand?" His hand remained firm over my mouth, so I nodded, desperate to cooperate if it meant surviving.

"Okay, I'm letting go now. One scream and you're done. Got it?" he pressed, and I nodded again, terror seizing me.

"Good girl," he sneered, his breath reeking of alcohol as he leaned in closer, making my stomach churn.

"My associates want to know where those stolen documents from the reliquary are," he said, loosening his grip on my mouth. But even though it was my cue to speak, I had nothing to say. Who was this guy? What on earth was the reliquary? And how could I talk my way out of this mess?

"I swear, I don't know what you're talking about. Please, just let me go. I'm begging you," I pleaded, hoping he'd believe me.

"Wrong answer," he growled, pressing the cold blade of a

knife against my throat. I didn't want to swallow, afraid of what a minimal slip on my part could mean.

"Last chance. Tell me what you know!" he demanded, his patience wearing thin.

Trapped and helpless, I realized I had no way out of this. This man would kill me whether I fought back or not. I didn't know anything about the reliquary, and something told me lying would only make matters worse. This man was dangerous, and with my awful luck, possibly even the same who broke into the house.

Driven by instinct, adrenaline, or perhaps stupid courage, I sank my teeth into his hand and stomped on his foot, seizing the opportunity to break free. But my escape was short lived. His grip tightened on my hair, yanking me back with force.

"Please, I really don't know anything," I sobbed desperately, feeling all hopes of escaping slipping away.

"Guess I can't play nice then," he spat, hurling me to the ground with brutal force. As pain shot through me, I realized with numbness resignation that I would not make it out alive. *Not like this. Not me. Not now.*

"Don't touch her again." The dark and riveting voice made our heads spin, and instantly I knew I was saved. Those same grey eyes that I had been hunting earlier stared back. "Step away, unless you want to lose a hand." Drake threatened, with a cool and collected voice that cut through the night like lethal steel.

"Drake," his name slipped through my lips like a reverence. His eyes found me at the same time, and my heart leaped in my chest.

The man laughed, twirling the silver blade in his hand.

Oblivious to the fact that Drake was stronger not to mention, immortal. Ignoring Drake's warning, he forcefully, yanked me to my feet. I cried out in pain as he tugged at my bruised arm.

"Don't get brave with threats, when I'm the one with the knife," the man taunted, pressing the cold steel to my throat once more.

I was petrified. All I could do was stare into Drake's eyes which were surprisingly calm before they blurred before me. Drake moved with lightning speed. With an effortless grip, he snapped the man's arm, the crack of bone echoing through the night, drowned out by the man's agonized cry. The knife clattered to the ground at my feet. The man's protests crushed by Drake's firm grip around his throat, lifting him effortlessly off the ground.

The haunted look shadowing Drake's face assaulted me. If I didn't do something, he would take the man's life and I couldn't allow it, not on my behalf, not while I was responsible for him being here. I placed a hand on his arm, and at the touch his head shifted, his gaze locked onto my fingers. I recoiled, withdrawing my hand, but his eyes found mine, and I stilled, lost into depths of onyx black.

"Please let him go. I'm ok. You don't have to do this," I pleaded, willing him to listen. He blinked and a semblance of control returned, together with the visible change of his silvery eyes.

"You want to spare him, after what he's done?" he questioned, his eyes narrowing in disbelief as I nodded, unsure of my own reasoning, but certain taking a life was not the answer.

Reluctantly, he lowered the man, until his feet touched the

ground. Drake loomed over him.

"This will be your only warning," Drake seethed, his tone clear and daunting. "If you come near her again, she won't be able to save you. I don't give second chances," with a look of disgust, Drake sent the man flying with an effortless shove.

The man fled, clutching his broken arm as he disappeared into the night. My eyes remained fixed on Drake's back, fear mingling with anticipation. Slowly, he turned to face me, his grey eyes unreadable as they studied me.

Hugging my arms around myself, I winced as I brushed against the bruise on my shoulder. "Are you hurt?" His voice, warm and gentle this time, washed over me, and I found myself unable to tear my gaze away from his.

"I'm ok," I replied, lost to the silvery depths of his eyes, and the frown that appeared on his face.

"May I?" he asked, stepping closer, towering over me. An intoxicating scent of sandalwood, pine and earthly forest numbing my senses. Grounding me in his presence. He was dangerous, and yet I could not move. I didn't want to. "Is it ok if I take a look?" he asked, and though my thoughts were a jumbled mess, I nodded in consent, unsure of what I was agreeing to.

With a sense of unease, I watched as he pushed the sleeve of my jacket down, exposing my bruised shoulder. His touch was gentle, and I stilled, lost in a haze, unsure if I was dead or dreaming.

"I'm sorry. Here," his palm closed around my shoulder, the touch sent a million butterflies fluttering through my stomach, followed by a comforting warmth spreading down my arm. I wanted to ask a million questions, but his eyes held me captive, and I was lost again, cocooned in a haze of comfort and warmth.

As he studied my face, I did the same, committing every detail to memory. The dreams I'd had of him paled in comparison to the reality before me. Drake was a God. Immortalized with strength and beauty, his features sculpted with an otherworldly perfection. A face like his could devastate armies.

Adjusting my jacket, he took a step back, and clarity returned to me in a rush. I touched my shoulder, surprised to find the throbbing pain gone, replaced by a warm, tingling sensation.

Drake stared back, his expression unreadable.

"Better?"

"Yes," I hesitated, confounded by him. A million questions lodged in my throat.

"Thank you," I whispered, the words feeling inadequate in expressing the gratitude I felt.

Stepping closer, his eyes never leaving mine, he spoke again, his voice tinged with concern. "That was a reckless move," he remarked, and I frowned in confusion, wondering if he was referring to my failed attempt to fight off the man.

"I had to defend myself. I didn't have a choice," I countered, but he shook his head, his expression hardening.

"Certainly, that was reckless. But I was referring to you, interfering," he said, and I stared at him for a moment... he was about to kill the man. "Don't ever do that again," he added, his face hardening, his tone leaving no room for argument. I took a step back.

"What are you saying?" I demanded, feeling a spark of anger fueling my reasoning. "That I should have just let you kill him?" His eyes darkened, flickering between silver and black before settling on silver once more. His fists clenched at his sides, a silent indication to his barely contained anger.

"Do you have any idea what you have unleashed? Any idea what I've become," he growled, his strides bringing him closer, and I stumbled back, my heart pounding in my chest. He paused, his gaze boring into mine, and for the first time, fear gripped me.

"Will you hurt me?" I blurted out, the question hanging in the air between us as I met the darkness of his eyes. They shifted before me, softening to their usual silver hue.

He considered my words for a moment, his expression a mixture of surprise and confusion. "That's an interesting question considering you know what I am," he mused, his gaze studying my face, as if it held some mystery he had yet to decipher. "No, I don't believe I ever could," he concluded; his frown deepening as if this realization was as much a revelation to him as it was to me.

"I have so many questions," I confessed, my gaze never leaving his. Drake smiled in response and its effect brought me to my knees. I had thought him capable of devastating armies with his immortalized perfection, but his smile clearly a weapon he rarely yielded, was poison to death itself.

"Those will have to wait," he said, his voice low. "Your friends are looking for you." he added, and I tore my gaze away picking up the noise of the crowd in the distance. Realizing how easy I'd lost myself in his presence.

Bending down, he retrieved the discarded knife, folding the blade and slipping it into his back pocket without another word.

"Will I see you soon?" I pressed, the words escaping before I could stop them, and a corner of his mouth shifted.

"Yes," he replied. Closing the distance between us until he was standing before me. I stilled as he raised his hand, the anticipation of his touch, sending a jolt of warmth coursing through me. But instead of touching me, he tucked a loose strand of hair behind my ear, his gaze never leaving mine. My lips parted; my throat suddenly parched.

"I should probably go," I whispered, breaking the spell. He dropped his hand, and a frown etched his brow.

Turning away, I took a few steps before pausing, glancing back at him over my shoulder. "Drake," I called out, and he met my gaze, his frown vanishing.

"Belynda," he replied, and I turned away with a smile. The sound of my name from his lips, echoing deep in my soul.

Once I reached the crowd and the lights, I couldn't resist stealing one last glance. I turned to where Drake had been standing, but he was gone, and a wave of disappointment washed over me.

"Where in the world have you been?" Lily grabbed my hand, startling me.

"I got lost in the crowd. I'm sorry," I lied, my eyes still searching for Drake.

"And your phone?" I frowned, patting my empty pockets. Damn it. It must have fallen when the man took me.

"I left it at home," I said, just as we spotted Ben and Oliver.

"Jesus, where have you been?" Oliver frowned; his tone filled with worry. "I've been looking everywhere for you. I was starting to worry."

Something had happen, I wanted to say, but like every traumatic event in my life, I shoved it aside.

"I'm fine. Is it alright if we go?" Oliver's gaze shifted to the dirt on my pants; the look on his face told me he sensed something was off but chose not to speak of it. Lily didn't seem to notice, and I was relieved because dodging her questions would have been challenging.

"Yeah, sure. Come on. I'll take you home."

I said good night to Ben and Lily, using my early curfew as an excuse, but the truth was that now that the adrenaline rush, and the Drake effect had worn off, I was in shock. All I could think of was the man with the knife, his reasons for coming after me. Mostly, I was anxiety ridden at the prospect of seeing Drake again.

The ride home was silent, but something was clearly on Oliver's mind. He pulled into the driveway and parked the car, unable to look at me.

"Will you tell me the truth? Did something happen to you out there?" He gripped the steering wheel, and for some strange reason, I didn't feel inclined to lie.

"A man attacked me," I confessed, barely recognizing my own voice. Oliver remained still beside me, his gaze fixed on me.

"How are you so calmed?" Honestly, I was surprised at that myself. I was coping better than expected, but I knew Drake's presence had a lot to do with it.

"I am a little shaken," I admitted. Oliver reached out to touch my hand, but I flinched away. I knew he meant to comfort me, but I couldn't control my reaction. It made me wonder why I hadn't responded the same way to Drake's touch.

"I'm sorry. I wasn't trying to be rude. I'm still a little jumpy, that's all."

"It's ok." Oliver gave me some space, absorbed in his thoughts for a moment. "Why you? Did you know the man? What did he want?" he asked, surprising me.

Good questions, but ones I had few answers to. I had no idea who the man was, but I knew what he wanted. I debated whether telling Oliver was wise, but I had confided in him thus far. Besides, it wouldn't make much sense to him anyway.

"Honestly, I don't really know. I could barely think straight. He kept asking me about stolen papers from a reli-quary or something like that, but I have no idea what he meant. Maybe he was just crazy."

I flinched as Oliver punched the steering wheel.

"I would have killed him." His sudden anger caught me off guard.

"No, you wouldn't have. Let's just forget it happened," I said, unbuckling my seatbelt.

Oliver remained silent but his anger oozed off him in waves.

"Goodnight." Oliver's tone was abrupt, and suddenly, he seemed eager to leave. One moment he was protective, the next, he seemed in a rush to be somewhere else.

"Goodnight. Thank you," I offered, confused by the boy's mood swings. I shut the car door, and he drove away from the driveway without another word.

As I watched the fading taillights disappear, I mulled over his strange behavior. I didn't want to dwell on it, but some-thing felt off, and my instincts were usually right.

7

SHADOW OF THE PAST

WHEN I TURNED AROUND, I WAS MET by a solid wall of muscle. A strong hand clasped firmly over my mouth to muffle my scream while the other one secured my waist, catching my fall. Panic surged through me, but in an instant, I relaxed into the man's hold, the familiar warmth and Drake's scent like a balm to my nerves. Eyes wide, I stared up at him. As my heart settled, he released me, taking a measured step back. A frown and a hard set of his jaw ruling his expression.

"Hello again," I said, pressing a hand against my beating heart and smiling with euphoric surprise. He regarded me silently, his eyes unreadable.

I glanced nervously at the porch steps and the windows, worrying Celest could come out at any minute.

Drake closed his eyes and tilted his head to the night sky, just as he had done the night I released him. He took a deep breath, and when his eyes returned to me, they seemed almost lighter, a silver sheen.

"He's not your mate," he said matter-of-factly, craning his head to the side with curiosity. "What is he to you?" he asked, and the shock of his direct question must have been evident on my face.

"Oliver?" I mused. Drake's eyes narrowed in the direction the car had taken, leaving no doubt about his lingering suspicion. "He's only a friend," I offered, feeling troubled by the strange need to reassure him.

"Mhhh," the sound reverberated from the depths of his throat. He straightened before me, and I wasn't sure how it was possible, but he seemed even taller. The material of his long-sleeve black shirt strained against the wide span of his shoulders. Butterflies returned to my stomach.

"Do you trust him?" he asked, and I blinked away the hazy thoughts distracting me. Did I trust Oliver? I mused over the question.

"In theory, yes," I admitted. "Why?" I asked.

"You shouldn't," he said without explanation, his tone disapproving.

I stared up at him with a frown. "Who should I trust then, you?" I asked with an edge of bitterness that didn't seem to faze him.

"I would advise against that as well," he replied. I stilled at his candor. If his words were a warning, every cell in my body begged me to ignore it.

"I find that hard to believe. I'll form my own opinions, thank you," I countered, meeting his gaze in challenge. He didn't back down.

"You mortals and your notions of romanticism," he said. "I suppose your assumption is based on my interference tonight?" He took a step closer as I stepped back, towering over me. Leaning down, he whispered, "I assure you, one insignificant act of kindness does not make me a hero."

"Why save me then?" I questioned, anger simmering against my will. "Are you saying you didn't care what happened to me?"

"I don't." His response was quick and cutting, taking me by surprise. What was more—it hurt.

What did one say to such a revelation? He stared down at me, a frown etched on his brow.

"I see." Arming myself with resolve, I pushed down the tears. His words had been hurtful and unexpected enough to crumble the walls of control I had built to shelter me from the night's events. He didn't care. He didn't care... I repeated to myself, attempting to understand. "Goodnight," I whispered, unable to meet his eyes as I turned to the stairs.

My body felt strangely detached from reality as I floated up the porch steps. He made no move to stop me. Not daring to turn around, I slipped into the house and closed the door behind me. The lights were off, so I imagined Celest must have gone to bed early. I leaned against the closed door, not knowing what to make of his reaction. Perhaps I was overreacting. After all, he didn't owe me anything, and he was right. I didn't really know him. He was only being honest. Brutally honest, but he wasn't a boy playing feeble tricks. He was dangerous, and he might not be a hero in his eyes, but he was one in mine. Even if he felt he had no valid reasons for saving me, the fact was he had.

Once again, guilt gnawed at me. If I hoped to survive in a magical world, I needed to learn how to navigate the intricate personality of an immortal man. I chided myself for acting so immaturely. The truth was, Drake confounded me. What did I expect? *Oh, you knew what you expected,* the voice at the back of my mind nagged. He was right about our notions of romanticism. I wanted him to say he cared—a bizarre notion, considering I had never been faced with such needs or emotions, and he was the last person I should pin any sort of sentiments to.

With a sigh, I opened the front door and disappointment settled in my stomach when I saw he was gone. As I made my way upstairs, I chose not to torture myself; he could take care of himself, he had proven as much.

THE SIGHT of Drake standing in the shadows of my room paralyzed me, and I was glad for the response; otherwise, I would have screamed.

"Are you trying to scare me to death?" I chided, leaning against the closed door, waiting for my fluttering heart to quiet.

"No," he said quickly. "I apologize." He seemed uncomfortable in the space of my room.

He stood by the open window, the reflection of my night light casting a shadow on the chiseled angles of his face. Drake had a strange magnetism that made him dangerously attractive in a compelling yet unnerving way. I would have to learn to control my reactions around him, though I wondered if that was even possible.

Loose tendrils of black hair fell over his brow, and now

more than ever, I appreciated the distance between us; otherwise, the intensity of his grey eyes would have indeed rendered me speechless.

"I apologize," he repeated, breaking the electrifying silence. His voice was a soft rumble, and I was glad for it.

"You don't have to. I'm fine." I pushed away from the door and walked to the bedside lamp, turning it on. My fingers shook under the soft light that bathed the room. I drew the curtains closed and shifted nervously around the room before sitting on the edge of my bed. His eyes followed me, silently studying my every move. "I'm just a little jumpy, but I'm better now," I added, leaning against one of the canopy posts.

His response gripped me with such force that my breath abandoned me for an instant. Drake smiled—a devastatingly striking smile. The strongest weapon in his arsenal, and by the look on his face, he knew just how lethal it was.

"The apology—is for my behavior downstairs," he explained with a subtle pause. His gaze fixed on mine, and I was glad I was sitting down. "I am a monster, and yet the thought of allowing that man, or anyone else, to hurt you is unbearable. This is my truth, mortal, and it confounds me because I do not trust you." The confusion on his face surely mirrored my own.

Suddenly, the walls that had fractured inside me stitched themselves back together with an electrifying pulse coursing through my body. I found myself smiling, even if he didn't trust me.

"You're forgiven," I whispered, allowing my eyes to linger on his. "Also, I don't expect you to trust me. You do not know me, yet," I added, unsure if it was even necessary to address the issue. The truth was, in his presence, I often lost my sensibility to think or speak with coherence.

He stared at me for a measured moment, then dipped his head once in agreement. His eyes traveled around the room and landed on my dresser. He took measured steps towards it, paused with curiosity, picked up one of my perfume bottles, and brought it to his nose. His eyes held mine over the bottle for a brief moment before he returned it to the dresser. His fingers grazed his jaw and chin, his thumb running over his lips, his expression distant, lost in memory.

"Can I ask you a question?" I whispered, and his gaze shifted to me, returning from wherever his thoughts had taken him.

"Only one?" he replied, the corner of his lips shifting into a faint smile. I smiled back, knowing one would never suffice my curiosity, but it would be enough for tonight.

"For now," I admitted.

"Very well," he acquiesced, leaning against the door. Arms crossed before him, his fingers tracing his lips.

"You seem intrigued by my scent," I began.

"Ah, yes." He cut me off, pushing away from the door, his gaze locking onto mine. "Your essence is unique." He stepped closer, stopping just before me, a hand braced on the post of the canopy above.

"Unique good or bad?" I asked, unable to discern by his unreadable expression.

"That's more than one question," he retorted, his eyes never leaving mine. "Both." His admission surprised me. "You carry Isabel's scent—a good thing," he whispered, leaning in. "But I have yet to understand why, and that is bad—so very bad." He stood before me like a god carved from stone. "Can you tell me why that is?"

I opened my mouth but no words came out. I shook my head in response.

"Lies," he hissed, darkness seeping from his lips. "You want to ask questions, yet you tell me nothing." His eyes roamed over my face with a desperate intensity. "I need to understand." He reached for a strand of my hair, curling it around his finger. "I know a thousand years are not kind to a mortal, and yet her essence is here. It lingers around you, inside you, defying all rational explanations." His eyes darted between my hair, my eyes, my lips, searching for answers.

"I wish I could explain," I whispered, but the frown on his brow told me my words weren't enough.

His hand circled my arm, pulling me to my feet. "No more lies. I deserve at least one truth. Why are they after you? How did you open that portal without them?" His grip tightened around my wrist, making me wince. Shocked by my reaction, he released me immediately. "Forgive me," he said. "Finding myself in this body, facing human emotions, can be over-whelming."

I stilled, absorbing the weight of his confession. Drake had lived in his dragon form during his imprisonment—a startling revelation.

Taking a deep, ragged breath, I steadied myself. He wouldn't hurt me. He had said so, but trusting him and under-standing the whirlwind of emotions was difficult.

"I know you want answers," I said, exhaling slowly. "But I do too. You can't accuse me of lying when you don't know me!" My voice rose, and I felt the heat of a flush in my cheeks.

I fought to catch my breath, my body feeling weightless, as if I were a feather suspended in the air.

Drake's hands pinned mine against the wall, his body trapping me. In a flash, he had moved us across the room as I had seen him do at the fair. One moment we were by the bed, the next we were here, his face and breath brushing my cheek. His scent was dominant, much like the depth of his voice.

"You're right. I don't know you," he admitted, and my insides trembled. "But I know Isabel. The thought of her gave meaning to my life in a world of darkness." His voice was filled with longing that weakened my resistance. "I don't know why, but her essence is close to you. It's a part of you." His nose skimmed across my cheek, then slowly down my neck, claiming my shoulder intimately. His lips glided softly over my skin, barely touching, and for that instant, I ceased to exist. I became his air, his anchor. In that moment, I would have stripped my soul bare if he had asked.

"It was her essence that brought me to you," he declared. "And it's been so long." His voice was thick with desire, his lips brushing against my skin.

In the recesses of my mind, I contemplated the unfamiliar need to wrap my arms around him, to ease his suffering and my own, but I could not move.

"Belynda, are you awake?" Celest's voice floated from the other side of the door, snapping me back to reality like a cold wave.

I shifted in Drake's hold, but he didn't move. His face

lingered close to mine for a moment longer before he inched closer. I stopped breathing altogether.

He halted barely a breath from my lips. So close that when he smiled, his warm breath caressed my skin. I licked my lips, his eyes tracing the movement.

"I should probably go," he whispered.

I simply nodded.

"Belynda," Celest called again, and this time Drake released me with reluctance. He streaked to the window with blinding speed, startling me, then looked back at me one last time before jumping from the ledge.

I had no time to overthink or reminisce. Celest was right outside my bedroom door. Quickly, I pulled the blanket around my shoulders and took a deep breath to calm myself. I opened the door a fraction.

"Celest?" I said, trying to sound sleepy.

"I'm sorry. I thought I heard voices."

I swallowed nervously. "Just my phone. I was getting ready to go to bed." I lied, remembering I had no phone.

"I'm sorry. Go back to bed then," she said, but paused. "Did you have a good time?" she asked.

"It was... uneventful," I replied, choosing not to elaborate. "Goodnight." I added, closing the door as she disappeared down the stairs.

I leaned against the closed door with a sigh, then walked to the window. I peered into the night, hoping for a sign that he would come back. Eventually, the cold seeped into my bones, and I knew he wouldn't. Not tonight.

I barely slept, my thoughts consumed by Drake: his eyes, his scent, the warmth of his body pressed against mine. Every word he had spoken replayed in my mind, every feeling he had sparked lingered. He wasn't lying when he said he had changed. Drake was a mystery I ached to unravel. He was angry and unstable, a dangerous combination, but who was I to judge? I couldn't even begin to imagine what he had endured. I anticipated trouble with him, but I wasn't afraid.

After hours of restless thoughts, my eyes finally surrendered to exhaustion. I drifted off, content with his intoxicating scent still lingering around me.

Despite only a few hours of sleep, I felt energizied. Drake was, without a doubt, the reason. Though I wanted to steer away from any complicated emotions, I couldn't deny the fascination. He loved Isabel deeply, and I already had enough troubles without adding heartache to the list.

Celest's empty coffee mug on the kitchen counter confirmed she was gone. She usually had a lot to wrap up after the book fair. Now that I could think clearly and everything didn't feel like a dream, I considered the possibility that Celest knew what the man at the fair was after. The intruders who broke into the house were clearly searching for something too, and her refusal to involve the sheriff only solidified my suspicions that both events were connected to her. She had warned me to be careful, but after last night, I wasn't sure that was possible. The more I thought about it, the more convinced I became that it was time to confront Celest.

The sun was barely visible over the horizon. It had been a long time since I had gone for a run early in the morning, but today, the anxiety was too much to contain. I needed to dispel it somehow.

I plugged in my earbuds and pulled my hoodie tighter, hoping to block the cold from my face. The rush burning inside me hadn't diminished as I jogged down the side of the old road, heading away from the town. I needed to avoid civilization altogether and clear my mind.

My lungs burned, and I welcomed the cold, fresh morning air. Despite my best efforts to eradicate him from my thoughts, Drake remained firmly embedded. Frustrated, I sighed and pushed my legs harder against the pavement, overcome by the crushing desire to see him again.

His revelation—that I shared Isabel's scent—puzzled and frightened me. I knew deep down he believed I had an explanation, but I needed answers too. Perhaps sharing what I knew of Isabel and her visions could help, but a part of me feared his reaction. Knowing she was gone, that her mortal body was no match against time, wasn't the same as accepting that she had sacrificed herself, her time here on earth, to ensure his safety. That truth, I feared revealing.

A prickling sensation slid down my spine, and like the day before, I felt the eerie sensation of being watched or followed. I plucked out an earbud to stay aware of my surroundings and slowed to a walk to steady my breathing.

"How little do you value your life, mortal," Drake's voice made me spin around with a start. His cautioning words went unheard. Instead, excitement swelled at the sight of him, and I fought hard to hide it.

I craned my neck to look up at him in the early morning light. He was even more breathtaking, if that was possible. His grey eyes didn't glow as they had in the shadows of the night, but they were still striking as they regarded me.

"How did you find me? I thought mystical creatures only came out at night?" I teased, uncertainty mingling with my curiosity. I took hesitant steps towards him, a playful smile on my lips as I pondered his mysterious nature.

He arched a brow, a flicker of amusement flashing on his face. "You might assume I haven't heard that before, but after living as long as I have, little surprises me," he replied, his age suddenly a tantalizing mystery. "To answer your question, creatures and immortals in the elemental Realms aren't bound by the same rules as humans."

I listened with rapt fascination as Drake spoke of his world. Despite standing before me as undeniable proof, it all still felt surreal.

I noticed his avoidance in explaining how he had tracked me down, but he had already confessed about my scent guiding him to me last night. Odd as it seemed, I found the idea strangely comforting and reassuring.

"I'm sure we're a lot more fragile," I mused aloud, voicing my thoughts.

"Incurably so, I'm afraid," he conceded, his tone tinged with a hint of regret.

"I can take care of myself, you know," I offered, attempting to project strength rather than appear as a vulnerable human. Yet, I struggled to convince even myself, let alone him.

"And yet, you lack common sense," he replied, his expression turning serious. "Why are you out this early and alone? Was last night not warning enough?" His voice lowered, dismissing any trace of humor.

Now thinking rationally, Drake was right. I had been reckless, ignoring my own safety. If only he knew it was my desperate need to see him that had clouded my judgment.

"Honestly?" I ventured cautiously, feeling a surge of bravery in being truthful, knowing he had been forthcoming with me.

"I would appreciate nothing less," he said, his gaze intense, capturing my breath momentarily. Staring into his eyes only reaffirmed my suspicion that I had been foolish to rely on him for protection. But how could I confess the truth without sounding utterly desperate?

"The truth is, I feel safe with you," I admitted, awaiting his reaction. His eyes urged me to continue. "I was reckless because a part of me hoped you'd find me." I looked down at my hands uneasily. "I wanted to see you," I finally confessed.

There. I had said it. It felt liberating, this honesty thing, and yet, I couldn't bring myself to look at him.

When I found the courage to meet his eyes again, I noticed they were lighter, a mesmerizing pale grey. His expression, however, remained unreadable. He didn't seem upset, which was confirmed when he reached out hesitantly and pulled out my other earbud. He inspected it with keen interest before returning his gaze to me.

"I seem to have conflicting feelings about your truth," he remarked, causing me to frown in confusion. After all, he was the one who had asked for honesty.

"It's reassuring to know that you trust me, yet to neglect your safety so thoughtlessly," he continued, pausing to emphasize his point. "You need to be more careful." His words carried a silent plea. "They won't stop coming after you until they get what they want."

Hearing the sobering truth from him put my precarious situation into perspective. "Drake, who are they? Why are they after me?"

His eyes narrowed in confusion. "You don't know?"

"No," I admitted, and his expression shifted from surprise to suspicion.

"Last night when you refused to tell the man what he wanted, I assumed you were lying. It seemed foolish to risk your life for that, but the guardians have sacrificed far more in the past to keep their covenant a secret. I thought perhaps you had gone rogue, which could explain why you were the only one present when I was summoned out of that hell hole," Drake paused, his voice darkening. "But if you claim you do not know them... I find myself lost again in the mystery of you." He locked eyes with me. "Who are you?" he demanded, his tone growing serious.

"I am just Belynda, and I'm still trying to wrap my mind around the fact that you're here, that I was able to release you," I admitted. "Despite what you think, I'm not magical. I've never been." I sighed, putting my earbuds away.

"Normal, human girls don't open magic portals," he pressed, his tone probing for an explanation.

I glanced around us; the middle of the road was hardly ideal for such a conversation. Drake, however, interpreted my hesitation differently. His expression hardened, and he adopted a guarded stance.

"Mortal, I will not play your games!" His intensity was

palpable. "If you want my trust and protection, there can't be any more secrets, do you understand?"

There was no anger in his voice, only a firm insistence on honesty. We needed mutual trust, but it seemed he was scrutinizing every aspect of my existence.

"Trust works both ways," I retorted. He shifted on his feet, stepping closer.

"Trust is earned," he replied coolly. "And that's rather difficult when nothing about you makes sense."

"What do you want to know?" I asked, sensing his eagerness for answers.

"Tell me about Isabel, your connection to her," he demanded. At the mention of her name, I realized she would forever be a presence between us—a lingering shadow from the past.

"Would you believe me if I said you're better off remembering the woman you once loved without tainting that memory?" My words seemed to strike a nerve, deepening the furrow in his brow.

"You don't get to make that decision for me. Speak now," his tone turned bitter.

He was right. Drake deserved to know, and I couldn't assume he couldn't handle the truth. Taking a deep breath, I gathered my thoughts.

"The way I see it, you can speak willingly, or I can resort to other means of persuasion. I'm sure you'll find the latter quite unpleasant." His words hung heavily between us. I was unsure if to perceive them as a threat or a warning.

"You wouldn't do that," I questioned, though a sinking suspicion told me otherwise.

"Wouldn't I?" he retorted, arching a brow. Drake's unpredictability was unsettling, especially when he chose to be intimidating.

I knew my own boundaries, but his remained a mystery. Reluctantly, I decided not to push further. I wasn't ready to test the extent of his powers, not yet.

"Fine. I'll tell you. I'd rather not push you any further today if I can help it," I conceded, noticing a flicker of amusement at the corner of his lips.

"A compromise, you're coming to your senses," he remarked.

"Is that what you call that?" I quipped. "I thought it was more of a threat. "Do it or die," I added, attempting to mimic his tone poorly. Drake's roar of laughter punctuated through the stillness and my very soul. It was like seeing a different man and it was warming, even if it was briefly and sporadic.

"You're wrong," he mused. "Dying—that wasn't an option," he continued, his demeanor serious once more.

It was reassuring to know that death at Drake's hands wasn't on the table. Yet, I couldn't help but wonder about his other abilities. Could he truly compel me to talk if I refused?

He fixed me with an expectant gaze. "Are you out to test my patience, human?" he asked, a hint of frustration in his voice. "I'm waiting."

Taking a deep breath, I resigned myself to the inevitable. "Let's see, where should I begin?" I muttered, struggling to gather my thoughts. His impatience only making me nervous.

I turned and started walking back towards the house. "Where do you think you're going?" Drake questioned, unmoving from his spot.

I paused and faced him. "I don't think the side of the road is the best place to have this conversation, do you?" I pointed out, and he frowned in agreement.

"Fair point," he conceded. In an instant, a rustle of wind blew against my hair, and he stood by my side.

"Shall we?" he asked casually.

I stared at him in wonder. "I don't think I'll ever get used to seeing you do that," I admitted, shaking my head to clear the image etched in my mind.

"I'll attempt to be more normal, for you," he offered.

"No, it's alright. It's just that when you do things like that, I feel like I'm in a dream, ready to wake up any minute. I'm still having difficulty believing you're real," I confessed. "So yeah."

Somehow, he seemed pleased by my admission.

"For what it's worth, you seem to be acclimating just fine," he offered, and I smiled. *A compliment...* He was indeed full of surprises

"Speaking of your super abilities, can you truly make me talk if I refuse?" I asked, unable to shake off my curiosity.

"Are you intrigued enough to find out?" he countered, his tone playful.

"No," I responded too quickly, earning a smile from the usually brooding god who leisurely walked beside me. Every time he smiled, the hardened lines on his face softened, making him appear even younger than his immortal age suggested. It was a surreal thought.

"You're not going to answer my question, are you?" I pressed, noticing the corner of his mouth shift with amusement.

"No," he replied simply.

One-word answers... I could deal with; it was the uncertainty of his abilities that unsettled me.

"Fine," I said, deciding to drop the subject, but to my surprise, he spoke again.

"The ability to compel is rare. In fact, I only know of one immortal with the gift," he explained, his gaze momentarily lost in the road ahead, adrift in a sea of memories.

"That's a relief," I voiced, hoping to steer the conversation away from coercive powers.

"A trivial concern, considering moments ago you were ready to speak—while I'm still waiting for you to begin," he remarked.

"Trivial?" I shot him a sidelong glance. "I don't relish the idea of being coerced into something against my will," I admitted honestly.

"I assure you, you would be willing," he retorted, his gaze shifting away from me.

"That's quite an assumption," I countered, and he slowed, taking my wrist and bringing me to a halt before him. I sucked in a breath, feeling my chest flush against his. Looking up, I saw darkening clouds forming in the background, but all I could focus on was his face—his eyes, his lips—as he leaned closer, a look I had yet to see on his godly features.

His breath caressed my cheeks as I closed my eyes, overwhelmed by the sensation. "If I wanted," he whispered, his hand gently closing around my throat, tilting it to the side, "If I desired," his lips vibrated close to my ear, his nose gliding along the exposed part of my neck, "you'd give yourself willingly—you'd beg to be taken and consumed," his thumb traced my lower lip, and when I opened my eyes, I found his grey ones, matching the storm forming overhead. "Make no mistake," he warned softly, sending a flutter through my stomach that agreed with his words. I wasn't sure I could deny him anything at the moment, and that was a dangerous realization.

"You are a witch," I whispered, trying to fight the haze as he allowed space between us.

"No, love, you are the witch," he corrected, his frown deepening, leaving me without a comeback. My thoughts remained fixed on the tone of his voice when he said *'love'*; I disliked it when he called me *'mortal'*.

My stomach chose that moment to grumble, betraying my nerves. "Hungry?" I asked, still unsure of his eating habits, but he smiled knowingly.

"Very," he replied with the same look he had adopted moments ago, and my stomach somersaulted, fully aware he wasn't talking about food. *Dear god—I was in trouble!* He made me crave things I had never thought of before. My entire body came alive, almost as if it had been dormant my entire life. Just waiting patiently, *waiting for him*. I frowned at the thought.

DRAKE SAT at the breakfast counter, his presence shifting the energy in the room. He watched me silently as I maneuvered around the kitchen, preparing breakfast. His elbows rested on the counter, fingers intertwined and brushing against his mouth. I realized it was a habit of his, that was very distracting.

"Are eggs and bacon okay?" I asked, unsure of his eating habits. He straightened in his chair.

"Yes," he replied with a hint of a smile.

I poured him a glass of orange juice, trying to ignore my trembling fingers. His eyes followed my movements with keen interest.

"Am I making you nervous?" he teased, his voice light, and I rolled my eyes.

"No," I lied, and his smile widened. *He knew.*

"Will you tell me about her?" he asked, his tone gentle yet pleading, which weakened my resolve.

"Isabel has haunted my dreams for years," I began, finally opening up about something I'd kept hidden for so long. "At first, I thought I was insane. It wasn't until recently that I realized those dreams were actually visions of her." I hesitated, watching his reaction carefully. His eyes remained calm, encouraging me to continue.

"Through her visions, I saw you," I admitted, taking a sip of my juice to steady myself. "The day you were sent to the dark realm—I..." I paused, searching his eyes for understanding. "It was like I was there, watching it unfold through her eyes. I felt what she felt, as if my body was possessed, yet a part of me remained slightly aware of who I was." Taking a deep breath, I felt a weight lift as I shared this with someone who wouldn't dismiss me as crazy.

"She had that gift," he whispered, his gaze locked onto mine. "Isabel often saw glimpses of the future."

"I see the past, and she saw the future?" I questioned, trying to understand how it worked.

"As I understand it, it can go both ways. Destiny is controlled by the fates, and what you see usually fits into their grand plan," he explained.

I blinked, attempting to wrap my head around it all. Now he was mentioning the fates and how they bent destiny...when I was still trying to cope with him being real.

"How am I supposed to survive in a magical world if I can't even grasp things like that?" I mused aloud, feeling over-whelmed.

"What I can't understand is how you've lived a life without knowing," he said thoughtfully. "The book you used belonged to the guardianship. Isabel was powerful, but even she couldn't open portals to the realms herself." His revelation made me freeze, suddenly understanding why Isabel couldn't release him herself.

"And yet, you managed it on your own. How is that possible?" he asked, his brow furrowing with genuine curiosity.

"I was hoping you would have an answer to that," I admitted, feeling a rush of uncertainty. "My entire life feels like a lie. Celest raised me after my mother died, and it seems like every-thing I've been told has been carefully crafted to keep me from the truth. I've only learned about the guardianship through Isabel's visions, but I don't know who I truly am, why I was cursed with these visions, or how I could release you when she couldn't." My confession hung heavy in the air, and I sensed that this time, he believed me.

"But you have an idea?" he added, almost a whisper.

"I have theories," I admitted.

I set down a plate piled high with eggs, bacon, and pancakes before him. His eyes followed my every move. Sitting beside him, we ate in silence, the air thick with an unsettling, electrifying heat emanating from him.

Out of the corner of my eye, I observed him cutting each

morsel with a surprising grace and elegance, a stark contrast to the dark and dangerous aura he typically exuded. Yet, he was a prince—*a prince of darkness,* a thought that unexpectedly made me smile.

As I washed the dishes, Drake disappeared into another room, likely exploring, and acquainting himself with the modern world, much like he had done earlier in the kitchen. Glancing at the kitchen wall clock, my nerves spiked, realizing Celest could return at any moment. The thought of being separated from Drake now unnerved me deeply.

Finding him in Celest's study, his back rigid, eyes fixed on the family tree painted across the wall, I knew what held his attention—*Isabel's* name.

"Ready to go?" I asked, breaking the heavy silence. His haunted expression shifted as he turned towards me.

"Show me," he demanded, his voice low, while his finger traced over Isabel's name etched on the wall. "This is why you refused to tell me. Show me how she died."

I hesitated, feeling the palpable shift in his mood. "Not here. Celest could return any minute," I urged, his eyes held mine, and after a few moments, they softened, but I could see it wasn't without difficulty.

"Where would you like to go?" he asked, surprising me with his willingness to comply.

"Anywhere but here," I replied honestly. Unsure of where to go.

"I know a place," he offered.

.   .   .

FOLLOWING him through the tall grass that bordered the lowlands behind the house, my curiosity grew. We bypassed the trees in the distance, and just as the skies above us closed, a slow, chilling drizzle began to fall.

Drake suddenly broke into a sprint, disappearing ahead of me through the tall grass.

"Where are you going?" I called after him, attempting to catch up. "Drake!" I cried; my breaths ragged from the running. He didn't respond, but I knew he heard me. Pushing myself to keep pace, after a few minutes, I recognized the old cattle barn looming in the distance.

In moments, the drizzle became a deluge. I tried in vain to shield my face from the rain by pulling my hoodie tighter, but it was already damp and clinging uncomfortably.

"Drake!" I screamed again, panic rising my voice. I couldn't see him anymore, nor where I was going through the thick, waist-high grass.

My distress must have been palpable because suddenly, there he was in front of me, extending his hand. Without hesitation, I took it, and he led us into a sprint, guiding me swiftly to shelter, never once letting go of my hand until we were safely under cover.

GLANCING around the old barn for the first time, I confirmed it was abandoned, save for a few broken haystacks.

"I hope this is okay," Drake said, releasing my hand.

"How did you find this place?" I asked, shivering. He studied me with concern.

"The night you opened the portal, I was weak," he

explained, watching my reaction closely. "I stumbled upon this place while searching for food to sustain my human form." Fascinating, I thought.

"Food?" I asked, puzzled, surveying the empty barn.

He smiled knowingly. "Livestock is sustenance," he clarified, and I grasped his meaning. I had countless questions, but I didn't want to appear impertinent.

"So, you were looking for cattle and found none. What did you do then?" I inquired, teeth chattering.

He shot me a worried glance. "I found provisions outside town, including clothes, if you were wondering." He was perceptive—I had been curious about that. I offered an apologetic smile, but I felt inspired, so I continued to try my luck.

"Besides cattle and regular food, any other unique dietary preferences?" I asked, recalling his impeccable manners during our meal. Discovering he could consume livestock made me wonder what else might pique his appetite, given he was after all a Dragon-shifter.

He laughed, his laughter infectious, bringing a smile to my lips. "My apologies. Explaining something so basic to me is unusual. To answer your question—regular food suffices. However, in my elemental form...I can be more resourceful," he admitted, and I frowned.

"Your element form, meaning your dragon form?" I asked cautiously.

"Yes," he confirmed, observing me with interest.

"You mentioned your human life force earlier. What did you mean by that?" I pressed, but he shook his head.

"No. No more questions about me."

"Alright, you don't have to answer that, but there is one

more thing I'm curious about. Please." I pleaded, attempting to coerce him, unsure if human charm extended to beings beyond our species. He walked around me.

"One," he agreed, a hint of amusement in his eyes.

"Why didn't you use your flying ability to get us to shelter faster?" I blurted out, catching him off guard.

Drake's mouth opened ever so slightly, which made me think that was perhaps the last question he had expected.

"I—I didn't think you'd want me to. You didn't seem pleased when I did it earlier. Would you have preferred that?" he asked, curiosity evident in his tone.

"Yes, of course! Just look at me, I'm soaked," I said, gesturing to my drenched clothes. Drake smiled, his gaze lingering on my trembling form as he stepped closer.

8

FIRE BOUND

THE COLD SEEPED THROUGH my clothes, invading my senses. I hugged myself tightly, trying to generate warmth, but my efforts were futile; I was drenched to the bone, and my small frame trembled uncontrollably.

Though we were sheltered from the rain now, I couldn't shake off the chill, despite the smoldering look in Drake's eyes.

"I'm so...cold," I managed, teeth chattering with each word.

Drake, too, was soaked, but unlike me, he seemed unaffected by the weather.

He approached me tentatively, stopping just a foot away. The heat radiating from his body was surprisingly comforting, even without physical contact.

I couldn't help but imagine how it would feel to have his arms around me, his warmth enveloping me. The thought made me shiver, and as I looked up, I noticed his eyes had softened to a lighter shade. His expression remained guarded, but there was a tenderness in the way he studied my face that weakened my knees.

Slowly, he cupped my cheeks with his hands, their warmth a soothing balm against my skin. His fingers slipped under the fabric of my hoodie, peeling it away from my face with gentle care.

"I can help," he murmured, his voice vibrating near my ear. I nodded gratefully, willing to accept any relief he could offer, basking in the warmth he provided.

His gaze locked with mine as his hands found the zipper on my sweater. With effortless precision, he undid it and eased the wet fabric from my shoulders, letting it fall to the floor behind me.

I couldn't decide which affected me more—the biting cold or the touch of Drake's hands. My body remained frozen, yet my mind burned with an unspoken desire to have him hold me.

For a moment, indecision flickered in Drake's eyes, but he quickly recovered. He wrapped an arm around me, his hand settling on the small of my back.

My mind was lost in a haze, overwhelmed by a rush of emotions I couldn't control. I felt consumed by them, drawn deeper into an abyss I couldn't retreat from. His warmth seeped through my damp shirt, though our skin didn't touch directly.

Maybe it was my hormones, stirred by his presence. Drake had opened doors to new emotions in me, powerful and unfamiliar. I wondered if my connection to Isabel was to blame for this irrational behavior.

Without thinking of the consequences, I placed a hand on his chest, then the other followed suit. Hesitantly, I rested my head on his chest, drowning myself in the exquisite heat radiating from him.

He didn't push me away. Instead, I adjusted my arms to encircle his torso, allowing my cold, shaking body to lean into him. He tensed briefly but gradually relaxed, his other arm wrapping around me and drawing me closer.

I was acutely aware that this moment couldn't last forever. When it ended, awkwardness might linger between us. But for now, I pushed those thoughts aside, content to be held like this.

Closing my eyes, I felt his warm breath cascade over my shoulder. Each breath comforting, a reminder that there was nothing simple or ordinary about Drake.

Once he noticed that my shivers had subsided, he allowed some space to flow between our bodies, and I was left reeling in disappointment.

I had a clear view of his face again, and a new wave of desires surged through me. I couldn't stop thinking about his lips, wondering how they would feel against mine. But I knew I couldn't cross that threshold—I'd never kissed anyone before, except him...in my dreams, but I was sure that did not count. Whatever was possessing me to act like this was beyond any rational explanation.

"Thank you," I murmured nervously, breaking the silence.

A faint smile tugged at the corners of his lips. "Anytime," he replied, his gaze holding mine.

I noticed the hesitation, and reluctantly, his hands finally left my waist, leaving me homeless of his touch.

"How are you so naturally warm?" I asked, hoping he had forgotten about our one more question bargain.

"My kind is bound by the fire element," he responded quickly.

His kind could only mean dragons, which were always depicted as fire-spitting creatures in my world. It made perfect sense for him to have control over fire. Yet, despite knowing he was real, I couldn't quite reconcile that image of a dragon with the man standing before me. It was a side of him I wasn't sure I was ready to fully accept.

"What?" Drake's voice broke my reverie, and I realized he had caught me staring. I shook my head to clear my thoughts.

"Hmm, nothing. I just can't quite imagine it, that's all," I said, shrugging.

"Imagine what exactly?" he asked, moving to sit on a stack of hay. I couldn't help but notice the grace in his movements. There was a regal air about him, reinforcing my earlier thought of him as *the Prince of Darkness*. I smiled to myself.

"Everything about you—it's all unreal to me. It's hard to imagine it, when dragons, magic, and the supernatural are considered myth and fantasy in my world."

He laughed yet there was no humor behind it. "Trust me—it's very real. Too real, if you ask me." His tone hinted at a discontent with his own existence. His legacy.

"Why would you say that? Aren't you at peace with who you are?" I asked, genuinely curious.

He shook his head. "It's not about who I am; but rather what I can become. Now that is something to consider."

His words from last night echoed his warning in my mind

"Do you have any idea what you have unleashed? Any idea what I've become?"

"What exactly is so bad about that part of you?" I pressed.

Drake fell silent for a moment, and I couldn't tell whether he was reflecting on his thoughts or if my question had unintentionally offended him.

Absently, he pushed the sleeves of his wet shirt up to his elbows. I gasped in surprise.

"What is that?" I blurted out, consumed by curiosity as I pointed to the long, black lines covering his forearms. The tattooed markings were intricate, the design reminding me of modern tribal tattoos but with an ancient, arcane aura.

The intertwined lines extended further up beyond his elbows, revealing only a glimpse of what lay beneath his rolled-up sleeves. I couldn't recall seeing the tattoos on the night I released him. Then again, fear had clouded my senses, and the darkness had concealed much.

Drake looked down at his hands, sighing heavily. "This is something else..." His voice trailed off, a troubled frown creasing his forehead.

"Something else that is bad about that side of you?" I probed gently, seizing the opportunity of his sudden openness.

He lifted his gaze, searching my eyes before he answering. "Yes, but certainly not the worst."

"And what exactly is the worst?" I pressed, aware that I was pushing my luck.

His eyes dropped to the floor, silence stretching between us. I waited, giving him the space to collect his thoughts.

When he finally looked up and his eyes met mine, I found a sadness there that struck me.

"The worst part is losing myself—not having control over my thoughts or actions," he confessed, his voice weighted with a burden I could feel in my own chest. As he spoke, I held my breath, urging him to continue. "It feels like every time it takes over me, I fall deeper and deeper into an abyss where no trace of my humanity exists," he added, his gaze shifting away briefly, but I caught a glimpse of what I could only perceive was shame.

"Even humans are far from perfect," I offered gently, hoping to alleviate some of the weight on his conscience. "There's darkness in everyone, Drake. But from what I've seen, there's more humanity in you than many of my kind."

My words hung in the air, spoken from the heart, and for a moment, he seemed lost in his thoughts, silent, and I couldn't place his expression.

"What is it about you?" He asked, mostly to himself as he rose. He sauntered until coming to a stand right in front of me.

"There is something so familiar about you and your essence that confuses my thoughts and emotions...I can't explain it." I stilled, as he brought a hand up, gently caressing the side of my face. "You are the embodiment of her, and the subtle taste of the ocean." He whispered. "It's as if she's here with us, yet here you stand before me, only you."

I became stone before him, unable to find words. "Show me now," he whispered, echoing his request from earlier in the study, and I remained still; spellbound by the shadows behind his eyes.

"How?" I replied, matching the subtleness of his tone. Drake stepped closer, tucking a wet strand of hair behind my ear, his touch making my heart flutter.

He studied my face in silence, his gaze lingering on my lips. Did he do it on purpose? Did he know that he made my heart race to a point where I couldn't recover? All my senses were heightened, every nerve tingling with the electricity crackling between us.

Raising his hand, he trailed his finger along my cheek. "It's simple. I promise I'm not going to hurt you."

The sincerity in his eyes was transparent. In that moment, I wanted to trust him. I knew he would protect me, and I had nothing to fear.

"I trust you," I whispered, the words hanging in the charged air between us. His eyes darkened briefly, a hint of emotion flickering across his face.

Leaning forward, he brushed his lips against my ear, his warm breath sending a shiver down my spine, and I stopped breathing altogether. "That's all I need," he murmured, his voice heavy with desire.

I bit my lip, wishing it were his instead. *How could I want him so much when we had only just met?* All of these emotions were new to me, yet they seemed natural around him. Earlier he had made me feel like I was standing at the edge of a precipice; now, I had leaped off its edge. But instead of falling, I was floating and never wanted to come down.

His glimmering eyes had me hypnotized. I inhaled sharply, feeling his hand at the small of my back as he drew me closer to him.

His other hand, which had cupped my cheek, now threaded through my hair, his fingers lightly grazing the back of my neck.

My mind was frozen, but my body was recklessly warm.

Without thinking, I surrendered to my senses, closing the remaining distance, forgetting about the consequences. The moment our lips met, it was as if a spark ignited, setting my whole being ablaze.

At first, he was as still as a carved statue, but then he responded with a deeper need and urgency that took my breath away. His lips moved against mine, his hands exploring my back, pulling me closer, while my mind screamed for more.

I didn't care about the consequences; all I wanted was him, in any way possible, in this moment.

My hands traced the warmth of his chest, feeling the firm muscles beneath my hands, before trailing to his back, where they tensed in response to my touch.

Curiosity sparked as my fingertips roamed his warm skin. I wondered how far his tattoo extended, a mystery hidden beneath his wet shirt. Strangely enough, he seemed to antici-pate my thoughts.

He smiled against my lips, and without breaking our passionate embrace, he reached behind his head and pulled his shirt up.

We broke away from our kiss so he could discard the shirt. I was desperate to find my way back to his lips, but my eyes were now enticed by his chest, shoulders, arms, and neck. Every surface where his tattoo extended.

"You have such a curious mind, I figured I'd rather show you, than tell you," he said, his smile leaving me breathless.

Mesmerized, I ran my fingers over the detailed patterns lines along his arms and chest. "How did you know?" I asked, realizing the meaning behind his words.

"Something else about me," he murmured. "I can see what

you see. A glimpse into your mind, but only when I do this." He brushed his lips against mine once more before withdrawing slightly.

It took me a moment to understand what he meant, before a deep blush spread across my face.

"Nooo..." I turned away, trying to hide my embarrassment. "But you said you didn't have the power to compel," I recalled from our earlier conversation.

"I don't," he confirmed.

"You're telling me that you could see what I was thinking while you kissed me!" He must think the worst of me, and I suddenly felt the urge to cry in shame or run—run far away. I turned around, burying my face in my hands.

"Hey, it's ok," he spoke, reaching to remove my hands from my face.

"Is it?" I asked, frustrated with myself and with him. "I just don't know what came over me. I feel so strange when I'm around you. It's like I'm possessed. But I know it's because of you. I've never done this before—this has never happened with anyone else." My words spilled out in a ramble, unable to contain myself.

Drake smiled warmly at my predicament. "Please don't be embarrassed."

He stood close, forcing my eyes to meet his. "If it's any consolation, you are a puzzle to me as well. I can't claim to have perfect self-control. I've always been devoted to Isabel, yet here I am. You've turned my world upside down since the night you released me. So please, don't be embarrassed for your thoughts." His expression softened. "Let's just say I'm glad you couldn't see mine."

A knot tightened in my stomach as I imagined what thoughts he might have had of me.

He ran his thumb over my lip, gently halting my nervous nibbling. "You're making it worse," he teased softly, his gaze intense and predatory urging me to forget my humiliation.

"You know, it's not fair that you can see into my head, but I can't see into yours," I remarked with a half-smile, trying to push aside my discomfort at the idea that he could see into my head.

Drake's brow furrowed slightly. "Trust me. My mind is not a place you want to be. I've been to the depths of darkness and back. So, no, I would never allow you to go there."

"But it's possible," I pressed, intrigued by the idea.

"The exchange can go both ways if our minds are open to it," he acknowledged.

The intrigue deepened, and I found myself drawn further into the enigma that was Drake.

"Then in theory, there is a way for me to block my thoughts from you if I wanted to?" I asked, half-teasing, half-serious.

He smiled, his brow arched knowingly. "It's not something you would be able to do. It takes the human mind a lot of practice and control to keep us out."

"Well, there goes my plan," I teased back, feeling a rush of relief and warmth as he caressed my cheek gently.

Unbidden, my hands returned to tracing the lines of his tattoo, following their intricate path along his arms and up to his chest. "It's beautiful," I whispered, captivated by the patterns.

Meeting his eyes, I sensed the magnetic pull between us

growing once more. He took hold of my hips and drew me closer, melding our bodies together.

Lowering his head, his lips brushed softly over my right shoulder, leaving a trail of heat along my skin. Each touch claimed me, in a way that I had never experienced before. Drake erased all boundaries I had ever known; I desired him beyond reason, and I could feel his own desire reciprocated in every touch.

Impatience, to feel his lips on mine again, I slipped my fingers in his hair and pulled him closer. This kiss was not gentle—it was urgent, it consumed us both.

His hands gripped my hips firmly, effortlessly lifting me until my legs wrapped around his waist. As the room spun around us, my back pressed against one of the barn beams. The sensation of the wood against my skin was nothing compared to the overwhelming desire to feel more of him. He settled between my thighs, yet I wanted him closer—if that was even possible.

Despite my inexperienced in matters of love and intimacy, I reveled in the knowledge that I was the cause of his pleasure. His lips moved recklessly down my neck and shoulder, biting and teasing, drawing soft sighs of pleasure from my lips. His hands roamed over my backside as I clung tightly to his shoulders, intoxicated by his scent.

My fingers tangled in the hair at the nape of his neck, pulling him even closer, lost in the moment.

"Isabel..." His choked whisper broke through the haze of desire, instantly sobering me. Cold realization washed over me, and I froze in his arms.

"Please forgive me. I—I didn't mean to," he whispered,

leaning his forehead against mine.

I wasn't angry. Hurt and disappointed, yes, but not angry. How could I be, when I knew all along that he loved her? It would always be Isabel.

"No, it's not your fault. You love her," I said softly, untangling my legs from around his waist. "I'm the one who is sorry, I don't know what came over me."

My body remained trapped between him and the wooden beam, but he didn't move an inch. Taking my hands in his, he kissed them gently, his eyes never leaving mine.

"I'm not apologizing for my actions; I wanted this," he confessed quietly. "I still do. You confuse me, and I don't know what's right from wrong anymore. When I'm with you, it feels as if—I'm with her."

His words carved a hole in my chest. I didn't want to live in Isabel's shadow, always wondering if he thought of her while he was with me. I needed to move past this moment. It had to end here and now.

"It was a mistake. We got carried away. Let's just finish what we started. You wanted to see, and I—I need answers."

He hesitated, then took a step back. I walked around him and picked up his shirt, handing it to him.

"I'll need to focus," I muttered to myself, not caring if he heard. Taking a deep breath, I tried to push down the hurt I was feeling inside as the images of Isabel flooded my mind.

"Ready?" I looked at him expectantly, swallowing the lump in my throat as he came to stand before me once more.

Strangely, he seemed nervous, his jaw tightening with hesitation.

"Whatever I see, you see?" I repeated for confirmation, meeting his gaze.

"But I need the physical connection," he reminded me, his voice softer now.

I grimaced, knowing that was the most challenging part of the exchange. I hoped that focusing on Isabel would be enough to keep my body from reacting to the feel of his lips against mine.

"I can do this," I said, trying to convince myself as much as him.

Closing my eyes, I focused on the first dream. The hooded figures chanted in my thoughts, and Drake took my face in his hands, pressing his lips to mine. It was bearable, only because deep down, I knew it was Isabel he desired.

Jealousy was indeed a powerful tool. I had no right to want this man—this creature. Clearly, he still loved her: body and soul and yet, I had allowed my feelings to swim in muddy waters with him.

I clung to the image of Isabel and Drake–it was the only way I could endure this exchange without crumbling under the weight of his touch.

In my mind, I replayed Isabel's argument with her mother. His hands held me tightly as Isabel's mother mentioned Xelraa. My thoughts drifted to their farewells, and I granted him time to relive the memory of his beloved's embrace.

His lips moved against mine with longing, but I didn't yield. He saw Isabel, he wanted her, not me.

I remembered awakening in the cottage, seeing how fragile

and devastated Isabel had looked. I recalled her tearful words, seeking his forgiveness for her perceived weakness. Instinctively, his hands caressed my face gently, as though comforting her.

I showed him the letter she had written, tracing her movements as she paced anxiously around the cottage before the ritual. I followed her path through the forest in my thoughts, replaying the ritual and her words as faithfully as I could remember.

He tensed when she mentioned the pureblood and the binding, as if he knew exactly what she was planning.

I focused on Isabel's face, illuminated by candlelight as she sat by the lake, dreading what lay ahead.

Drake sensed something was amiss. Pulling me tightly against him, his lips moved urgently against mine. But I needed to see this through.

In my mind's eye, I watched Isabel walk slowly into the lake until she disappeared beneath its surface. Drake's fingers dug painfully into my skin. His desperation was palpable as he waited for her return. I struggled against his grip, knowing he didn't need to witness the ending—he already knew—but he wouldn't let go. It became clear to me then: he needed to see. Even if it tore him apart, he needed to know how her story had ended.

Steeling my heart, I freed the shattering memory. Isabel's lifeless body floating to the surface, and as the dreadful images resurfaced, I winced at the sharp sting as his teeth bit into my lip.

I pushed against his chest, breaking his hold. My fingers touched my lips, confirming the trickle of blood. I turned to scold him, but no words came out. Drake stood stiff, trembling with a fury that wasn't cold-induced; it was a storm of rage and madness consuming him.

Physically, he was still Drake, but I sensed his demons would soon take over. The loving light in his eyes was replaced by the darkness of the deepest night.

"NO!" Drake's roar shook the barn. He streaked before me, his fists splintering one of the doors into a million pieces.

Fear gripped me. "Go!" he bellowed.

I grabbed my hoodie from the floor, clutching it tightly. Turning hesitantly to face him, I wished I hadn't.

The intricate lines tattooed on his arms seemed to writhe like black ribbons; smoke began to rise from his skin. I knew it wouldn't be long before his humanity was consumed by the monster he despised.

Terrified as I was, I refused to make the same mistake again. I couldn't leave him.

"I said go. NOW!" Drake thundered.

"No. I'm not leaving. Please, tell me what to do," I pleaded, my voice trembling.

"You must go. Please. I don't want to hurt you," he pleaded, holding his head in his hands as if in agony.

Reluctantly, I took one last look at him before turning and running into the pouring rain, not daring to look back.

I'm sorry, Drake. I'm so sorry. I thought, stumbling blindly through the storm.

9

THE LEGACY

THE HOUSE NO LONGER HAD THAT sense of safety I used to enjoy. In truth, I knew I would only feel safe once I saw Drake again.

It was almost three; the weather had eased up, but there was still no sign of him. I sat at my bedroom window, vigilantly watching the world outside, yet it did little to cure my anxiety.

Everything had spiraled out of control the moment I freed Drake, and now I feared for my own life as well. I couldn't bear the burden alone any longer and knew I couldn't keep this from Celest anymore.

With resolve, I found myself riding my bicycle through the soft drizzle. Tired of the lies, I sensed that Celest, too, had reached her breaking point. The rain intensified as I reached the library. The bell above the door announced my arrival, and Celest looked up from the counter, with a frown.

"Belynda?" she said, her surprise shifting into worry. "What are you doing here?"

I didn't respond immediately, steeling myself as I moved past the entrance and spotted the only two girls inside.

"I'm sorry, but we need to close early. I'm afraid I need to ask you to leave," I said. They collected their things, and I followed them to the door. Celest watched in utter surprise as I closed the door behind them and flipped the sign to "closed." Taking a deep, steadying breath, I glanced at the pelting rain outside before turning to her.

"No more lies," I declared. The horror-struck look on her face bolstered my courage. I moved to the cart of books, their spines suddenly revealing truths I had been too blind to see before.

I picked up one, *"The Guardian's Legacy,"* and placed it on the counter before her, my expression expectant.

"Belynda I—"

"I will have no more lies," I interrupted, my voice trembling. "My life is falling to pieces, and I haven't even lived yet." I wanted to cry, but the tears wouldn't come. Exhaustion had sapped my strength. All I wanted was the truth.

"You once told me that sometimes it's best not to become who we are destined to be. Do you remember that?"

Celest's mouth opened, and to my surprise, she pulled me into a hug. Her act of affection shattered my resolve, and tears finally flowed.

"I was being hopeful when I said that. All I've ever wanted was to find a way to keep you from this life that haunts you. Your mother never wanted this for you, and neither did I. But we were wrong to think we could change your destiny." Her words were a balm, soothing my anguish. For the first time, it felt as if the skies were beginning to clear. I wiped my tear-stained cheeks and stared at Celest as if seeing her anew. How could she have let me believe I was going crazy?

"I don't deserve your forgiveness, and I know it's too late for apologies, but I need to say it." Her eyes filled with tears, a rare sight—even when my mother died, she hadn't cried. "I'm sorry for not being the mother you deserved. I isolated you, followed an absurd plan, thinking it would protect you. I don't expect your forgiveness, but from this moment on, I promise you, I will do everything in my power to help you face this."

What could I say? A mixture of anger and relief washed over me as the weight of all the lies began to consume me.

"Please, say something. Anything," Celest pleaded, her voice desperate.

Both emotionally and physically, exhaustion was bearing down on me. I reached for the nearest chair and sat down before my legs could give out.

"What do you want me to say?" I stared at Celest, hoping my eyes conveyed the hurt she had caused. "Do you want to hear how much I've suffered because I had no one to confide in?"

"If that's all you have to say, then yes. I'd rather you blame me." Her voice was soft, resigned. Yet, there was no use in that anymore.

"Blaming you will not serve me. All I want is the truth. Now more than ever, I need answers."

Celest knelt beside me, grasping my hands. "I promise you, there will be no more secrets from now on. I will help you figure this out. I will stand by your side, no matter what."

I wanted to cling to my anger because, truthfully, she didn't deserve my forgiveness. But I couldn't. She had meant well in her own twisted and mistaken way; Celest was the only person who could help me with this mess.

Celest held my face in her hands, wiping my tears away with her sleeve. "Come. I want to show you something."

When I stood, my world turned on its axis, and I immediately sat back down. Celest looked at me, frowning.

"Celest, I did something. I don't know how to explain it because, to tell you the truth, I don't even know how I was able to do it."

"The fire bound—I know." Those three words were my liberation. She had my undivided attention.

"You know about Drake?" Celest smiled.

"I wasn't sure you could make it happen. At least, not without the knowledge or proper training. But when I learned that the council was summoned urgently two nights ago because of a high magic breach, I knew it had to be you." I stared at Celest as if seeing her for the first time. "You see, he is part of this destiny of yours that insists on happening no matter how hard we try to prevent it."

"Are you a Guardian?" I asked. She shook her head.

"No. Come, I have something for you. There is so much more you need to know."

I followed her into the office, a sense of unease sweeping through me. Sitting in one of the empty chairs across from her wooden desk, I waited patiently.

She pulled at one of the lamps on the wall, revealing a hidden partition beneath. Celest retrieved a small mahogany box from within and used the tiny key hanging around her neck to open it. She was full of surprises.

She sat on her chair, pushing the box towards me. When I opened it, the only item inside was a carefully folded letter. I looked at Celest, intrigued. I touched it, feeling the fragile, old paper. I hesitated, but Celest nodded encouragingly.

"Go ahead. I think you'll understand."

I twisted the letter in my hand, noticing a broken wax seal. My head spun, and a distant ringing filled my ears. I had seen this before, but not here. Not in this time. It was in my dream —this was Isabel's.

"How do you have this?" I demanded, my voice shaking.

"Let's just say that many people, over many years, went through a lot of trouble to secure this letter," Celest replied, her tone evasive.

"I hope you have a better explanation than that." I was tired of riddles—now was the time for clear answers.

"Belynda, as you have likely figured out by now, there is a whole different world out there beyond the one you know. I will explain everything, but this is a good place to start. It will help you understand better."

When I unfolded the delicate paper, fresh tears blurred my vision. I was correct. It was the last letter Isabel wrote before the ritual—the letter I had watched her write in my vision. The night she died. I wiped away my tears and read on.

A vision of death can be haunting...Yet I see only hope in this revelation. An end with a new beginning is the answer, not a sacrifice. If fate binds us together, death and rebirth will set him free...

I know this letter will find you, just as I have foreseen. Many will see these words before your light comes into this world. Many will fight against what these words represent and the prophesy it predicts, but many will treasure it and take part in its fulfillment. Remember that everyone has a place and purpose in this world and that fate and time have no measure. My purpose is clear now that the fates have shown me. I have seen it. The next pure blood will be born.

You alone will restore the peace and bring balance between the realms.

You alone will have the power to open the gates of the elements.

There will be no need for the misused powers of the council, for you alone will hold the sacred circle.

Beyond my knowledge will be your gifts but know that only in death will you discover your truest self.

Bonded through blood, water, and soul, together as one we shall be: you will bring him back to me.

The fates are on our side this time. The balance

has been tilted for hundreds of years by power and greed; no longer is there love and peace in the divided realms. It is our time to set things right. The fates and the elements have spoken and tonight I do my part.

Beautiful serpent... I know you will find the strength. Find the path where at rest we meet, and I will help you through. Give him all of our love and passion, for he is our future, our destiny. He will love us as one, for we are one and the same.

Tell him. Beyond death, I loved him, and your love is proof of that. Cherish every minute, every breath as I did in the flesh.

Beautiful serpent, you are my rebirth, my soul, together as one in life and death.

Embrace your destiny, for you are the chosen one, the last and only pure blood.

Isabel Adams Cromwell

I SWIPED at the tears streaking down my face, trying to assimilate the letter's context.

"How am I the pureblood she speaks of?" I whispered, mostly to myself.

"It's true," Celest confirmed softly. "That is her legacy and your life."

"What kind of life exactly is it? Is this the prophecy you spoke of? I can't do any of the things she said. And why does she call me 'beautiful serpent'?" I ran my hands over my face, trying to dispel the confusion that threatened to consume me. All emotions came crashing down on me at once—Celest's revelations, the memory of Isabel and Drake.

Celest squeezed my shoulder and handed me a tissue. "Your name comes from the druid words 'beautiful serpent,'" she explained. "The other things, as you put it...well, you have already done it. You brought the fire bound back on your own."

"I was lucky. Anyone could have done it if they followed the instructions." Celest shook her head, disapproval etched on her face.

"You don't know how wrong you are. It takes the power of the entire council to open any kind of portal, which they haven't been able to do for hundreds of years. Not without the Sacred Book. The fact that you could do it on your own without any proper training only makes me wonder what the extent of your powers could be." I knew she spoke the truth because Drake had wondered the very same thing.

"What about Isabel? She had gifts too. Why pass this curse to me?" Celest took the chair next to me, and I shifted to face her.

"She didn't have your powers, or the support of the council to bring him back. Through her visions, the fates presented her with a possible future: a future where time would eventually correct the past injustices caused by the legacy. Isabel's death triggered a change. Her mother tried to convince the council to reverse the sentence and warned them of the prophecy. But many refused. The council's cruelty unleashed a chain reaction that affected generations. Those who valued the prophecy and knew of Isabel's connection with the fates became allies. They conspired to steal the Sacred Book, leaving the legacy powerless to control the gates of the realms. Once Isabel's mother and father died, it weakened the power of the circle further. With Isabel gone too, there was no heir to ascend to their duties as guardians. Without all the required members and their Grimoire, the guardianship faded into darkness, becoming even more divided with time. So, you see, all that exists now is mostly a shell of power and corruption. There is nothing remaining of the sacred purpose for which the legacy came to be in the early ages."

I hung on to Celest's every word. As I did, my mind gained clarity about things that had before been nothing more than ideas, suspicions, or theories.

"My mind is so chaotic; I don't know what to think anymore. Part of me can finally breathe, knowing how the pieces of that story came to be, but it's too much to absorb at once. The lies, my human limitations are too ingrained in me to accept all of this." I glanced at the letter in my hands.

"There is no way around it. All these years, I have made countless mistakes, building lies upon lies in a desperate bid to keep you from your fate. I didn't know how far you had gone in your search for the truth until my brother Seymor called me and told me about the council meeting. All efforts to protect you had failed, like I failed to be there when you needed me."

I wanted to be angry with Celest, but I focused on staying sane long enough to absorb the information. She had been wrong to lie, but would I have done the same in her place?

"I am angry. I won't lie about it, but deep down, I don't

blame you. I'm just terrified, Celest. I'm scared, and I have no idea what to do next or what all of this means." The heaviness of the letter's words stared back at me.

"I know you're scared. So am I, but you are not alone."

I wasn't so sure. At that moment, I felt like a drifting island: alone and deserted with no idea who I truly was.

"Why me?" I glanced at Celest for answers. "How can I be bonded to her? How can we possibly be the same?"

"Reincarnation," Celest said, taking the letter from my hands and returning it to the box.

"Is that what she meant?"

"A soul binding, yes."

"But why me?"

"Those who believe in her words also believe in Isabel's connection with the fates. Her visions were a gift, and everything she foretold has come to pass so far."

"She says I'm a pureblood, but so was she. She could not accomplish many things, yet you think somehow, I'm better. Why?"

"Belynda, we believe that souls can transcend and evolve. Isabel might not have had the power, but you do."

I sighed with frustration, and Celest continued, "There is no way around it. Your mother tried; I've tried. This is your life —*her* life."

"But there are so many things that just don't make sense. If I am a pureblood, wouldn't that mean my parents were guardians?"

"Yes."

I turned to Celest at once. "My father was a guardian?" I

had played with the possibility, but it was a whole different story to have it confirmed. "You knew him?"

Celest seemed hesitant to answer. "I...*know* your father."

I stared at her, her words numbing my thoughts. I expected to wake up any minute. "My mother?" I swallowed the knot in my throat.

"Yes. Felsia is a guardian too," Celest added.

"She was?" The pained look on Celest's face made me uneasy.

"No, Belynda. She is a guardian. Your mother...she's alive."

The room started to spin, and my body swayed; the last thing I sensed was Celest's arms around me before the world turned black.

A PUNGENT SMELL saturated my head, slowly reawakening my senses. As my eyes refocused, I noticed that the strong smell came from the bottle of alcohol that Celest held close to my nose.

"Oh, blessed be. You scared me."

I blinked, confused as Celest held me. "What happened?"

"You fainted. I think you've had enough truths for one day." Celest pulled away, examining my face.

I closed my eyes and took a deep breath.

"NO. No," I said, blinking away the fogginess in my head. "I want to know now—I need to know, please."

Celest stared at me, weighing whether to continue. The resolve in my face must have been enough to persuade her.

"I wouldn't know where even to begin," she whispered.

"Tell me how you are involved in all of this. How do you know so much? Tell me about my mother and my father. Tell me, please. I need to know." My voice was edged with desperation.

"As a second born, I was not chosen to inherit the seat on the council—my brother Seymor was. However, I was sworn to duty and hired to find the location of the Sacred Book. Though, I had other reason's for spending so much time in the reliquary. Your mother had a vision that she was with child a few years before it came to be."

"My mother has the gift of sight?" My head swam with questions, but I didn't dare voice them all. I wanted to know everything, so I opted not to interrupt.

"She does indeed. It was her vision that set-in motion the events that followed. As I said, I was recruited to work at the reliquary with the purpose of finding the lost book; however, my real purpose was to find this letter. It had been lost for decades. For years, I searched until one day I found it, just like your mother had predicted. We knew then that the letter was not just the prophecy; it was written for you—future you. We couldn't remove it then, not without bringing suspicion to us. We decided to keep it hidden in the reliquary vault. We agreed I would keep watch over it until the time came to retrieve it. If the time came. As I told you before, we hoped that the visions would somehow change, but Seymor did warn us...we were wrong to go against what the fates had designed."

"This might not be the right time for this and perhaps this is the last thing you wish to hear but there are dangers that we will soon have to face. The guardianship has no idea that the prophecy is in motion, but they know that a manuscript is missing. What is worse, they are trying to prove that I'm responsible for taking it, and they believe that somehow it led me to the lost book and that I am keeping it from them. Now that they have sensed the high magic, it's only a matter of time before they come after me and perhaps you."

"They already have," I confessed, and told her about the man who attacked me at the fair and how Drake had exposed himself to save me. The blood drained from her face.

"It should have been me, not you." Celest paced angrily. "Thank the fates for his good timing. I must tell Seymor. If they sent someone after you like that without a care, it means they're desperate. They will come after him too."

"Were they the ones who broke into the house?"

"That's what I suspect. Now you understand why getting the police involved was not an option."

I nodded, the weight of her words sinking in.

"That means you cannot be going about alone anymore. They are likely watching us," she said, concluding what I had already suspected. Knowing Drake was watching over me provided some peace.

"Will you please tell me about my mother? How is she alive? Is she with my father?"

"No. Felsia and your father are not together. They had one encounter, but your father was lost to spirits and drugs at the time. He has no recollection of the encounter."

"You're saying my father doesn't even know I exist?" My fists tightened around the arm of the chair, suppressing the urge to scream in rage. So many lies...was there no end to them?

"Believe me. That is for your own protection."

"Why are you still telling me half-truths?"

Celest hesitated, her words painfully slow. "Belynda, your father... He is the head of the guardianship. He is the very person who likely sent that man to the fair after you and ordered the break-in at the house. He is the rotten core of the council."

"But he doesn't know who I am. Maybe if he knew I was his daughter..." Surely, he wouldn't want to hurt his own daughter.

"NO. Never. He cannot know. Your mother forbade it, Belynda. She has seen the future—you do not know what he is capable of!" Celest walked closer, her face pleading. "Father or not, he is not to be trusted. Do you understand?"

I wasn't sure what to believe anymore. I decided to give Celest the benefit of the doubt until I could decide for myself who my father was.

"Ok. But how can I believe anything my mother says if she has lied too? My entire life has been a carefully crafted act— even her *death*, Celest. How can you expect me to trust anything?"

"Please, don't blame your mother for keeping you a secret from your father. She had real reasons, Belynda. At first, she battled with her conscience, but as her visions evolved, she knew he couldn't be part of your life. She under- stood the kind of man your father was becoming and knew his ascension into the council's lead would ignite his thirst for power."

"I think it's best if I don't judge anyone until I know every- thing and can make up my own mind. So, please continue before I lose my courage and run out of here. Please. Continue."

"Very well. Your mother stayed here and continued her duties in the council until she could no longer conceal her condition. Then she decided to go to Rome, with Seymor's help, to give birth. We called in many favors upon her return to help conceal your identity. We adopted you legally, but Felsia insisted you take her last name. I have never been in the eye of the council. As a second-born, my life is inconsequential, so they never suspected a thing. For all intents and purposes, your mother was not your birth mother in their eyes, but you called her mother, and that's all that mattered to her. She knew, however, that she couldn't stay in your life. She had to leave."

The knot forming in my throat was suffocating; I could no longer hold back the emotions threatening to overtake me. "How could she leave me, Celest? How could she?"

"Belynda, you can blame her all you want. You can blame me too or curse the world around you, but the truth of what's to come will not change. I can't excuse Felsia's decision to leave you, but you must know that it was the hardest thing she ever did."

"But she could have spoken to me... tried to explain. Why pretend to be dead?"

"You were just a child." I swiped at the tears and pushed down my emotions. "It was the only way to ensure a clean break from the guardianship and any links that could lead them to you."

"Where is she now?"

Celest sighed deeply. "I can't tell you that. Felsia has truly kept her promise. She has reached out to Seymor through the years but never directly to me. Your mother thought she could change your fate by giving you a chance at a normal life—away from her and her ties to the guardianship. She even placed a binding spell on you when you were young, hoping to prevent you from coming into your powers. But we knew it hadn't worked when you had your first dream."

"But I remember my first dream. It was after she was gone."

"That wasn't your first dream. A few weeks before that, you had your first vision. That's what made Felsia decide it was time to leave, despite Seymor's constant reminder that fate couldn't be changed. Even then, she truly believed you would have a better chance if she broke all ties between you, her, and the guardianship. But when Felsia left, the dreams didn't stop, and I didn't know what to do. All I knew was that I couldn't tell you the truth. I had to try and give you a normal life. I couldn't contact your mother for guidance, and while I know it's a poor excuse for my lies, I didn't know how to deal with you. I will be eternally sorry for everything I have put you through. I don't know where to begin to make amends for the pain I've caused, but please, do not shut me out. Let me be here for you now."

"I can't think straight. My life is a complete lie. The father I never knew is a monster set on harming me; my mother, who I believed dead for years, is alive, and I'm part of some prophecy —the reincarnation of an old soul. I need a moment. Hell, I think I need a lifetime to absorb all of this, and even that might not be enough. I just can't."

"There is one thing I know for sure: you are strong. You

have endured more than most in your short years, and you are still here, fighting to understand. You have every right to feel hurt and betrayed, but time will help you understand and heal. You are a fighter, Belynda Hershton, and now you have the fire bound to walk your path. You are not alone anymore."

I faced a conundrum of information and emotions, but the thought of Drake helped me breathe. "How can I explain this to him without sounding insane?"

"Don't worry about that now. He's a fire bound. He will understand this better than you think. None of this is your fault; he will see that. Your lives are linked beyond time and reason, and like you, he will have to accept the fate that has been dealt for both of you."

My body felt weak, my mind on the brink of unraveling. There was only so much I could handle at a time—and there was still so much I wanted to ask. But for now, I needed to rest, to consolidate my thoughts, to somehow find the strength to accept this life, this proclaimed fate of mine.

"Can I keep this?" I asked, clutching the letter from the box, and waiting for her response.

"It's your legacy," Celest said, placing the empty box back in her armoire. "We should head home. There is always tomorrow."

I nodded and carefully slipped the letter into my jacket pocket. Daylight was almost gone, and the need to see Drake made me impatient.

The ride home was quiet. My eyes darted to every shadow on the side of the road, but who was I kidding? He wouldn't show.

As soon as Celest pulled into the driveway, I got out. Everything around me felt different; maybe Celest's revelations had changed me. The weight of the letter in my pocket was a constant reminder: I would never be the same again.

One thing hadn't changed—I missed Drake. Something inside of me felt hollow, like he was the missing piece.

A long, hot shower did little to quell my anxiety. Even my bedroom felt claustrophobic. Thoughts of Drake, Isabel, the council, my parents, and this pureblood legacy bombarded my mind. In the kitchen, I downed two pills to calm the headache threatening to consume me. I noticed the light in Celest's office was on, but decided not to disturb her.

For the first time in a long time, I went outside to the porch and sat on the swing chair. The cold temperatures descended, and the gray blanket of stars made the night feel even more melancholic. I hugged my knees to block some of the cold and rested my chin on them.

The squeak of the front door broke my reverie. I looked up to see Celest standing there.

"What are you doing out here? It's freezing. Come inside." Celest urged me, remaining at the threshold of the door.

With a firm shake of my head, I declined. "I needed to breathe. I wish I could just turn off my thoughts like a switch." My voice sounded distant and cold, even to me.

"I know you do, Belynda, but you need to rest. If you stay here, you'll catch a cold. You know it's not safe."

Couldn't she tell I was numb inside? The piercing cold against my skin was the only reminder I was still somewhat normal, not immune to the elements. "Please, Celest. Go to bed. I'll come in soon, I promise."

She hesitated at the doorway but didn't press further. "Goodnight, sweetheart."

"Goodnight," I replied, watching as she closed the front door and returned inside.

Sulking in my misfortune wouldn't make my problems vanish, but after everything I had endured, I deserved this moment to myself. How can someone's life change so drastically in merely a week? The more I thought about it, the less sense everything made. How did I change from Belynda—the ordinary, insignificant girl—to the blood and soul reincarnation of Isabel Adams? How? I didn't want magical powers or visions; I wanted to be normal.

Unbelievably, Drake was the only thing that made sense. Even though he was part of my legacy, he was the only one I chose not to live without.

My lips felt parched; the cold air burned my tear-stained cheeks, but I refused to move from my spot. The faintest sound of creaking startled me from my thoughts.

Celest stood at the door again, a somber expression on her face. "Belynda, you should come see this."

Alarmed, I followed her into the house and halted before the TV. The local news was on; the reporter gave some specifics, but all I saw were blazing flames consuming the fields outside of town.

"Drake..."

"He is a fire bound. An accidental fire in the middle of nowhere, with this rain...is no coincidence."

I willed my frozen limbs to move, but they remained stiff, unresponsive. A train of emotions crashed over me, leaving me unsure whether to laugh or cry. The memory of those magnetic grey eyes was my only anchor.

"I need to find him. I left him this morning; he was in pain and confused. He has nowhere to go."

"Belynda, all I know about shifters comes from books. If he's unstable in his elemental form, going out there now is madness."

"He won't hurt me," I willed the words to be true, yet they didn't sound convincing even to me.

"You don't know that."

"All I know is that through his rage, he begged me to leave —to run. He wanted to protect me, not hurt me. I need to find him. He shouldn't be out there alone like an animal. Please, you have to understand."

Celest glanced at the clock. "But child, it's dark out. Where would you even begin?"

"I don't care. I just have to do something."

I stomped into my room, heart pounding, and threw on something warm. When I returned downstairs, Celest stood at the door.

"You can't stop me," I said. "Drake is as confused as I am about all of this. He's alone out there. He deserves to know the truth."

"Believe me, I understand, but going out there now is reckless. Considering the threats we're facing, it's not safe for either of us. He, on the other hand, can take care of himself."

She was right, but I couldn't let another night pass without making things right with Drake.

"I know the danger, but if I don't go and try to find him,

the guilt will eat me alive. Please, Celest." My voice cracked, and I saw her resolve waver.

"If I can't convince you to wait, then I'm coming too. Whether you like it or not."

I didn't argue. Instead, I hugged her, feeling the barriers between us begin to erode.

A few minutes later, we stepped out into the night. The sky was clear, but a coldness settled over us like a blanket.

"Thank you for coming," I said softly.

"It's the least I could do. Now, where are we headed? We better get going."

I took the path I'd walked the night I released Drake. Celest was right—I had no idea where he was. But my instincts told me he wouldn't abandon me. I hoped he was close enough to sense my presence.

After thirty minutes, we reached the shadowy edge of the forest.

"How do you know he'll be here?" Celest asked, shining her flashlight into the trees.

"I don't. But he has nowhere else to go. Where else can he hide but in the darkness?"

"And how do we find him?" Celest's breath came heavy from the cold evening air.

"We don't. I'm hoping he finds us."

"This is your plan? We can't just sit here and wait. This is not a good idea."

"Not a good idea indeed."

Celest pulled me back as a deep voice echoed from the woods. I felt no fear. Instead, a wave of safety and comfort washed over me as he stepped from behind the tree.

"Drake!" I broke free from Celest's grip and ran toward him but stopped short. My thoughts and emotions pinned me still. I wanted to close the last two steps and fall into his arms, to drown my pain and confusion in his embrace. But I couldn't. Knowing the motives that united us, understanding the reason behind our strange connection, didn't justify the irrational feelings. Isabel's binding was the cause, but he didn't know that. I worried about his reaction. How would he look at me? Would he see me differently, hate me for carrying his beloved's soul?

Drake's eyes desperately searched my face. Though we had shared a moment—a lapse in judgment fueled by carnal thoughts and desire—he loved Isabel, not me. I reminded myself of that.

"Have you lost all sense?" Drake's voice was a mix of anger and concern, shadows framing the chiseled angles of his face.

"I saw the fire on the news. I had to know you were okay. It was my fault; I shouldn't have left," I said, searching his eyes, hoping he'd understand how sorry I was, how he wasn't alone.

His jaw tightened, as if he wanted to say more but held back. "That was not your fault. You were right to leave—I needed you to." He glanced over my shoulder at Celest. "But we'll talk about it later. Have you no care for your life at all?"

Drake's anger wasn't about Isabel or what happened this morning at the barn. He was genuinely worried.

"I'm as much at fault. I shouldn't have let her come out here, but there was no stopping her," Celest said. Drake's eyes shifted to her, an icy expression that mirrored contempt.

"This is Celest," I introduced, hoping to break the tension.

"A pleasure to meet you," Celest added, frozen in place.

"Is it?" Drake questioned, his cold gaze startling me. I glanced at Celest, seeing the shock on her face mirrored my own. "Earlier, I felt your doubts—your fears. How can you trust her when she's connected to them?" He paused, staring between Celest and me. "Something has changed," he concluded, his eyes scanning my face, sensing my distress.

I reached into my jacket pocket and pulled out Isabel's letter. Drake's breathing spiked, and I knew he recognized the scent, perhaps even the handwriting.

"What is this?" His frown deepened.

"This letter is for you, as it was for me," I explained, placing it in his hand. "Go ahead, it will clarify some things." Despite my fear, I encouraged him. Anticipating his reaction, I retreated and sat on a nearby branch, giving him space.

Drake produced a flame in his hand, igniting a small fire in the clearing. Celest quietly stood by my side. The soft light from the fire created dancing shadows around us; the chirping echoes from the deep forest anchored me as I watched him read the letter.

Fear gripped me as I realized I could face my legacy, but not without him. Drake was my lifeline.

He read the script twice and folded it, his expression blank but controlled. This time, the lines on his arms remained inked on his skin, and his eyes softened as he paced closer to where I sat.

"Are you alright?" he asked, surprising me. I stared up at him, confusion mixing with the effort to keep my tears at bay.

"I should be the one asking that," I whispered. His eyes roamed my face before he knelt, his gaze almost level with mine. "Please tell me what you're thinking," I pleaded, but his expression remained unreadable.

He closed his eyes for a moment, tilting his face to the sky and taking a deep breath. When he looked back at me, I saw a semblance of peace reflected in his eyes.

"Soon after you opened that portal, I realized this was not my time nor Isabel's. As a mortal, she couldn't be alive, and yet I found no rational explanation for her essence to follow you." His intense gaze warmed my cheeks, and I shifted my eyes to my hands resting on my lap. His warm fingers lifted my chin, stilling my heart as he gently forced me to meet his gaze. "Trusting you wasn't easy because I felt your bond to the guardianship, but this—" he paused, glancing at Celest. "After what you showed me this morning, this brings clarity—her letter puts everything into perspective. Her actions have meaning." His tone softened, and with it, my body relaxed. Relief brought the tears I had fought hard to contain. I covered my face, but he pulled my hands away.

"Why are you upset?" He leaned closer, his voice low, only for my ears.

"I was afraid you would hate me," I admitted, wiping away the tears. Drake's expression instantly changed to one of remorse.

"The only person I could ever hate is myself," he whispered, his revelation confusing me. "I am to blame for all of this." He hesitated, glancing at Celest, then leaned in, his lips almost grazing my cheekbone. "We will speak later, without the audience," he whispered, his thumb catching a tear from the corner of my eye. He straightened up, pinning Celest with a cold stare.

"Now you—I'm interested in what you have to say."

Celest looked like she wanted to run. She took a deep breath and sat down next to me on the fallen branch.

"Not tonight, please," I cut in. "I'm not ready to hear it all again. Not tonight, but I can show you." I paused, realizing how difficult the exchange had been. "If you'd like, I can show you," I amended, meeting his gaze.

"Very well," he conceded, and Celest visibly relaxed.

"Will you take me home?" I murmured, barely able to keep my eyes open. "I don't think I have the strength to stand for much longer tonight."

His eyes scanned me, assessing my state. After a moment, he nodded and walked over to the burning fire. With a simple wave of his hand, the flames vanished. I stared in awe, Celest's expression mirroring my own.

"You've had enough for one day. Although I think we can agree that this conversation is far from over," Drake said, glancing at Celest before making his way back to me.

"There is always tomorrow," Celest agreed, her voice steady this time.

I tried to take a step, but my body swayed with exhaustion. Drake was at my side in an instant, lifting me effortlessly into his arms. My protest died on my lips when I saw the resolve in his eyes—he wouldn't listen.

"I would let you walk if I knew you could make it," he murmured close to my ear, his voice a soothing rumble. I couldn't help but smile.

I relaxed into his embrace, resting my head against his neck, and inhaling his scent. The steady rhythm of his steps lulled me, while Celest's faint footsteps followed us. I wondered if she would object to having him stay at the house, but she remained silent. Drake's stride never faltered, his breathing even, unaffected by my weight.

"Are you sure you won't get tired and drop me on the way?" I asked softly, my lips brushing against his neck.

His hands tightened around me in response. "Do you doubt me?" he replied with a hint of a smile. I smiled back, involuntarily letting my lips graze his skin again.

"Keep doing that, mortal, and we both might fall before we get there," he added with a deep groan.

I smiled wider, avoiding his skin this time but secretly pleased to know that my touch affected him too.

IO
CONFESSIONS

MY *EYES WERE STARTING TO CLOSE* when I heard Drake's steps on the porch. He paused, and I guessed he was unsure whether Celest welcomed him or not.

"My room is just up those stairs," I said, trying to persuade him.

Drake dismissed my comment. "It's best if I leave," he said.

Before I could protest, Celest spoke up. "No. You should stay."

I saw the hesitation flicker in his eyes.

"I insist. Make yourself at home. There are extra rooms upstairs, and although we can't do much about clothes right now, I'm sure Belynda can find something for you," she added, glancing at the mud stains on his clothes.

"Thank you," he replied curtly but politely. It was clear he didn't trust her, and I knew it would take a lot for him to do so.

"Goodnight," she said to both of us, looking as though she had aged ten years in one afternoon.

Drake's eyes stayed on Celest's retreating form. She was clearly intimidated by him, and I didn't blame her. I knew firsthand how unsettling he could be.

"I think you can put me down now," I said with a smile, noticing he was lost in thought. Ignoring me, he marched up the stairs to my room.

At the top landing, he turned right and stopped by my bedroom door as if he had done it a million times before.

"How did you know this was my room?" I asked, intrigued as he pushed open the door.

"I tracked your essence across town. I think I can tell which room is yours if I'm five feet away from it," he said, a hint of impatience in his tone as he placed me gently on the edge of the bed.

""I'm sorry," I offered, unsure if I had offended him somehow. "Did I say something wrong?"

He sighed, running his hands over his face before coming to stand before me. He placed his fingers under my chin and tilted my face up to meet his gaze.

"I'm the one who should be apologizing. You've done nothing wrong. I'm angry at myself—for Isabel's sacrifice, for your suffering, all because of me."

"You're not to blame for my suffering," I said gently. "I would endure it all over again." As I watched him, I realized how true my words were. "I'm sure Isabel felt the same way. None of this is your fault," I whispered, trying to reason with him.

His eyes smoldered as he looked at me. "And her?" he said,

referring to Celest. "Are you sure you can trust her?" He searched my face. "Despite her hospitality, I..." he trailed off.

"I know. You have every right not to, but maybe if I showed you, if you knew what I now know, you'd think differently," I whispered, hoping he didn't find my idea too forward. Instead, his fingers tightened on my chin, and he knelt before me, his face level with mine.

"Show me then," he said. His thumb grazed my bottom lip, just over the cut he had branded me with, and his brow furrowed. "I'm sorry for this," he murmured, and I wrapped my fingers around his wrist.

"Will you tell me this isn't my fault, too?" he added, erasing the protest from my mouth.

I said nothing. He wouldn't hear it anyway.

"Show me," he repeated, and my lips parted under his warm fingers. Slowly, he inched forward, his lips brushing mine gently once, then again, searching my eyes each time. Then he kissed me, his mouth molding to mine, soft and warm, and I fought to concentrate on Celest's revelations.

Recalling the moment I ran from the barn; I allowed my thoughts of him to rise to the surface—the deep remorse I felt for abandoning him. His hand gently angled my chin, his lips just barely brushing mine. I recounted our exchange at the library—Celest's revelations, the confusion, fear, and anxiety that came with learning about Isabel's legacy. I worried he wouldn't understand, but his lips parted mine with a soft flick of his tongue, silently reassuring me.

His fingers stilled under my chin as I shared the painful truth that my father was the head of the guardianship, and my mother was still alive. The flood of emotions from all the lies overwhelmed me. But then I conveyed Celest's concern and her reasons for keeping me in the dark. Before I pulled away, I silently urged him to be more forgiving toward Celest. We needed allies, even if trust was difficult.

Drake pulled away slowly, his eyes searching mine.

"For your sake," he whispered, pushing himself up from his knees to sit beside me on the edge of the bed. "I should be the last to pass judgment." He leaned back, his feet still resting on the floor. I knew his words stemmed from his belief that he was somehow to blame for my hardships.

His expression was pained, reflecting the chaos in his mind. Likely still processing everything, like me. When the silence grew too heavy, I said the first thing that came to mind.

"I was afraid you wouldn't come back after today," I whispered.

Slowly, he turned his head toward me, his eyes drawing me in. I watched his chest rise and fall with each breath, wanting to be closer but feeling paralyzed in my own skin.

"Never," he admitted. "I needed time." His gaze drifted to the bed's canopy as he spoke, lost in thought. "I wasn't myself —I wasn't ready." His voice was lower, almost distant.

He closed his eyes, and I wondered if it was his way of guarding his emotions from me. Had he stayed away after the barn incident because he thought I'd judge him for losing control? It troubled me that he would think I'd reject him, but I understood why—he despised his own darkness. Hesitantly, I brushed my fingertips over his face, unsure of how he would react. His grey eyes opened, locking with mine.

"I was worried about you," I said softly. He sat back up, my hand falling from his face, but his gaze held mine.

"Your life is falling apart, and you're worried about me?" His words were sobering. "Do you even understand what is expected of you? What this legacy means?" He didn't blink, and the silence between us felt suffocating.

"I don't know what will happen. I am scared, terrified of what they could do...but I don't want to think about it. Not now. Not tonight. Not yet."

"No one will hurt you," he whispered, his words intimate due to our closeness. How could a person feel so sad, overwhelmed, yet happy? I couldn't be sure, but that's how he made me feel. Looking away, I felt a tear slide down my cheek. His warm fingertips reached for it, gently forcing me to meet his eyes, silently begging me to speak my mind.

"I've lost myself. This bond to Isabel..." I struggled to find the words. "How can I be both her and me? Please—tell me how, because I just don't know who I am anymore."

In a breath, his arms encircled my small frame, cradling me in his lap. It was enough to break my resolve. I cried, burying my face against his neck, staining the fabric of his shirt. He held me silently, attempting to shield me from my own pain.

Time stood still while I remained in his arms. The tears stopped, but I couldn't find it in me to release him.

"Tomorrow, everything will be clearer," he said, the echo of his voice, chasing away the stillness and shadows of the room. It felt strange breaking the comforting silence, but I knew it was necessary.

I stood up, and he followed, towering over me. Hesitantly, he brushed the back of his hand along my cheek. "Rest," he said.

He walked to the door and paused. "I almost forgot," he

said, reaching into his back pocket and producing my cell phone, which he placed on the dresser before walking out and closing the door behind him.

I stared at the door, placing my hand against it, wishing I could follow him or beg him to stay, but I didn't have the courage.

This tale of tangled souls and destiny was complicated enough without adding irrational feelings. I found myself irreparably drawn to him, yet I refused to acknowledge these emotions, unsure if he felt the same. The deep-rooted ache to be near him was ever present, but I couldn't tell how much of it was due to Isabel's binding. Did he feel as confused as I did? Did my presence call to him as his called to me? Or was I merely a vessel, with every touch and kiss making him imagine her instead of me? The idea poisoned my heart.

I lay in bed, my mind racing. Thoughts churned like restless waves. After a while, I pushed myself up and padded quietly to my closet, shedding my clothes for pajamas. As I slid open the drawer, guilt pricked me at the memory of Drake's mud-stained clothes. I should have thought of his needs sooner. I grabbed a pair of sweatpants and a worn band t-shirt.

Standing outside the guest bedroom, I hesitated, clutching the clothes to my chest. *Had he already fallen asleep? Should I return to my room?* Just as I turned to leave, the door creaked open. I spun around to find him there, leaning against the frame, a puzzled expression softening his features. In the dim light, the contours of his muscular frame, traced with intricate tattoos, seemed to pulse with life. My fingers twitched, wanting to reach out and run my hands over the smooth skin. But I didn't move. I couldn't. I shouldn't.

"Do you want to come in?" he asked, his voice smooth like a silent caress that traveled down my spine. A dangerous invitation. The way he looked...the lines of his tattoos, disappearing underneath the waistband of his low-hung pants...I averted my eyes.

"Uh, probably not a good idea," I managed, watching a smirk tug at his lips. "I brought you something to change into. I can wash your clothes for you," I offered, his eyes regarding me with an unreadable expression.

I cleared my throat nervously, trying to dispel the fog of desire from my thoughts, provoked by the brush of his fingers as he took the clothes from my hands. His warmth, electrifying my skin. "Would you like me to run you a bath?" I asked tentatively, studying his expression, which flickered between confusion and amusement.

"Why? Is my predatory, manly scent not enough for you? Have you ever seen an immortal bathe?"

I stilled, uncertain of the answer. His customs were unfamiliar to me, but he was right, his smell was alluring.

"I... I'm sorry. I didn't mean to offend you," I stammered, flustered. How could I have known the habits of immortals?

His laughter echoed down the hall, a rich sound that eased the tension in my chest. I couldn't help but smile in response.

"Forgive me. I couldn't help myself," he offered with a polite smile. "Immortals do partake in the pleasures of a good bath."

"You are awful," I said, playfully batting his arm, though it felt as effective as hitting a concrete wall. He grasped my hand swiftly, holding it longer than necessary before releasing me.

The charged space between us made me take a step back, clearing my throat. "Come, I'll show you," I said, leading him down the hall to the bathroom. I started the water running and pointed out where we kept the soap, guest toiletries, and towels. His dazzling smile made me uneasy, his eyes piercing me in silence, the corners of his lips twisting with amusement at private thoughts.

"You can drop your clothes outside the door, and I'll put them in the wash for you."

He stared at me with that heart-stopping smile.

"Is that all?" he asked in a playful, mocking tone. I rolled my eyes in response, before closing the door behind me.

Walking to the guest room, I spotted his discarded shirt by the foot of the bed. I picked it up and locked the door behind me. Passing by the bathroom, I found his pants on the floor outside. I paused, listening to the running water, imagining what an immortal god like him would look like—a thought I'd never considered before. Drake was dangerous because he made me want things I'd never imagined before.

Making my way downstairs, I was grateful Celest had chosen to retire to her bedroom. It meant she trusted me, even when I didn't trust myself around him.

Tossing Drake's jeans into the washing machine, I found myself unconsciously smelling the collar of his shirt. Immediately, I understood what he meant about his predatory scent, because I found myself enveloped in his alluring smell. I closed my eyes, lost in flashes of his haunting eyes, his lips, the smooth skin of his chest.

The water pipes shrieked, jolting me back to reality, signaling that he was finished. I threw his shirt into the washer and returned to the kitchen.

I made a turkey sandwich and a cup of tea, knowing he would likely be hungry.

The door to his room stood wide open, and I paused at the threshold, the food tray steady in my hands. He had his back to me, peering out the window as he toweled his dark hair. The low-hanging sweatpants revealed the flexing muscles of his back with each stroke of the towel. I was thankful for the weight of the tray in my hands, grounding me—otherwise, I might have swooned.

"Where...where is the shirt?" I bit my lower lip, my voice barely a whisper. Drake turned; his eyes almost glowing in the shadows.

"I couldn't possibly. It was too small." His explanation was simple, yet I laughed, picturing his struggle to fit into it.

"Let me help you." He took the tray from my hands, muscles rippling under his skin as he placed it on the bedside table. I couldn't tear my eyes away from the masterpiece tattoo that adorned his back. His body was a perfect temple, and I rocked on my heels, wanting to stay but knowing I shouldn't. I leaned against the door frame, trying to regain my composure.

"Thank you," he said, the wet strands of his hair falling over his eyes. I stilled as he strode towards me. The look in his eyes, smoldering, predatory almost. He braced a hand on the wall above my head, and my fingers instinctively reached out, brushing the tense muscles of his stomach.

I trembled with anticipation as he leaned in. "I smell of

strawberries," he whispered, his breath tickling my ear and sending shivers down my spine.

"It suits you," I teased, and his intoxicating smile drew me in. Our eyes locked, and the smile faded, leaving only the electric tension between us.

"Good night," I said, pulling my hands away from his skin and making my escape. I dashed to my room, but before I entered, I glanced back. He stood there, leaning against the door frame, watching me. It took every ounce of willpower not to run back and lose myself in him. With one last look at, I disappeared into my room.

Sleep eluded me, my thoughts consumed by Drake—his voice, his face, his touch. Thinking of him made all my worries vanish. As long as he stood beside me, I felt almost invincible. *Almost.*

DRAKE

Her quiet breaths seeped into the darkest crevices of my mind, drowning my unbridled thoughts. I chose to walk away—to put distance, completely aware that the monster inside me needed no encouragement. Leaning against the closed door of the guest chambers, I closed my eyes attempting to drown myself in her scent which lingered constantly on my body, my mind, my soul—*Isabel's scent.* Darkness moved over my skin at the thought of her, the haunting memory of her pale face on the lake's surface. The metal doorknob dented under my grip, and I released it, wrestling with the shadows barely contained inside me.

Being in my human body after so long was suffocating. It

meant following the rules of propriety, yielding to human emotions—human needs—I had long abandoned as a means of survival. The monster craved only darkness, living to consume and prey on the weak. Memories of the mortal's dreams took me back to a time when I considered myself worthy. But that man was dead. He vanished the moment I surrendered my humanity to the darkness.

Isabel could have had a long, happy life if I hadn't set my eyes on her. If I hadn't disregarded the covenant rules to follow my heart. I had doomed her, sentenced her to an early grave. I didn't deserve her or her sacrifice. I was a fool then for not fighting, and yet by fate's relentlessness, I found myself here once again, weakened by this mortal girl. The same inexplicable connection that had brought Isabel and I together seemed to conspire to bring us together one more time.

I pushed down the darkness threatening to overtake me and thought back to my time in Xelraa. Stepping away from the door, I removed my shirt and discarded it on the floor before walking to the window. Pushing it open, the evening breeze crawled in as I peered into the night skies. Since the night the mortal released me, I had done nothing but sleep under the stars, under the rain, surrounded by the forest sounds that brought me back to life. Xelraa had been a cradling expanse of decay and death. The smallest speck of beauty withered; only the strongest, foulest monsters survived, and I—I had learned to rule them all.

Breathing in the clear night air, I smiled, thinking of the girl down the hall. *Belynda...* Her name floated around my mind, and images of her face surfaced. Her spirited bright green eyes, the tilt of her defiant chin, her smile—her lips. The soft curve of her body.

"UHHH," I groaned, trying to extinguish those thoughts. She was innocent. She didn't deserve her fate, and I would be damned if I took any more from her. Bond or not, claiming her would be an injustice. I certainly wasn't worthy of her.

THE SOFT FOOTSTEPS prickled my senses, each sound pulling me deeper into awareness. I concentrated, picking up the sounds in her room, tracking her movements—her door opening, her quiet steps. I held my breath when her footsteps stopped outside my door. She hesitated, and so did I. She shouldn't be here, not with the way I was feeling. Yet, whatever humanity remained in me, and the monster alike, craved her closeness. Without thinking, I streaked to the door and opened it.

She turned around, her haunting eyes meeting mine briefly before drifting to my bare chest. The monster roared silently, clawing for release, wanting to take, claim, possess her.

"Do you want to come in?" The words slipped from my mouth, and I chastised myself for giving into the urges. Her gaze froze at the waistband of my pants before blinking up to meet my eyes. The monster crooned, pleased.

"Uh, probably not a good idea," she said, hesitating. I smiled, relieved to learn she had some sense of self-preservation afterall. At least one of us chose to keep a clear head tonight.

"I brought you something to change into. I can wash your clothes for you," she spoke, and my eyes darted to the clothes she clutched to her chest. I reached for them, letting my fingers brush against her wrist. She stilled, her reaction encouraged the shadows, the predator in me.

She shifted nervously. "Would you like me to run you a bath?" she asked. An image of her naked in the bath, on her knees before me, flashed in my mind. I smiled as the shadows danced, reaching to tease her.

"Why? Is my predatory, manly scent not enough for you? Have you ever seen an immortal bathe?" I teased.

She frowned, confusion marring her delicate features. "I... I'm sorry. I didn't mean to offend you," she stammered with a horrified expression. I laughed, trying to ease her discomfort.

"Forgive me. I couldn't help myself," I offered, with a smirk. "Immortals do partake in the pleasures of a good bath." And other pleasures as well, I wanted to add, but bit my tongue.

"You are awful." She flung her hand against my arm, impulsive and wild, too human, too beautiful. In a blur, I caught her hand and held it. In that second, I imagined a million ways to lure her into my chamber, to explore her body, to claim her. Her voice calling my name, begging for mercy, played in my mind. But none of those fantasies seemed worthy of her innocent eyes. I released her hand.

She felt it too—the tension, the sizzling currents between us. Her rapid heartbeat and the subtle flush of her skin betrayed her, even as her emerald eyes met mine with a feigned indifference. She was a vicious creature. I smiled at the thought.

"Come, I'll show you," she said, leading me to the bath chamber. I followed closely, mesmerized by the soft curves of her body. I barely heard her words, fixated instead on the micro expressions on her face, her perky nose, and full lips, her golden strands of hair that my fingers burned to touch. I shifted my thoughts. *What was wrong with me?* How could I protect her if I couldn't reign in the shadows and my impulses? She was innocent, for crying out loud!

"You can drop your clothes outside the door, and I'll put them in the wash for you." *Drop my clothes outside?* By the fates, she had no idea how alluring she was, what she was doing to me without even trying.

"Is that all?" I mocked, eager to get her out of the small space. My cock hardened at the defiant tilt of her neck as she closed the door behind her.

I jumped under the cascading waters, leaving my clothes by the door for her. I stilled, listening to her footsteps pause outside. I stared at the door, willing it to open, willing her to come in and give the monster the slightest excuse to play. But she didn't. As I heard her steps on the stairs, I wasn't sure which feeling was more rewarding—the relief knowing she was safe from me, or the disappointment that she was just out of reach.

Remnants of her scent lingered in the bathroom, each particle in the air tasted of her, a tantalizing reminder. I picked up a bottle of shampoo and inhaled deeply—strawberries, just like her hair. I lathered myself with it, knowing it would only serve to torment me further.

The cold water did nothing to quench my aching hardness. I groaned, the spray drowning the sound as I fisted myself, seeking relief. It felt strange, euphoric even, to feel such a human need after so many years without my humanity. It was wrong that she was the cause, but if I didn't find a way to appease the fire, to silence the monster's urges, she would end up paying, and I couldn't allow that. No, I didn't want that, I repeated to myself.

I slipped into the pants and frowned at the colorful shirt, discarding it altogether.

Back in the guest chamber, I returned to the window. During the years in Xelraa, in the sporadic moments of lucidity, I reminisced about Isabel and one other thing—the night sky. The only way to drown the grief, to not mourn my losses, was to return to the shadows, to lose myself to oblivion. Now, I craved *freedom*.

Her presence was unmistakable—her essence, her blood, her life force calling to me. The embodiment of Isabel, with a subtle taste of the ocean, pulsated from behind me.

"Where...where is the shirt?" I turned, watching her, breathing her in.

"I couldn't possibly. It was too small," I said, not dwelling on the fact that I had peculiar tastes. "Let me help you." I discarded the towel and took the tray from her hands. She was kind and thoughtful, I thought, as I turned to place the tray down.

"Thank you," I said, noticing her hesitation at the door. *Run, I thought. Leave now.* I warned silently, but the words never came out. Instead, I closed the distance with leisurely strides, my muscles coiling as I towered over her. Her hands shot out without warning, the muscles on my stomach tensing at her touch. *By the fates!* I needed a diversion, anything to keep me from pressing her against the bed, the wall, the floor.

"I smell of strawberries," I whispered against her ear. Her

body trembled, followed by the melodious sound of her laughter, which sent a jolt straight to my pants.

"It suits you," she teased, and I smiled. She always surprised me. She was dangerous, and she was so close. All I had to do was lean down, and I could claim her lips, as I had done before, but this time it wouldn't be to take in her story—it would be to make her burn. But she blinked, breaking the spell of our connection.

"Good night," she whispered, retrieving her hands from my skin, and retreating to her room. *Go after her. Claim her!* The voice in my head coaxed as I watched her hesitate at her door. *No...* I fought the darkness just as she disappeared into her room.

The soft bed dipped beneath my weight, and I closed my eyes, enjoying the rare sensation of comfort. It took her a while to fall asleep, but I heard the moment her breathing changed. It deepened, and with it, the muscles in my body relaxed. Whatever connection had been forged between us by Isabel's bond was undeniable. I needed her like I needed fire to exist, but I was terrified of hurting her. She was too innocent, too naïve, and she had no idea what I was, what I had become. What I could do to her if I allowed myself to let go.

Her presence invaded my senses even from a distance, a constant reminder of what I craved but shouldn't have. I turned onto my back, staring at the ceiling, trying to push away the images of her—her bright eyes, the softness of her skin, the sound of her laughter. She was a beacon in the darkness, a light I was desperate to reach yet terrified to touch.

In the quiet of the night, the monster stirred, restless and hungry. I clenched my fists, fighting to maintain control. No matter how much I wanted her, I couldn't let the shadows take over. She deserved better. She deserved safety and happiness, not the agony of my cursed existence.

But as the hours passed, the line between my desires and my fears blurred. The need to protect her warred with the urge to possess her. I was trapped in a nightmare of my own making, unable to move forward, unable to let go.

And so, I lay there, listening to the rhythm of her breath, a fragile tether to her humanity. She was my salvation and my damnation, the one thing I wanted most and the one thing I refused to have.

II
BENDING THE ELEMENTS

BELYNDA

THE MORNING LIGHT CREPT THROUGH MY WINDOW, and I lay still in bed as the events of the previous day rushed over me like a tidal wave. Pushing the blanket aside, I walked to the window. Celest's car was still outside, and it was way past my school hour, which meant I had slept through the alarm, and she likely didn't have the heart to wake me up.

I glanced at the closed door to the guest room, wondering if Drake was still asleep. My heart accelerated at the thought of him, so I rushed into the bathroom, not wanting him to catch me looking like this.

After a quick wash, I returned to my room and changed into jeans and a T-shirt, deciding to fetch Drake's clean clothes and bring them up for him to have something decent to wear.

The smell of pancakes and bacon floated up the stairs,

indicating that Celest was up early. What I didn't expect was to find Drake, fully dressed and sitting at the counter. Celest was nowhere in sight.

"Good morning," I greeted, attempting to hide my surprise. His eyes scanned my face, then traveled the length of my legs.

"Good morning," he replied, his gaze steady.

"You changed," I noted as he leaned back on the chair.

"She left them outside my door this morning," he explained, and I smiled, pleased to know Celest was trying.

As if summoned, she appeared.

"Good morning," she said, her voice soft. I noted the shadows under her eyes, an indication she hadn't slept much.

"Thank you for letting me stay today," I replied, walking to take the seat at the bar beside Drake.

"School can wait another day. I knew you'd be tired," Celest said, pulling the pancakes from the warmer.

"Are you hungry?" She looked at me, and I nodded.

"Did you eat?" I turned to Drake, who watched me silently. He smiled, leaning slightly closer.

"I have eaten, yes." His reply was casual, yet strangely alluring. I glanced at Celest, feeling self-conscious, but she was busy preparing my plate.

Celest placed the food before me, her discomfort palpable in Drake's presence.

"How are you feeling?" she asked, and I sensed Drake's eyes on me without needing to look.

"Tired. Confused," I admitted, picking up the fork.

"I'd be worried if you weren't," she replied softly, urging me to eat.

"What happens now?" I asked between bites.

"We wait," Drake answered.

"He's right. There's nothing we can do," Celest added.

"Do you think my father, or the guardianship will come for him?" I asked, my fork frozen halfway to my mouth.

"I suspect they will, eventually," Celest confirmed, glancing at Drake. "Your father has already violated countless rules. Once he learns of him, he'll use it as leverage to summon the council."

"They don't know I'm here," Drake interjected.

"That's unlikely. If your encounter with her attacker exposed your powers somehow, it's only a matter of time," Celest countered.

"I could leave," Drake offered, and I froze.

"You have nowhere to go," I said quickly, feeling a sudden emptiness in the pit of my stomach at the thought.

"He could return to his world," Celest suggested. "You have the power to open that portal."

"I will not leave her!" Drake's voice rang out, surprising me. "She will not face this alone." His gaze shifted between Celest and me, his tone leaving no room for argument. "When I said I could leave, I meant the house. It would be best for everyone if I kept my distance."

"No, where would you stay?" I blurted out too quickly, and he turned to look at me.

"Do not forget what I am, where I came from," he insisted. "I don't need comforts." He hesitated, glancing at Celest before returning his eyes to me. "Only to know that you'll be safe." I frowned, fighting the urge to beg him to stay. He couldn't leave.

"I'm not sure it will make a difference anymore," Celest said. "Leaving now will not help her." I was grateful for her words. "You protected her. They've connected you to her—to me. Whether they find you here or not, they will never leave us alone now."

Drake remained silent, but the frown etched on his brow signaled he was considering the options.

"You mentioned we had allies on the council," I said, recalling yesterday's hazy revelations. "Can't they help? Intervene on our behalf?"

"They can delay the summons," Celest replied. "Until they are all present, the conclave cannot begin, but they cannot stall it forever."

"I don't understand—if they don't agree with my father, why don't they stand against him?"

"They don't have the power. Stephen has elementals working with him."

"Elementals?" I asked, pushing my plate away, unable to take another bite.

"Gifted mortals—descendants of immortals that once walked this world, before me, before I..." Drake trailed off, dismissing the thought. "They can influence the elements to their will," he added, and I glanced between him and Celest, not fully understanding.

"Well, can't the rest of the council manipulate the elements too? Fight back?"

"No. They can't. Guardians are only descendants of witches. Some, like your mother, have gifts, but none of them have power over the elements," Celest explained, then paused to look at Drake before continuing. "But you do," she added.

"No!" Drake cut in, his fist tightening over the table. "She will not fight the elementals." His tone was dark and final.

Celest turned to me, her eyes wide with a silent plea.

"Drake, if this is my destiny, how do you suppose you'll stop it? Nothing can keep me from my fate." The weight of my own words hit me with force.

"I believe she can do it," Celest interjected, her voice trembling yet firm. "You can't deny the power of her gifts. She opened that portal all on her own."

I glanced at Celest, surprised by the courage she summoned to stand up to the Dragon prince. His face was a storm of fury and disbelief.

"I have never doubted her gifts," Drake growled, his voice seeped with venom. "But she has no idea how to control them. You forced her to suppress them her entire life, and now you expect her to summon them at will? To do what, go against the guardianship and elementals?" His energy shifted; he sensed it too. He stood abruptly, then paused, his gaze fixed on Celest. "Elementals have had an entire life of training to command their power. If you cared for her, you wouldn't entertain this idea."

Celest stiffened before me, clearly taken by Drake's argument. But this was no longer their decision—it was mine. My life, my destiny. Isabel had foretold it, and I had to trust in my abilities. I glanced at Drake, his presence a constant reminder that anything was possible.

"Celest, can you teach me what I need to know to bend the elements?"

Before Celest could respond, Drake was beside me in a flash, his presence shadowing over me.

"No, you're not listening. I know what you're doing." He gripped the back of my chair, his eyes dark and intense. "You think you have to rise to fulfill this proclaimed destiny, even after seeing the cost it brought to Isabel. I will not let you do the same to yourself. Do you understand me?" Drake was resolute, but I had to make him see that Isabel's sacrifice was not in vain. To my surprise, Celest spoke up, her voice steady and defiant.

"How can you judge me for hiding the truth from her when you refuse to see for yourself that there is no running from it? The fact that you are standing there is proof that Belynda is powerful and capable. I would give up everything if I could change things and offer her a normal life, but I've learned through my mistakes that there's no stopping the wheel of destiny once it's in motion. Look at yourself. The way you watch her, your need to protect her. You are only fooling yourself. No matter what you or I do, Belynda will face her destiny. Wouldn't you rather she be prepared?"

I stared at Drake, his presence drawing me in. Just as Celest had perceived, the tension between us was undeniable, an irrational pull. I watch his grey eyes become a dark storm of emotions spiraling out of control. My heart constricted, understanding his struggle to come to terms with Isabel's fate, blaming himself. As I watched the wave of emotions rolling over his face, I understood. He was afraid—scared he would lose me too.

"You will protect me," I whispered, as if the space belonged only to us. His eyes danced with shadows before he gently gripped my chin.

"What if I can't? What if I fail you like I failed her?" His whispered words were my undoing. I took his wrist and placed his hand against my cheek, wishing I could ease his guilt.

"Don't do that. She was responsible for her choices, as I am. Deep down, you know I must do this. It would make me feel better if you supported me, even if you disagree with my choices."

He straightened, resolve hardening his expression. "Fine, you want to learn, then I will teach you. But if this hell-bent legacy leads to conflict, you will let me deal with it. Give me your word that you'll stand aside, and I will agree to this madness."

I frowned at his terms, realizing he was missing the point. "You are asking me to promise to stand idle while you fight for me."

"Those are my conditions. Give me your word, or I will have no part in this."

I opened my mouth to protest, but I knew it would be in vain. "I promise," I said, the words meant to ease his mind. But deep down, I knew it was a promise I would break if it meant keeping him and Celest safe.

"When should we begin?" Celest beamed, pleased at the idea, and even I felt a flicker of excitement at discovering the extent of my proclaimed gifts, despite the lingering doubts.

Drake shook his head, still in disapproval, but he had already consented to help. "You said you would teach me," I pressed, and he sighed with resignation.

"After dusk," he conceded. "It'll be best if you're outside, closer to the elements." I offered him a smile, but he didn't return it.

"I'll leave you two to rest, maybe catch up," Celest said,

glancing between Drake and me. My heart sped up at the possibility of spending the day with him. "It's best not to raise more suspicion. I'll open the library and pick up some clothes for him while I'm in town," she added.

"Thank you," I said, walking her to the door.

"I'll see you later," she said, taking her coat.

"Be careful," I replied. She nodded, then walked out, closing the door behind her.

Drake remained still, rooted to his spot.

"Are you still angry?" I asked. His gaze locked on me, shifting between grey and black. He was clearly still upset, but there was something else in his eyes, something darker, and I had every intention of finding out what. "Tell me. What's bothering you?" I pressed, and he hesitated. "Please." I pleaded. His eyes roamed over my face.

"How can I..." he paused, stepping closer while holding my gaze, "...without hurting you?"

I stilled at his words. "Try," I whispered, a sinking feeling settling in my stomach.

He hesitated, the battle evident in his eyes. His fingers reached forward, tracing my cheek, then my lips, before he dropped his hand and turned away with a heavy sigh. He took a few steps away, but I couldn't let him go. Not like this. Not without knowing.

"Please tell me," I begged, closing the distance between us.

"I can't do this...you—" he said, stepping out of my reach. I frowned, hugging myself at what felt like his rejection. He was realizing he didn't want any part of this. He didn't want me.

"Tell me the truth, Drake. I've handled worse. I'm not a child; I can take your rejection."

His look was sobering, and I froze. Then he released a euphoric bark of laughter.

"What makes you think I'd reject or deny you?" he whispered, his eyes locking onto mine with an intensity that trapped me under his spell.

"Love," his voice dropped lower, darker, almost cradling my soul with its sound, "you might be able to control whatever impulses or thoughts you have of me, but I can't. That's why I'm trying to put distance between us. I've been without my humanity for too long, and the way you make me feel— scares me."

My thoughts swam incoherently at his admission, and I remained frozen as he leaned closer, his nose grazing my cheek.

"This is why we need some distance. I'm a fire creature. We are driven by desire, and you call to me in a way that numbs my senses," his breath caressed my neck. "You don't know how hard it is to stay away from you. Since the night you released me, I fought with myself day and night not to come to you sooner, to take you in my arms." His hands trailed down my shoulders and circled my waist, pulling me closer. I steadied my hands on his shoulders, remembering to breathe.

"I can't promise you that what I'm feeling isn't a product of your bond with Isabel, but what I know is that regardless of the cause, I am drawn to you. Being this close to you awakens things in me, and I'm afraid of losing control with you." He pulled back a fraction, his eyes searching mine.

"I'm not the man Isabel fell in love with," he confessed. "What you see is the shell of a monster that craves destruction. Even now, the darkness seeks retribution against the man who touched you, who thought he could lay his hands on you." His eyes darkened. "I should have ended his life."

"Why would you say that?" I frowned with worry. "Does killing come so easily to you?"

I needed to hear it from him. My convictions were no longer enough.

He weighed my words, staring into my eyes as if it pained him to speak. "I have killed before, Belynda." My name on his lips distracted me from the weight of his confession. "I could have killed him without a second thought," he added.

"You could have, but you didn't. You are not lost; you are not a monster."

He took my hand and placed it over his heart. "I wasn't good for her—I'm no good for you," he concluded.

I stilled in his arms, taking him in—his darkness, his shadows, his fear, his love, his insecurities. My heart expanded, realizing how irrationally I wanted him, despite our differences, despite having just met him. I *loved* everything he was.

I STRUGGLED to break away from his gaze, a dark hunger simmering in their depths.

"You are not the monster you claim to be," I whispered, my voice barely audible as I absorbed his words. His feelings for me were shadowed by the absurd idea that he was unworthy.

He shook his head, a shadow crossing his face. "You don't know what I'm capable of. Don't let my human essence blind you. The monster sleeps quietly within."

I met his gaze, knowing that words wouldn't convince

him. I would have to show him how unique and important he was to me.

"Tell me how you feel about this bond." I hesitated, searching for the right words. "I know you loved her, but what do you see when you look at me?" My voice trembled with my deepest fears. "Is it her face you see, her touch you crave, her lips you desire?" I had never been this open or forward, but since Drake, nothing was the same. I wasn't the same.

He sighed, his expression softening. "I did love Isabel, and I always will. She is part of you, and although her essence is ever present, it's your touch that I desire." His voice was almost a whisper. "After the rain—at the barn—when I first tasted your lips." He smiled, and I blushed at the memory. "It was your face I imagined when I closed my eyes, your lips I craved, your body I desired." He ran his thumb over my lower lip, and I parted them. The simple gesture set my body alight with needs foreign to me.

"I know you have doubts, as do I. Whether it's destiny or some divine force, I know what I want. You call to me, to my shadows, with a bewitching force I can't resist. My hesitation isn't from a lack of desire but fear of losing control with you. But know this—I burn for you, and that terrifies me." He tucked a loose strand of hair behind my ear, his piercing eyes tracing my face.

How could I respond to such a declaration? Any doubts I had vanished. It was clear he wanted me beyond reason, just as I wanted him. The current between us hummed with electricity, urging me closer. I wanted him—*needed him*—and he *burned* for me. His words echoed in my mind; my desire mirrored in his eyes. I wasn't afraid of him; I was desperate to be consumed.

The firm grip of his hands fell on my hips—tugging me against him. He leaned down, his lips brushing softly against my neck, sending shivers down my spine. I smiled, feeling light and free.

"You seemed perfectly in control last night," I teased.

He groaned against my skin, his grip tightening as he lifted me onto the edge of the table. "Did it seem that way to you?" he murmured against my cheek, his hands sliding to my behind, pulling me closer. He positioned himself between my knees, fitting perfectly. His warmth seeped into my skin like liquid fire. The tension between us grew, just as it had at the barn, and this time, he pressed himself against me, anchoring his hands on my hips and shifting me closer. Warmth and desire coursed through me. I braced my hands against the table as his hips pinned me. One hand moved to my throat, his mouth trailing a torturous path down my neck, collarbone, and chest. In the next instant, he was gone.

The feeling was like that emptiness one feels when dropped from the top of a rollercoaster. My breaths came unevenly, my body trembling as I steadied myself on shaking feet. As soon as I regained a semblance of control, I went in search of him. Had I gone too far, or perhaps not far enough? I frowned at the thought but decided I wasn't scared. I wanted more. I wanted Drake.

I found him in the living room, fumbling with the TV remote, a pained expression on his face, and a cushion over his lap. I smiled. He frowned.

"Why did you stop?" I asked, not daring to move from my spot.

He closed his eyes, and when he opened them, they were softer, but he wasn't smiling. "Because you don't want to be taken like that. Trust me. I wouldn't be gentle, and the monster wants nothing more than to sink its claws into you. Taste you, devour you." He frowned, shifting his gaze to the television. "I won't allow it." He concluded, avoiding my eyes. I smiled and, hesitantly, sat beside him, taking the remote from his hands since he clearly had no idea what he was doing.

"You should give yourself more credit, you know," I said.

He braced his arm on the back of the sofa, shifting slightly to look at me. "I'm curious to know why you think that?" he spoke, the edge in his voice slightly dissipating.

"You say you're unable to control yourself, but I think you're stronger than you realize," I said, noticing his eyes smoldering over my face, the corner of his lips twitching into a smile.

"I might be immortal, but self-control is not an ability I can claim," he replied, his eyes lighter, filled with mischief. I playfully hit his arm, and he caught my hand, bringing it to rest on the cushion over his lap.

The morning hours wove into noon as we remained in the comfort of each other's presence. I rested my head on the cushion on his knees while Drake played mindlessly with my hair. A sense of safety enveloped me, one I had never experienced before. In his arms, I felt at peace, safe, loved, and protected. Yet, my body buzzed with electricity. It hummed with currents, my skin prickling at the mere graze of his fingertips.

Each gentle caress intensified now that I knew how he felt. Every look, every touch was measured, restricted on his part. Although I understood his reasons, I wasn't sure I cared or feared them.

I knew I was young—a legal adult in society's eyes—but I never felt young at heart, unlike my peers. Perhaps being the vessel for Isabel's reincarnated soul had made me different. I had never been troubled with the woes of love or felt curious about exploring my body and discovering the pleasures of the flesh. Something every young adult experiences at least once in their young years, yet it never interested me. Not before the dragon prince.

Drake stretched beneath me, and I sat up, watching his heart-stopping smile as his fingers reached to stroke my face. "Are you hungry?" I asked, feeling a bit hungry myself and wondering if he was too.

"I could eat," he replied, and I smiled. He shook his head as if dispelling a thought and followed me into the kitchen. Taking a seat at the bar, he watched me silently as I moved about the kitchen.

"You're very skilled at this," he noted.

"Are ladies not apt in the art of cooking where you're from?" I teased. He ran his fingers over his mouth in a weak attempt to hide his smile.

"Servants are," he replied, reminding me how much I still didn't know about the prince of the Fire Realm, his home, and their customs.

"Of course, your majesty," I said with a mock bow, and he laughed, the sound warming my heart.

"Will you tell me about your life there? Your home, your

parents?" I asked. He blinked, as if going back to the past somehow pained him.

"In my realm, I was free. My father and mother were fair rulers; they loved their people." He paused; eyes distant. "I was different then." His frown deepened. "I hadn't become what I am now." His eyes darkened, shadows crossing his face.

The insatiable need to know him, to understand his darkest fears, drove me to continue despite the haunted look in his eyes. "Can I ask you something else?" My fingers mindlessly played with the hem of the apron.

"Anything."

"What was Xelraa like?" I asked. He stilled, his eyes turning to silver steel.

His body tensed visibly, and he hesitated. I wasn't sure if I should have asked, or if he would even answer. My intention wasn't to upset him, yet I seemed to have done just that. "Forget I asked. You don't need to tell me," I said, leaning over the counter slightly. His gaze held mine, anchoring himself to me.

"It's nothing more than the darkest, most sinister place anyone has ever seen. It's the Dark Realm, what you would call purgatory for us immortals—that's Xelraa."

"I'm not a follower of religious beliefs, but if purgatory is for the dead and you are immortal, what is the real purpose of the Dark Realm?"

"It's a prison. More precisely, a dimension of shadows, created to torture any soul that enters. The guardians used it for centuries to punish immortals from different realms who refused to follow their rules. But the shadow realm existed before them." I tried picturing such a place, but I couldn't.

"You said it was a prison. Were you locked in a cell all this time?" I asked. Drake regarded me with a look of uncertainty.

"There are no cells in the Dark Realm." He paused, gauging my reaction. "Imagine a place where the sun never shines, and the land is covered in never-ending fire. Water-bound creatures stand no chance at all in a place like this where earth, wind, and fire predominate. But even worse is the constant fight between species for survival."

Oh, Drake... My chest tightened as I pictured what it must have been like for him there. "When you told me you had killed before, was it there? In Xelraa?"

His silence somehow answered my question, and I sensed his shame. I was surprised when he responded.

"Yes." His confession was a strangled whisper, and I knew I had to ease his torment somehow.

"I'm sure you had no choice," I said, moving closer and leaning against the counter. "You did what you needed to do to survive." His eyebrows creased.

"Do you think that makes me any better?" His anger was palpable. "Belynda, I was born to lead. My father ruled the fire realm wisely and cared for his people. He cared so much that he closed his eyes to the guardian's decision on my punishment. I have never blamed him for it. It was I who made the choice. It was I who accepted this fate. It was hard for him, but he did nothing about it, even though he could have, even though he wanted to. I know he did it for the sake of our kind and to avoid a war, as did I, but also to respect my wishes, because he was a true leader. My father ruled with his human essence, you see. That's the kind of man I wanted to be. Even in a place like Xelraa, I should have been better. Like my father.

I should have died if necessary. Instead, I chose to live like a monster. Discarding my human essence made the loss of Isabel and my home endurable. It made me a cold-blooded predator. I craved the darkness, and it craved me, for I delivered."

Stunned, I searched for the words to bring him peace, knowing only time could heal the invisible scars. "I didn't know." I wanted to say I was sorry, though I knew he wouldn't want my pity. "I wish I could take it all away and erase the past. You are a good man, Drake, and deserving, even if you cannot see it." His gaze held mine.

"In your eyes, I want to be better—deserving, I do, but you should know one thing. I will end their miserable lives, without hesitation, if they so much as breathe near you." His eyes darkened. "They mean nothing to me—*nothing*."

"Do you think I would hate you or judge you if it came to that?" His eyes gave away his doubts. "I would never. I trust you. If someone dies by your hand, it will be because they deserved it."

"Will you listen to yourself? Your faith in me is beginning to affect your reasoning."

I pushed away from the counter, ready to rebuke his words, but noticed his grin. "You're laughing at me now?" I questioned, frowning.

"Yes, I can somehow find the humor in all of this. Can't you?"

I crossed my arms, recognizing his attempt to distract me. "Is deflecting your coping mechanism?" I asked, watching his smile vanish. "Why was it so easy to believe in Isabel's faith and not mine?"

"I wasn't a monster then."

"You are the same, trust me. If there's any truth to this bond between Isabel and me, which we know there is, my faith and regard in you is unwavering. I consider you worthy, just like she did. That won't change."

Frustrated, he ran his hands over his face. "Belynda, I gave up my human essence all these years, surviving as a monster. Embracing it again is hard. Now I'm faced with choices and guilt, and the one thing holding any shred of humanity in me is the need to keep you safe. You can understand why I don't wish to jeopardize that. I don't want you to hate me, but I'm willing to embrace the monster, and the consequences if it means you are protected. That is all you need to know."

The finality in his tone left no room for argument. He didn't see himself as worthy, so I would have to prove him wrong.

LUNCH WAS INSIGHTFUL. The talk of his home and his time in Xelraa left Drake edgy. I noticed the subtle shift in his eyes, the tensed muscles, and the furrow of his brow.

After lunch, I found him outside, sitting on the porch swing with his head resting against the back and his eyes closed. He didn't stir, although I knew he sensed me because he smiled and patted the empty space beside him.

I sat close, my thigh brushing his. With a deep sigh, he reached for my hand.

"Why are you out here?" I asked.

"It will rain soon," he said, as if that explained everything. I frowned, looking at the bright, sunny skies.

"Your human senses are limited," he explained. When I turned to him, he was staring at me. "Immortal senses are enhanced. We hear better, see better. My nose is particularly keen because of the predator in me."

"But the weather?" I questioned. He smiled.

"Believe me, it will rain soon." I didn't doubt his abilities. On the contrary, I was amazed every time.

"Do you like the rain?" I found myself asking, eager to know him. His thoughts, his likes, dislikes. His gaze shifted to the distant sky, where the clouds began to turn grey.

"Not particularly," he replied, but I sensed more behind his hesitation. "And yet, it's never been quite as beautiful."

"Why is that?" I glanced at his chiseled face, his gaze on the horizon.

"When you lose everything, you begin to appreciate the small things. The sun, the stars, the green of the forests, the rain—another's touch," he concluded, his gaze shifting to our hands. His thumb rubbed gentle circles over my skin. It was sobering to hear him speak like that. Drake was dangerous, and yet there was a gentleness to him that he couldn't see.

"I've answered your questions. Now it's your turn to answer some of mine," he said, and I peered at him, wondering what he could possibly want to know from my mundane, boring world.

"I'm afraid my life is abundantly dull, but go ahead," I said. His eyes danced over my face, from my eyes to my lips, and back to my eyes again.

"Why are you still untouched?" I stilled, my cheeks flushing at the bluntness of his question. Yet, I wanted to answer.

"I—I'm not sure." I frowned, staring at the soft droplets of rain that began to fall against the wooden stairs. "No one ever wanted me," I concluded.

"Doubtful," he said, tilting his head.

"It was never something I wanted," I whispered. "No one I wanted, not until you." I amended.

His eyes smoldered over my face, darker now, like the grey clouds covering the skies. The rain pelted hard against the porch rails and floor, drowning out all other sounds. It was peaceful and fresh, and my insides tightened as he slipped his hand to the nape of my neck and pulled me to him.

His nose brushed mine, and his lips followed, gentle and warm. They moved against mine leisurely. In a rush of boldness, I shifted and straddled him. He pulled back, hands gripping my hips, but he didn't push me away.

"You really have no idea how dangerous this is," he murmured, his voice low, his smile like a fog clouding my senses.

"I don't care, show me," I whispered, lost in his eyes. His fingers imprinted themselves on my skin, a deep roar erupting from his chest.

"You're testing my control," he whispered. My lips parted, and I brushed my thumb over his lips. His hips shifted into me in response. "You're playing with fire, love. You have no idea what I want to do to you." I pressed myself closer, his eyes almost glowing.

"Do it," I encouraged, my lips brushing his ear. In the next second, I was pressed against the verandah, my back firmly against his chest. His hand wrapped around my throat, his lips at my ear. The wood bit into my stomach, rain soaking my shirt, but I didn't care. His other hand draped around my stomach, fingers tracing the waistline of my jeans, slipping in, gliding over my skin. His hand slid down my throat, cupping my breast. I sucked in a breath, leaning into his touch with a breathless sigh.

"I'm tempted to fuck some sense into you," he rasped, pressing into me. "You'll either be the death of me," he whispered, "or condemn me to burn for yet another sin." Before I could catch my breath, he was gone. Vanished.

All I saw was a streak of black disappearing before my eyes as I stared through the curtain of rain.

"Drake!" I called after him and sank onto the swing to collect myself, knowing he wasn't going to come back. I wasn't sure what had possessed me to be so bold. I shouldn't have pushed him, but his reaction proved that he was the stronger one of us.

DRAKE

The shadows, recoiled under the pelting rain, the rival element serving to extinguish the burning within me. I lay on the forest ground, eyes closed, feeling the world alive around me. The cold drops fell against my face, her scent—Isabel's scent—lingering and torturing. I was foolish, and she was dangerous. With her innocence and curiosity, she had the power to devastate me, to light a fire that had been put to slumber for centuries.

Her touch made the memories of my time with Isabel glow with bright colors. I had allowed myself to be lost to the scent, and the memories of the flesh had betrayed me. Isabel's mouth on mine, her touch, her soft skin bending and willing as I made her mine, the memories distorted in my mind with glimpses of a golden-haired goddess of green eyes and white porcelain skin that I burned to consume, and yet I refused to. She was too good, too innocent to be tied to a monster like me.

BELYNDA

Already showered and changed, I watched the rain ease from my window and caught a flash of black crossing the driveway. So swift and subtle, if I didn't know of Drake's gifts, I might have dismissed it as my imagination. Taking the stairs two at a time, I met him in the entrance hall. Raindrops dripped from his black matted hair, his shirt clung damply to his skin, sleeves rolled to his elbows revealing the sinewy muscles and intricate tattoos. A puddle of mud and water gathered at his feet.

"I apologize," he murmured, his eyes bright and apologetic as he watched me.

"Don't worry about it. It's just water."

He shook his head and took deliberate, slow steps toward the foot of the stairs where I stood. "I meant for earlier."

I let my fingers trace along the line of his jaw, feeling it tense under my touch. "Shouldn't I be the one apologizing?" I teased. His lips quirked in response. "If anything, you deserve recognition for your restraint. Who knows, it might actually be one of your abilities, after all." His face lit up, his smile transforming him into something almost surreal in its beauty.

"You wouldn't be so eager to count me a hero if you knew

what I had planned for you," he teased back, a small smile playing on his lips.

"Tell me," I urged, but he stepped away, shaking his head. "Why not?" I pressed, and he paused, turning to face me.

"One day," he said, his gaze searching my face. "Your aunt is almost here," he added, and I took a step back, returning to the landing of the stairs.

Moments later, Celest's car pulled up outside. She entered, carrying far too many shopping bags. I moved to assist her, but Drake closed the distance with his unnatural speed, startling Celest and leaving me smiling in his wake. Despite his fears of losing control and his doubts about his own worthiness, his reaction was the gesture of a gentleman. It made me question if he was more like the man, he described his father to be than he believed.

"Where would you like these?" Drake's voice was neutral, yet I couldn't miss the unresolved tension between him and Celest.

"You can put them in your room," Celest offered softly. "They are for you."

"Thank you," Drake replied, his tone curt.

As Drake took the stairs, Celest inched up to me, her voice a hushed whisper. "Still unhappy about your training, I see." Her words conspiratorial, forgetting that Drake's supernatural hearing could catch every syllable. Suppressing a laugh, I nodded in agreement.

"I'm pretty sure he heard all of that," I murmured. Celest's expression became mortified.

"That's going to take some getting used to," she admitted, with embarrassment. " But I'm glad he changed his mind," she continued, less concerned now about Drake overhearing. "He understands he should give you the best fighting chance possible... he's just afraid, you know."

I did. I understood Drake's reasons better than he probably did.

"Yes. But can you blame him? He lost everything once," I said, feeling his presence.

"And my immortal life won't be long enough to make them pay if they try again," Drake added, his voice a dark shadow from the foot of the stairs. From the corner of my eye, I saw Celest shift uncomfortably, his warning unsettling her even if it wasn't directed at her. I also noticed he had changed his wet clothes. Celest had good taste.

"I'll prepare something for us to eat," I offered, trying to lift the heavy mood that had settled over Drake.

"I'll give you a hand. We have a few hours until sundown anyway," Celest said, following me into the kitchen.

Celest and I worked quickly, preparing a tuna casserole while Drake watched us, his eyes distant, lost in memories and time. At moments, it felt as if he wasn't in the room at all.

ONCE EVERYONE HAD CLEARED their plate, Drake's brooding expression remained fixed. His aversion to the idea of me fighting the guardians was clear in the hard set of his jaw and the way his eyes avoided mine.

Night fell as we left the house, the darkness deepening around us. My heart pounded with each step Drake led us deeper into the woods. The familiar path took on a sinister air in the twilight, shadows twisting into ominous shapes.

Drake stopped in a large clearing, and my breath caught. This was the place where I had performed the ritual that brought him to me. It felt like a lifetime ago, though it had only been a few days.

"This is it," Drake announced, turning to face Celest and me.

"Are you ready?" Celest asked softly. Drake took a step toward me, his eyes dark and his expression one of concern.

"You're worried. I can feel it. You don't have to do this," he said, his voice low and insistent. I shook my head, refusing to let him use my moment of indecision to alter my resolve.

"I need to do this. I want to—please," I replied, forcing my voice not to tremble. I looked up at him, pleading. His long, and weary breath of defeat served as encouragement.

"Celest, where do I start?"

"My knowledge on the subject is limited. Most of what I know, comes from books. But if you were able to work with the force of all four elements at once, you can certainly command them individually at will."

"Theories and feeble ideas," Drake responded, leaning casually against a tree. Celest offered him a discerning look, but he wasn't intimidated.

"Since you are the only one with the dominated skill, why don't you give her a demonstration?" Celest challenged. I was surprised when Drake strode toward me, a look of determination on his face.

"To clarify, not everyone has the power to bend the elements. Despite what some think, it's not possible unless you're naturally bound by them, as I am," Drake explained, glancing at Celest to emphasize his point. "When you opened the portal, you weren't bending them; you were using magic words to call on their spirit force. When an element is yielded to bend at will, you don't need magic words. Your life force has the power to call on it at will, like this."

Drake extended his hand toward me, and as he unraveled his fingers, a perfect ball of fire appeared, contained in the palm of his hand just like he had done the night before when he lit the fire in the woods. The flame danced effortlessly in his hand while Celest and I stared in awe.

"How did you do that?" I asked, spellbound by the flame. I tried to ignore the pang of disappointment as I realized that I was way over my head. Perhaps Drake was right. It was more complex than it looked. Drake closed his hand, and the fire disappeared.

"Belynda, don't get discouraged. I can see it in your face," Celest added gently.

"I'm not. I just—I don't know if I can do that."

"You won't know until you try," Drake said, offering encouragement for the first time. The look of disappointment on my face must have softened his resolve.

"Can you do that again, please?" I asked, not taking my eyes away from his hand.

Once again, he summoned the fire in the blink of an eye. This time, it expanded a few feet above his head as the flames stretched to form a sphere, manipulated using both of his hands. I noted how he commanded the fire with his body and mind, not uttering a single word. Drake startled me when he threw the ball of fire toward a few pieces of dry wood, igniting them instantly.

"I'm sorry. It's getting dark, and I thought we could use the light," Drake apologized.

I watched, mesmerized by the fire now burning on the ground. The softest touch on my arm brought my thoughts back to the present.

"Are you ready?" Drake asked, concern flickering in his eyes.

"Yes. Do I think or say something in particular to make the fire come?"

"Remember what I said: no special words. Bending the element is more like a feeling. It comes naturally to me, but perhaps you can visualize warmth and fire—feel the heat coursing through your body and will that power to be exerted out into the open."

"Okay, think about it, feel it...got it. Here goes nothing." I closed my eyes. "Wait, maybe you guys should step back in case something goes wrong."

Drake laughed, a deep, resonant sound. "Don't be absurd. I'm fireproof, remember? Do your worst."

I smiled nervously and glanced at Celest, who took heed of my warning and now stood a few feet away from Drake and me.

Closing my eyes again, I took deep, calming breaths to relax my mind. Focusing on the soft breeze brushing my cheeks and the silence of the woods around me, I did as Drake advised. I visualized my body enveloped in warmth, inviting images of burning flames into my mind. Once I felt the warmth flowing through me in waves, I opened my eyes and extended my hand. As Drake had said, I willed the warmth inside me to come alive and materialize. But it didn't happen. After a minute, I glanced at Drake, who watched me closely.

"It didn't work," I admitted, defeated, as Drake stepped forward.

"It takes time. Try again." He brushed his fingertips over my frozen cheek, leaving behind a trail of warmth.

Celest watched me silently from afar, nodding encouragingly.

REPEATING MY PREVIOUS STEPS, I relaxed my mind and focused on harnessing warmth within my body. Visualizing the heat rushing through me like a current, I extended my hands and opened my eyes, willing the fire to materialize. Nothing happened. Frustration tightened my chest, and I could feel their eyes on me.

"Belynda, I was wrong to put so much pressure on you. Perhaps he's right," Celest said, stepping closer. "It's not easy, but I believe you can do this. It just might take longer to achieve."

I shook my head, a sharp breath of defeat escaping my lips. "Well, that's exactly the problem. We don't have a lot of time. I need to make this happen!"

Drake's eyes flashed with darkness. "You don't need to do anything; I only need you to be safe. I've told you this already," he snapped, with finality.

Celest stepped closer, holding her ground before Drake's intimidating presence. "Can we please not re-hash that argument? Perhaps you should try another element." She encouraged, and I was grateful for her steady determination.

I glanced at Drake, seeking his approval, but his face remained impassive. "Let's give air a try then." My voice wavered. I closed my eyes with uncertainty and this time, instead of fire, I focused on the wind flowing around me. Concentrating on my breathing, I felt the currents within my body and allowed my mind to relax, visualizing the air twirling around me.

Drake's laughter shattered my concentration. I opened my eyes to protest but froze, mirroring Celest's look of shock. Two whirlwinds of air and dust—no taller than a foot—danced before me. I released a breath I didn't realize I had been holding, and the spectacle dissipated into dust. *What had just happened?*

"You are full of surprises," Drake said, his eyes filled with wonder and admiration.

"I knew it," Celest cried out, her excitement barely contained.

"What was that?" I asked, still stunned. "I didn't even get to will it forward. I just visualized it, and poof. I want to try that again," I said, my excitement bubbling over.

Drake's expression softened slightly, though he remained silent. Determined, I closed my eyes once more and felt the energy humming within me. When I opened my eyes, the whirlwinds had formed again. Holding my breath, I felt a thrill in the pit of my stomach at the sight before me. I took a slow and deliberate breath, and when the whirlwinds remained, I relished the control. Imagining the wind increasing, I willed the vortices to grow, forcing Drake and Celest to take a sudden step back. The wind circled in front of me until it reached the height of a tree. Then, I released it, watching as the dust particles settled at my feet.

"Remind me never to cross you," Drake said, the corner of his mouth shifting into a smile, but I still sensed his worry.

"You're special and powerful, don't ever doubt yourself," Celest added with such confidence, that I started to believe it too.

"What next?" I asked eagerly.

"How about you try using the force of the element to move or throw something?" Celest suggested.

This time, I had no issue creating the vortices of wind. I directed them towards a pile of fallen branches. With a clear image in my mind, I visualized the whirlwinds lifting the branches and smashing them against the trunk of a tree. As the wind slowly died, I exhaled, satisfied with the outcome.

"Did you see that?" I rushed to Drake, who was no longer smiling. "Please, I know you're worried, but can't you be happy for me?"

"Proud, yes. Happy, no," Drake said, his tone serious, "I worry that you think this is enough. I fear you will attempt something foolish because you believe you must, and you don't."

"But I can defend myself," I insisted. Drake raised arched a brow, skepticism etched on his face. "You don't think I can?"

"You're not ready. Not *yet*," he confirmed.

I felt the currents of power within me surge without warning. Overcome by the sensation and my irritation, I flung my hand in his direction and watched in horror as Drake catapulted backward through the foliage of the trees. He landed a reasonable distance with a loud thud.

"Drake..." I ran to him, Celest close behind. He was already standing and dusting off his jacket when I reached his side.

"I'm so sorry. I swear I didn't mean to do that. Please forgive me."

He stared at me in silence, my heart sinking until his lips shifted into a smile.

"Don't be," Drake said, a hint of amusement in his eyes. "I feel slightly better now, knowing that you're capable of tossing the council members around."

I laughed, but Celest didn't seem to appreciate the joke. "Well, not all of them anyway," I corrected.

"I can't wait to see what you can do with water," Celest said, her excitement mirroring my own. "Stephen will be so surprised; he won't know what to make of you." Celest added, and I stilled.

Her words made me freeze. A prickling sensation spread across my skin, ignited like a six sense. I spun, staring at Celest.

"Stephen...?" I questioned, but no... it had to be a coincidence, my subconscious reasoned.

Drake stepped protectively beside me. "Do you know him?" he asked with suspicion.

"Please tell me that my father is not the same Stephen— not Oliver's father..." I pleaded, desperately hoping it wasn't true. But the horror on Celest's face confirmed my worst fears.

"I wish I could, but I promised I wouldn't lie," Celest admitted. Her expression filled with regret.

I was mistaken to think that I was finally free of all the lies. If Stephen was Oliver's father—and mine—then Oliver was my *brother*.

"I wish I could make it all go away. I wish I could save you from all of these bitter truths," Celest pleaded.

I fought the urge to run away from it all, biting my lip to push back the tears that threatened to expose my weakness. Hurt, rage, or disappointment, I wasn't sure which emotion was greater. Drake pulled me into his arms, wrapping me in his warmth.

"We should probably head back," Drake suggested. This time, I didn't ask why. I could almost taste the change in the wind around us. Rain was coming.

I STAYED under the shower spray longer than usual, the knowledge that Oliver was my half-brother was daunting. The fates had spared me from having feelings for him, a small mercy at the very least. Whatever opinion I had formed of Oliver was now distorted. He had gone from a nuisance to a friend, to a possible foe. If, as Celest said, my father—the head of the guardianship—was to blame for the attack at the fair, it made me wonder if perhaps Oliver had something to do with it. His insistence on securing a date with me suddenly made more sense.

The bed sheets were warm, not as warm as drake's arms, but knowing he was just down the hall, was consolation enough. Since this afternoon, he had made it a point to stay away. Even after returning home, he excused himself. I sat at the edge of my bed, listening for him. Hearing the door of the bathroom, followed by the shower and a while after, his foot-steps as he retreated to his room. A part of me hoped he would knock on my door. That he would come, but he never did, and although I understood it was for the best, I felt a sinking sense of disappointment.

I found myself under the covers, trailing my hands over my lips, imagining his touch. Closing my eyes, I felt the grasp of his fingers around my neck, the length of his body pressed against mine. I released a breathless sigh, not recognizing myself.

Turning the bedside lamp off, I slipped my head under the covers, and prayed to the universe for divine strength to calm the tingling sensation deep in my stomach. The buzzing between my legs. The rush of adrenaline I felt at the thought of strolling down the hall and slipping into his bed.

I buried my face against the pillow and groaned with frustration knowing it would be a long night.

THE HAZY GLOW of the lamp's light fell on Drake's face as he stood before my window, shadows dancing against the darkness. His silver eyes searched mine for any sign of indecision, but he wouldn't find any.

The warmth of his fingertips sent shivers through my entire body as they brushed slowly over my lips, tracing my collarbone and neckline. His eyes darkened as his hand lingered, blushing along the side of my breasts. My breath emerged in a ragged sigh, the fire in his eyes mirroring my every desire. He pulled me closer, and I pushed against him, forcing him to sit on the bench by the window. I braced my hands on his shoulders and boldly straddled him.

It felt daring to have him fill the space between my thighs. My fingers laced through the dark hair at the base of his neck, pulling him closer.

He stiffened beneath me, his muscles straining against the fabric of his shirt. His hands glided under the warmth of my shirt, tracing the length of my back, leaving a trail of heat.

His lips trailed along my skin, then gently over my right shoulder. My body ignited, and I moved slowly against him.

The need for more of him drove me mad. I took his face in my hands, forcing him to look at me. The moment our eyes met; I lost all control. I leaned forward and brushed my lips against his—once, and then a second time. Gently, I bit his lower lip, and he welcomed me eagerly.

His tongue swept over my mouth; at first, the strokes were slow and calculated, but soon he claimed my mouth with urgency. Our lips moved as one with dire need, yet it was not enough to quiet the growing desire. The pressure in my thighs increased as his hands held me closer. I stirred in his lap, feeling the hard strain from his pants meet my core.

Drake groaned, breaking away from the kiss. He buried his face against my neck, his ragged breaths slowing.

"What are you doing to me?" he whispered, placing a light kiss on my cheek.

DESPITE THE CHILL in the room, sweat trickled down my neck as I sat up in bed. Tossing the covers aside, I switched on my night lamp, casting a dim glow over the barren room. The emptiness in my chest mirrored the starkness of my surroundings. It had all been just a dream.

I opened the windows, letting the cool air soothe my heated skin. The alarm clock read 3:44 AM. With a sigh of resignation, I brushed my hands over my face and slumped back onto the bed.

12

A LESSON OF POWER

BELYNDA

MORNING CAME, BUT I WASN'T READY TO move yet. My mind was riddled with remnants and flashes of Drake, Isabel, and the guardians.

With reluctance, I made my way to the bathroom, glancing at the guest room at the end of the hall. I leaned against the closed bathroom door for a moment, sighing before taking in my reflection in the mirror. The sleepless nights had taken their toll, but today, my cheeks were unusually flushed, and despite the lack of sleep, my eyes were bright.

I brushed my teeth, tamed some of my curls, and splashed water on my face. As I opened the door, I jumped.

"Good morning," Drake's voice paralyzed me. It traveled along my spine making me rock on my heels. He stood in the hall, fully dressed. My gaze took in the length of his legs, the way the dark blue jeans hugged his muscular thighs. The crisp black collared shirt was tucked in, sleeves rolled to just below his elbows, buttoned to his chest, revealing only the black lines of the tattoo that snaked along his neck and down his arms, ending just over his knuckles. Those long, skilled fingers —fingers I could still feel wrapped around my neck.

He cleared his throat, and I dropped my hairbrush, snapping out of my daze.

"Good morning," I replied. Before I could bend to collect the brush from the floor, he was there, materializing before me in a streak of black, holding the brush in his hand. I stared up at him, his smile growing at my obvious uneasiness.

"A bit uncoordinated this morning?" he noted with a wicked gleam in his eyes. "Must be the lack of sleep." He extended the brush to me. I stared between his face and his outstretched hand, riddled with suspicion. Could he know about my dreams? But that wasn't possible; he didn't have that ability; he had told me as much. What he did have were exceptional senses, and it wouldn't have been difficult for him to pick up on my restlessness. I took the brush from his hand, carefully avoiding his fingers.

When I didn't reply, Drake's smile widened. "I assume you'll be returning to your studies today?" he asked.

"Yes," I replied with a frown. "Unless I can convince Celest to let me take another sick day."

"Hmmm, you don't look sick to me. You look breathtaking, actually." Drake stepped closer, and I instinctively stepped back, pressing against the wall. He smiled, leaning in until his breath brushed my cheek as he inhaled my scent. "I'll see you downstairs," he whispered before straightening up and strolling down the corridor, disappearing around the curve of the stairs.

After collecting my bearings, I dressed and joined him and Celest in the kitchen.

Celest had outdone herself. The table was set with my favorites: blueberry pancakes, bacon, eggs, and toast.

"Are you hungry?" Celest greeted me with a smile. Her good mood was infectious, and I wondered if she felt relieved now that she had unburdened herself from all the lies.

"I could eat," I quipped, my eyes drifting to Drake, who sat at the table. He occupied the same spot where he had propped me up yesterday. His fingers trailed over the edge of the table, and I wondered if he was thinking about it. Warmth rushed to my cheeks at the memory, and his eyes darkened slightly. Subtle enough for me to notice, but only because I was looking. Yes, he remembered. I smiled and forced my attention to the plate before me.

We ate in silence, and I watched as Drake enjoyed his second serving.

"You should hurry up and finish. You don't want to miss your bus," Celest urged, glancing at the clock.

"There's no way to convince you to let me take another sick day?" I shot a side glance at Drake, who struggled to hide his amusement.

"Belynda, I know you are exhausted, but it's best if you return to school," Celest suggested. "If your half-brother is involved with Stephen's plans, then absenting yourself will only draw more attention. We don't want to make them more suspicious."

Her words brought me back to the harsh reality of the guardianship and our uncertain future. Slowly, my appetite disappeared.

"I think it's a bit late for pretenses. And I have my doubts about Oliver's involvement," I said. Drake braced his arms on the table's edge. His disapproval was clear. "Oliver knows I was attacked, but he seemed genuinely upset. He was angry even," I admitted.

"He is not to be trusted," Drake said, his tone final. I chose not to respond and fuel his dark mood.

"Belynda, you can't be sure," Celest argued. "For all you know he could be lying."

"She's right," Drake added, surprising me. Seeing him agree with Celest was almost unsettling.

"Well, then I guess it's settled," I said, shaking my head in disapproval but choosing not to argue further. The truth was, I didn't know Oliver well enough to vouch for his innocence.

"Your transportation is close," Drake declared.

Celest glanced at him with fascination, clearly puzzled by his abilities, just as I often was.

I stood from the table and headed upstairs to my room, sensing Drake's presence behind me. I grabbed my bag and spun around, coming face to face with him. Drake leaned casually against the door frame, his eyes scrutinizing me.

Despite his agreement that returning to school was the best course of action, his worry was evident. It was in the furrow of his brow and the hard set of his jaw. Taking slow steps, I closed the distance and stood before him.

"I will be fine. I promise," I said, my voice soft as I lost myself in his eyes.

His gaze held me silently for seconds that felt like an eternity. His fingers traced my cheek, and I saw his struggle for control, and even though I burned to reach up and kiss him, I didn't.

"Please, just promise to get along with Celest while I'm gone," I pleaded.

"I thought you had more faith in me," he replied with a raised brow, a smirk tugging at the corner of his mouth. "I'll behave. I'm not going to bite her head off."

"I'm sorry. You're right."

"Don't apologize," he said softly, his fingers tracing my face. His eyes held mine, the silver in them shimmering. "I know what I am. If I wasn't a monster, you wouldn't have to worry or ask."

"You're not a monster," I retorted firmly. "Shadows and all, I will never hate you. What must I do to prove it?"

His eyes darkened briefly before returning to their usual silver hue. "I believe you care for me. The question is: will you feel the same when you glimpse the monster within?"

I opened my mouth to offer a protest, but the sound of the bus horn cut me off. "This conversation isn't over," I groaned. With hesitation, I did what I had wanted to do since I woke up this morning—I stood on my tiptoes ignoring his stoic posture and brushed my lips against his. "Now I have something to look forward to." I smiled, feeling warmth spread through me. "I have to run," I whispered, leaning back.

His eyes danced with amusement as I walked away, leaving him standing in my room.

. . .

CELEST WAS ALREADY out on the porch, waving to the driver to hold. "Please be patient with him," I asked, giving her a quick hug.

"Don't worry. We'll be fine," she replied, and her smile was reassuring.

As I took my seat on the bus, I glanced back at my bedroom window. Drake's silhouette was there, a dark figure against the light. I smiled, knowing he could see me in detail even if my human eyes failed to do the same from this distance.

The ride to school was short but gave me enough time to revisit the recent events. Despite my belief that Oliver had nothing to do with the incident at the fair, I couldn't help but grow uneasy for our encounter.

Stepping off the bus, I scanned the table where they usually gathered. Oliver wasn't there, but Lily was. The moment she saw me, she jumped from Ben's lap and rushed over, just as the bell rang.

"Good morning," I said.

"Good morning. I didn't see you yesterday," she noted. " I tried your phone but got your voicemail."

"I wasn't feeling well, that's all," I lied, knowing the truth was far too risky to share. I had hoped to confide in her after the ritual, but things had become more complicated than I had anticipated. Involving her wasn't just madness; it was dangerous.

Ben joined us, walking closely next to Lily but absorbed in a text message as we made our way into the building.

"Good morning, Ben," I offered. He glanced my way and

returned the greeting, and I couldn't help but wonder why Oliver wasn't with him today.

"Was Oliver alright when he dropped you off Saturday?" Lily asked, and I stilled at the oddness of her question.

"Fine. Why?"

Lily shrugged. "Ben is worried. He's not answering his calls. He didn't show yesterday for class or practice and isn't here today either."

"You know him. Maybe he found another poor soul to torment," I joked, trying to brush away any rising concern. However, I couldn't control it. The doubt settled in the pit of my stomach. *What if he wasn't, okay?*

"That's what I said, but Ben thinks he's been acting strange lately."

"No comment. He's always been weird to me," I teased, trying to act as naturally as I could around them.

As my English Literature class concluded, I was torn between relief that Oliver hadn't shown and concern that something terrible might have happened to him. He wasn't my problem, but the thought always crept back into my mind.

The rest of the day dragged, my thoughts spiraling in circles. It was only the memory of a pair of hypnotic grey eyes that kept me tethered to reality as I watched the clocks.

When the final bell rang, I was the first on the bus, eager to escape.

MY EXCITEMENT CRUMBLED when Celest's car was absent from the driveway but then I realized she had perhaps gone to work, which left me wondering what had been of Drake. What he had done to occupy his time.

I froze on the steps as the front door swung open. Drake leaned casually against the frame, arms crossed before him, eyes fixed on me with a subtle hint of a smile playing on his lips.

"Those were the longest six hours of my existence. I guess my human side is yet to come to terms with the excess of time," he mused.

I smiled sheepishly, knowing it had nothing to do with his adjustment to humanity—or time, for that matter—because I had felt the same.

"You were not the only one tormented," I admitted, feeling his eyes roam over my face. He shifted, allowing me to pass, then closed the door behind us.

I hesitated by the stairs, the tension between us palpable yet neither of us made a move.

"Are you hungry?" I asked hesitantly, attempting to diffuse the simmering tension, but he didn't move, only his eyes darkened.

"Innocence be damned, I will burn!" he declared, blurring before me. I blinked, and suddenly he was pinning me against the wall, trapping me with his body. My bag strap slid down my shoulder and dropped to the floor. His nose skimmed over the skin of my neck, breathing me. I held my breath as he inched closer, his lips now with a clear intent.

The measured movements of his mouth against mine stirred strange things within me. He moved painstakingly slow, teasing and probing, pressing his body tightly against mine. I gasped in surprise as he lifted me effortlessly, my legs instinctively wrapping around him. His lips continued their slow assault.

Time ceased to exist. My surroundings dissolved. I only became aware again when the soft cushion of the couch met my back. His weight braced over mine, his lips trailing down the side of my neck. This time, I didn't mind his ability to see my thoughts; he was all I could think about. His touch—his kisses, burned away all my inhibitions.

"Drake..." I whispered, worshipping his name on a breathless sigh.

"Ughrrr," he groaned, pulling back abruptly. He sat at the edge of the sofa, arms braced against his knees, avoiding by gaze. "It won't happen again," he stated, with finality.

"Are you the only one who gets a say in this?" I challenged, sitting up with a frown.

He turned his head, his eyes pinning me. "Yes, seeing as you lack common sense when it comes to your safety." My frown deepened.

"You would never hurt me," I insisted.

Slowly, his eyes became lighter, his gaze softening. "I would forfeit my life before yours. But there are many ways I could hurt you without taking your life."

"You wouldn't," I pressed, staring into his eyes. "I know you wouldn't," I added. He bit his lip, shaking his head as his eyes shifted to the ceiling, before returning to me.

"Does your offer for a meal still stand?" he asked, and I knew he was only attempting to divert the conversation.

I nodded slowly. "Come. I'll make us something." I chose not to push him further. Drake remained an enigma to me, and perhaps he was right about my senselessness. If I were sensible, I'd heed his warnings—or at least, take them into consideration.

DRAKE

The human world cradled me—the symphony of subtle sounds the only distraction against the measured course of time. Every space in this home, every item, I memorized. Along every line, of every book, and yet, I found the most comfort in her space. Her chamber became my sanctuary, the place where her scent lingered uninhibited. Laying on her bed, I allowed my eyes to close. Isabel's essence—now Belynda's essence—assaulted my body.

My muscles coiled in response, my mind transporting me to long-forgotten memories of my time with Isabel, memories I had suppressed to survive the shadows. Images of Isabel's pale complexion danced in my mind, mingling with thoughts of her body, her touch—a silhouette of comfort I had long forgotten. Every pore in my body remembered what she had felt like, and though a part of me mourned her memory, our time together, my love for her felt rekindled in the face of the mortal girl. *Belynda...* Her name flowed in my mind, like remnants of a spell woven to trap me. Isabel's binding, assumingly, and despite my reservations, I felt drawn to accept this fate—to be destined for her, even if I refused to claim her.

Staring up at the canopy of her bed, I debated my options. Returning to my home in Druleska seemed the most viable solution, yet I couldn't bring myself to consider it. Abandoning her was out of the question, and I didn't know what it would take to open a portal to the Fire Realm.

I sat on her bed and opened the drawer on her night table. Her journal sat there, beckoning me, and I took it without hesitation. I smiled at her peculiar ink strokes, yet found warring emotions as I read through her notes—sadness, curiosity, and something I dared not admit even to myself—as I watched my name scrawled neatly in her last entry.

By the fates, I want her. Closing the journal and returning it to its place. This savage need to claim someone had never been so strong. Not with Isabel, or with any other that had graced my bed before, in my long immortal existence. Forsaking my humanity and emotions had a price, and I knew this was the cost. The beast had been denied for too long, and remaining human, gentleman enough, required a herculean effort when all I craved was to shred the clothes from her flesh. To watch her porcelain skin blush under my belt, her knees raw before me. Her soft lips around me, her bright green eyes peering up, begging for mercy.

I shook my head, trying to dispel the images I had conjured. So lost in them, I completely missed the tires screeching on the road. In a flash, I was downstairs, attempting to steady my breathing and listen for hers. The sound of the engine faded, and only the thumping of her heart remained, accelerating with each of her steps.

I OPENED THE DOOR, leaning against the frame. The moment her eyes found me, she smiled, and I crossed my hands before me, struggling to contain myself, to thwart the maddening desire to close the distance, take her over my shoulder, and devour every shred of innocence she possessed.

"Those were the longest six hours of my existence. I guess my human side is yet to come to terms with the excess of time," I voiced, and she smiled, a subtle shade of crimson rushing to her cheeks.

"You were not the only one tormented," she confessed. Her admission did little to placate the clawing needs of the beast within me. On the contrary, knowing she was as eager to see me as I was to see her brought me to the edge of my control.

I let her pass, her pure scent assaulting me as I closed the door behind her. I turned, watching her brace her hand on the stair rail, her eyes drawing me in, a silent spell. Fates help me, I wanted to lose myself in her, to claim her in any way possible.

"Are you hungry?" she asked, and the last shreds of my resolve wavered. *Yes*—the monster and the human in me were starving, but not for food.

"Innocence be damned, I will burn!" I roared, closing the distance before she could take a breath. Her body yielded under my touch, her delicate curves fitting perfectly against me as I secured her against the wall. My nose skimmed down the smooth skin of her neck, her scent feeding the shadows, the hunger, and I was lost the moment my eyes fell on her parted lips.

My senses became lost to the shadows. Pressing into her, I claimed her mouth as my own and her touch as my salvation. My hands cupped her behind, pulling her, lifting her as I pressed into her, her legs wrapping around me. She wanted this, and who was I to deny her? The shadows cooed as I laid her down beneath me, pressing into her, reveling in the high of her touch. My tongue branded the skin of her neck, committing every pore of her body to memory.

My name rolled from her lips on a breath, and it stilled the shadows, restoring a semblance of control.

"Ughrrr," I pulled away with reluctance, attempting to reign in the impulses. I avoided her eyes, which I could feel burning into me. "It won't happen again," I stated, unsure if I was trying to convince myself or her.

"Are you the only one who has a say in this?" Her voice was steady. She was angry, and I confirmed it when I glanced at her. A visible frown marred her brow. She had no idea what she was asking for or how enticing she was without even trying.

"Yes, it seems you lack common sense when it comes to your safety." Her frown deepened.

"You would never hurt me," her words were soft, gentle even, and yet they had the opposite effect on the fire coursing through my veins. A warring need to protect her and devour her in the same breath.

"I would forfeit my life before yours," I declared, knowing the words to be true. "But there are many ways I could hurt you without taking your life," I warned, afraid that if she didn't resist me, if she didn't fight for her innocence, soon it would be lost.

"You wouldn't," she pressed, staring into my eyes. "I know you wouldn't." I bit my lip to stop myself from cursing and shifted my eyes to the ceiling, praying for strength. By the fates, she had no idea how wrong she was. She was clueless to the fire burning in my veins. How I willed my immortal body to remain stone before her presence, instead of unleashing the monster and fucking her senseless. I shook my head to dispel the thought, seeking any form of distraction from the burning desire coursing through me.

"Does your offer for a meal still stand?" I asked, trying to shift the conversation, to put distance between us and clear my senses.

Her eyes told me she knew exactly what I had done, and yet, she didn't press me, something I was thankful for.

"Come, I'll make us something," she agreed, and I watched her silently as she rose to her feet.

"I'll join you in a moment," I said, and her eyes hesitated over my face, a silent attempt to make sense of the man before her, but it was useless. Not when I barely recognized myself.

I LISTENED KEENLY to every move she made in the kitchen, every breath and sigh beckoning me, yet I couldn't bring myself to move from my spot. What I needed was to take to the skies, to unleash my fire in the only way that wouldn't involve taking what I most desired—*her*.

"Dinner is ready," her soft voice called, startling me. Too preoccupied with my beastly needs, I had blocked out my senses and completely missed her approach. I rose to my feet and held her eyes, every step carrying me closer to her. Her fragile mortal body stood at the end of the hall, her face impatient, her eyes filled with a million questions I likely would never get to answer.

"Is everything okay?" she asked, her gaze holding mine with unwavering bravery.

"It is," I reassured her with a smile, even if my insides were clawing to break free, begging me to take her and satiate this fire—this hunger—one way or another.

SHE SAT BESIDE ME, and I focused on the food before me, forcefully shutting off my senses in an attempt to ease the flames coursing under my skin. I permitted myself one glance at her, albeit briefly, engraving in my mind the delicate tilt of her neck, her rosy cheekbones, the silky lock of her hair tucked behind her ear, the delicate movements of her lips as they parted. She was a goddess, and I ached to immortalize her in this very moment. To preserve this vision of purity and goodness because it was fragile, and it hung precariously by a threat whenever she was near me.

"Did you enjoy your steak?" she asked, distracting me. Our eyes met briefly, and I nodded.

"Exquisite," I said, my eyes trailing the movement of her napkin as she brushed it over her lips. *Damn the fates!*

"How about some ice cream?" she asked. I paused, unsure about consuming anything with the word ice in it, but smiled courteously, nonetheless.

"Ice and fire are not complementary," I offered, allowing her to draw her own conclusions.

"Ice can hurt you?" she asked, horror on her face.

"I never said it could, but I prefer to avoid it," I explained. "It makes my element restless."

"Then, no ice cream for you," she said. "Do you mind if I have some?" she asked, as if I would deny her anything in this moment.

"There is no need to ask," I granted. She hesitated but then left her seat. After rummaging through the icebox and kitchen compartments, she settled on the counter before me with a bowl and spoon in hand.

"It's strawberry," she declared, taking a dollop, and depositing it in her bowl. "It's my favorite," she added, and I smiled, picking up the familiar yet different scent like the shampoo bottles in her bathroom.

"I can tell," I replied, watching her with keen interest. She dipped her spoon and brought it to her mouth. Her tongue darted out, tasting the creamy stuff, and my cock twitched in my pants. *Hell, and damnation*, I was going to burn, and she with me. I covered my mouth with my fingers, trying not to close the distance and lick the cream from her lips. I watched her savor the damn thing. Never in my immortal existence had I experienced such a stimulating response from watching someone eat.

"What?" she questioned; her eyes bemused.

"You could say I'm intrigued," I spoke, and her smile grew. She dipped the spoon once more and extended it in my direction. I met her gaze, and her brow rose, daring me to taste it. Drops melted onto the counter. I smiled, leaning in, holding her wrist with my hand. Her pupils dilated as I closed my lips around the spoon. The ice cream melted in my mouth. The coldness, sweetness, and texture were an experience.

"Mhhh," I murmured, holding her gaze. She swallowed nervously. She was aroused; I could see it in the flush of her skin, taste it in her scent. In that second, I saw my hand around her delicate neck, my tongue exploring the valley of her breasts, peeling her out of those tempting tight pants she often wore.

"Drake…" she spoke, her quiet voice pulling me out of my thoughts. I sucked in a breath, hating myself for allowing my mind to be so weak. I released her wrist and stood up.

"I'll be back later. Before training."

"Wait!" she called, and I paused. "Tell me where you always run off to at least," she asked with curiosity.

"To the mountains," I allowed, "where I can be free and keep myself concealed from human eyes." It wasn't the guardianship rules I cared to uphold, but I understood why the need for secrecy was important; mortals were not ready to learn about us.

I excused myself, ignoring the million questions written on her expression, and extricated myself from her presence.

THE WIND SHRIEKED, whooshing against the expanse of the beast's wings the deep mountains containing its shadows. As the sun began to set, I knew it was time to return. Both the human and monster within me were tempted, lured, and eager to be near her, but at least we did so with a better grip on reason.

Belynda and Celest conversed quietly in the kitchen. I hesitated as I slipped through the attic window.

"Is he upset?" The old woman asked, and her question was followed by a long pause. I stopped at the top of the stairs, unsure whether to interrupt.

"Aren't we all?" Belynda spoke, and I stilled, waiting to hear more. "We all have demons to face. I sense Drake's biggest battle is with himself," she added. The mortal witch was more perceptive than I had thought. She wasn't wrong.

Quietly, I descended the stairs, feeling uncomfortable prying.

"If I have learned anything, it is that one cannot change what is written. Sometimes it is best to accept things for what they are and make the best of them," Celest added. I wondered if she would think the same if she knew I wanted to ravish the young woman standing before her, *her protege*. I cleared my throat, announcing my return, and their backs stiffened. I smiled, attempting to ease their discomfort.

"Are you ready to go?" I asked, still unsettled by the idea of Belynda fighting.

BELYNDA

Dark clouds blanketed the night sky, and the cold air cut through our jackets like knives. Drake, of course, remained toasty warm and unaffected. As we reached the denser part of the woods, he released my hand and summoned a ball of fire, molding it effortlessly in his palm like a torch.

My heart sank. I had failed to control fire, and trying again filled me with dread.

"We're deep enough here," Drake said as we stepped into a small clearing. Like before, he gathered a few dry branches and lit them—the fire, casting a dancing glow of light.

"Belynda, you should give fire a try again." Celest urged; she took a few steps away from me in the process.

"No." Drake's commanding voice pierced the silence. "She should try another element. Perhaps one you feel more connected to," he added, glancing my way.

His motives were clear. He didn't want me to feel discouraged if I failed again. Bending air had been easy enough, but fire remained a challenge. I could feel it and I was certain he could too.

"I think I'll try earth first," I said, looking at Celest. She nodded reassuringly.

"Just relax, close your eyes, picture the element, and command it," Drake instructed, gathering a fistful of dirt from the ground, and blowing it into the air. "You can do it." He stepped back to stand beside Celest.

"Okay. Here goes nothing." I closed my eyes, took a deep breath, and felt my body relax as the fresh air filled my lungs. The cold numbed me but helped clear my mind. I pictured the dirt particles moving beneath my feet, separating, and shifting. My eyes fluttered open as my body began to tremble. At least, I thought it was my body until I saw the earth breaking before my feet.

"I did it!" I shrieked.

"I had no doubt, Belynda. You are more powerful than you imagine," Celest praised.

Drake remained silent, but his eyes, and the subtle hint at a smile, told me he was pleased. Proud, even.

"Now reverse it," Drake directed.

This time, I wasn't afraid. I knew what I had to do. Without hesitation, I closed my eyes and visualized the earth coming to rest and joining together. I felt the vibration, but I didn't open my eyes this time and instead waited until there was only calm surrounding me. When I opened them, I was greeted by Drake's heart-stopping smile and an ecstatic look on Celest's face.

"I think your abilities are an understatement," Celest said.

"I have to agree. I've never seen anyone take control or summon an element as effortlessly as you have," Drake added.

"Water could be a challenge, though, and fire is still a problem," I said, frustration creeping into my voice.

"You'll be fine with water," Drake murmured.

"Why?" I questioned, but he avoided my eyes.

"Just a hunch," he added, and although there was a strange undercurrent to his tone, I didn't question it.

"But there's no water around here. Am I supposed to conjure it out of thin air?" I retorted.

Drake smiled. "There's no fire, yet I summon it," he pointed out, reminding us of how little we truly understood. "The elements are always around us. Just because you can't see them in their natural forms doesn't mean they're absent. Air isn't just the wind; it could be your breath. Earth isn't just the ground; it's also trees and rocks. Fire exists as body heat and lightning."

I had always thought Drake's warmth was a *dragon* thing, but now I realized it might be his ability to control fire. *Fascinating.*

"How do you think these trees grow? There's water beneath it all. You also have rain. You can command the element forward, and believe me, if you have control, the element will yield to you no matter what."

Could it be that simple?

"Water it is then..." I moved away from them, hoping Drake's hunch was right, and I was able to bend water. As my body relaxed, I stretched my arms out, palms down, and imagined water erupting from the ground, forming flowing strings rising from the forest floor.

"She's incredible," Celest whispered, her words prompting me to open my eyes. I gasped as multiple ribbons of water wove an intricate maze around me. I willed the water to circle Drake and Celest, my smile growing at the sight. Satisfied, I visualized the water returning to where it had sprouted, watching it creep back into the earth.

"That was surprisingly easier," I said, with a frown, as I still felt the strange tingling in my body at the elements magic.

"How so?" Drake asked, a darkening spark of curiosity in his eyes.

"It's hard to explain. It felt more natural, effortless, familiar," I frowned, unsure if my explanation made sense. "Even now, I can still feel its power." I added, staring at my hands, which looked completely normal to the naked eye, but felt electrified somehow.

"I see," Drake said, his gaze shifting past me, lost in thought. "Can you try changing the element's form?" Drake asked, and I frowned unsure what he meant.

"How?" I looked at him for guidance.

"Turn water into ice," Drake replied, and I frowned.

"Ok." I said, feeling nervous once again.

As the ripples of water resurged from the earth, I visualized it transforming, solidifying, but it didn't change. I glanced at Drake and shook my head. "I don't think I can."

"Try again, this time touch the water." Drake urged.

I did as he asked, I bent down, and dipped my fingers in the small sprout coming from the ground. I closed my eyes, feeling the cold on my fingertips, imagining the element transforming.

When I opened my eyes, the sprout of water had frozen,

forming an umbrella of ice, that looked like a magical mushroom close to the ground. I smiled and looked up at Drake and Celest.

"I wish Seymor could see this. You're beyond all our expectations. Your father will have to renounce his seat, whether he likes it or not. The time has come for the guardianship's power to dissolve."

"Do you think it will be that easy?" I questioned, failing to hide my skepticism.

"I pray to the fates that it is. Many members agree it's time for him to step down. The rest are just followers, too scared to confront his tyranny. But if he bends, they all will."

"Do not be fooled, he will *not* bend." Drake interrupted. "Men like him will fight or die. He hasn't risen to his position by yielding. He will step down the day his soul turns to ashes, and I will make sure that it does if he refuses to remove himself willingly." Drake's words hissed through the air.

The shiver that crept down my spine had nothing to do with the cold, or Drake's threat to end my father's life. While Celest's optimism had given me hope, Drake's words sparked the fear slowly growing inside of me. Irrationally, I worried mostly about Drake. I refused to imagine a life without him.

"There is always that possibility," Celest added. "But I feel strongly that Belynda's power will take Stephen by surprise. That will be the chance we need to make him bend if he doesn't do it willingly."

"You're both forgetting that I'm not ready, not yet. I'm still unable to bend fire."

"Perhaps you weren't ready before. Try again," Celest urged.

I glanced at Drake, unsure. His silence was the only encouragement I knew I would get. Celest stepped back, but Drake remained still. Closing my eyes, I visualized the heat within my body—a challenging task given the cold. I took deep, soothing breaths, picturing a bright flame moving within me. Extending my hand, I willed that flame to materialize in my palm. I wished it with all my being, but when I opened my eyes, the disappointment on Celest's face was my confirmation: I had failed once again.

"What am I doing wrong?" I asked, frustration tainting my voice. "I'm doing the same as I did when calling the other elements."

Drake walked closer; his expression calm yet intense. "Why are you so concerned over this? You've surpassed everyone's expectations. You don't need to control fire; you have me."

"You might be right," Celest added, her eyes distant as if she were seeing something we couldn't. "Maybe that's why the fates brought you together."

Drake looked down at me, considering her words.

"No one has ever controlled more than one element. The fact that you can command three is more power than the fates have ever allowed a mortal or immortal to possess. They've never entrusted that much to one individual. It makes sense that they brought you two together: he completes you, and maybe he's the reason you can't bend fire," Celest added, her words a theory, but they lessened my disappointment at failing to bend fire.

"Could that be possible?" I searched Drake's eyes, waiting

for confirmation. He knew more about the fates and the realms than either of us.

"Is possible. When the Fates are involved, nothing is certain. They are dark and twisted. They always get what they want, but the path is never straightforward. But she's right," he said, glancing at Celest. "They would never grant so much power to one person, not without a reason."

"They have a reason," Celest offered. "If they're behind this prophecy as Isabel says, then I understand why they'd make an exception. The fates want you to succeed, but they won't allow you absolute control of all the elements." She looked at Drake, then back at me. "In a way, they're providing you with access to all the elements without giving you full command over them."

"Why would they do that? What would they have to lose? They could strip me of my powers at any moment if they wished," I asked.

"I'm sure it doesn't work like that," Celest replied.

"They could," Drake corrected, "But they won't, as long as you serve their purpose."

I realized we only had theories about why I couldn't yield the fourth element, but that was fine because I had Drake.

"So, if I'm unable to bend fire, I guess my training is over?"

"It means you've proven you can bend water, air, and earth, but you still need to practice," Celest said.

"Drake, could Isabel bend the elements?"

"She could only bend earth," Drake confirmed.

"Then where do my powers come from if not from the bond we share?" I asked, glancing between Celest and Drake. The look on their faces confirmed my suspicion: no one knew.

"The fates are a complicated lot. They ensure the wheels of life turn in all realms. You were given these gifts because your life is already mapped out; you have what you need to fulfill the path they set for you. Nothing with destiny ever makes sense. Even when we think we have free will, the wheel always turns. It comes at you without reason or cause, but they are always behind it," Drake explained.

"You're right. That makes absolutely *no sense*. I don't see any choice here. The fates toy with us like we're pawns in their game."

"We believe their plans are greater than that. They don't meddle in our lives for fun; there's always a purpose, usually for the greater good, even if the road seems sick and twisted or ends badly for some of us," Drake added.

"Yes, sick and twisted indeed. What about your fate, being sent to Xelraa? What about Isabel's fate? We both know how hers ended—the ultimate sacrifice."

Drake's expression darkened, and I hated myself for the harshness of my words.

"Whatever their plan is, it brought me here with you," he concluded. I couldn't argue with that. I was grateful, even if part of me wondered how long the fates intended us to stay together. If Celest was right, and Drake completed me for a greater plan foreseen by the fates, what would happen when we fulfilled that purpose, and they no longer needed us? Could they sabotage our union in a heartbeat? After all, they controlled our destiny.

I wanted to cry in frustration, but my anger kept the walls firm and my tears in check. Isabel's fate made me wonder if one of us would face the same sacrifice in the future to fulfill the fates' plan.

The walk home was eerily quiet. Thoughts of the fates wouldn't leave my mind, and I had to put an end to them. I couldn't live in fear. My time with Drake was now, and I chose not to waste it. Jogging a few steps to catch up with him, I took his hand. He squeezed mine gently in return.

"Are you okay?" he asked, his eyes peering down at me.

"I will be," I admitted, walking beside him.

"Understanding our world can be overwhelming."

"Yes—yes, it can," I admitted, and he pulled me closer, draping an arm over my shoulder.

"We should pick up the pace; rain is coming," Drake said, tilting his face to the night skies. His eyes searching the clouds.

"You forget I'm particularly good at bending water," I offered. Drake's eyes shifted to me, a deep furrow on his brow.

I reached for his hand, feeling the warmth of his skin against mine. "What's wrong?"

He shook his head, his expression distant. "Nothing. Nothing at all."

But the way he said it made me feel like there was so much more he wasn't telling me.

13
DARKNESS AND LIGHT

WE REACHED THE HOUSE, drenched to the bone. The forewarning of the impending rain and my still-developing ability to command the element was not enough to prevent it from reaching us faster than expected. Although being caught under the pouring rain with Drake had its benefits, I thought as I nestled deeper under the covers of my bed.

The water pipes shrieked, signaling that Drake was done, and I trembled under my sheets, wondering if he would come. A soft knock at my door made my heart race. I sat up in bed, clutching the covers to my chest.

"Come in," I called. The door opened a fraction, and Drake peered in before pushing it open the rest of the way. My eyes betrayed me, roaming over his naked torso as he stood there, still toweling his damp hair, a frown on his face.

"You showered quickly," I noted, my teeth chattering.

"Not quickly enough. I could hear you shivering over the

running water." His lips moved in explanation, but I was momentarily distracted by the drops of water that fell from his hair and traveled over his chest.

"Have you come to offer your help?" I asked, and he lowered the towel from his hair, letting it drop to the floor. He turned around and closed the door behind him. I thought he was going to leave, but instead, he walked to the foot of the bed. My eyes followed, appreciating the ripple of his muscles. The pajama pants—courtesy of Celest—fit him perfectly, hanging dangerously low on his waist.

"Move over," he said, crawling onto the bed. My god, he looked so sexy, I almost forgot how to breathe. He lifted the covers and slipped under the sheets beside me. He didn't touch me or made a move to pull me closer. He simply lay on his side, his head on the pillow, his eyes regarding me in silence. The heat that emanated from him was like oxygen for a drowning sailor.

"You have no idea how incredibly good this feels," I whispered, every inch of my body aware of his presence.

"I'm glad I get to please you in some way," he replied, his voice like a smooth caress that prickled my skin.

"Surely, there are endless ways you could please me," I teased, provoking his shadows completely aware of the dangers, and yet, my mind and body refused to take heed.

His eyes changed, darkening. "Certainly," he replied, his lips drawing my gaze.

I imagined the sensation of running my fingers down his shoulders, recalling the day at the barn, my exploring fingers over his skin. As my shivers subsided, a fluttering sensation grew in my stomach, traveling lower between my thighs. The corner of his mouth shifted, and I closed my eyes, attempting to quell the blush creeping on my cheeks.

When I opened them again, his grey eyes were locked on mine, the distance between us becoming unbearable.

"Why are you looking at me like that?" I whispered, as if my words could draw him closer.

"How exactly am I looking at you?" he teased, smiling.

"Your eyes are lighter," I pointed out. "They seem to shine whenever you're having wicked thoughts," I admitted sheepishly, humoring him.

A heart-stopping grin spread across his lips as he lifted his head from the pillow and leaned closer, pressing his lips to mine. Warmth and tingling sensations lingered even after he pulled away.

"Wicked thoughts indeed, but I'll settle for keeping you warm," he conceded, his gaze still holding mine.

"Do you promise not to disappear if I touch you?" I asked.

My gaze traced the subtle arch of his brow. "I do it for your sake," he whispered.

"Yes, you've said as much," I replied. His eyes roamed my face, and his lips parted to respond, but I saw how much effort it took to deny my request. So, I did what I wanted. I reached forward, feeling the smooth skin of his face. He was so beautiful, it hurt to imagine my life without him. I committed every detail to memory, seeing him anew, as if for the first time, or perhaps truly appreciating his perfection for the first time.

My fingers trailed across his lips, feeling their fullness and softness, exploring the sharp angle of his jaw. He closed his eyes, seeming to enjoy the journey of my touch across his skin.

"Can we stay here like this, forever?" I ventured, uncertain but hopeful.

Drake held my gaze, his eyes echoing my own longing and resignation. He shifted, slipping his arm under my head, and pulling me close to his chest.

"We can. At least for tonight," he murmured, pressing a kiss to the top of my head. I stilled in his arms, my hand resting over the exposed muscles of his stomach. His body tensed slightly, mirroring my own, but neither of us moved. I knew if I followed my impulses as before, he might leave, and I was too content in his arms to risk it. So, I focused on my breathing, and as my body relaxed, so did his.

Drake held me in silence, both of us aware that forever was an illusion—especially with the menace of the guardians looming over us, the abyss of his immortality and my fragile humanity, not to mention the unpredictable plans of the fates. I succumbed to sleep in his arms, the weight of that realization heavy on my mind. Time, it seemed, was our greatest enemy.

TYRUS

Pulling twenty-four-hour shifts for Mr. Radcliff was out of the ordinary. I had grown accustomed to his summons at ungodly hours, but this... I didn't know what to make of it. Leading his security team and managing business affairs was one thing; realizing the depths of his corruption, knowing I was complicit, was another. I surveilled the hideout of the lowlife who had assaulted that girl at the fair and cringed. I had done many things for Mr. Radcliff that I wasn't proud of, but that had been the hardest to stomach. Thoughts of my daughter, just a few years younger, made it even more difficult.

Extinguishing my cigarette with a pinch of my thumb and forefinger, I felt the exhaustion of the nearly dawn hour weigh on me. There was no movement inside the cottage, but I knew he was there. It had taken my team three days to track him down after he disappeared without reporting back to me. My orders had been clear: gather information and report.

The look on the man's face as I kicked the door down was priceless. He was drunk with sleep and spirits, an empty bottle lying beside his bed. He cowered in a corner, hands raised defensively.

"I've done nothing, Tyrus. I don't want any trouble."

The coward. He had the nerve to assault a girl but not to face me. I wanted to pound his face, but my guilty conscience reminded me I was as complicit as he was.

"I just want to talk. That's all. Take a seat," I said, motioning to a chair. He shakily complied, a far cry from the man I had hired just days ago.

"Why didn't you report back to me Saturday evening as agreed? I need to know what the girl said."

"Look, I don't know what kind of government experiment you guys are involved with, but I don't want any trouble. All I know is that I've never seen anything like it. That guy was not human."

I stared at the fidgeting mess before me, genuinely intrigued for the first time.

"What guy are you talking about, Hugh? Did you see the girl?"

"Oh, I saw the girl, alright. She said nothing. I couldn't get her to talk because he came out of nowhere. He was fast—really fast. He grabbed me by the neck like I was nothing more than a rag-doll. I tell you... I've never seen anything like it. There was something off about him. Something not right."

Just when I thought things couldn't get more complicated.

Leaving the sorry excuse of a man behind, I exited the cottage. Normally, I would have warned against sharing our business, but this time it wasn't necessary. The man looked like he wanted the earth to swallow him whole. Whatever he had witnessed had clearly shaken him enough, to leave him in such a state. While I wasn't sure how Mr. Radcliff would react to this development, I sensed he would be in one of his moods upon learning that someone—or something—was protecting the Hershton girl.

I drove down the pathway to the Radcliff residence, dreading every second. Entering quietly through the back door where the staff were having breakfast, I wasted no time with formalities.

"Is Mr. Radcliff awake?" I asked.

"Yes, Sir. He's in his office. I'll inform him you're here immediately."

"No need. I know the way. Thank you."

The staff member seemed ready to object, but I ignored him, striding down the corridor toward the devil's domain and knocking forcefully on the oversized mahogany doors.

"Come in," his gruff voice instructed. I took a deep breath before entering.

"Mr. Radcliff, Sir. I apologize for the early hour," I said respectfully, though he cared little for sensible hours, especially when it came to business.

"Out with it. I've been waiting for a report since Saturday, and you know I'm not a very patient man."

No, he certainly wasn't. Lately, I wondered if he even possessed a soul.

"I spoke with Hugh personally. I'm afraid he couldn't extract any information from the girl, but we may have encountered another complication."

His eyes abandoned the newspaper he was reading, focusing intently on me.

"I'm listening."

"Hugh mentioned the girl wasn't alone, Sir."

"What exactly is the problem? I thought you said he could handle himself?"

"He believes the man he encountered wasn't human, Sir," I admitted, sounding almost incredulous saying it aloud. Yet, with Mr. Radcliff and his cult, and the young ones he called elementals, I had witnessed enough unexplainable things to know there was more to the world than met the eye. Under the circumstances, I felt emboldened to voice it, despite sounding somewhat unhinged.

"Sir, I've never seen a man more terrified. He said he'd never witnessed anything like it."

"An immortal?" he murmured, barely audible. For the first time in the years I had worked for Radcliff, a shadow of concern clouded his expression.

"Sir, are you alright?" I asked, pulling him from his reverie.

"Tell me everything."

"He said he tried to interrogate the Hershton girl, but a man appeared out of nowhere—unbelievably fast and strong. He held Hugh off the ground by his neck like a feather."

"I see," he muttered, deep in thought. "Do you think Hugh will talk?"

"He won't be a problem, Sir. But what about this... situation?"

"Undoubtedly," he replied.

"Do we know who he is, Sir?"

"Actually, the question isn't who, but what he is."

I stared at Radcliff, struggling for words.

"Our generation has never faced such a challenge, but we've always known it was a possibility with the high magic we've encountered. Now we have confirmation." His eyes met mine. "If an immortal creature has entered our realm, we must find it, determine what it is, and return it to its place of origin."

Mr. Radcliff was into some scary weird stuff, but never had I confronted a problem like this. I had two options: embrace the madness or run. The latter didn't suit my nature.

"Sir, I must admit this is beyond my expertise, but I will ensure my team remains vigilant and informed. I'll also set a permanent surveillance on the Hershton house in case he reappears."

"That's a start. But I'm starting to think this could work in our favor."

"Sir?" I asked cautiously. Was he losing his mind?

"This is the evidence we needed to convene the council. Once they learn of this breach and that an immortal is protecting them, they will have no choice but to support my decision to bring in Celest, and perhaps even the girl."

"Sir, with all due respect, I doubt they'll approve of Hugh and the circumstances that led to his encounter with the immortal."

"Do you question my competence?"

"No, Sir. I didn't mean—"

"The council only needs to know of our encounter with the immortal. No need for specifics. Once Celest and the girl are in our control, it will be their word against ours. Given the unprecedented threat, my actions will appear reasonable."

Was he deluded by his own supposed wisdom?

"Sir. If there is nothing else, I'll inform my team."

"Leave. Arrange for the council's emergency meeting this afternoon."

"Yes, Sir." I left the devil's office, each step feeling like it pulled me deeper into his web. I tried to push aside the guilt, reminding myself that this was just a job. I didn't know enough about the supernatural world to question his motives.

BELYNDA

A pleasant scent and warmth surrounded me as I stirred in bed. My eyes adjusted slowly to the soft fragments of light peering through the open curtains. I turned over and was startled by Drake's piercing silver eyes.

"Hey," I said, pleased to see that he had stayed.

"Hey," he replied with a grin. How was it possible that he could look this breathtaking even upon waking?

He reached out, his fingers brushing some of my hair behind my ear. I grimaced, knowing I probably looked a fright compared to his unnatural, godly appearance.

"How do you do it?" I whispered.

"Do what?" His puzzled look made him even more charming.

"Look this good without effort." I explained, a grin widening across his lips. "It's inhuman."

"The one gift I'm blessed to have, I suppose," he teased. I reached out hesitantly, brushing my fingers along the line of his jaw, feeling the muscles tense under my touch.

"I'm glad you stayed," I admitted. He took my hand, kissed it, and then secured it against his chest.

"Did you sleep well?" he asked, his gaze holding mine.

"Better than I have in a long time," I offered truthfully. "Did you?"

"I seldom do," he replied, and I frowned. "Sleep is not important to my kind," he explained.

"You don't sleep?" I shifted onto my elbows, watching him with curiosity. A million questions sprang to my mind.

"I do," he amended. "It makes it easier for me to hone in on my element, but it's not necessary. Not the way it is for humans or other immortals."

He was so unbelievable. "When will you ever cease to amaze me?" I questioned, realizing that he and his world were still a great mystery to me.

"Never," he leaned in and placed a soft kiss against my lips. "I can't reveal all my secrets now, can I?" His breath fanned my face. He was devastatingly irresistible.

"You seem more in control this morning," I noted, attempting to contain my smile. He surprised me by wrapping his arm around my waist and pulling me atop him.

"I'm trying," he spoke, his chest vibrating with his voice. "But it's not without effort." He shifted beneath me, my thigh brushing the stiffness just below the waistband of his pants, and I froze. "Exactly," he added, swiftly extricating himself from underneath me.

"Where are you going?" I protested as he reached for the door.

"My self-restraint needs another cold shower," the heart-stopping smile on his face doing strange things to me.

He closed the door behind him, and I fought the instinct to follow. What the heck was wrong with me? I groaned and buried my face in my pillow.

The time he spent in the shower was torturous. My mind burned with thoughts and images of him. Granted, I was inexperienced but not naïve enough to not understand my body and its needs. After all, I was eighteen years old with raging hormones. My fingers glided over the sensitive spot, pulsing between my legs. I imagined what he would look like—ripped, taut muscles glistening beneath the water, his strong hands, his fingers. I fantasized how they would feel over my skin.

The pipes shrieked, and I stilled, returning to my senses. I stared at my closed door, my heart beating wildly, matching the pulsing between my thighs. I groaned in frustration, realizing that with his enhanced senses, perhaps continuing wasn't wise.

The moment I heard him return to the guest room, I dashed into the bathroom and took his initiative, settling for a cold shower myself.

LIKE THE LAST TWO DAYS, Celest was up early. Over breakfast, we talked about continuing my training after dusk. Drake offered to teach me offense and defense tactics, and I was excited to learn more. I was also pleased to see him more relaxed about the idea, though I knew deep down, he was still worried.

The thought of spending even a minute away from him seemed unfathomable, let alone six hours, but returning to school was inevitable.

"Will you be okay?" I asked, pivoting to face him as we reached the front door.

He dipped his head, placing a swift kiss on my cheek. "I'll manage," he said, his breath fanning my skin as he smiled.

I lost myself in his eyes, wanting to confess that I would miss him, but I held my tongue. Our situation—the feelings forged between us—were complicated enough. It was too soon to speak of love, even if every pore in my body felt it, every thought, every beat of my heart recognized it when I looked at him.

SCHOOL—I grimaced as I stepped off the bus. It felt pointless. After losing a year when my mother died, I was the oldest in my class and already felt like an outcast. With so many more important things to worry about, school seemed trivial. I was graduating in a year, and I knew fractions and social studies wouldn't help me in my world. Nothing I learned here could prepare me to fight against the elementals and the guardianship.

Then there was the issue of Oliver. I didn't know what to expect from him, and his continued absence from school only unsettled me further. Despite telling myself I didn't care, the truth was that I did, especially after learning Oliver was my half-brother. Three days out of school was no coincidence; something was wrong. Lily was equally concerned about him, but I reminded myself there was nothing I could do.

The hours dragged by even more slowly than the previous days, and I knew it was because of my irrational need to see Drake.

TYRUS

The sleepless nights were starting to catch up with me as I waited outside the meeting chamber, straining to hear through the thick doors. Some of the louder voices carried through as Stephen broke the news of the breach and pushed for an immediate in-person summon. As expected, the usual members met his demand with reluctance. I recognized Seymor's voice; he had every right to question Stephen since his sister was the one being brought to trial. Sylvie and Ren backed him up, but the shocking news of facing an immortal creature swayed the rest of the council to side with Stephen's petition.

The doors to the antechamber opened, and in walked a somber-looking Oliver.

"I'm here to see my father." His tone suggested that whatever he had to say would only worsen Mr. Radcliff's mood.

"Kid, it's not a good time. He's meeting with the council, and he doesn't sound happy."

"Honestly, Tyrus, I don't care. I'm done with his bullshit." I walked away from the chamber slightly, hoping no one inside had heard. Oliver followed.

"Seriously, you need to relax. Whatever you plan to accomplish with this attitude? It's not going to work. You have a better chance when you've cooled off."

"He lied to me and went behind my back. He sent some scum to attack Belynda at the fair—I know he did." The kid had more morals than I gave him credit for; maybe I should take a page out of his book.

"And what exactly do you plan to gain by confronting him?" Surely, he knew there was no point. I did. It was the reason I was in this mess to begin with; the reason my conscience was heavy every time I closed my eyes, blurring the lines between right and wrong.

"I'm just tired of being his pawn. I'm ready to tell him he can shove his guardianship legacy. I don't care for it."

"Oliver, I don't always agree with your father's decisions, but how do you know he's wrong? Are you willing to put your hands in the fire for this girl? Can you honestly say she and Celest are innocent, and your father is at fault? He just got the council's vote for an in-person summons. They should be here in a few days."

"You know exactly what he's after. Can't you see he's just using them to find the manuscript? That damn book he's been obsessed with for years. He doesn't care about them or the rules. Power is his only goal—nothing else. He certainly doesn't give a damn about his own son, so..."

"I think it's more complicated than that. We've learned that an immortal creature breached our world when the portal was opened."

"What do you mean by an immortal creature?" I had hoped that, with his guardianship training, he could share more information about whatever this thing could be. But by the look on the boy's face, he was as clueless as I was.

"Something or someone, not human, protecting the girl."

Oliver paced in front of me, lost in thought.

"How do you know this exactly?"

There was no point in lying to him; he already knew his father had sent someone after the girl.

"All I can say is that whatever that thing is, it helped her."

"I take it you guys have this from the source. Further proof that my father is responsible for her attack. For fuck's sake, man. How could you stand and do nothing?"

I deserved that...

"I have no excuse. I'm just doing my job here and right now; I don't know who the villain is and who isn't. Can you blame me?"

"That's on your conscience, man. Whatever this immortal thing is, I'm glad it intervened and helped Belynda. I've known my father long enough to know he is rotten to the core. I've only had to listen to this girl for a few days to know she is no monster. Whatever she is, she doesn't deserve this. So, you tell me who the villain is."

Perhaps the boy was right. Heck, I knew deep down that he was, but I was trained not to ask questions. My position and rank came with a seal of top-secret discretion.

"Maybe you're right, but there's nothing either of us can do now. I think you should go home and take a shower. You're a mess. Did you even go to school today?"

"What's the point?"

"The point is that you don't want your principal calling your father—that should be reason enough. You don't want any more trouble for yourself, trust me. Go home and sleep on it. There is nothing you can gain by confronting your father. Just stay out of his way. That's what's best."

"You're right about one thing. There is no point. No one can make Stephen change."

He turned to leave but looked back before reaching the doors. "You know nothing good has ever been said about cowards."

With that, Oliver strolled out of the chamber, leaving me to mull over his words. I wasn't sure if he was referring to himself or me, but I certainly felt like a coward.

BELYNDA

To my disappointment, Drake wasn't waiting for me. Instead, I was greeted by Isabel's sword, her cup, and the sacred book resting atop the small table in the foyer.

Drake wasn't in the living room, kitchen, or office. Frowning, I took the stairs. The door at the end of the hall was wide open, but I discarded my bag in my room first, returning Isabel's belongings to the secret compartment before making my way to the guest room.

Drake stood before the window, fully dressed, hands in his pockets. He turned his head, his eyes finding mine.

"Hi," I said, stepping into his room.

"Hello," he replied, the corner of his mouth twisting into a grin, but he didn't make a move to close the distance.

"How was your day?" I asked, leaning awkwardly against his door.

"Uneventful," he offered. "Did you see him?" he asked, and I frowned.

"No. Oliver didn't show, and I'm beginning to worry," I admitted, and this time he took a step closer.

"You have problems of your own to worry about." His eyes held mine. "He isn't your concern," he added.

"I can't help myself," I allowed. Although I could tell he wanted to say more on the subject, he didn't. "Thank you for bringing back her things," I added, attempting to shift the subject.

"It was overdue," he replied, his head tilting slightly, while he ran his thumb over his bottom lip.

We stared at each other, neither one moving. My heart pounded fast in anticipation, silently willing him to close the distance, for I didn't have the courage to breach the space. Did he feel the currents of tension flowing between us? Or was I the only one hypnotized by him?

"What are you thinking?" he asked, surprising me, and I hesitated, unsure if I should offer the truth.

"I—I'm wondering if you can feel the energy?" I said, motioning with my hand between us.

"Why do you think I'm keeping my distance?" he said, the silver in his eyes darkening like clouds of a grey storm. "I smell your scent, taste your excitement." He whispered. "I see the way your pupils expand; I can hear your heart accelerate." I sucked in a breath.

"Are you going to kiss me?" The words left my lips on a breath.

"Kiss you?" He laughed out loud, the sound echoing against

the walls of the room. As his laughter died, his eyes darkened, and something shifted in my stomach as he closed the distance. His frame towered over me, pressing me against the door. His eyes pinned me as his fingers came to my mouth. His index and middle finger traced my bottom lip, and as they parted, he slipped them inside my mouth. I held his wrist, my eyes locking with his, and when my tongue moved around his fingers, he released a deep-rooted growl. He gripped the back of my head with his other hand, fisting my hair, forcing his fingers deeper into my mouth.

"The shadows seek more than your lips," he rasped, and my body reacted, arching into him.

I pulled on his wrist, removing his fingers from my mouth. "Let them take what they need, please," I whispered, my senses abandoning me, and for a moment, I saw myself reflected in the blackness of his eyes.

He claimed my mouth without warning. His lips were rough and unyielding, and I welcomed his fire. I gripped his shoulders, and his hands squeezed into my hips, lifting me slightly, pulling me against him, to feel the hardness straining between us. He was magnificent, wildly unhinged as he threw me on the bed, startling me. My eyes found his as he pinned me against the bed, securing both my wrists above my head with one of his hands while his lips moved with mine in an intoxicating rhythm of strokes and dips of his tongue.

He abandoned my mouth with a groan, and in the next breath, he was on his feet, putting distance between us. I watched him, breathless.

"You can't keep doing this," I protested. "We both want this. Please, stop punishing yourself and me." I pleaded, extending my hand to him. "Come back."

He smiled mischievously and closed the distance, leaned his fists on the mattress, and planted a chaste kiss on my lips.

"Your aunt is almost here. I'm more than glad to lay back and join you if you think she will approve."

I sat up on the bed in a second, frantically attempting to fix my hair. Drake leaned casually against the bedpost, clearly amused by my predicament.

"I don't think it's much use," he teased, watching me run my fingers desperately through my strands. He reached with his hand, tracing his thumb over my lips, before leaning close to my ear, his breath warming my skin. "Your lips are red and plumped. You can't hide the fact that you have been thoroughly kissed," he smirked, evidently pleased by this. "I think it's best if I go stretch my wings," he added, strolling to the window. I stood from the bed's edge and followed him. He jumped from the window effortlessly, and he turned to me, offering me a smile before disappearing from my sight.

I took in the afternoon breeze, and it served to cool down my body. Drake was overpowering and dangerous. With him, I never saw reason. Just as he had warned, a minute later, Celest's car turned up the driveway.

I SAT ON MY BED, the door slightly ajar, absorbed in finishing my homework when Celest's knock interrupted my focus. The concern etched on her face immediately set off alarms in my mind—my first thought jumped to Oliver.

"What's wrong?" I asked as she hesitated in the doorway, her expression grave.

"I just spoke with my brother," she began, glancing briefly

down the hall. "Where's Drake?" Her worried expression unsettled me.

"He's out stretching his wings. He often seeks freedom, especially after spending so much time in the shadows," I explained, offering insight into the Dragon prince's mind.

"That makes sense," she acknowledged and her understanding of his need for escape made me wonder how much she knew of his prison.

"Do you know much about Xelraa?" I asked, my curiosity piqued, after the sparse explanation Drake had offered.

Celest shook her head. "Not much. From what little I've gathered, it's not a place you escape without scars. It was forged at the same time as the other realms, but where the other ones thrived with life and light, Xelraa, served to contain darkness, shadows, and evil."

"Why create such a place?" I mused aloud, pondering the necessity for such a creation.

"I wish I knew," Celest admitted. "But magic thrives on balance. Light can't exist without darkness," she reflected wisely. Drake, I realized, embodied this balance—both shadow and light intertwined.

"I hope he's being careful not to expose himself," Celest added, "Not just to protect the guardian's secrecy, but because the world isn't ready for the truth," she added.

"He is," I assured her. "He knows," I added, recalling he had said the same not long ago. "Could you tell me what's happened?" I asked, and the somber look returned to her face.

"I'll explain everything over dinner," she replied, "I'll get started."

"I'll join you in a moment," I offered, watching her retreat from my doorway.

It was remarkable how much my relationship with Celest had transformed. Unlike before, I eagerly anticipated our time together. Her acceptance of Drake certainly eased things, but there was more to it now. With no more need for secrecy, she appeared different—more open, more loving. And she offered invaluable insights into the magical world that still eluded me.

"Will I get to learn about the realms?" I asked, intrigued.

"I think you should. If you hold the power to open the gates to these worlds, it seem prudent for you to understand them," she replied. Her words gave me something to consider that I hadn't thought of before. If we manage to ease tensions with the guardianship, would Drake consider leaving? Returning to his home? A knot formed in my stomach at the thought. Wanting to keep him here felt selfish, but I couldn't imagine letting him go. Although if the moment came and he wanted to leave, I would never deny him his happiness or his freedom.

DRAKE

The wind shifted from the north as I donned my clothes, the subtle change in the breeze pricking my senses with new scents—unfamiliar humans, and they were closer. I slipped on my shoes and streaked towards the Manor, dusk slipping into the blanket of night. Like a predator, I watched from a mile away as the men took post, undetected by the human eye but not by me. Contemplating my options, I entertained the idea of slipping behind them and snapping their necks before they even had a chance to blink. *Yes*, the monster agreed, but I knew better than to allow my shadows to make decisions in the mortal world.

My return to the house was stealthy. I streaked through the field and jumped onto the roof, probing at a second-floor window that faced the back of the Manor, and it yielded under the force of my hand.

Celest's voice rang clear. Though I still harbored objections over the woman's actions, I could no longer deny her affection for Belynda. The moment Belynda's eyes fell on me, her entire face lit up, and with it, my dark soul.

"Just in time," Celest said, "Dinner is ready."

I glanced between them, still debating whether to turn around and dispose of those men out there, but a small part of me urged me to reconsider and not take matters into my hands without consulting them.

"I'm afraid there won't be any training this evening," I offered, both sets of eyes turning to me at once. "There are men watching the house as we speak," I continued before they could argue.

"Stephen..." the old woman whispered. "He knows, and he's not wasting any time," she added.

"I can go back out there, make them disappear," I offered, a part of me hoping they would concede.

The old woman shook her head, and the look on Belynda's face told me she didn't agree either.

"The last thing we want is to give Stephen any more reasons to come after us."

"That hasn't stopped him before," I argued.

"I know, but what he doesn't need is more proof against us to present to the rest of the council," she explained. "My brother Seymor called today. An official summon has been made to all council members. He expects them to arrive within the next four nights."

"They know I'm here," I realized. There could be no other reason for the urgency.

"I'm afraid so. He doesn't know what you are or why you're here, but they know there was a breach."

"What does this mean for us?" Belynda asked, a worried look crossing her face. I burned to reach for her and assure her everything would be okay, but I wasn't as sure of that myself.

"It means Stephen is ready to ask for a vote to bring us in and employ any means the guardianship has to find him, at whatever cost."

"What if we give them something they want?" Belynda suggested, and I knew whatever it was she had in mind, I wouldn't like it.

BELYNDA

"We have nothing to offer them," Celest said, and I paused, realizing she didn't know I had the sacred book. I had never told her because I always assumed she knew I had used it to release Drake.

"We do," I said. "I have the book Stephen has been looking for," I added, and Celest stared at me with confusion. "I didn't just use my powers to bring him back," I explained. "I found the book, along with other belongings of Isabel," I confessed.

"How... where?" Celest was genuinely surprised, which told me she had nothing to do with how they got there to begin with.

"Hidden in my room, in the hollowed space beneath the windowsill. I found it by chance."

"Felsia..." Celest whispered.

"Do you think it was her who placed them there?" I had wondered the same myself.

"I don't know what to think anymore. It's possible, but I can't reason why she wouldn't have told me. Unless it was there even before her, and she had no idea." That was always a possibility.

"Do you mind bringing it down, please?" I asked, and Drake hesitated.

"Her belongings came to you because they were meant only for you. What you are considering is a bad idea."

He was probably right, but if I had any way of saving us from the guardianship, I would take that chance, even if giving up her things somehow felt like a betrayal of her sacrifice.

"Drake, please."

He gave me a long, pained look, and without another word, disappeared up the stairs in a blur, returning in a few seconds with the book in his hand. He placed it on the table before me, and I pushed it towards Celest before taking a seat myself.

"It might not be much, but perhaps..."

"This is priceless," Celest muttered, her fingers tracing the delicate pages. She glanced between Drake and me.

"He's right. You don't know Stephen like I do. This book will only give him the power he's always been after and serve as our sentence to burn." Celest paused, correcting herself. "Well, we would burn. As for Drake... I don't know. Perhaps it would give them the power they need to send him back."

"No!" I jutted away from the table. "That's not an option."

"You're right, it's not," Drake said, taking my hand. "And you burning or giving him that book is not an option either."

"Then what do we do? Sit and wait?" The impotence was driving me mad.

"How long do we have?" Drake added, too calm and collected for my liking. I sensed that a storm was brewing inside him, just beneath the surface.

"Stephen needs to wait for all members to arrive and deliberate before making a decision. Seymor has assured me that at least two other members will delay their arrival as much as possible. If all goes according to plan, that should give us a few more days—or at least a week—to work on Belynda's training."

Drake laughed, but there was no humor behind it. Celest and I exchanged glances.

"Is this what your brother and these men are hoping for? A few days to have Belynda take full control of the elements? Please tell me that you can see how ambitious and absurd the idea is?" Drake pushed back his chair and stood up, eyes never moving from Celest. "I told you before, and I will tell you again, she is not fighting anyone."

No, not this again.

"Drake. You saw what I can do with the elements. I can help."

"This is not a game," he thundered. "How can you be sure

that we can trust anything your brother says?" Drake added, bracing his fists on the table.

"I know it's hard for you to trust the guardians, but Isabel's legacy would have been lost if it weren't for them. Trust me when I say that many members of the council are tired of Stephen. They don't agree with his ideas, but they are too afraid of him and the control he yields over the elementals to do anything about it. I know you worry for Belynda, as do I, but you know that you cannot go against fate. Belynda was born to end this; you are proof that nothing we do will change that."

Drake's anger was palpable, but he said nothing else on the matter. Even though he couldn't argue against the truth, I could see in his expression that he would never concede to the idea of me fighting.

AFTER THE TENSE evening and the disagreements, Drake retired to his room, leaving the dinner table quieter than usual. The weight of imminent danger was amplified by the unsettling presence of the men lurking outside our home.

I stared out my bedroom window, but all I could see was darkness. The clock read fifteen past midnight, and although I had to be up early for school, sleep eluded me.

I closed my door and made my way to Drake's room, knowing he was awake and likely still upset. The door was slightly ajar, so I knocked once and pushed it open. He didn't move from his position by the window. His back was stiff, the room bathed in darkness except for the small nightlight behind the desk.

"Do you mind if I join you for a while?" I asked. "I can't seem to fall asleep."

"No, you're welcome to stay," he said without turning around. I studied him and paced around his room, noticing the few books on his night table. I picked one up in surprise, and when I glanced at him, his head was turned toward me, his eyes watching.

"I wanted to catch up with the world," he explained quietly. "Celest offered some reading material." I nodded and placed the book back on the table, his eyes returning to the darkness beyond the windows.

I sat on his bed and rested my back against his pillows. He looked like a statue standing in the darkness. At times, it seemed as if he wasn't even breathing.

"Are they still out there?" I asked. He shifted, his fists tightening at his sides.

"Yes." His response was terse, the coldness in his tone making the hairs on my skin prickle.

"Will you come lay down for a while?" I asked, hoping to pull him out of his dark mood.

He didn't move or reply. His eyes remained fixed on the darkness, his back stiff, hands tucked deep in the pockets of his jacket.

"Are you okay?" I pressed, sitting up on the bed. His grey eyes turned to me.

"I'm okay." He offered, before facing the window again. "But you were right about what you said to her." He spoke without turning, and I wasn't sure what he meant. "My biggest battle is with myself." He added, and I knew he had heard my conversation with Celest.

"I'm sorry."

"Don't be. It's the truth…I battle my demons and my instincts, and—just like now—the fear of losing control. Perhaps your aunt is right; one cannot change what already is. I should stop fighting my instincts and go down there…make them disappear." His last words flowed in a menacing low breath that chilled my soul.

He was so absorbed by his thoughts that he didn't notice me slipping from the bed. I placed my hand on his arm, and his bright eyes burned into mine, startled by the touch.

"I think it's only natural to want to hurt those who seek to harm you and those you care about, but killing them won't fix things," I offered. "I know how much you battle against the darkness for control. I saw it at the barn; I see it every time you try to keep your distance. You are not a monster, Drake. I know it's hard, but the fact that those men are still out there is proof that you can fight your shadows. Every day, your human instinct surfaces more."

"I've told you before, your faith in me has no boundaries, and you lack common sense. At the barn…I could have hurt you. I really could have."

"I refuse to believe that. Your fire was taking over, and you still had enough reason to send me away, even after I refused to leave. No, I don't believe you could have hurt me." He turned to me, and for the first time, the expression on his face softened as his fingers traced the contours of my face.

"Drake?" I spoke, unsure if it was the right time, but I was suddenly curious.

"Yes?"

"Back then, when you first met Isabel, how was it?"

He took a deep breath and lowered his hand from my face, taking a step back.

"That's a long story, and you need to go to bed. We can talk about it tomorrow."

"I'm just curious. Was she ever close to you while your Dragon took form?"

There, I said it. Drake instantly seemed troubled by the question.

"Never." He hesitated, likely wondering where I was headed with this. "I couldn't..." The tone in his voice told me it wasn't just fear that had held him back from revealing to Isabel, and me, his Dragon form. Perhaps also shame.

"I don't believe you would hurt those you love, even in your Dragon form."

"That's a theory you and Isabel both shared. However, I'm not willing to test it."

"You've never been around a mortal while your element took over?"

"My kind served guardians since they became the protectors of the realms from the very beginning. However, that was a long time ago; I was different then. I had not lived or endured Xelraa either. Nor do I know what my alter ego is willing to do or not do, and I'm not willing to risk it—not then with Isabel and certainly not with you now."

"I disagree. I think we need to test this theory once and for all. I'm willing to prove to you that you are incapable of hurting me."

Drake frowned, staring at me.

"Perfect. You want to do this now? In your room?"

My heart skipped a beat, and I hesitated, caught off guard by the idea.

"Sure, if you want." I caught the tremble in my voice, except I was not about to coward now. Drake stared at me in silence, a smile forming on his lips.

"I know you're eager to test your theory, but I'm not. Not where your safety is concerned. Besides, I wouldn't want to destroy this room."

"Oh..." I had not thought that through.

"Yes. *Oh* indeed."

"I still think we should try. Perhaps not tonight or here. But I would like to try."

Watching me closely, I knew inside he was fighting with the decision and his need to keep me safe.

"It's the only way we will ever know if we can be together." I delivered the final blow, though I knew nothing would keep me away from him, only death itself.

"We will discuss this further, but you need to go to bed now. Perhaps you're right. After all, you seem to possess the ability to calm me down." Drake picked me up effortlessly in his arms, and I cried in surprise, wrapping my arms around his neck for support.

"Put me down." I squealed in protest.

"I don't think I will. I'm enjoying this."

Oh, two could play at that game, I thought as I leaned in and pressed my lips against the side of his neck. His laughter reverberated between our bodies.

"I know what you're doing. It's not going to work."

"And what exactly am I doing?" I teased breathlessly as I continued my gentle assault. My mouth moved slowly across the warmth of his skin; I knew I was starting to affect him when his hold around me tightened and his breathing became shallow. I kissed the edge of his jaw, then up to the corner of his lips. He was affected, yet made no move to release me, so I ventured further. He walked down the hall and into my room, kicking the door closed with his foot.

I knotted my fingers through his hair at the base of his neck, claiming his lips with an urgency I did not realize I possessed. Yet it was the softest reach with my tongue that made his resolve crumble.

"You are a wicked little minx," he murmured against my lips before spinning me effortlessly to straddle him.

Drake pushed me against the bed and lay on me, supporting most of his weight with one hand while the other held me tightly to him. His lips melted against mine, his tongue invading me without restraint. I wanted him closer. His free hand moved over my breasts, then down my side and around my thigh, bringing my leg up around him.

Pushing himself against me, my legs locked around his torso, bringing him closer. His movements were a slow taunt.

"I burn for you," he whispered against my lips, his breath dense with need.

"Please...don't stop," I begged, pulling him back to my lips. I didn't want to reason with these feelings—I only wanted him. As he stilled, motionless on top of me, I knew nothing further would happen.

"You are a temptress, sent from the pits of hell to tempt me and make me lose my mind," Drake said with a playful smile.

"It's your fault for teasing me like this," I offered playfully.

His laughter echoed throughout my room, and I was intoxicated by it.

"Love, you did all the teasing. I merely reacted." I threw my hands on the bed and untangled my legs from him with a groan of frustration. "Are you upset?" he asked with a bemused expression.

"No. But you clearly possess more self-restraint than I. Much more than you give yourself credit for."

He pulled himself up. "Perhaps you're right. I definitely feel very human. Now go to bed."

"Wait. Stay." He glanced at me hesitantly from the door.

"I know I asked you once to trust me, but you shouldn't," he remained by the door. The darkness in his eyes beckoning me to understand.

"I do trust you. Please, stay." I pressed. "I don't want to be alone," I added, and I saw the resolution in his face.

"Fine. I'll take the floor."

I laughed out loud at his absurdity.

"Surely you can sleep next to me, Drake." I sat up, pulling the covers. "I'm sure you don't bite." I teased.

He was on top of me in a blink, his hands held most of his weight as he hovered above me.

"Perhaps I should," he grinned, fanning my face with his breath, "to teach you some common sense." He bit my bottom lip softly before pushing himself off me. "Now, sleep. I'll take the floor."

"Don't be ridiculous. We can share the bed—if you want to, of course." I added, afraid of sounding too desperate.

"You know it's not for lack of want, but if you want me to stay, I will take the floor." He moved a loose strand of my hair behind my ear and then ran the back of his fingers across my cheek.

I stared at the ceiling. Despite his insistence on the absurd idea of taking the floor, when he had slept next to me before, I didn't push him. I didn't want to stay alone. Not tonight.

"What are you thinking about?" he asked after a while, likely sensing my inability to find sleep.

It was hard to pinpoint one thought because my head swam in all directions. However, the most troubling image was the proclaimed legacy of mine.

"Mostly about figuring out what to do next. I mean, how do I bring balance to the realms? How can I fulfill this prophecy?" I asked.

"That's the beauty of prophecies; they seem to find you even when you're not looking. Aren't we proof of that?" he said, his voice smooth. "Don't worry about that now. It is your destiny; you don't have to look for your fate. It will present itself to you as the fates see fit. Only then will you know what to do."

I thought about his words, which surprisingly made me feel better. He was right; I shouldn't be trying to figure out what to do. Everything would fall into place. The fact that he was here was proof of that.

DRAKE

I burned to close the distance and wrap my arms around her as I had done the night before, but being near her without taking from her became more difficult each time. The monster and the man within me yearned alike—to slip under her covers, to feel the prickling of her skin under my fingertips. I closed my eyes, imagining my tongue exploring the valley of her breasts.

Sitting on the floor, I watched her sleep. She was scared; even if she didn't say it, I knew it was the reason she had asked me to stay. Now that she had found sleep, I felt it was safer for her if I left. I lifted the covers and gently pulled them up to cover her arms. My hand reached out to stroke her face, but I stopped myself, not wanting to wake her.

The need to protect her, even from myself, was primal and overwhelming. There wasn't anything I wouldn't give to keep her safe. As this realization washed over me, I felt the birth of a forgotten feeling. *Love.* By the fates, I loved her.

14
FACING DEMONS

I **FOUND BENJAMIN PACING OUTSIDE THE HALL OF** the antechamber. My expression tightened at the sight of him. Despite his quiet demeanor and friendship with Oliver, the kid always gave me a bad impression. He was too eager to please Mr. Radcliff and the council.

"He will see you now," I spoke curtly; it was no secret that I disliked him. He offered me a smug smile before closing the doors. I was about to walk away, but something told me to stay, so I listened.

"Young Benjamin. What can I do for you today? What are you doing here this early?" Mr. Radcliff asked sternly as usual.

"I'm sorry, Sir. I just thought you might be interested in what I have to say," Benjamin replied with an air of admiration that sickened me.

"Well, stop wasting our time and spit it out, boy."

"Sir. It's the Hershton girl." I stilled by the doors at the mention of her name, knowing Benjamin had nothing to do with her. *What was he up to?*

"What about her?"

"Mr. Radcliff, the girl wears the Cromwell seal in a necklace." I wasn't sure what Benjamin was talking about, but judging by the silence that followed, he had Mr. Radcliff's undivided attention.

"Are you certain of this?"

"Yes, Sir. I am. I wasn't at first, but I am now."

"Does Oliver know about this?"

"He does, Sir. He asked me not to say anything. He said he would bring it to your attention..." I knew it. My instincts were rarely wrong.

"But he has not..." Mr. Radcliff didn't sound happy. I knew this meant more trouble for Oliver, but I was glad he had kept whatever he knew of the girl to himself. Perhaps he was right to call out his father after all.

"Sir, if I am honest...I believe Oliver's interests lie elsewhere." If I didn't know better, he was purposefully trying to get Oliver in trouble.

"Yes. With that wretched girl." Mr. Radcliff's footsteps echoed around the chamber.

"Thank you, Benjamin. This is just the excuse I needed. As for this conversation, let's keep it between us for now." I allowed some distance from the door.

"Yes. Of course, Sir."

"Good. Now go to school and call Tyrus in on your way out. We have much to do." I braced myself, knowing I wouldn't like his orders.

BELYNDA

The pounding at my bedroom door jolted me awake, followed by Celest's voice.

"Belynda, are you up? You're going to be late for school."

School...Celest. Oh god, Celest.

I flipped the covers and realized Drake was not on the floor or in the room at all. Celest knocked one more time, and I jumped.

"Belynda, I have to go into the library. I left something in the oven for breakfast." She called from the other side of the door. I opened it.

"Thank you. I was so tired that I must not have heard the alarm. Is everything alright at the library?"

"Yes. I'm just hoping to receive some news from Seymour, and I'll feel restless here at home until I do." She was right. At least at the library, she would be occupied. Then, I remembered the men who were watching us.

"Wait. Those men are probably still out there. Have you spoken to Drake?"

At the mention of his name, the door from the guest room opened, and Drake stepped out. He stared at us from the end of the hallway, appearing very refreshed, dressed in black trousers and a knee-length coat, courtesy of Celest.

"I don't think you should expose yourself like that," Drake added as he approached, obviously having heard our conversation. "They are gone now, but not for long. Being alone makes both of you an easy target."

"Well, Drake can go with you to the library. I should be safe at school."

I didn't need to look at Drake to know he disapproved, but I appreciated his silence.

"I don't think it's necessary. All we know is that they are watching. They don't know he's here with us, and if they wanted to harm us, they would have already done so. Besides, I'm sure Drake has better things to do than babysit me."

"I don't mind; it will give me time to catch up on my reading," added Drake, surprising me yet again with his chivalry. While he still didn't completely trust Celest, I was grateful he was showing some kindness. It was an effort for him.

"You don't have to do this. Really. I will be fine," Celest added.

"No. I insist. But if you'd rather have your space, I can accompany you, and once I know you're safe, I'll return. I'm sure you can call if you need me." Celest preferred that idea.

"Ok then. We'll wait for Belynda to leave safely on the bus," Celest said. "Come on down. I'll serve you some breakfast while she finishes up." Celest returned downstairs, and Drake followed, but not before flashing me a smile. I ignored him, closing the door behind me and rushing to the shower.

I WALKED towards the entrance hall, and he followed closely, but before I reached for the door, he paused and pulled me to him. His warmth cloaked me as his arms came to rest around me. Reaching for my hand, he brought it up to his lips for a kiss, disregarding the fact that Celest was in the kitchen.

"Don't forget I'm only a call away. I mean it...if anything happens. If someone even tries to touch you..."

"I know..." I smiled, amused. "You will rip their heads off."

I lifted my chin to look at him, but he wasn't smiling. "I was joking," I added, but he didn't seem to enjoy my humor.

"Belynda, I'm serious. It scares me that you don't see it. That you don't fully understand or accept what I am capable of."

"Drake, I know that you would hurt anyone that tried to hurt me, and I would do the same in a heartbeat for you. However, I prefer teasing you rather than feeding the dark cloud now brewing in your eyes." He seemed shocked by my assessment but, as he took in my words, the corner of his mouth lifted.

"A dark cloud, you say," he smiled then. "You are very perceptive but even better at distracting me." Sweeping down towards me, he captured my lips in a swift and final kiss.

"You need to go."

On cue, the horn of the bus sounded outside. I stood on my tiptoes and tangled my fingers in his hair, staring deep into those grey eyes of his.

"You are the one who distracts me," I accused with a smile before pulling away from him, but he drew me back and brushed his lips against mine before letting me go with a satisfied grin.

"Don't miss me too much," he said, and I smiled.

As fate would have it, Oliver was the first person I saw as I stepped off the bus. With one glance my way, he turned and walked in the opposite direction. Relief flooded me, knowing he had finally decided to leave me alone. But concern quickly followed; because that wasn't the Oliver I knew. He looked unkempt and tired, a stark contrast to his usually polished appearance. His clothes were wrinkled as if he had slept in them, and he had clearly skipped shaving for a few days.

As I walked to class, I tried to remind myself that Oliver was not my concern. *I don't care about him,* I repeated like a mantra, but it shattered the second I took my seat next to his and glimpsed the dark circles under his eyes. He wasn't right. I could pretend all I wanted, but I did care. My gut told me that the bastard we shared as a father had something to do with Oliver's erratic behavior. Perhaps Celest was right after all. Maybe Stephen had used Oliver to get close to us. If everything I had learned about Stephen was true, I could imagine the sort of life Oliver had growing up with that monster as a dad. I didn't know Oliver well, but I knew enough to recognize that he wasn't completely devoid of feelings. There was always a choice, but I wanted to believe that if he was involved with our father's schemes, it was against his will.

Oliver glanced my way, and I held his gaze. His eyes bore into me, but I couldn't decipher what I saw in them—desperation, frustration, loneliness. I wanted to speak to him but didn't know where to begin. There was no easy way to broach the subject without revealing too much. I couldn't just say, *'Hi, are you being manipulated by your scumbag father, who also happens to be mine? Oh yes, that makes you, my half-brother.'* No, not the best idea.

"Are you okay?" I whispered.

He nodded and attempted to smile, but it was so forced that he couldn't even manage it. He wasn't okay, but I wasn't in a position to pry.

When the bell rang, my thoughts were muddled as I tried

to find a way to approach Oliver. Most of the students had fled the classroom, but Oliver had not moved. This was likely my only chance. As I turned, Oliver did too, but he surprised me by speaking first.

"I'm sorry about the fair. What happened to you...I shouldn't have forced you to go; I just—" He trailed off, unable to find the words. If, like me, he was bound by the secrets surrounding the guardianship and his father, it would explain his hesitation. The fact that he somehow felt responsible for what happened to me by apologizing only reinforced Celest's suspicions that he was involved. Whether he was to blame directly or indirectly, at least he apologized. I wanted to confide in him, but this legacy bound me too. While it was easy to believe he was forced to do his father's bidding, it was another thing altogether to confide in him.

"Honestly, Oliver, I'm okay. What happened was not your fault. You can't control what crazy people do. Look on the bright side, okay? You had your date, and now you can just go back to ignoring me, alright?" I tried to lighten the mood, but he wasn't buying it.

"Just know that it has never been my intention to hurt you, despite whatever has happened, or might not have happened —my fault or not. You must believe me."

Oh, Oliver, what in the world is your father doing to you? I wanted to voice my thoughts aloud, but the unspoken truth seemed safer now. If neither of us said it, we could at least go on pretending he was simply referring to a bad date. I stared at him a while longer, and I knew then that I couldn't blame him. He was just another pawn in his father's game—my father.

"I know that; I might not have known it a few weeks ago,

but I do now. I know you're not the insensitive idiot I thought you were." At my comment, he smiled. "Please don't torture yourself anymore. There are no hard feelings, honestly."

"You know, I wish I had your courage. To be who you want to be without any pretenses. You wouldn't understand." He was far from the truth; I knew very well what living a lie was like—not having true friends, at least none who genuinely knew who I was. I was glad I had Drake and Celest now, but I wondered who Oliver had.

"Well, sometimes in life, we are forced to be something we are not, even against our better judgment. Something tells me that perhaps you're stuck in that situation too."

Oliver stared at me with a confused look.

"Perceptive," he said with a small smile.

"Not perceptive. It's just obvious." I gestured to his appearance and the wrinkles in his clothes.

"I'm a mess, aren't I?"

I laughed softly. "A little," I admitted, as the students for second period started to arrive. "We're going to be late." We gathered our bags and walked out together. Like he had done the week before, he walked me to class. The bell rang as we reached the door, signaling that we were late as the last few students rushed into their classes.

"Thank you for the chat, and again, I'm sorry."

"Will you stop apologizing? Trust me, there's nothing else to say, okay?" I studied him, trying to convey everything I couldn't. His shoulders visibly relaxed, and I turned back to enter the class, but I didn't feel right leaving him like that.

"Oliver, one more thing." He paused, looking back. "If you ever need anything, or to talk, don't forget you have my number." After all, he was my half-brother, even if he didn't know it.

"Thank you. I'll keep it in mind." He smiled and strode off without another word.

Perhaps this school day wasn't a total waste of time after all. I had dreaded seeing Oliver again, but it had been surprisingly liberating.

When lunch came around, things seemed to have regained some form of normalcy. Lily and Ben sat with the rest of their group; Oliver appeared to have regained some spirit and was back to being the center of attention. I doodled my way through the rest of my classes, my thoughts lost in the memory of a pair of grey eyes I could not wait to see. It was inexplicable how much I could miss him after having him in my life such a short time. The constant need to be close to him was intoxicating, and when I closed my eyes, I could almost smell his fading scent in the collar of my jacket.

When I got home, the house was empty. Celest was not back yet, and to my surprise and disappointment, neither was Drake. I wandered through the silent rooms, trying to shake off the creeping fear. He could take care of himself; my worry was unfounded. He would be back soon. The door to Celest's study was open, and I found myself drawn inside. I paused across her desk, staring at the large picture containing the family tree. So much history was here: the history of my ancestors. I walked around the desk, searching for Isabel's name. A cold shiver trickled down my spine, knowing how her life and mine were bound. This hell-bent legacy had brought me to

Drake, and for that, I was thankful. I didn't care much for the added responsibilities, but I would take all the lies and crazy prophecies if it meant we could be together.

A soft sweep of wind moved my hair, and I turned to find Drake at the door. His eyes held mine as he closed the distance between us, drawing me into his arms and burying his nose in my hair.

"I'm sorry, I should have known you would worry."

I pulled back to stare into his gray eyes, my hand reaching up to touch his face. "I know you can take care of yourself, but I couldn't help it. I keep thinking you'll disappear and never come back," I admitted, voicing my worst fears.

"I will never leave you. That is the one thing you can always be sure of." His reassurance warmed my insides.

His eyes shifted to the wall behind me, and I knew what he saw. Her name, like a beacon in the distance.

"Are you okay?"

He had told me many times that he was fine, but the thought was never far from my mind.

Drake turned to me, his fingers brushing the side of my face. He captured my chin between his fingers and his lips brushed mine softly. When he pulled away, his eyes held my gaze.

"Isabel is part of our past, but she is also bound to our present and future. To answer your question, yes. I'm okay now that I know the truth. Isabel is no longer an unfinished story; she is part of a chapter in our lives that has now ended, and you, Belynda, are my future." I stared back at him, lost in his eyes. His words, served to ease my mind.

· · ·

LIKE THE NIGHT BEFORE, the house remained under watch, and training wasn't possible. Though I wanted Drake to stay with me, I felt self-conscious asking out of fear. He would insist on taking the floor, and I hated causing his discomfort. Every passing minute brought us closer to facing my father, and I feared what would become of us if we failed against the elementals.

DESPITE IT BEING FRIDAY, a day I usually welcomed with better spirits, today felt different. I was restless. An uneasiness prickled over my skin as the bus left the driveway.

As I reached school, thoughts of my uncertain future with Drake resurfaced, even though I knew dwelling on them was a waste of time—especially if the fates had any say in it. Still, my mind kept drifting to the worst outcomes.

I spotted Lily sitting with Ben and waved at her as I headed to my usual spot beneath the tree. It was comforting to know she had found someone who made her happy, and Ben did exactly that. Waving me over, Lily smiled, and in that instant, I was glad I had kept my secrets to myself. It felt better knowing she was safe.

Still, I couldn't help but wonder how she would react if she knew the truth. Would she laugh and call me crazy? Or maybe she would have been an excellent ally. Either way, she was better off not knowing. At least with Ben, she had the chance of a long and happy future. As I studied them again, the bell rang, and I tried to dispel the envy in my stomach at the ease of their relationship.

Mrs. Gill glanced at me as I entered the class before

returning her attention to the attendance book. Surprisingly, Oliver was already seated at our table.

Our table. I smiled at the thought, remembering how ready I had been to murder him just a few weeks ago. Now, I wondered how he would react if he knew I was his half-sister. The father we shared might be evil and corrupt, but I had no hard feelings towards Oliver. However, I didn't fully trust him. While something deep inside of me insisted he was nothing like our father, being wrong was not an option I could afford.

"Feeling better today?" I asked, noticing he appeared more like his usual self. His clothes were fresh and clean, and his hair was perfectly styled.

He grinned, running his fingers through his hair. "I guess you could say that."

I smiled back, glad to see him out of the funk he was in. "Oliver, about our arrangement."

"It's over, I know. Don't worry," he interrupted.

Although we seemed to have built some sort of connection, I figured it was best to leave things as they were and stay away from him, at least for now.

"I think it's for the best. Don't you?"

"Yeah. It is." He smiled, but it didn't reach his eyes.

He kept to himself for the remainder of class. When the bell rang, I was sure he would say something else, but he packed his books away.

"I'll see you around," I called after him.

"See you." He barely glanced my way before disappearing out the door. He was one strange boy. That was something we seemed to have in common.

• • •

THE DAY DRAGGED on in a haze. In my final class, I found myself staring out the window, lost in thoughts of Drake and the uncertain future ahead of us. I knew it was useless to dwell on it, yet I couldn't ignore the facts. We were from different worlds, his immortal existence and my fragile humanity were an abyss, destined to tear us apart.

Suddenly, I felt a presence and turned to see Mr. Miller standing over me, his expression stern and disapproving.

"Ms. Hershton, is there something outside that window more interesting than my lecture?"

"No, sir," I replied, feeling all eyes on me.

"Then you won't mind answering my question," he said sharply.

"I'm sorry, could you repeat it?" I asked, knowing I was on thin ice as his face flushed with irritation.

"You'd know if you weren't daydreaming during my lesson. Stay behind after class," he instructed.

For a moment, I wasn't entirely sure what had happened. *How had I ended up with detention?* This wasn't good...not good at all.

Glancing at the clock, I realized I would miss my bus home. I needed to call Celest.

As the bell rang and students began to file out, I hoped Mr. Miller might reconsider, but he left quickly.

The assistant coach, in charge of detention, entered a few minutes later, followed by a few other students, poor souls like me, destined to remain here.

"Mr. Porter, can I step out to make a quick call? I need a ride," I asked, hopeful he would understand. He nodded, preoccupied with writing our assignment on the board. The hallway was empty, and the school grounds were eerily quiet. Alone, I dialed Celest's number, but it went straight to voicemail. Redialing anxiously, I drummed my fingers on the lockers. Still no answer. She must still be at the library. I tried the library's number next, and she didn't pick up either.

What was I going to do? I didn't want to worry Drake by calling him; there was nothing he could do from there. I needed a ride.

Just as I was about to call Celest again, Mr. Porter poked his head out of the classroom.

"We don't have all day, Ms. Hershton," he reminded me.

Grimacing, I followed him back inside. Detention dragged on, a pointless exercise in penance. By the time we were finally released, I had filled nearly ten pages with the same sentence:

"I will pay attention in class from now on."

My fingers were numb, and the skies threatened to pour with rain. Still without a ride, I sought shelter under a nearby building as a light drizzle began. From where I stood, the school parking lot looked empty.

I dialed Celest's number for the fifteenth time, growing increasingly anxious with each unanswered call. *What was I going to do?* As a last resort, I decided to call the house.

With each unanswered ring, my hopes evaporated. No answer—what was happening? I couldn't stay here, my stomach twisting with unease.

Pulling my hood tighter, I started walking. Within minutes, the heavy rain thundered down. My boots squished with each step, hood clinging to my face as I pressed on. A loud horn blared behind me, making me jump. The car screeched to a halt, and for a second, fear gripped me.

"You look like a drenched cat," Oliver smirked, rolling down the window. "Get in. I'll take you home."

A million thoughts raced through my mind as I hesitated, uncertain. "Belynda, it's pouring, and your house is on the way. Trust me, please. Get out of the rain." Reluctantly, I opened the door and climbed into his car.

"That wasn't so hard, was it?" Oliver smiled as he started the car again. I took a deep breath, trying to relax.

"Thank you. I'm sorry about your seats," I murmured.

"Don't worry. They'll survive." He sped towards my house, and soon, we fell into a comfortable silence.

When he pulled into the driveway, my fear and suspicion had morphed into gratitude. "Thank you for the ride, I mean it."

I moved to open the door, but Oliver gripped my arm firmly. "Belynda, I don't know why you thought walking home alone was a good idea, especially after what happened at the fair..." His voice trailed off, a pointed look in his eyes.

"I know. I'll be careful. Thank you again for the ride." I stood on the porch, watching him drive off into the rain. Stepping into the warmth of the house, I closed the door behind me, only to cry out in surprise as a blur streaked past me. Drake stood before me, holding me against the door.

"Are you okay? What happened? Why was he with you? Belynda, I was worried sick," Drake's shadows danced around him.

"I'm fine," I whispered, hands on his face to calm him. His eyes reflected the storm clouds outside.

"Do you know how worried I was when you didn't show up?"

"I know. I was stuck at school and missed the bus, but I tried to call." Drake's brow furrowed. "I called Celest, her cell, and the library, but no response. I even tried the house, but you didn't answer."

"I went looking for you. I got there just in time to see you get into his car." Drake stepped back, running his hands through wet hair. That's when I noticed his dripping clothes.

"I spared his life, because I know he's your brother," Drake confessed, a haunted look in his eyes.

"I'm ok. He didn't touch me."

"I know, and yet, I followed the steady beat of your heart the entire time, fighting the urge to…" He bit out the words, fighting his shadows.

"Shh, stop," I interrupted, placing a finger on his lips, stopping him from torturing himself further. "Oliver is not to blame for his father—*our* father's sins."

"The boy doesn't know of your parentage. I don't believe he is a victim, and neither should you."

"He had nothing to do with it—I can feel it."

Drake gently gripped my chin. "You always place too much faith in people who don't deserve it." His warm lips met my cold mouth, silencing any protest. "I trust your judgment, but I need you to promise to keep your guard up. At least until we're certain he can be trusted."

Knowing Drake, I knew he wouldn't easily change his opinion. If his relationship with Celest was any indication, Oliver would have to go to extreme lengths to earn Drake's trust.

"I promise." He didn't seem entirely convinced but dropped the subject. "Have you heard from Celest at all? It's unlike her not to answer."

"She was fine when I left her this afternoon—busy, buried in the back going through old books." If Drake had been with her until noon, she might not have heard the phone. It wouldn't be the first time.

"Perhaps she missed your calls?" Drake added, as if reading my mind. "You're shivering. You need to get out of those clothes and into a warm bath."

He was right, so I didn't argue when he led me upstairs. After showering, I half-expected to find Drake in my bedroom, but it was empty. I quickly dressed and checked the guest room, but he wasn't there either. As I reached the foyer, I saw him resting on one of the sofas with his back to me. I approached quietly, but he sensed my presence before I got close.

"BELYNDA, I knew you were there. Trust me." Drake's voice broke through the silence as I walked over, defeated, and sat down beside him. He had changed out of his wet clothes as well.

"Just testing your hearing abilities," I teased weakly. "I'm still worried about Celest. Maybe I should try calling her again." I had already tried her cell and the library's phone, but there was still no answer.

"I'll wait until sundown. If we haven't heard from her by then, I'll go check on her," Drake offered, trying to ease my worry. I nestled my head in the crook of his neck, comforted by his scent which grew more familiar each day. It was the perfect balm to ease my mind. His scent was both appealing and predatory. It teased my senses making it impossible to resist.

He tried to cradle me on his lap, but I shifted and straddled him instead. His hands firmly held my thighs, his thumbs tracing circles over my skin. The heat that radiated from him, soaked into every part of my body.

His eyes held a storm of emotions, and I sensed that he was still troubled by what happened with Oliver. Then there was also his own battle, the one he fought against himself to repress his desires—his shadows.

Our shallow breaths became one, as I leaned in, pressing my lips to his. His grip tightened on my thighs—a warning, perhaps—but I couldn't stop myself. Drawing closer, I weaved my fingers in his hair, losing myself in his warmth, taking his air as my own. He was at the edge of the precipice; his restraint slipping away while mine had vanished long ago.

"You don't know what you do to me," he murmured, his voice thick with desire.

"Tell me..." I teased, breathless.

He brushed his fingers along my jawline, tracing down my neck. Closing my eyes, I tilted my head back, allowing his exploring hand to continue. A shiver ran through me as his lips grazed against my neck.

The urge to be closer to him was overwhelming; each movement from my body deliberate and tortuously slow, drawing a groan from him.

"I need you, Drake. Please," I pleaded. In a blur, my back was against the sofa, his body pressed over mine. I pulled him closer, my legs wrapping around him as his need pressed against me. His body moved over mine and the friction was thrilling. Gasping, I felt his lips searing a trail down my neck, igniting my senses.

Reaching for the hem of his shirt, I pushed it up, exploring the solid contours of his back. My fingers traced his spine, and for the first time, I felt the immortal prince of fire shiver under my touch.

Drake leaned away and removed his shirt in one fluid motion, discarding it on the floor. He was a vision. His skin and muscles were as solid as marble, yet smooth and soft beneath my touch. My fingers glided over his chest and down his arms with appreciation; he was breathtaking.

His gaze pierced my soul, holding me captive as his body moved against mine, leaving me breathless. His lips claimed mine: demanding and unyielding.

"Belynda... we can't," Drake managed to say between the moments he spent devouring my mouth. I didn't listen. I wanted to stay in this oblivion.

"Wait. Wait. Wait..." He pulled away reluctantly.

"What is it...?" I touched his face, struggling to catch my breath. Did he not feel the same? "It's okay if you don't..."

"Oh, I do. Trust me. I want nothing more." He laughed, though there was no humor in it.

"Then what is it? You can trust me." I struggled to understand.

"I know I can. It's me I don't trust." He shifted back to his knees. "Belynda, I'm afraid I'll lose control and hurt you. I've told you this."

Silly, silly man. I sat up and kissed him.

"Hey... I trust you, but you need to trust us. What we feel is beyond time and reason. Your elemental is part of who you are. I know you would never harm me. But you have to believe it too; otherwise, how can we be together?"

It pained me to say it, but he needed to understand. Drake had to face his demons. He cupped my face and placed a soft kiss on the edge of my lips, searching my eyes. I stared back into the gray storm reflected in his.

"I promise I'll try. I just need time. I was lost to the darkness for too long, and even though you've made my human emotions resurface, I need to be certain I'm in full control if I want to be that close with you." I couldn't fully grasp the darkness he spoke of, but I understood patience, and that's all he was asking for. I could live with that.

"So, time... does that mean no kissing then?" I teased, and he smiled.

"No. I think those boundaries are safe for now." Pulling my legs astride him, his lips claimed mine once more: gentle but fluent. He stroked and teased, and I did the same. There was no better torture than this. I imagined his hands trailing down my back and over my hips, pinning me closer to him, and to my delight, he did as I imagined. I broke away and grinned.

"Although it has its privileges, it really isn't fair that you get to see into my head." I protested. He smiled mischievously and kissed me again. However, this time it was different. His lips melded with mine like a dance that clouded all of my senses. Fierce and relentless. In my mind's eye, I watched us, bound to each other. I broke away to remove my shirt; the gray color of his eyes smoldered as they took me in. His hands glided over the curve of my breasts, leaving warm trails behind as he branded them with soft kisses. Drake pulled away, and I struggled to free myself from the daze. As I caught my breath, I realized my shirt was still on, and Drake was smiling, pleased.

"What was that?"

He tucked a strand of hair behind my ear. "Well, you said it wasn't fair I got to see into your head, so I gave you a glimpse of mine."

I was speechless. "That felt... *real*." I whispered, wondering how much more I didn't know.

"It's harder for mortals to distinguish between what's real and what is merely a desire or a thought. Especially when we open up our minds to them."

"But not impossible...."

"No. Not impossible. It just takes practice and a little self-control. If you lose yourself completely to your senses and what you are feeling, it's harder to distinguish the thoughts." If only it were as easy to keep a cool head when he ignited my senses.

"You said I could learn to keep you out of my head. Is that the same concept? Staying focused. Not losing myself in the feeling?" By the expression on his face, he didn't like the idea of being shut out, so I smiled.

"Yes. In theory. But it's harder to keep us out." Oh, he was so sure of himself... I made a note to try extra hard to make it happen.

"And why is that?" I needed his advice if I wanted to succeed.

"Humans are overcome with emotions. I guess it's much harder to control yourselves when we are close and allow the exchange."

"So, you're saying we are easily dazzled."

"Clearly."

"Oh really... I bet you anything I can resist your charms." I feigned offense at his claim that humans—myself included—were weak to immortal allure like his. Yet deep down, I knew the truth; I was lost to him from the moment those grey eyes found me.

"I'll wager no such thing."

I didn't argue further; any attempt to stay away from him was a lost cause from the outset. He smiled, and the silver hue in his eyes darkened. Picking me up effortlessly, he made his way up the stairs without skipping a breath.

Laying in bed, I took my time exploring the intricate lines of his tattoos as my fingers traced around his arms, up to his biceps, chest, and abs.

"Why do they look different from the last time I saw them?" I questioned, realizing the patterns and symbols were not etched the same way over his skin. His fingers trailed over my wrist.

"They come alive when I free my fire, and every time the darkness is absorbed back into my human body, they set in different ways." *Fascinating,* I thought.

"What do they mean?" I asked, absentmindedly tracing one of the intricate symbols. His closed eyes fluttered open.

"They are runes from the ancient world. Only those with royal blood are born with them. But none with the same." *Interesting...* He held my exploring hand above his heart. "This one means courage." No matter how hard I tried, he always managed to surprise me.

"What about this one?" I traced the lines on his right shoulder.

"That one represents wisdom."

"Why only royals?"

"No one knows why. The elders believe they are gifts: qualities that the gods bequeath us. I don't quite agree, though."

"Why not?" He traced the lines on his left bicep, a furrow on his brow.

"This one would be for integrity." He shook his head and moved to the one on the side of his ribs. "Protector...shall I continue?" He propped himself up on one elbow and traced down his abs. "Discipline..."

I realized then why he disagreed with the elders' beliefs; he couldn't see the meaning of those words reflected in himself.

"Why are you so hard on yourself all the time? You are courageous," I argued, tracing above his heart and then his right shoulder. "You are wise," I continued, "And I don't think I've met anyone more honorable or with more integrity than you." I moved my hand to his side, then his abs. "You are a protector above all, and I can testify to your discipline." It was the truth. As an immortal man, he could have taken me, yet he had shown a herculean restraint to keep my virtue, my innocence, as he often called it.

"There was a time when the old and innocent part of me would have believed that, but not now. Not after abandoning Isabel and knowing I'm to blame for her fate."

"Hey. You're not to blame for her choices. That's not how I see it. You were brave and honorable in your judgment. You accepted your punishment for your people."

"What about being a protector... how exactly did I protect her? How could I pretend to possess such a quality after all the lives I claimed for the shadows?"

"You protect me. You can't save everyone, and not everyone deserves to be saved."

"Your faith in me is relentless."

"Someone has to be the wise one."

"And here I thought I was the one bestowed with the gift of wisdom."

"Oh, hush." I jabbed him in the side, and he laughed.

TIME PASSED, but neither of us could muster the strength to leave each other's side. Outside, the storm had slowed to a drizzle, and I shifted slowly over Drake, glancing at the clock on the night table. It was close to six.

"Can you please pass me my phone?"

Drake retrieved it from the table and placed it in my hand. I hit the redial button and was once again greeted by Celest's voicemail. I tried the library next, and after the twelfth ring, I hung up.

"I'll go check on her," Drake offered, perceiving my silent concern.

"Please be careful." Placing a kiss on my temple, he climbed out of bed. He walked at a human pace, and I watched, bemused, as he put on his shirt.

"I won't be long."

"Be careful," I repeated, my eyes, trailing behind him until he disappeared from my sight.

Reluctantly, I pushed myself out of bed and peeked through the curtains. He was too fast for my eyes and the thought had me wondering about the men watching the house—if they were still out there. Drake had not mentioned them, so perhaps they were gone, or maybe... he had gotten rid of them. *I frowned at the thought.*

Restless, I busied myself organizing the room. I didn't realize how tense I was until I heard the front door open no more than twenty minutes later. I rushed down the stairs, but the color drained from my face as I reached the foyer and saw Drake's expression.

"What happened? Where is Celest?" I asked, panic rising.

A few droplets of rain trickled down his forehead as he entered the kitchen.

"She's gone."

"What do you mean?"

"They've taken her," he said, his brow creased as he ran a hand along his jaw.

My heart dropped. All feelings of hope evaporated, replaced by fear.

"Nooo." I shook my head, my sight blurred. Drake pulled me to him and I fought against the tears shocking me.

"I'm right here. I won't let them hurt you," he said, his voice vibrating between us.

I pulled away, peering up at him. "How do you know? Did you see them?"

Drake shook his head. "I recognized their scent, and I'm inclined to believe that she didn't go willingly," he confessed, and a million possibilities rushed through my mind.

"Why?" Drake's brow furrowed. Hesitant, his eyes scanned my face. "Don't lie to me, please."

"I found traces of her blood." His admission rang in my ears, but I remained frozen, fighting against the sudden rush of anger and frustration. "I also found this." Drake reached for his pocket and offered me Celest's cell phone. "I thought it might be useful."

All of my missed calls illuminated the screen, and I felt a pang of guilt for not getting to her sooner. I scrolled through her messages, but there was nothing that could help us. I returned to the call history, noticing two calls made to her brother, Seymor, around noon. If he was on our side as she had claimed, then he needed to know.

"She made two calls to her brother. It must have been just after you left. We need to speak with him. Tell him what's happened."

"No." Drake took the phone from my hands, and I stared after him as he turned towards the stairs. I followed.

"We have to, we need to do something to get her back," I argued.

"I trust no one," he declared, his back, stiff and unyielding as he took the stairs.

"Drake please." I tried to reason. "Celest trusted him. He could help." Drake paused at the top of the stairs and his eyes pinned me.

"We're leaving, this very moment," he said, and I froze, staring in awe as he marched towards his room.

"Leaving?" I hesitated, before following him. "Where?" I asked, confusion clouding my mind.

Drake turned before opening the door. "Anywhere, away from here. Unless you give me leave to kill them all, I'm taking you as far away from here as possible." I stared at him with disbelief.

"No. I'm not." I shook my head, my feet refusing to move further. "I won't abandon Celest or run from my fate." Drake's eyes shifted, darkness settling in them as he strolled back to me.

"Then if you refuse to go, you must promise to let me deal with them. My way."

Over my dead body, I thought, but nodded in agreement. There was no way I'd let him face this alone. I thought I'd made that clear.

"I'm becoming very familiar with that look of defiance. This isn't a game. I'm not entertaining the idea of you facing them, but if it were to come to that, you lose your strongest weapon—the element of surprise."

His idea was sensible, but he still didn't get it. "I won't let you fight alone."

"I know...it's not an easy compromise. I'd rather pull you over my shoulder and carry you as far away from here as possible," he added to prove his point.

"But you won't, because I would never forgive you," I said with finality, and the darkness in his eyes told me he would do what he had to do against all odds.

"Perhaps but I'm heeding to your wishes against my instincts. That's why I need you to hide your powers. Promise me, no matter what."

"I promise..." I said reluctantly, feeling the weight of that promise, knowing it would haunt me.

This time, he seemed to believe me, his expression softening "Belynda, I..." he trailed off, his gaze smoldering over my face. "I don't want you to hate me, but I will do everything in my power to keep you safe, even protect you against yourself."

"I don't want you to protect me!" I yelled, with frustration and impotency. He stilled, a deep furrow on his brow. "I want you to find Celest. Trace her scent. Bring her back." I cried, almost pleading with desperation.

His eyes shifted before me. His shadows danced over his fists. "I can't, I won't. Don't ask me to. I won't leave you alone. I won't risk losing you." I stared at him, trying to reason with him.

"You still don't think I can take care of myself, that I'm strong enough to do what is expected of me?" I stared up at him, anger coursing through me. His eyes softened for a moment.

"Belynda, it is not your ability and skills that I doubt. I'm the one who is not comfortable testing the theory of you being a heroine and getting killed in the process. I'm not completely heartless. I want to save your aunt, but not at the expense of putting you in danger."

I watched the expression set over his face, and I knew then that he wouldn't budge.

"Then forget my promise. I will go find her myself," I declared. His fist braced against the wall, halting me.

"Over my dead body," he seethed. I stilled before him.

I blinked away my tears, shifting my gaze to my hands before returning them to him. "You were the one who told me that my future would present itself as the fates saw fit. What if now is my time to face Stephen and end the guardianship?"

"Enough!" he barked, and I flinched. I had never seen him this upset before. He hesitated before turning his back to me, and I watched the tendrils of black swivel around his fingers as he strolled down the hall.

"You can't protect me forever," I whispered, trying to reach him.

He paused outside his room. He turned to me, his eyes piercing, and I glimpsed his unspoken answer in the bottomless pits of black. He would. Even if he had to burn this world to do so.

THE EVENING HAD TURNED GRAY, mirroring the night sky as the last moments of happiness and bliss we had shared were now overshadowed by Celest's capture. Drake had chosen to isolate himself in Celest's office while I retreated to my bedroom. With every fiber of my being, I realized I loved him all the more for wanting to protect me—and I would do the same for him. However, I wasn't powerless, a damsel he needed to save. If there was any truth to Isabel's prophecy and I was the one to bring an end to the guardianship, what I needed was his trust, his support. Staring out of my bedroom window, I prayed for something to ease the guilt I felt for not being out there searching for Celest right now.

My bedroom door opened, and I turned as Drake entered, carrying a plate with sandwiches and a glass of milk. He placed it on the dresser; he no longer seemed angry, and although we weren't arguing, it just felt strange to have this silent distance between us.

"Are we ok?" I couldn't help expressing the crushing fear inside of me. He walked over, his fingertips running gently down the side of my cheek.

"Eat. You'll waste away with worry otherwise. You need your energy for whatever is to come, and rest." He avoided my question, even if his touch spoke volumes. We were ok, yet his unwavering belief that he had to protect me at all costs, left us at an impasse for now.

I reluctantly reached for a sandwich and took a bite, offering him some, which he declined. "I've already eaten. That's for you."

I took another forceful bite and a sip of milk. "I don't know if I can get any rest considering our situation."

"You have to."

"And you? When do you rest?" I said, and then remembered, he didn't need to. He held my gaze.

"I don't need it. Eat. I'll check on you later." He traced my cheek again and walked out of the room without another word. He could pretend all he wanted, but he was as worried as I was.

Not long before midnight, the heavy rain returned. The water was soothing, it always helped calm my anxious mind.

"Is it your habit to fall asleep by your window on rainy nights?"

His words stirred me from sleep as he picked me up effortlessly, tucking me into bed. Between the sleepy haze, I realized what his words meant. He had carried me to bed that night—I hadn't sleepwalked as I had suspected. He had been here in my room, even before the night of the fair.

"It was you," I whispered, my eyes heavy.

"Yes. I'm here now. Sleep." Nestling close, he settled beside me.

DRAKE

I watched her sleeping from beside me, and I cradled her closer. Her face, pale reminding me of Isabel's figure edged over the lake's surface, the memory darkened my mood further.

She had said she would never hate me for being a monster, yet I had seen the anger on her face, felt her contempt earlier. I was selfish, heartless, a monster, but I couldn't bring myself to let her go. She refused to leave, and without knowing it, she was sealing the guardianship's fate. If we stayed, the moment they came for her, they would cease to exist. Innocent or not, I would end their miserable lives to keep her safe, even if she came to despise me for it.

She stirred in my arms, and I eased my hold on her.

"No." Her sleepy voice made me freeze. "Please, save her." She whispered in her sleep, wrestling against the sheets. Something tightened in my chest.

The shadows wrestled with the light inside my head. My actions had made her unhappy. She was worried about Celest, and I couldn't deny that a part of me felt something for the loss of the woman.

Her scent would likely be washed away by now from all the rain, but I could try tracing it. Maybe if I managed to get her back, Belynda would see reason and come away with me willingly. Celest could come along too, if that's what made her happy.

The shadows crooned with reluctance to abandon her side. Leaving her was dangerous; she would be unprotected, the darkness reminded me.

"Please don't." She murmured. "I'm not going." The shadows stilled inside me. I was her nightmare. The notion crumbled something inside me, and I pushed away from the bed. Rising to my feet, I searched her night table for her journal and wrote her a note.

I wanted to protect her, but if she came to hate me, if she came to despise the monster, I would lose her. Neither monster nor human were ready to let her go. The shadows ebbed under silent compromise as I left her sleeping form.

BELYNDA

Coldness prickled my skin, and I stirred in bed to find Drake was gone. My eyes adjusted to the darkness of the room, and the heaviness of reality came back to haunt me. *Celest.*

A neatly folded piece of paper on the pillow caught my attention. Switching on the lamp, I read over the soft strokes of pen, running my fingers over Drake's writing.

> I've gone to find her. I will bring her back.
> This is my promise, but you must keep yours—
> Drake.

I GLANCED at the clock on the night table: 4:05 AM. I rose from the bed and left my room. His door was slightly ajar, and I entered to find his bed perfectly made. As I turned to leave, a silver gleam on his dresser caught my attention. Celest's phone.

I hesitated, knowing Drake had warned against calling her brother, and yet, I couldn't help but think he was wrong. We needed all the help we could get, and he couldn't see that. His obsession with protecting me clouded his judgment. Finding Seymor's number, I hit the call button as I walked downstairs.

"Celest?" A British accent echoed through the speaker, taking me by surprise.

"Uh, hello. It's not Celest."

There was a short pause on the line.

"Belynda, is that you?" He asked with apprehension.

"Yes. I'm sorry, I didn't know who else to call."

"Where is Celest?" His concern confirmed I was right to call. Seymor didn't know.

"She was taken from the library."

The long pause at the end of the line unsettled me. "Belynda, listen to me carefully. If Stephen has sent for Celest without the council's consent, it means he doesn't care about the consequences of breaking the covenant."

"Then what can we do? There must be a way to help Celest. We can't just sit around!"

"You do nothing for now. You need to be careful. Do not attempt anything foolish. I'm in the States. I'll be there soon."

"But Celest said the only way to stop Stephen from reaching a decision was if the entire council was not present to vote."

"We're past that now, especially since Stephen has decided to go after her and break the covenant. He will have his way with or without the vote. The only thing we can do is be there and exercise our right to question his decisions. I know you're worried, but your safety is far more important than all of ours, and Celest knows that as well as I do. So please, be careful, and whatever you do, do not underestimate Stephen. Stay close to the fire-bound. Do not leave his side. He will protect you." I frowned.

"Drake went to find Celest," I said.

"He shouldn't have done that." I heard the disapproval in his tone. "He won't be able to get her back without a confrontation. He should be with you. Your safety is more important."

I wanted to say it was my fault. I was the one who had begged him to help her when he had refused, but I held my tongue. Everyone around me had suddenly gone mad. Celest's life was just as valuable as mine.

"If you think your return to the council will help, then you should hurry."

"Please be careful. I'll be in touch." Seymor ended the call, and I knew Drake would be furious, but I didn't care.

I thought about what Seymor had said. If getting Celest back resulted in a confrontation, I knew Drake would put an end to it all without hesitation. He would accept the consequences and the losses, and I would hate myself for having driven him to it.

I shook my head to dispel the idea and prayed it didn't have to come to that.

15

NO BROKEN PROMISES

TIME PASSED, AND DREAD BEGAN TO SETTLE OVER ME. Drake hadn't returned, and it was almost dawn. Anxiously, I paced by the entrance hall. The loud creak on the porch floorboards, almost made me cry with relief. *Drake was back.* I pulled open the door and froze.

took a deep breath, surveying the hunting party standing outside. Under the soft porch light stood two young women, likely in their twenties, and a boy not much older than myself. Hovering behind them were two burly men. It didn't take introductions to know who they were. I closed the door behind me and stepped onto the porch. Drake's voice echoed at the back of my mind, *"Stay safe. Hide your powers."*

"Hello?" I offered, breaking the silence.

"Your name?" demanded one of the girls with short, raven hair, unmistakably an elemental. She couldn't be this rude and smug if she didn't have a shield for that unpleasant attitude. I wasn't intimidated; knowing I had power over three elements gave me the courage I needed.

"This is my home. Shouldn't I be the one asking that? After all, you're the ones knocking on my door at this early hour." My tone was firm, though I realized in my position, I should have been more cautious.

The girl didn't appreciate my response, evident from the icy, venomous smile she returned. It unsettled me, and I realized I should have been less candid.

"Ah, yes...where are my manners? I must say you're quite bold...but I'm afraid I have little patience for idle chitchat and introductions." She turned to the blond girl beside her with a sinister smile. "Alexia here will handle the introductions."

The blond girl hesitated, but it was the boy who spoke up. "Amirth, that's not what we agreed upon."

The raven-haired girl shot him a murderous look, and he shrank back, clearly indicating who was in charge. I needed to be cautious with her.

"Alexia, do introduce yourself," she commanded.

The blond girl seemed unsure, and the moment her eyes turned to me, my world tilted on its axis. My vision, thoughts, and the world turned. Everything slowed down yet moved too fast for me to understand what was happening.

Pain surged through my body. Gasping for breath, I struggled to stand. The moment clarity replaced shock, I realized Alexia was an air elemental. The force of her summoned wind had shot me over the porch rail.

The world seemed to move in slow motion, my senses dulled yet hyper-aware. Cold metal pressed against my throat, grounding me to the grim reality. Drake moved swiftly, snapping one of the guards' necks. A horror scene rested before me as the man's body slumped to the ground.

DRAKE

The trail had been lost—washed away under the rain, dissipating just over the mountains. *Go back,* the shadows urged, growing more unsettled. But my senses caught a faint trail once more, only for it to die again. *Forget the woman and go back!* Darkness beckoned, and I was tempted to listen. I had been gone for too long. I had made a promise. I knew if I continued, I would eventually find another trace. Even if it took me days, I would find them. Yet, the monster was restless. I had to return, make sure she was safe first.

Ignoring the new trail my senses picked up, I turned around and streaked down the mountain, back to her.

As I neared the house, my nose prickled, alert to new scents. This time, I didn't hide in the woods. Instead, I raced up the road, straight to the Manor.

Her piercing scream turned my soul to ice. I reached the house just in time to see her hit the ground. Darkness cradled me as I moved with inhuman speed, twisting the neck of the man closest to me. Her eyes met mine, horror reflected in them as I let the man's body slump to the floor.

I took a step toward her but was catapulted against the porch rails. I was up in an instant, racing to her, but the earth broke open before me, creating a chasm that swallowed me. I clawed my way up and shot out of the hole, landing before the elementals. Darkness seeped from my pores, and in that instant, I embraced the shadows.

"Drake!" she screamed, her voice cutting through the haze, as the other man pulled her to her feet.

"Look at me," I beckoned her. "Everything is going to be alright." I said, knowing in the depths of my darkness that I wouldn't hurt her, nor would my shadows, but they would take everyone else. I took a deep breath, and as the storm of madness began to consume me, I felt a prickling at my back. I turned, and her face blurred before me. My body swayed as I turned towards the road, my senses numbing as the two men. Whatever magic they had used on me, was working.

"No..." Belynda cried out, as my knees hit the ground. Terror gripped me as her form began to blur.

"You promised..." I whispered, before a dark blanket of night settled over me.

BELYNDA

Drake's body fell heavily against the ground. The sound, like a crashing boulder echoing in my head.

"NOOO. Let go of me! Drake, wake up! What have you done to him?" I screamed, blinded with fury, kicking, and struggling against the man's hold.

"He'll live. It's just a tranquilizer," the elemental boy said, approaching Drake. In the dim light of dawn, I saw them then —multiple silver darts embedded in Drake's back. I followed their gaze across the road to see two emerging figures. The larger one held the gun.

"Please," I begged, struggling against my captor. I had never been one for violence, but all I wanted was vengeance.

Amirth laughed, and it took every ounce of my willpower

not to break my word and use my powers. She was an earth elemental, surely vulnerable to water. I had promised not to fight back—not yet anyway. Closing my eyes, I saw only Drake's pleading eyes, his last words. He was right if they hadn't killed us yet, it meant they were taking us, to where they had Celest. I would wait patiently and then, I would make them pay.

"The demon doesn't belong here. But you already know that." Amirth said.

"You don't know a thing about him. You're the monster," I spat at her feet, forcing her to take a step back.

"You stupid girl. If I didn't know you would break so easily, I'd teach you a lesson. Tyrus, put her out," she ordered, glancing at the man who held the gun.

"I'm sure we can deal with the girl without—" The man began to argue, but Amirth snatched the gun from his hands and fired a dart into my leg.

Even as darkness closed in around me, I held onto my promise—it was the last thought before everything went silent.

TYRUS

"Next time you hesitate on my orders, you will have Stephen to answer to. Is that understood?" I kept my mouth shut and my fists clenched. I was a powerless human—a soldier, but still powerless. Amirth had the ability to crush me without even lifting a finger. If that wasn't enough to keep me in place, knowing she was a cold-blooded monster did. I pulled out my radio and ordered my men to bring the car. The sun was rising, and we needed to move this show out of prying eyes. We loaded the unconscious man-creature into one of the Jeeps and placed the girl in my car. I was glad Amirth chose to ride with the creature. I wasn't sure I had much patience left in me today.

The girl lay motionless in the back as I drove deeper into the mountains, sparing a glance in the rearview mirror, I felt conflicted. Oliver wasn't going to be happy about this or the fact that his best friend had been the one to betray her to his father.

"Sir," the radio interrupted my thoughts.

"Speak, Thomas."

"Sir. The man is starting to shift."

It couldn't be. One tranquilizer was enough to knock out an elephant for an hour, and it had been no more than thirty minutes. He should be out cold for hours.

"Dose him again, then. We don't know what we're dealing with here, so make sure you keep him under until we're there."

"Yes, Sir."

I didn't like this one bit. I glanced at the sleeping girl once again and sighed. *What the hell was I doing? This was wrong...*

I took out my phone and dialed the only person I thought could perhaps intervene and help her.

BELYNDA

Bright dots swarmed my mind, intensifying the throbbing pain inside my head. My voice sounded foreign to my ears as my groans of pain echoed against the walls. After a while, the unbearable ache in my head began to subside. The unsettling stench of humidity assaulted my senses, but I welcomed it. It meant I was still alive. Opening my eyes slowly, I adjusted to the darkness.

Where the hell was I? Was I dreaming? Had I traveled back in time? I had only seen the likes of this place in movies with castles and dungeons. The naturally carved walls connected to cobblestone floors. There was a wooden door with metal bars —undoubtedly, it was not a twenty-first-century hotel accommodation. This was my prison cell. The musky stench of humidity and mold overwhelmed my senses. As my eyes adjusted to the darkness, I could see more details. Deep cracks slithered down the walls; water slid down slowly through the built-up moss. Wherever this place was, it had to be underground.

I touched my leg where the dart had hit; it was no longer tender, so I probably was unconscious for a while. A tiny window was open at the top of the door. While it wasn't large enough to escape through, it was enough to look outside. Using the metal bars on the door, I pulled myself up and clung to them, stilling as a dizzy spell raked over me. *Just breathe*, I reminded myself. I was strong. I could do this.

As I glanced through the small opening, disappointment settled in. There was only a stone corridor, poorly illuminated by a dancing glow: a light that could only come from torches or candles. Somehow, I had expected the lair to be more modern—at the very least, in tune with the times. It was surprising that although they had evolved, they still chose to operate in such an ancient fashion. For all I knew, we were not in Cummington anymore. Yet there was one thing I understood for certain. I had to find a way to get out of here and find Drake and Celest. I could use my powers, but I had made a promise.

I inspected the rock walls that surrounded me, contemplating the idea of using my earth element to break free. I reached the same conclusion—I couldn't give myself away. They had to come for me. It was only a matter of time before they realized that they didn't have the sacred book.

The only thing I could do was help to speed up the process. This time I stood without support, glad when the wave of nausea evaded me.

"HELLO?" I yelled. "Is anybody there? Can someone hear me?"

The only answer was a resounding echo.

"This is no use," I whispered.

I should have included lock-picking in my training. Slumping onto the humid floor, I leaned back against the door. I fought the tears that threatened to weaken my spirit. I refused to give up. Drake and Celest had to be okay. I just had to wait.

Minutes passed, and I occupied myself by playing with the water elemental. At the flick of my wrist, the constant dripping from the roof and walls ceased. Yet the overwhelming silence drove me mad, so I allowed the water to flow once more. After bending the element to stop and start its natural flow several times, I willed it to gather in front of me: a shaped water mass that I raised to my eye level. I smiled, satisfied, and poked the floating water blob.

The sound of approaching footsteps startled me, and I released the element. The water collapsed and splashed my pants. I stood quickly, staring through the small opening of the door.

"Hello. Let me out!" I shouted as the moving silhouettes came to a halt in the corridor, standing outside of my door.

"No need to shout. We haven't forgotten you."

I tensed at the sound of the voice. It was Amirth, and hovering behind her was the one who shot Drake.

Do not fight...stay calm. You only get one chance, I repeated to myself as they fumbled with the keys.

"Where am I? Where is Drake?" I commanded, staring at Amirth as the other man held my arm, guiding me down the corridor.

"Silence!" Amirth snapped.

The lit torches alternated as we moved down the corridor, bringing to life the creepy catacombs. We walked for a good five minutes, turning left and right through the labyrinth of corridors that all looked the same. This place was huge. It would be next to impossible to escape without getting lost.

Soon, we found ourselves in a connecting hall. Amirth slowed her pace and turned to us.

"Take her to the chamber. I will join you shortly," she ordered, before turning down the opposite corridor.

Tyrus kept me moving quickly. We were alone; it would be easy to knock him out without exposing my powers. *This was my only opportunity.* As I was about to summon air, we reached the end of the corridor, and I was distracted by the stark change around me. The walls were less rustic yet still eerily cold. It was definitely more modern than the dungeons we had left behind. There was no other way to continue but through the double metal doors in front of us.

"Where are you taking me?"

Perhaps I could persuade him to let me go—after all, he had hesitated to shoot me before.

He didn't speak. Instead, he pushed me through the doors, and I froze.

A worried-looking Oliver paced on the other side, and when he saw me, relief flooded his face. A knot formed in my throat, and I repressed the urge to cry, unsure if it was the hurt from his deceit or the hope of seeing a familiar face. Tyrus released my arm, and Oliver took a few steps, closing the distance, surprising me when he pulled me in for a hug.

"I'm so sorry," he said. I remained frozen, not knowing what to do or say or what to make of this situation. "Tyrus called me. I'm sorry it took so long for me to get here."

"You're behind this? Please tell me you had nothing to do with that man attacking me at the fair or the reason that I am here."

I wanted to believe there was some good in my brother, even if he didn't believe it himself.

"I swear I didn't know it would come to this. I never meant to hurt you. You have to believe me. There are people behind this—others that I cannot excuse or fight against."

"I know your father is. But you...I was never sure about you." I confessed; he stared at me with a searching look.

"I take it you're not completely innocent in this. How much do you know about the guardianship?" Taking my necklace in his hand, I knew what he was looking at—the family crest. For the first time, we weren't hiding from one another.

"Some. But apparently, there's a lot we don't know about each other."

"You should know that I don't justify my father's actions. He can't do this and expect to get away with it: assault, kidnapping...the council needs to hear about this. That's why I'm here. But first, we're getting you out. Then, I expect a long explanation."

"No, wait...not without Drake and Celest." Oliver glanced at the man, confused.

"Tyrus..."

"I'm sorry. I'm afraid that's impossible."

"What is she talking about?" Oliver pressed.

"Your father gave the orders. Celest was brought into the chamber yesterday for interrogation. The one she calls Drake... well, that's a whole different level of complicated. He's secured in the chamber as we speak and under strict orders. How do I put this? He's not...quite of this world."

"Is that the immortal who breached through the portal? The one who helped you at the fair?" Oliver stared at me, waiting for answers, but I had no idea how to respond. "An immortal...Belynda, I would hate to think that my father was right about you."

"He isn't. We have done nothing wrong. I promise. Despite what everyone thinks, Drake is not a monster. Everything this legacy has taught you is a lie. There are bigger forces at play. You just have to trust me when I say that he is bound to my destiny, and I...I love him." I didn't miss the way he flinched as I spoke the words I hadn't dared speak before.

"You love him? An immortal?" He ran a hand through his golden hair. "I'm sorry. I need a minute."

I had been right. Oliver had feelings for me. Impossible feelings.

"Oliver—us…we can never be together."

"Why not?" He paced back towards me, staring into my eyes. I couldn't tell him. No, it wasn't my secret to tell.

"I admit that up to a few weeks ago, I hated you. Though that's all changed now that I see the real you. I like you as a friend, Oliver. Like the brother I never had. Anything else is not in me to give." He rubbed his temple, pacing again. Yet when he turned, he faced Tyrus with a look of resolve.

"Are you sure there isn't anything we can do to get them out?"

"I'm afraid not. Not from the chamber. Most of the council is present, and so are the elementals and a team of my men."

"You could order your men out."

"You know that even without my men, we can't just waltz in there and pick them out from under your father's nose. Not with the elementals about too, unless you've got some magic powers I don't know about, son."

"Yeah…well, you know I didn't inherit that family trait."

They laughed, and I finally understood. Oliver was not the firstborn, so he hadn't inherited the guardian gifts. But I had…I was Stephen's firstborn. To my surprise and relief, Oliver didn't seem disappointed by the idea. On the contrary, he seemed glad to have been spared from the family trait. I released a sigh of relief, knowing power wasn't what he sought.

"I've realized that there is no running from one's fate. So, if there is no way to get them out, I will face your father and the council. You'll be there and so will Tyrus. You can speak on my behalf, and perhaps we can make the council see reason. As long as we have them on our side, we have a chance."

Oliver and Tyrus looked at each other, then back at me as if I had grown two heads.

"You don't know what you're saying. You can't go in there," Oliver pressed. "You underestimate my father. He won't hesitate to kill us all if we become a threat to him or his legacy."

Fear slid down my throat like a silent knife.

"I'm not afraid. There is no other way; there isn't a place I can go where he won't find me. If I can't walk out of here with Celest and Drake, I'm staying and facing your father...whatever the outcome."

"She's a tough one, isn't she?" said Tyrus.

"Hard-headed is more like it," Oliver countered. "I won't change your mind, will I?"

"No."

"Follow me then." Pushing open the two heavy doors, he strode through. "Watch your step, and whatever you do, stay away from the edge. These steps are a slippery death trap."

As I followed him into the consuming darkness beneath us, I gasped.

The torches illuminated the descending spiral stairs. Ahead of us, there was only darkness. For once, I did as I was told without complaint. He was right, one wrong step and it would all be over.

The further we descended, the more convinced I became that the guardian's lair was in another world and time. I glanced at the dancing shadows on Oliver's face, and then at Tyrus, who hadn't said much. Could I even trust him? He had shot Drake but had hesitated with me. Perhaps like Oliver, he could see the wrong in all of this but couldn't do much about it. I could work with that. I could make him see—give him a chance to redeem himself.

Every step we took was more frightening than the last; I was closer to facing Stephen but also closer to Drake.

"How much farther is it?"

Oliver's steps didn't falter.

"Almost there." *I wanted to throw up.* This was it.

"Can you tell me more about your father?" Oliver was silent for a measurable time, but then he stopped, reaching behind, and taking my hand.

"I wish I could tell you that you have nothing to worry about, but I would be lying. I'm sorry. No son should have to say this, but my father is a cruel man. One way or another, he will get his way. He always does. The council will have you answer for your involvement with the immortal and how he came to be here by whatever means necessary. I beg you...please reconsider this crazy idea. Let us help you out."

"That's not an option. I already told you; I'm not leaving without them. I'm not afraid." I pulled my hand from his. "What about you? Where do you stand in all of this? Is there nothing you can do?"

Oliver glanced at Tyrus.

"We will do everything we can, I promise. But Tyrus is right; we are no match for the elementals." They wouldn't sacrifice themselves for me, nor would I have expected it. But perhaps they would stand aside when the time came for me to do my part.

"I understand. Will I see any other familiar faces? I'd rather not have any more surprises."

"Ben will likely be there. He's in line to inherit a seat from his father."

"Ben? Lily's Ben?"

Oliver confirmed with a firm nod. "Maybe he'll be willing to help us too."

"I wouldn't count on that," Tyrus offered.

"Oh..." That I had not expected.

"Let's just say that Ben is not as charming and quiet as he pretends. He is the reason why my father moved to collect you; he told him about the necklace you're wearing and the Cromwell crest inside of it."

One would have thought I'd be used to all the lies and betrayals by now, but I wasn't. The truth hurt every damn time.

"Does Lily know?" If she did, it would devastate me.

"No, and I'm not sure she could handle the truth, to be honest."

Neither could I, but I didn't agree with Ben lying to her; lying to my friend, even if technically, I was doing the same.

"I wonder why the necklace caught his attention." I felt the stone grow heavy on my chest and Oliver glanced at me. It wasn't hard to guess what he was thinking. I was the one wearing it. I should know its value.

"It's unique, actually. The Cromwell name has been part of the council since the first circle of guardians. However, their line died a while back. So, you can see why my father would be interested in knowing how you have it; I have to admit even I am curious myself."

I was too afraid to reveal the reason to Oliver, scared to announce my connection to Isabel. Our bond and the prophecy were likely the reason the necklace came to be in my family's possession. The Cromwell legacy died with Isabel.

"The necklace was a gift from Celest. I don't really know how it came to my family, or much else for that matter."

Oliver laughed without humor.

"You know, I thought I had you all figured out. I wish we had more time to talk. To start over. Things would have been different without so many secrets between us."

Oh, Oliver...it was impossible.

"We can still be friends..."

"Yes. You've said that already."

"Can you tell me where we are?" I asked, trying to shift the subject.

"Only a few hours' drive up the mountains."

I was right. This place was deep underground, considering the humidity on the walls. We reached the end of the stairs, greeted by another set of iron doors. Tyrus pulled them open, and the lights momentarily blinded me.

"Your eyes will adjust," Oliver added as he guided me through an open chamber, illuminated by hanging chandeliers. I couldn't believe my eyes: the high vaulted ceilings, the massive columns...it was a place of fairy tales. In this case, more like the evil lord's lair. Nonetheless, it was like nothing I had ever seen.

Tyrus came to a halt, and Oliver's back stiffened. Something about his sudden change told me that beyond the doors awaited our final destination.

"I take it this is it?" I murmured under my breath. For the first time, Tyrus faced me with an earnest expression.

"A word of advice. Tell them what they want or give them

what they require. Oliver is right. You have no idea what you're dealing with."

Perhaps it is they who have no idea. I wanted to voice my thoughts but instead held my tongue.

"Thank you. Thank you both." I glanced at Oliver and detected the fear written on his face. He closed the distance between the wooden doors and knocked twice.

A minute later, both doors opened simultaneously, exposing a grand room. The high vaulted ceilings were extensively adorned with hanging iron chandeliers, each filled with hundreds of candles, bathing the entire space with light.

This place made me feel like a young debutante, entering the grand ballroom to be presented to society. It was breathtaking and terrifying all at once.

As Oliver and Tyrus guided me across the threshold, the magic of the place began to fade.

Gathered at the far side of the chamber was a group of men wearing long dark robes. I didn't need an introduction; Isabel's revelations were still vivid in my mind. I had not forgotten what their gathering looked like; it was the council members, and surely among them, Stephen.

The collective exchanges and murmurs resounded around the chamber walls like the buzzing of bees. Taking a deep breath, I continued to follow the commotion taking place on the other side of the room.

The closer I got, the faster my heart pounded, and I finally saw what the uproar was about. *Drake...*

A tranquilizer dart shot at his chest. How many times had they done that to him? I fought the tears brimming in my eyes; Tyrus caught my distress and leaned in, to whisper.

"He's alright. He's strong. That's the only way they can contain him."

"It's still not right; he's not an animal." Breaking away from Tyrus and Oliver, I ran towards Drake. He was unconscious, but even so, he stirred at my touch.

"Drake, come back to me. Come back, please." Tyrus pulled me away, gripping me around the waist as I struggled to get free.

"Let go of me. You monsters! Don't do this."

"Belynda, stop. Get a grip. Please." Oliver pleaded next to me, but all I saw was Drake on the floor. I punched and raged against Tyrus, but he didn't budge.

"Enough!" The resounding voice came from behind. The echo and silence that followed were enough to chill my bones.

Standing barely ten feet away from me stood Stephen. I knew it was him. *Finally, my father...* There was no doubt in my mind. I would recognize those eyes anywhere. After all, I saw them every day in the mirror.

It was strange to see my resemblance mirrored in someone I had come to despise so much. As I stared at his face, I noticed the hardened lines on his forehead and the dark expression he held.

He could never be my father: this man with the dark aura had no regard for anything else except himself and his purpose. That much was clear.

The hinges on the wooden doors creaked in the distance, and as they opened, my heart caught in my throat. Leading the procession was Amirth, flanked by Alexia and the red-haired boy. However, this time, it was the man following behind who had my attention. They held up Celest, who was slumped over their shoulders, barely able to stand. Her clothes were torn and soiled. As they released her in front of Stephen, Celest noticed me, and a semblance of despair marred her face. My own tears brimmed, fueled by rage.

"I'm so sorry," she cried, crumbling to her knees. Glancing at Drake's stiff form with a look of horror, I realized then why she was apologizing. She thought he was dead.

"He's not dead," I said. She looked at me with a gleam of hope, just as Drake stirred.

Groaning, he fought to regain consciousness. Those tranquilizers didn't seem to have much of a lasting effect on him. It must have been his fire element, burning it away.

"Just in time," Stephen's voice broke through the silence as Drake pushed himself up from the cold stone floor and onto his knees. The rest of the council members kept their distance, evidently afraid of the immortal before them. On the other hand, Stephen appeared perfectly at ease as three elementals flanked him.

"Belynda..." My name on Drake's lips was no more than a breathless whisper, but it made my skin tremble. Pulling the darts from his chest, he dropped them against the floor. Glancing around until his eyes found me, he stood, and everyone took a step back. Without anyone to stop him, he moved toward me.

Tyrus held me firmly, but I felt his grip loosen as Drake drew closer. The man who now held the gun took a deliberate step forward, aiming the weapon at Drake. Stephen raised a hand to stop him.

"That's enough. We need him conscious for this. You may leave us; we can handle it from here."

Tyrus signaled for his men to retire, and they did without question. I watched them exit the chamber. Tyrus, however, remained behind me, standing next to Oliver.

Drake reached for my waist and pulled me to him. All my strength crumbled at his touch, and the tears flowed as I clung to him, breathing in his scent in case it was the last time.

"This is certainly unexpected, but it explains your girl's tenacity to defend the immortal," Stephen spoke directly to Celest. "What I still don't understand is how the portal was opened without the council."

"I already told you how. I did it." Celest declared defiantly, staring up at Stephen.

"Oh... Celest. Haven't you had enough?" Stephen moved the strands of matted hair from her forehead with a look of contempt and disgust. "Don't attempt to make a fool of us. We both know you don't have that power, which only proves you're trying to protect someone or hiding something." His attention shifted to Drake. "We all know it is not the beast." His words made my blood run cold.

"You are the beast!" The poisonous words flowed from my lips without reservation.

"It's alright," Drake whispered against my ear, and it bothered me even more knowing that he believed his words too.

"No, it's not okay. *He's* the animal. Look at what they've done to Celest. They are the monsters."

"That's enough," Stephen interrupted impatiently. "If you don't tell me who opened the portal this very instant, then I will give your girl a reason to call me a beast." He struck Celest across the face without warning, and she cried out.

"STOP IT!" I launched forward on instinct, but Drake held me back.

"This isn't right! They deserve a fair trial," Oliver yelled.

"You dare speak for them! You forget your place," Stephen roared.

"And you forget the rules you're bound to." Oliver took a step back and turned to the council. "You can't stand and watch idly while my father breaks the covenant."

Low murmurs erupted among the council members.

"Enough." Stephen's commanding tone silenced the buzz of voices. "I'm waiting," he pressed, determined to get answers.

I tried to go to Celest, but Drake refused to release me. "Don't. Not yet. You wanted me to trust your brother. Let him have his chance," Drake whispered, his voice low and calculating as he pulled me back.

I pushed against him again in vain. He was unyielding like stone.

"Stop this, or I will be the first witness on trial against you when her brother and the rest of the council members arrive. I promise you that," Oliver threatened.

"Look at you. If you showed the same devotion to the guardianship as you do for that girl, I would be proud to call you my son."

I felt so much rage, wishing to scream at Stephen for being such a coward.

"That's a lie. We both know you don't care about anyone but yourself—not the guardianship or me. All you do is feed off the power that this position gives you. You are abusive, manipulative, and a coward who enjoys the fear of others."

Stephen laughed like a madman at Oliver's accusations. "Look around you. How do you think this legacy was preserved if not with blood and sacrifice? I made the decisions that none of them were willing to make."

Stephen turned to face his council members. "He speaks of the covenant: a thousand-year-old rule only in place to hold us back. The faulty rules of the covenant allowed him, an immortal, to breach the gates we were meant to protect. The covenant stops us from making decisions—important decisions that can save or end us all. What makes you think the breach will end with him?" His words served to unsettle the council members and, like he had expected, to instill fear.

The doors to the chamber opened and everyone's attention fell on the three council members that strode in. Celest's face lit up with relief.

"Seymor..." she whispered. He looked older, and his eyes appeared tired. The resemblance between the pair was uncanny. A spark of hope ignited in me with his arrival; Seymor and the two other guardians didn't join the rest of the council.

"Sylvie, Ren... Seymor. A pleasure to have you back in the conclave. It's been a while," Stephen offered with a tight, cold smile.

"I'm afraid I can't say the same... What the bloody hell is going on here, Stephen?" It was the lady who walked in with Seymor who spoke, questioning the spectacle before her. Seymor, I realized, was still frozen, shocked by the state of his sister.

"You have crossed the line here." Seymor finally spoke. Without preamble, he moved toward Celest's side.

Amirth looked at Alexia and the red-haired boy — the message was clear. They took a step forward, and Seymor froze.

"You can't do this. You have to let her go."

"I don't think I will. You see, your sister here has betrayed the guardianship. She's hiding information from this council and is yet to explain how the portal allowing the immortal's breach was opened. She claims she did it herself, but we all know she doesn't have that kind of power. Perhaps she would care to explain now that you're here."

"Whatever your accusations are against her, this is not the way. You've broken the covenant. That's enough to stand trial right beside her."

"Is this what this legacy has been reduced to? Rules. Doesn't everyone see the danger we face by having this immortal in our world? The exposure, the mess we have in our hands. Who wants to accuse me of breaking the covenant? Rules that somehow only exist to protect creatures like him."

The murmurs of the council rose, echoing around the chamber.

"He's right. Celest might be your sister, but I'm sure the council would like to remind you that your duties to the guardianship come first." The familiarity of that voice had me searching among the council members. It was Ben. He glanced at Oliver, as if conveying the same message to him. He would choose his calling over their friendship.

"You don't have the right to speak for the council," Oliver snapped.

"Neither do you," Ben countered.

"But I do," spoke the man beside Ben. "And I believe I

speak for everyone when I say that we face something we may have never faced before. My son is right, Seymor. You must put aside any ties that may blind you to the truth." I had never met Ben's father, but I knew it was him the moment he spoke. *Like father, like son.*

Although the same didn't apply to Oliver and our father; he had proven to be nothing like him, and Drake was starting to see it too. Isabel's mother had chosen the guardianship over her own daughter. I would not see that happen again; I prayed Seymor would show more common sense than Isabel's mother had.

"You certainly don't speak for me," said the man beside Seymor.

"Or me," added the lady by his side.

"And definitely not me," Seymor concluded, staring at Ben's father.

"I believe I speak for the majority of the council," Stephen interjected, trying to conclude the argument in his favor. "And the way I see it, if you're not here to protect the legacy and what it stands for, you're against it."

"This is not a dictatorship. That is the very reason why the covenant is in place. The council must vote."

"Ren, Ren. You and your ideals are always getting in the way. You want a vote? Fine. Then we vote. All those who agree with me, say 'yea,' and those opposed and stand by the covenant say 'nay.'"

Loud murmurs turned into chaos with a mixture of responses. I counted each in turn.

"Yea, yea, yea, yea, yea."

Sylvie, Ren, and Seymor called their vote, and my heart

raced. "Nay, nay, nay." Then another older man who stood with the rest of the council. "Nay."

"I vote yea, and as you can see, I call the majority. Are you satisfied, Ren?" His face was euphoric. Oliver was right. Power was like a drug to him. I no longer struggled against Drake. He held me as we watched the spectacle unfold. I wasn't sure what would happen now that it was evident where most of the support lay.

"Stephen, I have always pledged my support to the guardianship, but I will not let you hurt my sister."

"Then you and everyone who opposes my decision and that of the council will be treated as a traitor, just like her."

Ren, Sylvie, and Seymor whispered in the silence, and the elementals deliberately gravitated closer. Seymor seemed to argue with the other two members, but it was Ren who spoke up.

"We will hear what Celest has to say on the matter."

I stared at Seymor, evidently displeased by this but refusing to look away.

"Very well." Stephen strolled back to Celest and pulled her forcefully by the arm. "I will give you a chance again to explain how you claim to have opened the portal yourself."

Celest looked at Drake and me, then at her brother. "I already told you. I found a spell in the reliquary. I did it myself."

"You're lying. No such spell exists that would allow a single guardian, let alone a human to open the gates of the realms."

"You don't know that. It was you who had me searching

for the Sacred Book all these years—I found it and used it." The murmurs of the council erupted once again.

"Give us the book then." Her eyes flickered to me, then back to my father.

"I won't."

"You won't?" His loud voice echoed around the chamber. His patience thinning.

"It was destroyed." Celest said, and my father's face turned murderous.

"Celest, you are testing my patience, you truly are." He withdrew a small dagger from one of the pockets on his robe and gripped her arm, turning her to point the blade against her throat. "If you won't speak, perhaps someone else will do so on your behalf."

Celest shrieked as the tip of the blade bit into her skin. I couldn't stand by and watch this. I struggled against Drake's hold, but he didn't budge. Oliver and Seymor protested, but no one else moved. The elementals positioned themselves in front of Stephen as if daring someone to act.

He pulled Celest at his whim and pressed the blade harder.

"Show them what you can do," Drake whispered against my ear, and I stared into his eyes. The subtle nod from his head encouraging. "You can start it love, I will end it," he whispered.

A fresh trickle of blood flowed from Celest's neck, and the panic was clear in her eyes, before she fainted, her body slumping against his. My logic clouded, and my sight became a blur. I stared at her ashen face and the other faces around me, but they were all out of focus. All I could hear was the sound of my erratic breathing, then the earth began to shake beneath our feet. The whole place vibrated, and even the walls trembled. I willed the stone floors to crack, and they did so willingly, allowing me to escape from Drake's hold. Everyone wore the same look of confusion. Drake had been right. Surprising them was my strongest card.

"Amirth—stop!" Stephen's commanding voice echoed over the loud uproar.

She looked at him, then at me with a puzzled expression.

"It's her, Master. She's an earth elemental."

For the first time, Stephen looked at me with keen interest and horror.

"Do something. Stop this at once!" he barked at the elementals, who stood frozen while he sought shelter amongst the rest of the council.

My concentration broke as a strange feeling of weightlessness took over my body. Drake's arms abandoned me, and I saw the chamber's ceiling fly before my eyes as my body moved through the air. I felt life escape my body as my back collided against the stone on the farthest wall. My previous experience with Alexia's power had been nothing more than a roller-coaster ride. This time, she held nothing back.

My back throbbed as excruciating pain tore across every part of my body. I fought to catch my breath as the blow knocked the air from my lungs; the pressure on my back and chest made it impossible to stand. Someone held my hand, and I held on to them like an anchor.

"Belynda, breathe, just breathe. I'm here." *Oliver...* Where was Drake?

I lifted my head in time to see the horror scene unfold. Drake held Alexia suspended in midair, her neck in a tight grip while she fought to break free and catch her breath. Smoke slowly came out of her mouth.

Amirth screamed, and the earth parted, forcing Drake to break his hold on Alexia. I tried to move, but it was useless. The red-haired boy, who had remained a peaceful bystander until now, raised his hands and erected a wall of fire in Drake's path. Drake stepped right through it unfazed.

"You will have to do better than that." Drake moved swiftly, returning to Alexia, who could barely stand. I stared, horrified, as she lifted her head towards Drake and used her last efforts to catapult him against the ceiling, then back against the floor before collapsing herself.

Amirth and the boy ran to her, bending protectively over her frame. As seconds passed, the pressure on my lungs eased, and I could finally breathe again.

Was it all truly happening? I glanced around the chamber towards Drake as he struggled to his knees. Oliver leaned beside me while Seymor and Ren used the commotion to help Celest. A moment too late, I realized that Stephen had used the unrest to his advantage too. I knew it the instant their strange chanting reached me, followed by a startling cry.

The roar echoed in the chamber and pierced my ears, but it was terror that gripped me the moment I realized it was Drake. He twisted on the floor in agony.

"DRAKE!" I screamed. *I had to go to him...*

"Stop. You're hurt," Oliver said, holding me.

"I have to help him." I managed the words with effort, pushing away from Oliver to stand. *Please give me strength*, I prayed to no one in particular—the fates, Isabel, or any divine power that could help me move. I willed myself to take a step, and a warm, calming sensation flowed through me. I wasn't sure if it was an adrenaline rush or if my prayers had been answered. I fought against the pain that pierced the right side of my ribs while Oliver supported most of my weight. I swayed, but he kept me upright.

With his help, I reached Drake and kneeled beside his still body. He no longer roared in pain, which gave me a shred of hope.

"I'm okay, I promise."

Oliver seemed reluctant to leave my side, but he finally gave us some space and retreated to Tyrus's flank. Taking Drake's hand, his eyes opened. There was something wrong and I knew it instantly: his eyes were bleak, devoid of light. No fire.

"What have they done to me?" His plea only confirmed my fears.

"Tell me what's wrong. Drake, what is it?" Stephen stood, his disciples at his side and a satisfied expression.

"What did you do?" I demanded. "Haven't you done enough?"

"It's gone... the fire," Drake whispered. "All gone. I'm *human*." It wasn't possible, and then I heard Stephen's laugh.

"How do you fix this?" I cried.

"So many questions, yet I still get no answers," he replied. "I would like to know about your power. An earth elemental kept from me..." He glanced between Celest and me, waiting. I remained silent, which only provoked him further. "You will tell me!" he ordered and, without warning, pulled me forcefully to my feet. Drake launched himself between Stephen and me, and he tumbled backward.

"I might not be as strong, but you will have to kill me before you lay a finger on her again." Drake stood protectively in front of me. Stephen's sinister laugh echoed around us as he retreated to the rest of his men.

"We certainly don't want to do that. It is not in our interest to kill you now."

"Of course it isn't, Stephen. Dear," the pleasant voice evoked another buzz of murmurs among the council members. I felt the earth shake beneath me, though as Drake's arms anchored around me, I realized it wasn't the earth that trembled, but me. It felt like Alexia had knocked the air from my lungs again.

"Are you alright?" Drake's voice was like a distant echo. It wasn't my imagination. There, in front of us, stood the ghost of my mother. Everyone stared — Stephen, in particular.

"Felsia..." It was Stephen who broke the hum of voices.

I couldn't find words; the bottled-up need to cry was lodged in the back of my throat.

"Is it really you? How is it possible after all these years... why have you come back now?" I glimpsed the confusion and suspicion on his face as he tried to make sense of the situation.

"Because now is the right moment. This is how it's destined to be."

"You... so many years, Felsia, you abandoned your duties to this council, leaving us weak. You were loyal to me... tell me you have nothing to do with this elemental and the breach. Tell me!" He raised his voice, but my mother was unfazed.

"Oh, Stephen." I watched in slow motion as she took gradual yet deliberate steps toward Drake and me. "Your greed for power blinded you long ago. It made you a tyrant and has kept you from seeing the truth."

She reached my side, gently brushing away the tears from my cheeks.

"This elemental, as you call her, is my daughter." She looked into my eyes, and any feelings of resentment evaporated. I hugged her back with all my strength.

"Shhh, it's alright, my darling girl."

"Your daughter?" Stephen repeated with suspicion and disbelief. My mother turned to him and smiled.

"Our daughter, Stephen. She is our daughter." Gasps extended like a ripple effect among the council members.

"A pure-blood." Ren looked my way, and suddenly all I heard was *"pure-blood, pure-blood"* spoken among the crowd. And one other voice. *Oliver's.*

"My sister..." I met his eyes and watched his expression transform from one of surprise to horror.

"Silence." Stephen roared, quieting the buzzing room. "You come back after all this time only with lies," he accused. "All I have is that poor excuse of a son. *He* is my firstborn. Whatever you claim, she is no daughter of mine."

Tyrus placed a hand on Oliver's shoulder, and I stared at the monster in the eye with all the hatred I could muster.

"You're right; you have no daughter because I would never call you a father. You're a disgrace to humanity. The *real* monster." He stormed across the chamber like a demon blinded by rage.

"Do you think anyone will believe you?" He turned to my mother. "This is Celest's adopted daughter. An earth elemental that was kept from me, from *us*," he amended in front of the rest of the council.

"Did you aid them in opening the portal?" He asked, trying to regain control of the situation.

"That wasn't necessary. You see, Belynda has many gifts because she comes from you and I."

"Impossible. I refuse to hear any more of this absurd tale."

"You can pretend it's not the truth. But deep down, you know we—"

"There was no we—no us. You said nothing happened..." Stephen tried to reason against my mother's revelation.

"I lied." She confessed with a smile, and it served to irritate the monster further.

"You lied, you lied!" He looked ready to punch something. "And you expect us to believe any of this?"

"Have you forgotten the most sacred prophecy?" For the first time, Stephen seemed unsettled. "Yes, I believe you do remember."

"Oh, Felsia... nothing you say is credible, but I do admit, you had me there for a moment." He laughed, approaching the rest of the council.

"Gentlemen, it seems that our end is near, and this child is our doom."

Some laughed, while others murmured among each other.

"Is it possible?" One of the members that voted in Stephen's favor spoke up.

"Of course not," Stephen rebuked. "She might be an elemental, but she is no guardian. This legacy is untouchable and I don't know what you plan to achieve with this web of lies, Felsia, but you will pay nonetheless."

"Surely, we cannot discard the possibility. If she is your daughter…" The same man who had spoken before interjected. "It would certainly explain how the portal was opened. Every member of this council knows that our combined efforts are not enough to open the gates, not anymore. Not without the twelve seats of the conclave." Stephen squeezed his fists tightly together, visibly upset by the defiance.

"There is no pure blood. They have found the Sacred Book, and they will return it to the conclave, even if it's the last thing I do. We will make the covenant whole again with the book and reinforce our power. I will hear no more of this. Tyrus, lock them away but leave the girl. We'll bind her, like the immortal."

"Is that what you did to him?" I questioned.

Stephen addressed the council. "Great power only comes with knowledge—knowledge she doesn't seem to possess. Is this the pureblood you speak of? She is nothing more than a pawn in a bigger plan intended to break our bonds."

"Stephen, don't you think it's time you let them think for themselves?" The murmur within the council intensified, and Stephen's impatience grew as my mother continued to explain. "Belynda, he isn't human. They trapped his element's power within his human essence or, as you say, his soul."

I glanced at Drake and saw relief flow through him at her admission. I realized then that though Drake despised the monster he thought he was, he would never be whole without his fire. Being human wouldn't have been enough for him. With that realization, I felt the heaviness of what that truly meant, unable to picture myself in his life forever.

"I don't have a soul…" Drake whispered, and I knew why. He thought he was damned for his sins.

"You do. All beings, mortal, and immortal, have a soul. The guardians are to blame for that misconception. They allowed creatures outside the human realm to believe that, to expel any unions between our kind and yours. But in truth, there have always been other reasons. Isn't that right, Stephen?"

"They will never be human. That is why it is us who were chosen as keepers of the gates."

"Perhaps that was then but times have changed. When the fates chose us, they did so because they believed in our humble spirits and our ability to be rational. But mostly, they thought we could love one another as equals. Our time is up, Stephen. Whether you believe it to be true or not. Nothing will stop the fates' plan. It is Belynda's path to set things right."

Without warning, Stephen was on me. He barely managed to push me, yet it was with enough force to knock my head to the floor.

I winced as a warm sensation smothered the side of my face. My vision clouded until I gradually became aware of my surroundings once more. My mother hovered protectively over me.

"You're bleeding." She pressed her scarf against my head to stop the flow of blood. Faintly, the commotion in the back-ground heightened my awareness, and I realized that Drake was restrained against the floor by an unseen force. I glanced around and sure enough, Alexia had recovered enough to hold him down. When I glanced at Stephen, I felt an overwhelming satisfaction. He looked disheveled; a cut on his bottom lip was evidence enough that Drake had managed to get to him.

Stephen spat out the blood and moved toward Drake with determination.

"STOP!" I shrieked as Stephen reached Drake's side and kicked him. "Please STOP!" I shouted while Stephen continued his relentless assault. The beast was deaf to my pleas and Drake could no longer shift, even though he fought against the force of air still holding him down.

"Belynda, look at me." My mother shook my shoulders for attention. "Can you stand on your own?" She asked. I nodded and slowly she helped me to my feet.

"Listen to me. This is the only chance you will get." Her voice was low and measured. "Don't doubt yourself. Your powers are greater than anything in this realm."

"I'm not afraid," I said, and I meant it.

"I need you to create a distraction. I'm going to take Celest out of here first. Tyrus and Seymor will help us out." I looked at her hesitantly and nodded. Celest... I searched until my eyes found her.

"Yes. Save Celest."

"I will come back." She promised, and I smiled in an attempt of reassurance, but a part of me knew this was the end. It would be them or us, and I would fight for Drake until my last breath.

"Don't doubt yourself." Her words were the incentive I needed.

WITH A GUST OF WIND, Alexia flew across the chamber, landing against the wall like I had done earlier. I enjoyed giving her a taste of her own medicine. I had everyone's attention then, like

I had hoped. I needed their focus on me so my mother could move Celest.

I smiled at Stephen. Without giving them a chance to recover from the surprise, I willed the stone floor, ceiling, and walls to break and crumble.

"Go now. Quickly," I urged my mother, and she used the commotion to reach Celest.

Dust fell from the ceiling rocks, and the noise as the stones fractured around the hall caused a wave of panic. Paintings and chandeliers shook; some fell off their hinges, but Sylvie and Ren stood their ground with Oliver. Meanwhile, Stephen shielded himself with Ben, his father, and two other council members, hiding behind two large pillars. My mother was already on the move with Tyrus and Seymor's help.

It was clear that the loyalty of the elementals was to one another. Amirth and the boy leaned protectively over Alexia, who lay unconscious on the floor despite the chaos.

Summoning water would be my third and final act — I had no control over fire. It occurred to me that perhaps there was no need to harm Stephen or the council to end the guardianship. They just had to believe, witnessing the depths of my powers to finally fall back and accept that my mother had spoken the truth. I was the pure-blood, and the legacy would fall.

The water flowed like waterfalls, erupting from the crevices in the walls and floor.

As the water reached Drake, his body stirred, as if the element sprung him back to consciousness.

"It can't be." The disbelief in Stephen's voice and his allies carried over the chaos, and even the elementals took pause.

The rage in Stephen's face was visible, and that was all it took for me to realize I was wrong. He would never allow it — even if the truth were obvious, he would never stand aside. I was suddenly at a loss. I couldn't kill him. Thinking I could and *actually* doing it were two different things. I glanced at Drake, torn. He winced in pain but managed to get on his knees.

He examined the chaos around him, stopping when his eyes focused on me. The horror in his face frightened me, even more than the scream that followed.

"BELYNDA, NOOO!" His warning wasn't enough to stop Stephen's dagger as it pierced my back.

The chamber stilled. Even time seemed to pause as I turned in shock, feeling the blade tugged violently from my spine and plunged again into my side.

"NOOO!" Drake growled, but his voice was far away. I touched the blade and stared at my bloody hand. The room spun around me, and my knees gave; firm hands caught me before I hit the ground.

The familiar scent encircled me, and I was safe and at peace.

"Stay with me," the angelic voice whispered. I glanced at the beautiful angel standing above me.

"I love you, Drake." My eyes fluttered closed, too heavy to bear.

"No... look at me. I'm not losing you. Do you hear me?" I wished to look at my dark angel again, but I couldn't find him.

"Please, forgive me for this. I love you more than my own life. Forgive me."

A sharp pain tore through me, pulling me back to hell. I heard the metal blade clash against the stone floor as Drake dropped it. I screamed, but his lips silenced my pain; they were my anchor. My body felt heavy, but the pain slowly slipped away. I floated then and dreamed of Drake.

The dragon flapped his wings forcefully in the air, suddenly landing on all fours before me. I reached my hand hesitantly, and the creature nudged its head against my hand.

'Dragh, cuir às do mo bheatha beatha dhaoine,' the Dragon spoke, sounding like Drake. 'Dragh, cuir às do mo bheatha beatha dhaoine.'

The dragon repeated but I didn't understand. Then unexpectedly, the Dragon vanished. I saw only darkness, but I could hear it in the distance...

"Breathe..." Drake's voice was a soft caress in the wind. "Breathe." He was closer now, more demanding. As I inhaled, my throat burned. Fire crawled inside of me, burning, sealing, and binding my wounds. I twisted and turned in agony, scorching inside.

The cries of terror were real, though I didn't want to hear them. I wanted to go back to Drake. My fingers felt the hard stone floor beneath me, yet I could no longer feel Drake's arms. Panic rose within me, as intense as the fire that still burned inside.

My eyes opened, and I was still dreaming. The Dragon was back, but this time, he wasn't calm. He created an inferno in what appeared to be the remains of the guardianship's chamber.

I pushed myself from the floor, but the beast turned its head, staring at me briefly before returning to wreaking havoc with its inferno.

The heat in the chamber intensified; this dream felt too real.

"Belynda, you must move. Now!" That voice. I knew that voice... it was my mother's. "Help me get her up."

"I'm... alive?" I whispered.

Someone tugged at my arm more forcefully.

"Belynda, snap out of it. You're alive, and so am I, but we won't be for long if we can't control him," Oliver shouted, and as the fog lifted from my mind, I saw Oliver's face.

"Drake... where's Drake...?"

Suddenly, everything came flooding back. The knife, what Stephen had done... on instinct, I ran my hand over the side where the blade had been embedded, but there was no pain, no trace of any wound. If it weren't for the blood soaking into my shirt, I would have thought I had imagined it all.

"How...?"

"There's no time to explain. We need to go before this place collapses on us all," my mother urged, but I was frozen. I stared at the fire-breathing creature a few meters from us, finding it hard to believe that any part of Drake could be in there. Then again, the beast had shown me mercy so far. This wasn't a dream; the way the creature had looked at me and the fact that we remained alive while the dragon continued its devastation had to mean that a part of Drake was still in there somewhere. There was a faint glimmer of hope.

"I will get close. He won't harm me. I can make him change back."

My mother looked concerned.

"That's the problem. He can't take his human form."

I blinked, not understanding her words.

"Of course he can. He has done it before; he can do it now."

My mother shook her head.

"No, he can't. He gave up his human life force to save yours. He can't turn back now."

"NO!" Horror struck me as the faintest of words came back to me. His plea... to forgive him. A plea that hadn't made sense then, but now it did. How could he do this? Sacrifice his humanity to save me?

"We need to go... now." The urgency in Oliver's voice brought me back as parts of the ceiling began to collapse.

"I can do it. I'll be fine. I know he's still in there. He has to be."

My reassurance wasn't enough to erase the worry from my mother's face, but she squeezed my hand in encouragement.

I took deliberate but small steps towards him; he must have sensed my movement because the enormous beast turned its head to face me. I held my breath, waiting for a rain of fire, but it didn't come. Smoke spilled out from the beast's nostrils as it stared down at me.

I extended my hand, just as I had in my dream — only this time, I didn't feel at peace or weightless. My hand shook, and my heart pounded. I kept my eyes on the dragon, and it stood there, observing me expectantly.

"I know you're still there, Drake," I spoke softly. "You need to stop this, or we will all be hurt." The beast flapped its massive wings, sending ash and flames swirling from the ceiling.

I closed my eyes but kept my hand extended; the beast nudged my hand once more with its nose. My hand trembled, but I don't think he noticed. Slowly, I allowed my fingers to touch his soft yet peculiar skin. In response, the beast grunted.

"I'm okay, but we need to go."

The beast snorted again and stretched out on its front legs, causing my hand to move further up its head.

Encouraged now, I caressed him slowly and realized that his moody grunts were in response to my touch. He liked it. It was hard to visualize this beautiful yet lethal creature as Drake, but I forced myself to remember that he was still in there.

"Drake, I need to know if you can understand me. We have to go. Can you give me a sign?" The beast swiped its long tail and wrapped it around me. I yelped in surprise but contained my scream. Gently and effortlessly, he lifted me and placed me next to my mother and Oliver.

"I think I just had a heart attack watching you two," Oliver whispered.

"Their bond is incredible," my mother said, taking her time to admire the Dragon before us.

"I think he understands. We should go now."

"There is a passage through the ritual room that leads to the woods. It connects to the loading entrance. I think it's big enough for him to follow us," Oliver suggested.

"Lead the way."

Oliver and my mother moved swiftly through the debris towards the tunnel where the council members had retreated. As I looked around us, I watched in horror at the charred bodies. The memory of Isabel's words flowing into my mind

"You will all burn for this." Her warning promise, laid before me.

The reality of Drake's actions was brutal, and it wasn't until that moment that I truly understood his grief and self-hatred. However, as horrific as everything was, I had never once doubted my love for him. He had sacrificed himself to live only within the shadows, and even though he had never said it, I peered at the dragon beside me, realizing that his love for me was unconditional too.

I called upon the water element to extinguish the remaining flames, leaving the scene of devastation behind as I followed Oliver and my mother.

The ritual room Oliver had mentioned had been spared from the flames. My mother took my hand, and we hurried along. There was so much I wanted to ask her, but none of it seemed to matter now — only Drake. If he couldn't change back to his human form, then it would be impossible for him to live in my world. Despair consumed me with every step I took, unable to picture my life without him. The impending truth of what was to come made it hard to breathe. I turned back and glimpsed the massive Dragon as it followed a few paces behind us.

The next corridor we took was barely lit, but as Oliver had promised, the path was wide, and the ceiling was high enough for Drake not to feel constricted.

"Oliver said this would lead us to the forest. But what then?" I asked my mother. "If he can't change back…, how can he stay?" I was sure Drake could sense my anguish even in his dragon form, so I fought to push back the tears while attempting to control the panic in my voice.

"We will find a way. I promise. In the meantime, we need to find a temporary solution. We can't take any risks." Hearing my mother's reassurance gave me hope. After all, she was a guardian with vast knowledge.

"What can we do?"

"For now, we can bind him," she offered.

"Bind him?" I didn't like the sound of that, not after everything he had suffered already. "I don't think so."

"I can't think of any other way. Unless you're willing to send him back through the portal?"

"No. That's out of the question." I was torn, and it was clear to see.

"It's only temporary. I promise. We will find a way to bring him back."

"How exactly do we bind him?"

"He won't like it. He will need to submit himself willingly, and most elements don't take kindly to being subdued by other elements." I was beginning to realize just how much I had yet to learn.

"I'm sure Drake will do whatever it takes to stay." I watched him, and the sudden glow in his eyes was the validation I needed.

"There is a lake not too far from here. Water and ice will keep him contained and hidden."

My heart broke. I couldn't look back. How could I do that to him? Keep him frozen like some prehistoric beast.

"We're almost at the exit," Oliver announced. I glanced ahead, but there was only darkness. After a few more meters, I felt the breeze, and sure enough, there it was. The high foliage of the forest trees greeted us. As Drake emerged, he expanded his wings and, without warning, took off in flight. He soared above the trees, and after circling a few times, he came back down to the clearing. He was happy to be free, which only made the decision to confine him harder.

My mother took me by surprise, pulling me into an embrace.

"I was so scared. I thought I'd lost you for a moment. If it wasn't for him... what he did..."

"I'm okay."

"I know. You have grown so much," she muttered.

Suddenly, reality crashed down on me. My mother was here after all these years. I pulled back to look at her; she hadn't changed much.

"I have a lot to explain. I know I do, and this is not the time or place. I just want you to know that leaving you was the hardest thing I have ever had to do, but it was necessary to protect you. I wanted you to have a normal, happy life. I thought if I left the circle, Stephen and the guardianship would weaken, and perhaps there wouldn't be a prophecy. I was right about one thing: the guardianship did weaken, but the prophecy continued its path. I knew the moment you released him that there was nothing else I could do except allow everything to follow its course and be at your side at the right time."

"How did you know?"

"Seymor. He helped me. He has kept me informed."

Suddenly, I remembered.

"Celest, where is she?" I gasped, alarmed, remembering her previous state.

"She's fine; Seymor and Tyrus took her to a doctor we can trust."

"What about Stephen?" She glanced at Oliver, and the look of terror in her eyes said it all.

"I'm sorry. I never meant for anyone to get hurt."

Oliver took my hand.

"Hey. I don't blame you. Not after what he did to you."

He was right. I would be dead if it weren't for Drake's sacrifice. Rage burned within me then as I stared at him in his dragon form, unable to change back. Why did he always have to be the one paying the price? Is that why the fates had brought us together, to make him suffer?

Sensing my distress, my mother held me.

"He will need you to be strong now more than ever," she whispered.

Taking a deep breath, I pulled away and swiped at the tears. She was right; this wasn't the time to wallow in self-pity. It was time to find a solution.

"How do we reach this lake?"

I didn't know of any water bodies near enough — or large enough — to contain Drake.

"It's deeper in the forest. No one comes this far into the mountains. Let's go; we're near enough from here to continue on foot."

Drake didn't wait. Once again, he broke above the tree line and flew low enough to show us the way. I watched him in awe. Drake didn't like to follow; he was a leader, born to rule.

As we ventured through the trees, my thoughts consumed me. Drake must have understood; he had to know our intentions. Why else would he be guiding us? How else would he know of this lake if it was so hidden and remote? Perhaps he had come across it during the time he was out here alone. Suddenly, I found myself lost in his memories: the night I released him, all the moments we had shared flashing before my eyes. I loved him. I would not allow him to live like this forever.

As we broke into a clearing, the serene glimmer of the water's surface brought me back to reality. This was it—the moment I had been dreading.

The ground shook as Drake landed a few meters from the water's edge. I approached him slowly, my heart breaking with each step.

He exhaled and crouched, bringing his face to my level. I reached for the soft spot between his bright eyes with trembling fingers —eyes that stared back at me without blinking. I could see my reflection clearly within them.

"I know this isn't easy for you. I have no right to ask you to do this. Not after everything you have already given up for me." He huffed, nudging his warm snout against my cheek gently. I imagined what Drake would have said: he wasn't sorry for what he had done. Could it be possible that he felt the same, even in Dragon form? All of that agony and fear about hurting me and losing control. I was in the most vulnerable position yet alive because of him. Leaning in, I gave him a gentle kiss, and he offered a low grunt in response.

"I don't want this," I whispered, trying to hold back the tears. "But it's the only way to keep you with me."

As I said the words, Drake stood at his full height and turned towards the lake. He glanced back, then walked deeper into the water, fluttering his massive wings, and creating a ripple effect around him. As he reached the middle of the lake, he stopped fighting. His body sank deeper and deeper until only his head remained. Turning to me, the look in his eyes tore me apart.

"I will find a way to bring you back. I promise." The words escaped my lips so softly, yet I knew he could hear them. "I love you."

The feral growl as he submerged underwater was my undoing. My knees caved, and I tore at the ground with my hands.

This was his and Isabel's story repeating itself all over again; she had promised to release him from Xelraa and failed. Did he fear the same fate now? *No!* I couldn't do it.

The softest touch on my shoulder pulled me back.

"It's now or never. He suffers more if he remains subdued underwater. You must freeze him now, Belynda," my mother warned desperately.

She was right; we had come this far. There was no other choice. Not now.

On my knees, I crawled to the water's edge and touched it with my fingertips. Perhaps it was the flow of my emotions or the fact that Drake was deep under the surface, but strangely, the water felt electrified: pulsing and alive. I willed the element to transform, watching in despair as the water solidified quickly, away from my fingertips.

It was done, yet the pain inside my chest solidified too; I was frozen like Drake at the bottom of that lake.

"Belynda, you're not alone anymore. We'll find a way."

Oliver didn't speak but offered me his hand. I stood up and looked at the lake as my insides shattered.

We reached the edge of the woods, fear gripping my insides — a fear that threatened my future with Drake. *What if I couldn't find a way?* I fought the thought that threatened to extinguish my life completely, refusing to let my story end like Isabel's. I had no time to waste. His life, his freedom, depended on me.

The fates will be on our side, Drake, I thought before turning my back on the glimmering silver lake.

Acknowledgments

Writing this book has been a memorable journey for me and my family, Jason, Junior, and P.M. thank you for your love and support. To all the friends who helped in the process, Joan, the S.N Morgan team, and Yaha, thank you for being there. Thank you for believing in me and pushing me to follow my dreams. Without your support, this book might still be unfinished....

Morgan Vela

About the Author

Morgan Vela is a debut author of romantic fantasy novels. Her stories join with shifters, witches, and dragons and explore other realms—while magic fills the pages of her stories, romance guides her imagination.

I have made up stories in my head for as long as I can remember—I have seen dragons and magic-filled worlds since I was young. I have traveled long and far and lived many lives through the pages of books I've read. This freedom of believing in the impossible, even briefly, made me want to share my stories. And so, my journey began as a writer.

My debut novel 'Vanished' is in paperback at Barnes & Noble and Amazon. It is also available as an eBook through Kindle Unlimited. 'Vanished A Guardian Story' is Book One of the Vanished Series. 'Throne of Fire' is the sequel, followed by 'Tides of Destiny,' book three in the series. The fourth book and last of the series, 'Shadows and Light,' is projected to be released summer of 2024.

ALSO BY MORGAN VELA

VANISHED SERIES

A Guardian Story

Throne of Fire

Tides of Destiny

Shadows and Light (Coming Summer 2024)

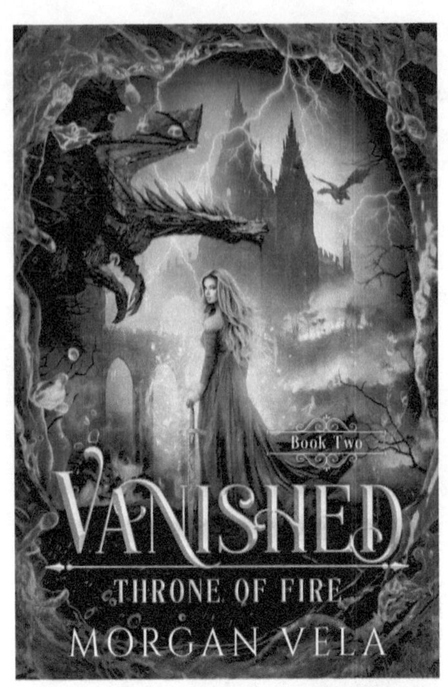

Book Two
VANISHED
THRONE OF FIRE
MORGAN VELA

Book Three
VANISHED
TIDES OF DESTINY
MORGAN VELA

STAY CONNECTED

Morgan Vela Author

www.morganvelaauthor.com

9 798988 455219